A Rare Ruby

Dee Williams

headline

First published in 2002
by HEADLINE BOOK PUBLISHING

First published in paperback in 2002
by HEADLINE BOOK PUBLISHING

1

ISBN 0 7472 6451 1

Typeset in Times New Roman by
Letterpart Limited, Reigate, Surrey

Printed and bound in Great Britain by
Mackays of Chatham plc, Chatham, Kent

HEADLINE BOOK PUBLISHING
A division of Hodder Headline
338 Euston Road
LONDON NW1 3BH

www.headline.co.uk
www.hodderheadline.com

Dee Williams was born and brought up in Rotherhithe in East London where her father worked as a stevedore in Surrey Docks. Dee left school at fourteen, met her husband at sixteen and was married at twenty. After living abroad for some years, Dee moved to Hampshire to be close to her family. A RARE RUBY is her twelfth novel, following eleven hugely popular previous sagas set in Rotherhithe.

Thanks have to go to Carol and Diane, who work at our wonderful Horndean library. They are always willing to help find books for me, which have been invaluable for finding out about laundries and bagwash in the 1900s and 1920s.

I would like to thank Ron Brown of our local *Evening News* for his interesting article about laundries which planted the seed for this book. Ron, I have used the bits you couldn't.

This is also for Chris Lloyd of Tower Hamlets Research Library for finding me photographs of the working conditions that some of the girls and women had to put up with.

I would also like to use this opportunity to thank Christine for the beautiful prom dress she made for my granddaughter Emma. She looked lovely. There will be another to make in two years' time for Samantha.

Many thanks, everybody.

Chapter 1

Ruby Jenkins pushed the kitchen door open with her bottom and dragged the heavy bundle of dirty laundry tied up in a sheet through the doorway. The smell of boiling washing filled the house. She took off her coat and beret and flicked her dark hair away from her eyes. She would have to get her mother to cut her wild hair soon – it was getting out of control. Ruby stood for a moment or two looking at her father sitting hunched in the chair next to the fire. Every time she looked at him, she couldn't believe this was the man who'd gone off to be a soldier just five years ago, 10 September 1914. Thomas Jenkins had been so proud when he came home from work and told them he had joined the army. He had taken the King's shilling. He was going to fight for his King and country. The reason she remembered it so well was because it was the day after her ninth birthday.

Her father looked up. 'Hello, love.' He grinned. 'All right then?'

Tears filled her brown-speckled eyes and she nodded. He used to be a tall, upright man; now he was broken and sad.

'I'm cold,' he said, pulling the old blanket he always had wrapped round his shoulders tighter.

'That you, our Ruby? You got that washing?' yelled her mother from the washhouse at the back of the house.

'Yes, Mum.' She smiled when her mother called her 'our Ruby'; it made her feel very precious. 'Mum, Mrs Barton said could she have it back be Friday.'

Mary Jenkins came into the kitchen. She pushed back her damp hair and wiped the beads of perspiration from her forehead with the bottom of her overall. 'Well, let's hope the weather stays fine. It looks a bit like rain – that'll be all I need.'

It was almost the end of October; Ruby's fourteenth birthday had come and gone. There hadn't been any celebrations and she had wanted to find work immediately, but her mother told her she would be more use at home; she needed her help doing the washing and collecting and delivering it. Ruby would have loved some money to spend on herself. She never had any as every penny had to go to help the household. They weren't the only ones suffering. As she walked round the streets in Rotherhithe it upset her to see the many sad men, who once must have had good jobs, standing with trays hanging round their necks, selling matches, bootlaces and the like. Worst of all were the cripples sitting on the pavement with a cardboard sign next to them saying: 'Kitchener needed me. Now I need you' that made her turn away. Ruby had nothing to put in the cloth cap in front of them. And she knew things would get worse for everybody now the weather was beginning to turn wintry.

She stood in the kitchen and took in all the poverty they now had to endure. So much of their home had finished up in the pawnshop with no hope of it ever being redeemed. All they owned was a table and four chairs, none of them matching, and two very tatty brown brocade armchairs that Ruby and her younger brother Tom had found in a derelict house. They had laughed and giggled as they dragged them home but it wasn't really funny when the horsehair stuffing constantly spilt out when anyone sat on them. She looked at the cracked mirror over the fireplace, which came from another of her and Tom's scavenging expeditions. Even her mother's prized possession, the brass fender that had 'Waste Not Want Not' written on it, had long since been sold. Only a solitary clock stood on the mantelpiece; there were no ornaments.

In one room, Ruby and Tom slept on a thick feather mattress. There was no bed and only one blanket: they used coats to cover them. Last winter had been bitter and they had had to huddle together to keep warm. Ruby had hated scraping the frost off the inside of the window every morning. She remembered the chilblains she'd had on her hands and feet and said a silent, desperate prayer: *Don't let it be so cold this year*.

Her mother and father shared the other room. Her mother had determined to keep her bed, she said it reminded her of happier times. Ruby recalled the day she came to this house with her mother to look at the rooms. Mr Cox, the old man who lived there, said he would be prepared to move upstairs and let them have the downstairs for a minimal rent, just two shillings a week. That was a lot less than the five shillings her mother had struggled to find each week when they lived further up the road at number sixty Hill Street. Mr Cox was a bachelor and lived alone, and as part of the agreement her mother had to do his washing and cooking, as there weren't any facilities upstairs.

Ruby didn't like him. He was short and fat, and smelt of beer and stale pee. She hated it when he threw his dirty washing down the stairs. She would pick up his dirty underpants and socks as if they were about to bite her. If she came out of the closet and found him standing there, she always wondered whether he had been watching her through the knotholes in the wooden door. Sometimes, when he came down and sat at the table with them, Ruby found his eyes were on her. Thankfully most of the time he ate upstairs alone. Once she had told her mother her worries, but Mary had dismissed them as being silly.

'Why would he be interested in a slip of a girl like you? He's been good to us and he sits and talks to your father. So don't you go upsetting him with your childish notions.'

Ruby was shocked when she found out from the girls at school what men wanted from young girls. Was it just childish notions?

She particularly hated it when her mother was cooking something special Mr Cox had bought for himself, which her family would not be sharing. The succulent smell of meat or fish would almost make her mouth water.

Every time Ruby passed her old house a lump would come to her throat and she'd give a little smile at her fond memories. The front room with its lace curtains always gave out the lovely scent of lavender polish when the door was opened. Her mother used to polish the brown leather three-piece suite with so much pride. The front doorstep was religiously whitened every morning. Gawd help you if you stepped on it and left a dirty footprint, you'd end up with a clip round the ear. Now all that had gone. Ruby looked down at her black button boots. They were scruffy, dirty and too small for her, they hurt as they rubbed the many darns in her lisle stockings. She remembered when her boots were new; now the soles were worn through and there was only cardboard stuffed inside between her feet and the ground. The thought of the winter and wet feet made her shudder. Before the war her father had worked in the biscuit factory. He'd had a good job and they hadn't gone hungry and her mother hadn't had to do other people's washing – and, best of all, she'd gone to school. One at a time she gently ran her boot up the back of her legs to try to bring the shine back.

'Ruby, bring that load out here and sort through it,' her mother interrupted her thoughts. Mary Jenkins was a proud hard-working woman who kept the two rooms and kitchen with its range for cooking, plus the washhouse, which had running water and a boiler, as clean as she could. They were lucky they only had to share the outside closet with the old man, not like some round their way. Sometimes as many as six families had to share. Her mother fed them as best as the pittance she got for taking in washing allowed, making sure Mr Cox upstairs always had the best of whatever they had.

Ruby smoothed down her grey frock. It had once belonged to her mother and fitted her well enough, but now her bosoms were developing it was getting tight and cutting under her arms. How she wished for some new clothes. Tom was now wearing a pair of his father's trousers that her mother had cut down to fit him. They were much too big and the legs hung down well below his knees. She said he would grow into them. Tom hadn't complained, he said they would help to keep his knees warm in the winter. As far as Ruby could see things were never going to get any better. She sighed as she pushed and heaved the bundle into the washhouse. Even though it was cold outside the heat and steam in the small room was overpowering.

Her mother, a thin wiry woman, was at the sink scrubbing shirt collars and cuffs up and down the wooden washboard. Her straight grey hair always escaped from its hairclip and fell round her face. She tucked the offending hair behind her ear. 'Somehow that woman always manages to get a navy sock in her load. It's not the first time that everything's gone blue and I've had to wash that load all over again. I've nearly finished here, so when you've done that you can help me take that lot out of the copper and put it through the mangle,' she said over her shoulder.

'Can Tom help me?'

'He's had to go and get me some soap.'

Ruby tied the thick sacking apron round her waist and stood on the box next to her mother. Although she was as tall as her mother now she felt safer on the box as she leaned over the bubbling copper. Very carefully she wound the washing round and round the stick. She was always terrified of splashing the boiling water over herself as she pulled up as much washing as she could hold, then gently lowered it into the tin bath that stood next to her.

Her mother helped her carry the tin bath to the deep sink and tip the clothes out just as Tom came bounding through the scullery.

'Just bumped into that Ernie Wallis. D'you know, he told me he was gonner take some of Mum's customers away from her.'

'I'd like to see him try,' said Ruby.

'Don't stand there looking at your sister, give her a hand.'

Ruby shivered as she ran the cold water over the clothes and pummelled them up and down. When she'd rinsed them, she twisted them to get out as much water as she could, then lifted them into the tin bath again. 'Tom, grab that handle.'

Between them they lifted the heavy bath and after many stops to rest, managed to manoeuvre it into the small back yard. Ruby took a breath when the cold hit her wet apron then penetrated through her thin clothes and on to her stomach.

'That Ernie Wallis is a big bully,' said Tom, peering under the fringe of his dull blond hair. He was nine years old, small and thin for his age, and the image of his mother. Although he looked frail, with two hands he expertly turned the handle on the big mangle as his sister fed the sheets through the wooden rollers and then placed them into a wicker basket.

Ruby gave him a big smile. It wasn't fair. They couldn't afford the slate he needed to write on at school, so he didn't go. Although Ruby tried to help him with his sums and reading, it wasn't the same as going and sitting in a classroom. She had loved going to school, and her teacher, Mrs Grey, was always saying that Ruby was a bright girl who should go far. But when her father had joined the army she'd had to stay at home and help her mother. And, after the war had ended, her father couldn't work any more so they had had to move from their house.

'I'm gonner bash that Ernie Wallis when I grow up,' said Tom.

'I don't think Mum will like that.' Ruby was grinning.

Tom quickly glanced around and moved closer to his sister. 'He called Dad a silly old fool. He said I'll be like him when I grow up. I won't, will I?'

That remark took the grin away from Ruby. 'Course you won't. It was the war what done that. Dad's shell-shocked.'

'I ain't ever gonner go to war.'

'You won't have to. That was the war to end all wars. Come on, help me put this lot on the line.' Ruby thought about Ernie Wallis. He was tall and good-looking. When they'd both been at school she'd looked up to him. In fact, like most of the girls, she had adored him, but he always ignored her. When his father had been killed at the beginning of the war he'd been very upset and had had to leave school to help his mother support his three younger sisters. The last time she'd seen him he'd been pushing a pram with furniture on it; he hadn't spoken to her. Was he taking the contents of their home to the second-hand shop? Was that why he was nasty to Tom? Was he angry with what life had thrown at him?

Ruby and Tom's hands were freezing as between them they pegged the sheets on the line. Ruby pushed the clothes prop under the rope so the washing could catch the slightest breeze.

'Can's see it drying much today,' she said, picking up the wicker basket.

That evening Ruby sat with Tom at the old table, trying again to teach him how to do his sums. In the washhouse, damp washing hung from the airing poles close to the ceiling. A line had been strung up under the mantelpiece, and the clothes horse, full of Mrs Barton's washing, was taking all the heat from the fire. Ruby watched the steam gently rising.

'Mum, I was talking to Milly in the dairy, she asked me if I knew of anyone who had a room to let.'

'Well, we ain't got a room. Ruby, I've told you before – I ain't gonner have strangers walking about this place taking the mickey out of your father.'

'But Mum, at least you'll have a couple of shillings every week. It's gotter be better than having all this washing all over the place every day, and having to pawn most of our things, and I could go out to work.'

'That's as may be. But as I said, I don't want anyone laughing at him, and I certainly ain't having that means test man round. And I can't see him' – she raised her eyes to the ceiling – 'letting me have anybody else move in. What sort of job d'you reckon you could get anyway?'

'I don't know.'

Suddenly her father began coughing. Ruby looked over at him. Her heart went out to him as he grinned back at her. Her mother must love him very much. She never got cross, nor shouted at him, even though his not working made life so difficult for them all. Ruby didn't know where she got such patience from.

★ ★ ★

The following afternoon Ruby was in the dairy across the road, talking to Milly. Ruby liked Milly even though she was years older than Ruby; Ruby had known Milly all of her life. At one time, before Milly had to help in the dairy, they had played together and Milly would get told off for banging a ball on the wall of the shop. Milly's parents owned the dairy, but they were getting on now. Most of the time, since her father had been taken ill and couldn't stand all day, Milly was in the shop alone, although sometimes her mother would come down. Milly was nearly twenty, and knew most of what was going on round about and, despite their age difference, loved talking to Ruby.

'Did you tell your mum about that poor young girl who wants somewhere to stay?'

'Yes, I did, but you know me mum. 'Sides, we ain't got much room.'

'She's got this baby.' As Milly leaned over, her big bosoms rested on the counter. She was the only person Ruby knew who wasn't skinny. 'Her baby's only a few weeks old. I think her old man's in the Navy so he's away a lot. She wouldn't be any trouble.'

'Where's she staying now?'

Milly looked up at the door, pulled her cross-over apron tighter round her and leaned forward. She lowered her voice. 'She's with that Mrs Mann and her daughter. You know, they live in the next road.'

Ruby nodded, her dark searching eyes full of expression. 'They frighten me.'

'They frighten everybody with their ranting and ravings about the Lord coming and taking all the wicked ones.'

'Does this girl come from round here?'

'Don't think so. I ain't seen her hereabouts. 'Sides, if she did I reckon she'd be staying with her parents.'

'I'll ask me mum again. How does she pay her rent?'

'She must get some sort of allowance.'

'Now this weather's turned Mum might think twice about it. All that washing hanging about – I don't think it does me dad any good, sitting with all that steam round him.'

'How is your dad?'

'Mum don't think he'll ever be any different.'

'Shame. He was such a nice man.'

Ruby watched as Milly put a dollop of dripping on the scales. She took it off and put it on a sheet of greaseproof paper, then very quickly added another lump. 'What is it, bread and dripping for tea?'

Again Ruby nodded.

'That'll be tuppence,' said Milly.

Ruby smiled. 'Thanks, Milly.' With the wind and rain beating against her face, Ruby hurried across the road.

'Mum, Milly was telling me about this woman what wants a room. She's got a baby and her husband's away, she lives with that Mrs Mann.'

Mrs Jenkins's head shot up. 'Ruby, we've only got three rooms and a washhouse, and we was lucky to get this much space. Where would she sleep? And I can't see Mr Cox being very pleased about it.'

Ruby knew they could have trouble with him, but her mother needed the money. 'She could come in with me and Tom. P'r'aps she could bring a mattress. She could sleep next to us.'

Mary Jenkins picked the iron off the hob and, turning it over, spat on it making it sizzle. 'I can't see her paying to sleep on the floor. She must be better off where she is, she must have a room. Why does she want to move?'

'Milly didn't say.'

She smiled at her daughter. 'You're a good girl. Now you

10

carry on with this while I cut the bread and make a bit of toast for tea.'

As Ruby moved the iron back and forth over the washing she began to think of ways to help her mother out. She should try to get a job. But what? It couldn't be for long hours, as she needed to help her mother till Tom was old enough and strong enough to collect and deliver on his own.

As Ruby made her way to the market the following morning, her heart gave a little leap when she saw Ernie Wallis in front of her. He was pushing a pram piled high with bundles of washing along Rotherhithe New Road. Ruby knew he was fifteen; he was taller but thinner than her. He had a mop of dark hair that fell over his vivid blue eyes: no wonder all the girls at school had been in love with Ernie Wallis. She grinned. He was having a great deal of trouble getting the pram down the kerb as one of the wheels was badly buckled.

'What are you looking at?' he asked when he caught sight of her.

'You,' she said confidently.

'Well, don't.'

'I can look at who I want.' Although Ruby was shaking in her boots she just had to speak to him – hold his attention. She didn't want him to ignore her any more. 'Where are you going with that lot?'

'Mind yer own business.'

Ruby was interested. He didn't live round this way. 'You told our Tom you was going to take some of me mum's customers away from her.'

He laughed. 'That brother of yours can be a right wimp.'

'And that wasn't very nice telling him he'll grow up like me dad.'

'Yer. I shouldn't have said that. I was having a bad day.'

11

So he could be nice, thought Ruby. Since she was angry about his remarks she wanted to tell him off, but she also wanted to keep close to him. 'D'you go to work?'

'Course.'

'Where d'you work?' she asked as they continued along the road together.

'What's it to you?'

'Just interested, that's all.'

'It's only temporary at the moment. I'm looking for something better.'

'Trouble is so are a lot of men.'

'Know that, don't I? You gonner follow me?'

'No. I'm going to the market. Where are you going?'

'As I said. Mind yer own business.' He turned off and went towards Lower Road.

What was he doing going down there? Ruby wanted to follow him, but she knew he'd be mad at her and she didn't want to get into his bad books as she still had feelings for him . . . but could it lead anywhere?

She wandered round the market looking for anything that was cheap or had been thrown away. Her mind was going over what Milly had told her about the woman who wanted a bed. She had to convince her mother that this would be good for them. Perhaps the woman would help her mother, then she could really start looking for work?

It was late afternoon when Ruby was delivering Mrs Barton's washing. She was standing on Mrs Barton's doorstep when Mrs Flynn, the next-door neighbour, came out.

'Been looking out the window waiting for you. Could you do a little job for me?'

'Yes, if I can.'

'I'll pay yer.'

Ruby's eyes lit up. 'What is it?'

'Could you be a love and take me washing to the bag-wash? Me feet's playing up something rotten and I can't be dragging this lot down there.'

'Would you like me mum to do it for you?'

'No, ta all the same. I use the bag-wash off Lower Road. All I have to do is stuff it in a pillowcase and they wash it like that – that way I don't lose any.'

'You wouldn't lose any if me mum did it.'

'From what I gather your mum's got enough on her hands. Besides, they put it in the big dryers afterwards. It comes back just damp and I can manage that.'

'Is it ready?' asked Ruby.

'I'll just get it. I'll give you a couple of pence for your trouble. You'll have to bring it back tomorrow.'

Ruby was overjoyed. Was luck on her side? Could she earn a bit more? 'That's all right.' After she'd collected Mrs Barton's money she loaded the old pram with Mrs Flynn's dirty washing and made her way to the laundry.

Ruby stood in front of the imposing entrance. Under the large brick arch, which had the name 'Stone's' painted on it, the cobbled path led to a dark, dreary-looking building with small narrow windows. It looked more like the workhouse than a laundry. Gingerly and very carefully, Ruby pushed her pram round the horse dung and past the delivery cart that had 'Stone's Laundry' in large letters on the side. The horse was busy munching on his nosebag; there wasn't a sign of the driver. Steam hissed and rose from the drains. When she got up to an open door, the noise from machinery took her by surprise.

'Yes?' said a stern-looking woman coming up to her.

'I've brought Mrs Flynn's bag-wash.'

'Have you now. Has she put her number on it?'

'I don't know.' Ruby looked about her in bewilderment. This was the first time she'd ever set foot in a place like this.

'Give us it 'ere.' With that, the woman lifted the heavy bundle of washing out of the pram as if it weighed just a few pounds. 'That's all right,' she said, looking at a number that was drawn on the bolster case the washing had been stuffed into.

'When will it be ready?' asked Ruby.

'It's a bit late today. Call back tomorrow, about midday, we shut at four on Saturdays.'

'How much will it be?'

The woman threw the bundle on the scales. 'D'you know if it's all whites?'

Ruby nodded. Mrs Flynn had told her that.

'That'll be sixpence for the washing and tuppence for the drying.'

Ruby almost gasped at the prices. Her mother didn't charge that much.

'You pay when you collect.'

Ruby thanked her and left, but not before she had a quick glance around. Could this be the answer to her prayers? Could she set up some sort of business like collecting and delivering washing? A lot of people didn't do their own washing and her mother couldn't really take on any more. Her mind was going over and over as she walked home. Would it be possible for a young girl to start a business? Would people laugh at her? Her mother would tell her not to be silly, but everybody had to start somewhere. Was that what Ernie Wallis did? If so, he wouldn't want her intruding and taking his customers away. She smiled to herself. But after all, all's fair in love and war.

Chapter 2

That night, as Ruby lay on the thick feather mattress next to her brother, she was still deep in thought. If Ernie Wallis could collect and deliver loads of washing to the laundry, so could she. She didn't want her mother to take on any more work; this way would be much better. Perhaps if her business grew, she could expand, get another old pram then get Tom to help her. She smiled to herself as Tom turned over and snuggled close to her. Was she being too ambitious? She could only give it a try. She put her arm round Tom. She loved him so much. It would be wonderful if they could really make a go of this. Her father always used to say that you never make a lot of money all the while you work for someone. Tomorrow she'd ask Mrs Flynn if she knew of anyone else who wanted their washing taking to the laundry, then gradually she could build up her reputation. She drifted off, dreaming happy dreams.

It was well past lunchtime before Ruby managed to get to the laundry. She was worried Mrs Flynn might be waiting for her washing. There wasn't anybody outside near the big metal scales, so she went in. The room was tall and white with a huge counter, a stack of brown paper and balls of string. She stood and waited for someone to talk to. The door at the side was slightly ajar. Ruby carefully pushed it open. She could see a young girl sorting through a pile of washing.

Ruby nervously said, 'Hello.'

The girl looked up and put her hand on her heart. 'Bloody 'ell. You frightened the daylights out of me. What d'yer want?'

'Sorry. What're you doing?'

'The worst bloody job here.'

Ruby looked about her embarrassed. 'Why is it?'

'Would you like to sort out blokes' smelly, shitty pants?'

'No, I suppose not.'

'Well, don't stand looking at me then. What d'yer want anyway?'

'I've come for Mrs Flynn's washing.'

'Well, you've got to go and see Mrs bloody snotty-nosed Watson. She's the charge hand.'

'Where will I find her?'

'Sniffing round old man Stone, I shouldn't wonder.'

'Who's he?'

'The owner. You're a nosy cow, ain't yer?'

Ruby looked down. 'Sorry.'

'Look out, here she comes.' The girl put her head down and continued to sort through the dirty washing.

'Yes?' asked Mrs Watson, coming up to Ruby.

'I've come for Mrs Flynn's bag-wash.'

'Well, you wait out there.' She pointed to the open door. 'You shouldn't be in here.'

'Sorry. I was just looking for someone to ask.' Ruby grinned at the girl and followed Mrs Watson.

Ruby was full of expectations when she delivered Mrs Flynn's washing, but her high hopes were soon dashed when Mrs Flynn told her she hadn't heard of anyone else who took their washing to the bag-wash, but promised to let her know if she ever did.

At first Ruby was downcast as she began to walk home, but then she suddenly remembered what her father had told her many years ago. 'You don't get nothing for nothing in this world, you've got to strive for it.' With renewed enthusiasm she began to knock on the doors of the big houses.

The first three were polite and said their maids did their washing. At the next house she was sent down to the basement and the woman told her to bugger off. After a lot more refusals her feet hurt and she was cold and hungry, and she was beginning to lose heart. It was the next house that sent her on her way home with her tail between her legs.

The woman opened the door. 'Yes?'

Ruby gave her the biggest smile she could and said politely, 'I was wondering if you sent your laundry to the bag-wash and if so would you like me to collect and deliver it for you?'

The woman looked her up and down. 'I wouldn't trust you with my dirty washing. I don't suppose I'd ever see it again. Now get off of my doorstep before I shout for a policeman. Who would give a scruffy-looking kid like you their dirty washing?'

With her head down, Ruby turned and walked away.

She turned the corner and almost bumped into a young woman who yelled at her, ''Ere! Watch where you're going.'

'Sorry.'

''Ello there. You're the kid what come to the laundry this morning, ain't yer?'

It took a moment or two for Ruby to recognise her. At work her dark hair had been scragged back from her face and covered with a cloth hat. Now she was wearing a wide-brimmed black hat with a floppy rose on the brim, which almost covered her face, and her black coat looked as if it had

17

been made for her as it fitted her well-formed figure perfectly. Ruby half smiled. 'Yes.'

'You look a bit down in the dumps.'

'I'm all right.'

'What's up? Your old man bin giving you a pasting?'

'No.' Ruby went to move on.

The girl put her hand out. 'Just a mo'. This morning you was full of questions, so what's wrong now?'

How could she tell this stranger that her hopes of having her own business had been dashed? She would think she was daft. 'I'm all right.'

'I'm just off to the market. Fancy coming along?'

'No. I've got to get home.'

'Well p'r'aps another time. By the way, me name's Elsie, what's yours?'

'Ruby.'

'Ruby. That's nice. Might see you at the laundry one day. Bye.'

'Bye,' said Ruby. She stood and watched Elsie walk away in her good boots, swinging her handbag as if she didn't have a care in the world. Ruby was letting her thoughts drift. That's a nice hat and coat she's got on, must have cost a bit. I wonder how much she earns? Ruby wished she had a job. Did they want any workers at Stone's laundry? Elsie was now out of sight. Perhaps she could help her get a job? Ruby began to walk in the same direction as Elsie.

There was the usual hustle and bustle at the market. The stallholders were shouting about their wares. Kids were running around screaming and yelling. One stallholder was hanging on to a young kid and giving him a clip round the ear for pinching things. Ruby could see the boy, who was about six, looked terrified. There was a chill wind, but he didn't have a coat and the dirty tatty shirt he had on was ripped up the side. His trousers were many sizes too large for him and held up with a length of webbing tied round his waist. Ruby suddenly caught sight of Elsie striding up to the man. Although she was slight and a lot shorter than he was, she pulled him round. Ruby couldn't hear what she was saying, but the wagging finger and the movement of her head told her he was getting a right mouthful. Ruby smiled. Elsie was very gutsy.

Elsie put her arm round the young boy's shoulder and began to walk away. Ruby went up to her. 'You was very brave standing up to that man.'

She grinned. 'Didn't see you watching.'

'I came to ask you a question.'

'Did you now.' Elsie still had her arm round the young boy's shoulders. He looked scared stiff. 'Can't bear to see these kids bullied. I know what it's like to be hungry. 'Ere y'are, lad.' She opened her bag and gave him a ha'penny – 'Can't afford any more' – then snapped the clasp of her bag shut.

'Cor. Thanks, missus.' The boy clutched the money and ran off.

'That was very generous of you,' said Ruby.

'I 'ave me moments. Now, what was it you wanted to ask me?'

'I was wondering if there's any jobs going at Stone's?'

'Dunno. Wouldn't like to say. Mr Stone don't always tell me his business.'

'You talk to Mr Stone?' asked Ruby, wide-eyed.

'No, course not, you silly cow. I was just pulling your leg.'

Ruby bent her head; she felt so humiliated.

Elsie had moved on. 'Come on,' she called over her shoulder. 'You know, you're a funny little thing. One minute you're all talk, the next you go all shy.'

Ruby fell in step beside her. 'Have you worked at Stone's long?'

'A couple of years. How much, missus?' she asked the woman on the second-hand clothes stall as she held up a thick black skirt.

'To you, dearie, a tanner.'

Elsie put the skirt to her waist. 'I'll give you thrupence.'

'I've got a husband and six kids ter feed.'

'You should send him out to work then.' Elsie laughed. 'That'll tire him out, then you won't have any more.'

'Saucy cow. Give us fourpence and it's yours.'

Elsie handed over her money and took the skirt.

'You must earn a bit to be able to buy a skirt just like that,' said Ruby.

'Not really. I've had me eye on that for a couple of weeks. I was sure she would have sold it be now. D'you like it?'

'It's very nice.'

Elsie tucked her arm through Ruby's. 'Look, why don't you come to the laundry on Monday and I'll let you know if Mrs Watson is in a good mood. If she is then you can ask her about a job.'

'Thanks, Elsie.'

'Have you got any family?'

'Yes, me mum and dad, and I've got a brother.'

'Have you now. Has he got lovely eyes like yours?'

Ruby felt herself blush. 'I ain't got lovely eyes.'

'I reckon you have, and how old is this brother?'

Ruby laughed. 'He's only nine.'

'Shame.'

They continued walking along. Ruby learned that Elsie was nearly eighteen, and she was the middle daughter. Her father worked in the docks and she was only working in the laundry till her older sister Jenny got her a job in the tea factory.

'It's a lot better pay, and cleaner,' she said, stopping at a stall that sold lace. 'Trouble is, jobs don't come up there very often.'

Ruby felt so happy. As they slowly moved on, she found Elsie was eager to tell her her life story. Elsie's father had been in the army and had returned fit and well, but her mother died during the war and the girls were left to look after themselves. Elsie told her things had been very hard while her father was away. Ruby listened very intently, but said very little about her own family.

'I must get home,' said Ruby. 'I look forward to seeing you on Monday.'

'I might not be so cheerful then, sorting out dirty washing!'

'Bye.' As Ruby walked through the market her head was full of the prospects of a job. She so desperately wanted to bring in some money. It must be wonderful to go up to a stall and buy a skirt. Anything would be better than her mother's cast-offs and clothes from the jumble sales that were unwashed and smelt of mothballs.

She decided not to say anything till she was sure of getting a job. But how would her mother manage? Ruby'd just have to get up early and collect the washing before she went to work, and then deliver it when she'd finished. With everything settled in her mind, Ruby too found she had a spring in her step. She went to the back of the greengrocer's stall and began sorting through the mouldy potatoes he'd put out.

At last it was Monday. Ruby couldn't wait to get to the laundry. As she hurried along the road she saw Ernie Wallis in front of her – and her heart sank. She didn't want to catch him up; she didn't want him to know what she was doing. But as he struggled with his pram she knew she would have to speak to him.

'Hello, Ernie, seem to be seeing a lot of you lately.'

'What you doing round this way again?'

'Just going to the laundry, same as you.'

'Where's your washing?'

'I ain't got any today.'

'So what you doing round here then?'

'As you said to me the other day, mind your own business.'
When she walked past him her heart was thumping. Why did
he always have this effect on her?

The first person Ruby saw when she walked in the packing
room (where, Elsie had told her, the best jobs in the factory
were), was Mrs Watson. She looked desperately at the closed
door behind which she knew Elsie could be.

'It's you again. Whose washing you come for this time?'

'I ain't come for any washing. I was wondering if you've got
any jobs going?'

'Were you now? And what makes you think you'll like
working here?'

'I don't know.'

Mrs Watson's face suddenly broke into a wide grin as she
looked beyond Ruby.

'Hello, my son. And how are you today?'

Ruby quickly swung round. She was face to face with Ernie
Wallis.

'Hello, Mrs Watson.' He gave her a sweet sickly grin, then
he turned on Ruby. 'What's she doing here?'

'Come looking for a job.'

'Her mother takes in washing. I reckon she's after your
customers.'

Ruby couldn't believe her ears. 'What?' she screamed out.

'Is that your little game, madam? You'd better get out then,
before Mr Stone comes down and throws you out.'

'I didn't. I wasn't. You mustn't believe him. It ain't true. I just want a job.' How could he do something like this? She looked at him. 'Why are you saying this?'

'Just looking after me own interests, and that of Mrs Watson here.'

Mrs Watson gave him a smile. 'Come on, lad, let's get this lot sorted.'

Ruby stood and watched them push the pram away. In just a few days her hopes of starting up her own business and working had been dashed. All the love she'd had for Ernie Wallis had gone. Why had he done that? She could kill him for it. She marched defiantly down the road. She would show him. She wasn't going to give up that easily, but she knew, deep down, things never went that smoothly for the likes of her.

It was very quiet when Ruby pushed open the kitchen door. She stood for a moment unable to take in all the mess.

'What happened?' she asked, rubbing her nose. The smell of soot filled her nostrils and was going to make her sneeze.

'Bloody chimney, that's what.' Her mother was busy pulling the washing off the clothes horse.

Ruby looked at her father who had soot over his face. He began to laugh.

'And you can bloody well stop laughing,' shouted her mother.

His face suddenly crumpled and his laughter stopped. Ruby had never heard her mother shout at him before.

'Got to wash this lot again. Mrs Prince wants it back tonight. I know she takes these sheets to the pawnshop till Friday. Those poor kids won't be able to have any dinner till then.'

'You put them in the copper, I'll clear this mess up.' Ruby got down on her hands and knees and, with the small dustpan and brush, began carefully to sweep the soot away. She didn't want it flying all over the place.

Her father grinned as he sat silently watching her. She wanted to laugh; he had rubbed soot over his face and left dirty streaks. Ruby wondered what was going through his mind. Normally nothing that happened around him seemed to affect him, but today he was different: he was taking an interest. Ruby looked at her mother; she had never seen her so tense and distressed.

When the room was clean and the washing back on the clothes horse, Ruby sat at the table and looked up at the small clock on the mantelpiece. It had been a wedding present from her mother's mother and father. They would have been upset if they could see what had happened to their daughter and her family. Like her father's parents, they had been dead a long while, since before that dreadful war had started. Ruby wished she had a gran and granddad, it must be nice to visit old people who knew your parents when they were young.

Her mother sat at the table. 'Cheer up, love. I know this has been hard work, but thanks for clearing the mess up.' She touched her daughter's hand.

At first Ruby couldn't speak. 'That's all right,' she whispered. 'But it ain't that.'

'What is it then?'

'Nothing.'

'I know you're at a funny age, and everything seems worse than it really is, so come on, what is it? What's upset you? I'm sorry I shouted at your dad, but he seems to have forgotten it.'

Ruby looked at her father clutching the poker and staring into the fire. He always told her he could see pictures and wanted to draw them. What was in his troubled mind?

'Ruby, where was you this morning?' asked her mother.

'I went for a job.'

'What? Where?'

'At the laundry.'

'And?'

'I didn't get it.' Ruby went into great detail of how she'd first thought of starting her own business, then how she'd met Elsie, and then how Ernie Wallis had dashed her hopes of getting a job. 'Don't laugh at me, Mum. I want to help. I don't want to live like this.' She waved her arm at the clothes horse. 'I want to be able to go and buy a skirt.'

Her mother went to her and held her close. 'I won't laugh and I can understand how you must feel. You're growing up and I'm sorry things are so hard. But I'm sure they'll get better.' She gently pushed her daughter away. 'Look at your dad. I do believe he's improving a little.' She smiled. 'Who knows, one of these days he may even go out to work again.'

'Do you really think that, Mum?'

'As I said, who knows? You're a good girl, Ruby. D'you know why you was called Ruby?'

Ruby shook her head.

'Your dad always said you was his bright little jewel and very precious. He was right, you know, and to us you are indeed a rare Ruby.'

Ruby smiled. 'Mum, can't we have that woman come and stay here? It will help, if only through the winter.'

'I was thinking about it when all the soot fell down. Do you really think we could manage?'

Ruby quickly wiped her nose on the bottom of her frock. At last she had got her mother to change her mind. 'I *know* we can.'

'Pop over and tell Milly then. But the woman might have got something be now.'

Ruby was out of the door and across the road in no time.

Chapter 3

It was a week later and a cold damp Wednesday afternoon. Ruby had just returned from delivering washing when there was a knock at the door.

'That'll be Mrs Norton,' said her mother.

'I'll go,' said Ruby.

'She come round earlier and brought a flock mattress she said she got from the market. It's a bit stained and some of the stuffing's coming out, but I can soon fix that. Just as long as it ain't got any bugs in it. Can't stand bugs.'

On opening the front door, Ruby was very surprised to see a young and pretty girl on the doorstep, standing beside a scruffy pram with a torn hood. A few bags were wedged in next to a tiny baby that was almost hidden beneath a pile of covers. She didn't look old enough to be married and have a baby. Ruby had thought she would be a much older woman.

'Hello. You must be Ruby. I've heard a lot about you,' she said. 'It was ever so nice of your mother to take me in.'

'You'd better come in.' Ruby stood to one side as Mrs Norton manoeuvred the pram into the narrow passage.

She was the same build as Ruby, slim and not over tall. Her fair hair had been pushed under her tight-fitting shapeless black hat, but a few strands had escaped and hung down in curly tendrils. Ruby noted that her black coat had seen better days. She gave Ruby a smile as her bright blue eyes darted nervously about her.

Mary Jenkins came into the passage. 'You can leave the pram here for the moment, but we'll have to find somewhere else for it. We might be able to get it in the room with you.' She looked up at the stairs. 'I don't want him complaining.'

'This is so very kind of you.'

'As I told you earlier, you'll have to muck in with us.'

'I don't know what I would have done if I'd had to stay in that house much longer. Not that we were allowed to stay in all day.' She lifted the baby from the pram; it had a long off-white frock, but wasn't wearing any socks. 'We had to go out every morning and not get back till six. It wasn't so bad in the summer when I had a job, but now I've got the baby and the weather's on the turn.'

'That's terrible,' said Mrs Jenkins. 'Didn't you have your own room?'

'No. I had to sleep on the sofa in the front room, it was very uncomfortable. So you see the floor in your house has got to be better.'

'I don't know about that,' said Mary Jenkins.

'I know I shouldn't speak out of turn, but I expect you know that the Manns are very religious and they had Bible meetings every day. That's why I had to get out: they used the front room for all their chanting and praying. I can't walk the streets with the baby, not with the winter coming. I'll be able to pay you rent.' Mrs Norton smiled and her blue eyes lit up. 'This must be my lucky day. I've managed to get a little job.'

'You've got a job?' asked Ruby. 'Where?'

'Ruby,' said her mother, shocked. 'I'm sure Mrs Norton will tell us if she wants to.'

'I'm sorry,' said Ruby. 'But as jobs are so hard to get round here, I was just wondering . . .' Her voice trailed off.

'Please, call me Beth. I'm going to work for that Mr Thompson in the Royal Albert.'

'The pub!' queried Mrs Jenkins.

'Yes. I'm going to do his cleaning.'

'But I thought Mrs Moss did that.'

'She did, but she had a bad fall and broke her arm, so she'll be off for a bit. As I said, I was lucky. I met her when she was at the cottage hospital. I was there with little Danny here.' She patted her baby's back.

'Oh dear,' said Mrs Jenkins. 'Nothing serious, I hope.'

'No, not really. He's having a bit of trouble with his . . .' She stopped and looked about her. 'His little thingy,' she whispered.

Ruby wanted to laugh, but knew she mustn't.

'We should have been Jews, then this wouldn't happen.'

Ruby wanted to ask her mother what she meant, but she could do that another time.

'What about the boy when you go to work?'

'Mr Thompson said I could take him with me.'

'In that case, then you are lucky. Take your bits in the room you'll be sharing with Ruby here and my son Tom.'

'This is very kind of you, Mrs Jenkins.'

'As I said, we need the money. Ruby, give Mrs Norton a hand. When do you start working at the pub?'

'Tomorrow.'

Ruby lifted the two bundles from the pram and put them on the floor.

'Come on, son. I think it's time for your feed, then a nap.' Beth Norton took a brightly coloured crocheted blanket from the pram and wrapped the baby in it.

'What time do you have to do your cleaning?'

'In the morning, about seven.'

'That's all right then. I'll be up long before then.'

Ruby could see her mother was trying to put Beth at ease, but there was a kind of undercurrent she couldn't understand. Was Mary worried at what Mr Cox might say? Would he throw them out? That was a threat that hung permanently over them. But surely her mother could tell him?

'You said your husband was in the Navy. Does he come home very often?' asked Mrs Jenkins.

'No.' It was very abrupt. 'I haven't seen him for a while. Not since I had the baby.'

'That's awful. You must have been very young when you got married.'

'Yes. I was.'

'I don't think he'll be able to stay here when he comes home.'

'Don't worry about that. He's the other side of the world.'

'Will he know where to find you when he does get back?'

Beth Norton blushed and looked flustered. 'Yes, I did write and tell him, and Milly in the dairy said she'll show him where I'm staying, but I don't know how long it'll be before I see him again. It could be months.'

'I expect he'll be pleased to know he's got a son. Most men like that.'

'I hope so.'

'Shall I make a pot of tea, Mum?'

'Yes, and I must get on. There's always washing and ironing to be done in this house.'

'I don't mind giving you a hand if you ever need it.'

Ruby could have kissed Beth Norton. Perhaps some of her luck was going to rub off on to them.

In the kitchen, Ruby put the kettle on the hob.

'What's that?' asked her father when the baby cried.

'It's all right, Dad. It's our lodger's baby.'

'Baby.' He smiled and sat up. 'We got a baby?'

'Yes, Dad. A little boy.'

'I like babies. Where is he?'

'Mrs Norton's just feeding him. She'll be in in a minute.'

'Can I hold him?'

'We'll see.' Ruby felt sad as she watched her father sink down in the armchair again and pull his blanket round his shoulders.

'Who's that?' he asked later, pointing at Beth Norton when she came into the kitchen.

'Mrs Norton. Our lodger. You know, I told you about her,' said Ruby, who was standing at the table, ironing.

Beth sat next to Mr Jenkins. 'Hello, this is my baby. His name's Danny.'

'Hello, Danny.' Thomas Jenkins gently took his hand.

The way he looked at the baby, Ruby thought her heart would burst.

Mary Jenkins came into the room. 'You finished that ironing yet, love?'

'Just got to do the last few handkerchiefs and pillow cases,' said Ruby.

'When you've finished that you can take Mrs Bell's washing and collect the dirty lot.'

'Where's Tom?' asked Ruby.

'Collecting from Mrs Morris. It's getting dark and I don't like him going round that way, they're very rough.'

'Can't he come with me?'

'No. I want him to fetch some coal when he gets back. You'll be all right.'

'But it'll be dark be the time I'm finished.'

'I'll put Danny on the floor then I can finish off that

ironing for you, Ruby. Is Mrs Bell's very far?' Beth Norton asked Mrs Jenkins.

'The buildings.'

'The buildings?' she repeated with a look of horror on her face.

'Do you know it?'

'I've heard about it,' she said quickly.

'It's not too far and, Ruby, if you go now it won't be too dark. And you don't need to take the pram.'

Ruby shuddered. She didn't want to argue, but she didn't like going round to the buildings in the dark. They were near the docks and were very old and dirty with broken windows. She had been told that a lot of women who lived there entertained the sailors and dockers. She was always frightened when she had to step over a pile of rubbish that sometimes turned out to be a tramp or a drunk. Her mother never went round there so she really didn't know what it was like. Rubbish filled the stairway and gangs of boys stood on the corners, and she had heard some terrible tales of what they did to girls on their own. What if they stole the money? Her mother should have sent her out earlier, before it got so dark.

Outside it was raining that fine drizzle that made everything feel dreary and damp. Ruby dragged her coat round her and pulled her hat down over her flyaway hair. She hurried as fast as the flapping soles of her boots allowed. The sound of the ships' mournful sirens filled the air and as she went past the high wall surrounding the gasometer, she could hear footsteps; someone was walking behind her. She couldn't look round. Fear made the sweat run down between her tiny breasts. As they got closer she wanted to run, but knew she would fall over if she tried. The sole of her boot had started to come off and was beginning to slow her down. How she hated all this poverty. Why couldn't she get a job like Beth Norton and not have to go out on nights like this to deliver washing?

'What you doing round this way, Ruby Jenkins?'

Although she could have flung her arms round Ernie Wallis's neck she was so relieved to hear his voice, she was still very angry with him.

'Here, you ain't coming round this way looking for washing, are yer?' he asked as he fell in step with her.

'No, I ain't. And I don't want to talk to you after what you told that Mrs Watson.' Deep down Ruby knew that wasn't true, she wanted to talk to him more than anything else in the world, but she wasn't going to let him know it.

He laughed. 'I shouldn't worry about it, they're always looking for girls to work there.'

'D'you think I should try again?'

'Don't ask me. So what are you doing round this way at this time of night?'

'I'm just taking some washing back.' She had to think quick. 'It's me mum's friend.'

'Well, that's all right then. I can't hang about chatting. I've got to get a move on.'

'The woman ain't that well and Mum's doing her a favour.' Ruby knew she was blabbering on, but she wasn't going to tell him the truth and she really wanted him to walk with her.

'So, where does this friend live?' he asked as his pace quickened.

She crossed her fingers. She couldn't tell him the address or who it was as her mother might lose a customer. 'She's in the road next to the buildings.'

'You shouldn't be round here in the dark, you know, it ain't safe. I can walk a bit of the way with you, but I've got to go to the pub.' He hesitated. 'Me mum likes a tipple. Come on, I've got to hurry.'

'Thanks, Ernie. I don't like being out in the dark.'

In silence they quickly moved on. Ruby was sure he would be able to hear her heart beating. The sound was filling her ears. Was it through fear, or just being with him?

When they reached the pub, he said, casually pushing open the door, 'See you one day. And, Ruby, try for that job again.' With that he was gone.

Ruby slowed down. Well, his mother must certainly be in need of a drink. Or was it him? Surely he wouldn't waste his hard-earned money on beer; after all, he was the only bread-winner. And what did he mean, try again? Would he have a word with that Mrs Watson? She smiled as the glimmer of hope took hold, but when she continued on her way, she kept glancing nervously over her shoulder nearly every step of the way.

Inside the buildings the smell of stale pee took her breath away. She peered round the bend in the stairs. It was dark and eerie. Oh, how she hated this place. During the day screaming kids filled the stairs, stopping her going on as they tried to pinch the washing from the pram. Tom always took a stick to them, but he wasn't with her now. Why didn't her mother let him come with her? They could have got the coal together. Tonight the stairs were empty and she could hear the sound of her breathing above the hissing from the gas lamp; it didn't have a mantle and the shadows on the walls frightened her. Shouts and swearing were coming from behind most of the closed doors, yet from one there was the sound of somebody playing a piano. It was very tuneful. At last she knocked on Mrs Bell's front door.

She knocked again when there wasn't any answer. She wanted to cry. Had this been a wasted journey? She was cold and miserable. She banged again, only much harder this time. Why did Mrs Bell live in such a terrible place? She was always well dressed and had lovely undergarments. He mother never let her iron the delicate fabric, as they looked very expensive and she was worried Ruby might scorch them. Tears welled up in her eyes. She banged again.

'All right. All right. Keep yer hair on.' A thickset man wearing only trousers and a vest pulled the door open. The hair on his chest sprouted out from the top of his vest. His braces were dangling down and he didn't have any shoes or socks on. 'Well, what d'yer want?'

'I've brought Mrs Bell's washing back.'

'Have yer now? Rita!' he yelled. 'There's a kid out here with yer washing.'

'Give her the money then,' came a voice from inside.

'I ain't giving her no money.'

'You can be so bloody annoying at times.' A thin woman came into the passage. She only had on a white cotton petticoat with pretty rosebuds on the bodice. Ruby had seen it many times. Her hair was all over the place and Ruby could see she had a lot of make-up on even though most of it was smeared round her face. She pushed past the man and gave Ruby sixpence. 'Thanks, love. Can you collect the dirty stuff tomorrow? Only I ain't stripped the bed yet.'

The man put his thick hairy arms round Mrs Bell's waist. 'Come on. Let's get back to bed. I want me money's worth.'

'Shh. You'll shock this little girl here.'

Ruby now guessed what she did for a living. The girls at school had told her all about women like that. As she walked away the thought that was filling her mind was: I bet she earns more in a night than me mum earns all week. And it can't be all that hard work.

Ruby hurried home, jumping at the shadows. She let her

mind wander to Beth Norton and Mrs Bell. Everybody seemed to be making money except her. Even Ernie had money to waste on beer. By the time she turned into Hill Street, giving a sigh of relief at being home, she had made a decision. Tomorrow she was going back to the laundry to see Elsie and try again to get a job.

Chapter 4

Ruby carefully took Tom's arm from across her waist. She'd had a restless night; the baby seemed to be crying all the time. She'd tried stuffing bits of rag in her ears, but that hadn't helped. She was glad when she heard her mother moving about.

'I hope Danny didn't disturb you.' Beth Norton's voice came from out of the darkness.

'No, no, course not,' said Ruby.

'Does he always cry like that?' asked Tom.

'No. He must feel a bit strange, being in a new place.'

Ruby couldn't see that. He was only a baby. How would he know a strange place when he was sleeping in his own pram that had been pushed hard under the window? All night Ruby had felt the wheels with her feet.

She waited till Beth Norton was out of the room, then quickly dressed and walked out into the kitchen. As usual at the beginning of the day, the range had been black-leaded and the hearth whitened. Despite being so short of money her mother still had standards she liked to keep up, and that Mr Cox would complain if the front doorstep wasn't kept up to his satisfaction. On the range, the lid on the black kettle gently bobbed up and down. The room felt warm and comforting. In the washhouse, her mother had already got the fire under the brick boiler well alight.

'Hello, love,' said her mother as she pounded the washing down in the boiling water. 'Did you sleep all right?'

'Not too bad.'

'Right, I'm ready,' said Beth popping her head round the door. 'Wish me luck.'

'Course we do,' said Mary Jenkins.

Beth closed the door.

'That baby makes a bit of a racket. Did it disturb you?'

'A bit.' Ruby wasn't going to let on how much; after all it had been her idea that Beth Norton came to live here. 'I expect he'll settle down,' she added.

'I hope so. With these thin walls, I'm expecting him upstairs to come down as soon as he gets up.'

'Mum, what if he says she has to go?'

'I don't know. Remember, it was your idea. Don't worry. I'll think of something. There's a bit of bread you can toast, then I want you to do all that ironing.' As her mother went back to pounding the washing she added, 'There's a couple of shirts that want buttons on, so put them to one side.'

In the kitchen Ruby looked at the pile on the chair. She knew that it would take her all morning.

In fact it wasn't till late afternoon that Ruby finally managed to get out. Beth had come home from her cleaning and had been telling them all about it. How Ruby envied her when Beth said she would be getting seven and six a week. To Ruby that was a fortune – but Beth did have to go in every morning, including Sundays.

'The floor's in a bit of a state. I don't think Mrs Moss could get down to give it a good scrub, but my knees can stand it. And he does let me have hot water. I'll be able to give you two and six a week all the time I'm working there.'

'How did you manage before?' asked Mrs Jenkins.

'My husband gave me money before he left, but I don't know what I'll do when Mrs Moss comes back. I don't wish anybody any harm, but I hope she don't come back too soon.'

'We never know what's round the corner. At least it'll give you a chance to get back on your feet, and who knows, your husband might return very soon.'

Beth just smiled.

Elsie had told her they didn't finish till seven o'clock so it was dark when Ruby finally got to Stone's. She didn't want to go in as she didn't want to upset Mrs Watson. She hung about hoping Elsie or someone would come out. The door opened and Ruby caught sight of a figure hurrying round a corner. 'Elsie,' she called.

'Who's that?'

'Me. Ruby.'

'I ain't Elsie. Who are you, and what are you doing here?'

'I wanted to see Elsie.'

'Wait here, I'll see if she can get away.' The young woman, who was much the same build as Elsie, disappeared inside.

After what seemed to be for ever, Elsie came out. 'What're you doing here?'

'I had to see you.'

'Come on then. I'm just going to have a pee, but don't breathe in, will you?'

Ruby quickly followed her but stopped when the smell took her breath away. 'What a pong!'

'It goes with the job.'

Above the sound of Elsie peeing in the galvanised bucket, she shouted to Ruby, 'I thought you was looking for a job?'

'I was, am. I did see Mrs Watson, but someone I know told her I only wanted a job here to get some work for me mum. She takes in washing.'

'Who'd do a thing like that?'

'Ernie Wallis.'

Elsie came out pulling up her knickers. She straightened down her skirt. 'That's just the sort of thing he would say.'

'You know him?'

'Everybody knows him. Right charmer he is.'

'I know.'

Elsie laughed and gave her a small punch on the arm. ''Ere, you ain't fallen for him as well, have you?'

'No, course not. I knew him at school. All the girls liked him then.'

'Well, he ain't changed. There's a few in there that'll drop their drawers for him any time he asks.'

Ruby didn't answer. She was too shocked.

'Look. I'll have a word with old Watson and see if I can't sort something out for you.'

'Thank you, Elsie. When shall I come back?'

'I'll go and see her now. She's in a good mood today. Think she might have been out with old man Stone last night.'

Ruby could have kissed her. Was some of Beth Norton's luck rubbing off?

It was ages before Elsie finally came out again. 'You can come in and see her now. I don't hold out much hope, but good luck anyway.'

'Thanks.' Ruby followed Elsie.

'So it's you,' said Mrs Watson when she caught sight of Ruby. 'I'll say this for you, you're persistent.'

Ruby hung her head and said softly, 'It ain't true what Ernie Wallis told you. I ain't looking for work for me mum. She's got more than she can cope with already.'

'Has she now. Well, she might want to send some round here to us?'

Ruby shifted her weight from one foot to the other. She hoped the sole of her boot would stay in place.

'We might be needing someone in the washroom. It's hard and heavy work. You don't look very strong, do you think you could cope?'

Ruby looked up. Her smile was beaming. 'Yes. I know I could.'

'Well, you don't look very strong to me. But you can be on trial for a week and we'll see from then on.'

Ruby could have flung her arms round this woman. 'When shall I come here?'

'You can start Monday. Be here at seven-thirty. You'd better wear some waterproofs on your feet, it's very wet work. And don't be late.'

'I won't.' Ruby couldn't tell her these boots were all she had. 'Mrs Watson, what time does Elsie finish?'

'In about a quarter of an hour.'

'Can I wait for her? I want to thank her.'

'You can wait here. And I don't want you two chatting all the time you're working otherwise it'll be out of the door for both of you.'

The last thing Ruby wanted to do was to get Elsie the sack. 'I won't.'

Ruby listened to the chatter and shouting that came from behind a closed door. She was so excited. She had got a job. She had forgotten to ask how much she'd be getting, but that didn't matter at the moment. She would be working with other girls and women. It seemed that Beth Norton had brought them good luck after all.

'Where have you been?' asked Mary Jenkins, straightening up

from bending over the ironing. 'I've been waiting for you to give me a hand with this lot.'

'I've been to get a job.'

'What d'you mean, get a job? Where?'

'The laundry. I start on Monday.'

'What?'

'I'm working in the washroom.'

Her mother brushed her troublesome hair from her face. 'That's hard work.'

'So Mrs Watson said. But I don't mind.'

'What they paying you?'

'I don't know.'

'You don't know? Didn't you ask?' Ruby could see her mother wasn't happy about it.

Ruby shook her head. 'I was so pleased at getting the job I forgot to ask.'

'Will I have to do all Ruby's jobs now?' asked Tom.

'Looks like it. Let's hope it'll be worth it.'

'I'm on a week's trial.' Ruby was disappointed at her mother's reaction; she had thought she would be a little more enthusiastic.

'Honestly, Ruby, I don't know how we're going to manage. Tom here can't do all the collecting and delivering.'

'Don't worry. I'll do the big loads after work.'

'Go over and get a couple of eggs for tea.'

Ruby went across to the dairy with a heavy heart.

'You look like you've lost a shilling and found a tanner. What's up?' asked Milly, her bright red cheeks shining. 'Has that Beth settled down?'

'She seems to be happy enough. She works up the pub.'

'I know. She told me. So what's the trouble then?'

'I'm going to work at the laundry.'

'Good for you. Mind you, it's bloody hard work. I couldn't

do anything like that. So what's making you look so fed up?'

'I thought Mum would be pleased.'

'And ain't she?'

Ruby shook her head. 'I think she's worried about Tom taking the washing out on his own. Mum don't like him going round the buildings.'

'I'm not surprised at that. Can't say I'd fancy going round that way after dark.'

'I had to go round there the other night.' Ruby giggled. 'The woman had a man in there and she only had a petticoat on.'

Milly leaned further over the counter. 'No. Was it her husband?'

Ruby shook her head.

'I've heard a lot of that goes on round that way.'

'Now we've got Mrs Norton's money coming in and if I can hang on to me job, Mum might not have to do so much.'

'You're a good girl, Ruby.'

Ruby blushed. 'Can I have two eggs please?'

'Tell you what. I'm feeling in a good mood tonight. You can have three for the price of two.'

'Thanks.'

Carefully Ruby crossed the road. Suddenly she was sure things were going to be fine. Everything seemed to be happening at once: she could feel that all the bad times were behind them. As the sole of her boot flapped about, the thought that brought a smile to her face was, perhaps next week her mother would let her keep her first week's wages. It would be great to go to the second-hand stall in the market, or the pawnbrokers, and get a smart new pair of boots. She knew she should get waterproofs, but hopefully and if she showed willing, she might not be in the washroom too long.

Chapter 5

It was a typical November Monday morning when Ruby left home: cold, dark and damp. She knew her mother wasn't happy about the situation as she was tight-lipped and had hardly said a word.

Outside the factory Ruby scanned the crowd of women. Finally she caught sight of Elsie. Ruby called out her name.

Elsie's face broke into a grin. 'Hello there, love. All right then?'

'Bit worried.'

'I hope she don't give you a rotten job.'

'She said I might be in the washroom to start with, but I'll be grateful for whatever she gives me. Thanks for putting in a good word for me.'

'Don't thank me till you know what you'll be doing. Look out, here she comes.' Elsie stood back.

'Follow me, Miss Jenkins,' said Mrs Watson. 'Have you known Mr Wallis long?' she asked over her shoulder as they marched through a huge room.

'We was at school together.'

'Nice lad, and very good to his mother.'

Ruby didn't answer. Her eyes were darting about her as she took in the large noisy machinery. The room was very warm. Two women were lifting heavy lids on presses that hissed at

43

them. They took out flat sheets and together carefully folded them. The women sitting at a long table ironing went quiet when they walked through; a couple of them grinned at her.

Ruby was intrigued to see the irons were attached to the ceiling by a length of tube. 'These gas irons are the very latest thing. We try to keep up-to-date here at Stone's,' said Mrs Watson. She stood at the door and called: 'Miss Cotton. This is Ruby Jenkins, she's here to give you a hand.'

Miss Cotton was a big woman with arms thick like a man's; it appeared she was in charge of the washroom. When Ruby walked in, she couldn't believe it; the place was swimming with water.

Miss Cotton looked down at Ruby's boots. 'They ain't gonner last five minutes in this place. Ain't yer got nothing better?'

'No. But when I get me wages I hope to get some new ones.'

'New ones won't last five minutes neither. You want a good pair of waterproofs. Now come on, I'll show you what to do. First of all you'd better put this on.' She gave Ruby a thick rubber apron that reached almost down to the floor.

Ruby noted that all the other women were wearing the dark red aprons. She was intrigued and a little worried when told to help put washing in the huge boilers. They were lit with frightening gas jets that hissed continually. She hadn't seen anything like this before. She then had to move on to another boiler and help take the washing out. The heat was stifling and the water gradually crept up her legs. Her arms and back ached; she was tired and uncomfortable. When somebody blew a whistle all the other women stopped work. Ruby looked round in amazement.

'Come on, love,' shouted one woman. 'It's dinner break. You've got half an hour to eat yer sandwiches.' The woman patted the wicker laundry basket she was sitting on. 'Come and sit be me.'

'Thanks.' She plonked herself down. 'I didn't bring any sandwiches.'

''Ere, 'ave one of mine. D'yer fancy a drop o' beer?'

'Don't drink beer.'

'Go on. A little drop won't hurt yer.'

'Wouldn't mind. It's very hot in here.'

''Ere, don't swig too much, we don't want you falling about drunk all afternoon.'

'She might finish up in one of the boilers,' shouted someone behind.

'Christ, I hope not, she'll come out all white,' came from another.

Ruby handed back the bottle. 'Thanks. I didn't think we had a break.'

'You lot,' shouted her new-found benefactor. 'This little 'en ain't got nothing ter eat, so how about passing over something?'

An assortment of things landed on Ruby's lap. She had never seen such a variety of food.

'Me name's Doris. What's yours?'

'Ruby.'

'Old Mrs Watson certainly chucked you in at the deep end.'

'Have you been here long?' asked Ruby, her cheeks full of thick fish-paste doorstep.

'A few years. This must be the worst job in this place. Mind you, the pay ain't bad.'

'And she can't do anything else,' shouted another elderly lady.

Ruby wanted to ask her why she was still in this room if she disliked it so much, and what sort of wages they got, but she didn't want to appear daft. How many people start work and not know what wages they're going to get?

''As she got a grudge against yer?' asked Doris.

'No, I don't think so. What's the best job in here?'

'Packing room. But like most jobs yer get paid piecework in there. We don't, that's why most of us stick at it.'

Ruby must have looked bewildered. 'Piecework?' she asked.

Doris continued, 'Yer get paid fer every bit of work yer do, so yer 'ave ter be quick, otherwise yer don't earn much. And another thing, yer have ter be able ter read in the packing room. Can yer read?'

Ruby nodded. 'Wouldn't you like to work in there?' she asked.

'Na. I ain't very good at tying up parcels; I'd be all fingers and thumbs. 'Sides, I can't read, so Gawd only knows what would finish up in 'em. I could just see the look on some posh tart's face if she got some old bloke's combs.' Doris threw her head back and laughed.

Ruby was amazed that the women could laugh and talk so easily while working in such a dreadful place.

When the whistle blew for them to finally stop for the day, it was seven o'clock. Ruby felt she had been in the washroom for a week.

Outside the cold wind cut through her thin coat. She pulled it tighter across her small bosom. The street gas lamps spluttered above her head and a fog was coming off the water. Sounds echoed; everywhere there was an eerie yellow glow and the ships' foghorns added to the ghostly atmosphere.

'Ruby! Ruby, wait.'

Ruby caught sight of Elsie making her way through the throng. Coming up to Ruby, she put her arm through the younger girl's.

'You all right? Where did you finish up?'

'In the washroom.'

'No! The old cow. She done that on purpose. She don't want you to stay.'

'Does she do that to everyone?'

'No. Some ask to go in there as they get more money than the rest of us. Some of 'em have got little 'ens and drunken old men at home, so they have to earn as much as they can. You won't find me in there. I'd tell her where to stuff her job.'

'I'm on a week's trial.'

'Well, see how it goes.' She stopped. 'I go down here. See you tomorrow.'

'Bye. And thanks.'

Ruby was dead tired as she slowly made her way home, but she knew she would stick at it just to show Mrs Watson and Ernie when she saw him again. She shivered. Her feet were wet and cold and her chilblains were back and driving her crazy. She knew she mustn't scratch them in case they got infected. Perhaps she could put them in the piddle pot tonight; that might help to stop the itching. She almost prayed that her mother didn't want her to deliver washing tonight. The bottom of her thin frock was wet and clung to her legs with every step she took. She didn't feel elated at being at work, just miserable, but she mustn't let on to her mother.

'Hello, love, had a good day?' asked Beth smiling when Ruby pushed open the kitchen door.

The kitchen was warm and cosy. How Ruby envied Tom, her father and Beth sitting at the table having their tea.

'My God. Look at the state of you,' said her mother, leaping up. 'Get those wet things off before you catch your death.'

Slowly Ruby unbuttoned her boots. Her fingers were red and sore. She was having trouble holding back the tears. She rolled down her damp stockings. Every movement was such an effort.

'You'd better get that wet frock off as well. I'll hang it on the clothes horse, it'll be dry by the morning. I don't think you'll be able to deliver Mrs Bell's washing tonight.'

'I'll do it in the morning, before I go to work.'

'You can't, she won't be up.'

'Perhaps I can help out. I can do it when I finish tomorrow,' said Beth. 'I like to take Danny for a little walk in the afternoons. Tom can show me where she lives.'

Ruby wanted to throw her arms round Beth. She also wanted to cry, with joy, fatigue and relief that she didn't have to go out tonight. 'Is it all right if I go to bed?'

'Don't you want something to eat?'

'No thanks, Mum. The women gave me a lot.'

'The women fed you?'

'I didn't take nothing with me.'

'I hope they don't think I starve you?'

'Course they don't. I must go to bed.' She pushed open the door and fell onto the mattress; instantly she was asleep.

The shouting woke her.

'When I let you live here I didn't think you'd take in lodgers.' Mr Cox's voice was loud and booming.

'She ain't a lodger. She's my sister's girl and she moved here to be near the docks when her husband comes home.'

'Well, tell her to keep that bloody kid quiet.'

Ruby couldn't believe what her mother was saying. She was telling him a lie. She waited till she heard him stomp up the stairs, his feet crashing on the bare floorboards, and then she stood up.

'Mum, what's happening?' she asked, wandering into the kitchen.

Her father was holding his head and rocking back and forth.

'What's wrong with Dad?'

'Mr Cox came in shouting, and you know how much that upsets your father.'

'It's my fault really,' said Beth Norton softly. 'It seems Danny kept Mr Cox awake this afternoon.'

Ruby put her arm round her father's shoulder and held him close. 'It's all right, Dad.' She looked up. 'It's taken him a long while to come down and shout about it then,' said Ruby to her mother.

'He was asleep when I took his tea up and I think he was just waiting for an excuse to come down and say something. I don't think he likes hard roe on toast.'

'I heard you tell him that Beth was your sister's daughter. You ain't got a sister,' said Ruby.

'I know that, but he don't. Now, d'you fancy some roe on toast?'

'Yes, please.' This was indeed a rare treat. Perhaps things were going to work out now her mother had accepted that Beth Norton was going to stay – well, for the time being anyway.

All the rest of the week while Ruby worked, she was pleased that Beth helped Tom collect and deliver the washing.

On Friday night Ruby waited impatiently for her wages and to see if Mrs Watson was going to let her stay.

'Ruby Jenkins,' Mrs Watson called; her long finger beckoned her. 'Here, just a minute.' Mrs Watson was standing in the doorway. She wasn't going to come in a room that was ankle deep in water.

Slowly Ruby made her way over to her.

'So, you've managed to stick at it then? I didn't think you'd last a day, let alone a week.'

Ruby managed a weak smile.

'I'll hang on to your wages till tomorrow. Just in case you don't turn up. You finish at four tomorrow.'

'Do you want me to work next week?'

'Do you want to?'

Ruby nodded.

'I'll talk to you tomorrow.'

'You staying then, Ruby?' asked Doris.

Ruby broke into a grin. 'Looks like it.'

'Good for you, girl. Who knows, she may even give yer a better job.'

'D'you think she will?'

'Dunno. Wouldn't like ter say.'

On Saturday Ruby took the envelope Mrs Watson handed her.

'I want you to carry on in the washroom on Monday.'

Ruby's heart sank. She wanted another job, but knew she couldn't argue.

Mrs Watson turned and walked away. 'Have a nice weekend.'

Ruby quickly tore open the packet. Inside was a ten-shilling note. She wanted to sing out. She had got her first week's wages. Ten shillings.

Even though it was cold and she had wet feet, Ruby was glowing while she waited outside for Elsie. 'You look nice,' said Ruby.

'Always like to tart meself up a bit on me half-day. You look pleased with yourself. You staying?'

Ruby nodded.

'Good for you. Where're you going to be next week?'

'I've still got to stay in the washroom, but I don't mind. I got ten shillings.'

'Well, I'll say that for old Watson, I don't think she's twisted you. I told you that's the best-paid job. Nearly everybody else is on piecework.'

'Are you on piecework?'

'Yes. I still only get about ten bob, the same as you; sometimes I can make a bit more, but not very often. It depends on what I have to handle. Sometimes I have to hold me nose the stuff is so rotten and stinky. There're a dirty lot of buggers about. I think some of the old women in the ironing room get a bit more than that, especially those that iron the toffs' shirts.'

Ruby looked at her wage packet. 'I hope me mum'll be pleased.'

'She should be. You've worked bloody hard for it.'

'I'm going to the market to get some new boots, can you come with me?'

'Why not? I might get a better deal than you.'

They stepped over the horse dung and pressed themselves against the arch when the horse pulling the laundry van came racing through.

'You should be more careful,' yelled Elsie. 'That's Frank Stone, he's one of the boss's sons. You wonner watch him. He's always after the girls. He's even got some of them the sack.'

'Why?'

'Think he was worried some of 'em might blab about what he got up to. He's married, you see.'

'That ain't fair.'

'That's life, love. His younger brother Ben ain't so bad.'

'You know everybody.'

'I make it me business – you never know if it might come in useful some day.' Elsie pointed to the horse and cart. 'So don't get involved with him. He thinks he owns the place.'

Ruby laughed.

'What's so funny?'

'Well, he will own the place one day, won't he?'

'Oh, you. Come on, let's be moving on.' As always, Elsie tucked her arm through Ruby's and they marched off together laughing.

Wandering round the market Ruby priced up the boots on the second-hand stall. The pair she wanted was two shillings. She didn't want to spend that much on herself. After they had been back three times, Elsie had managed to get them down to one and six.

'I'm going to wear them home.' Ruby sat on the kerb and put them on. 'Well, what d'you think?' She paraded up and down in front of Elsie.

'They look very nice.'

'They're a bit big, but at least they ain't squashing the chilblains on me toes, and I might even grow into them.'

Elsie grinned. 'You daft 'aporth.'

'I feel so happy. Thank you so much for everything you've done for me.'

Elsie looked embarrassed. 'As I said, you're daft. I ain't done nothing.'

'You got me the job and now the boots with a quarter knocked off. I'll buy you a present next week.'

Elsie stood in front of her. 'Now you listen to me. You look after your money, you work bloody hard for it.'

Ruby's mouth turned down.

Elsie grinned. 'Tell you what, you can buy me a Christmas present.'

'But that's weeks away.'

Elsie laughed. 'You'll have more time to save up and spend on me then. I'm only joking. As I said, you look after your money.'

Ruby was so happy. She couldn't believe her good luck: to have found work *and* a friend. At the flower stall Ruby couldn't resist buying her mother some flowers. As it was the end of the day, they had been reduced to tuppence. Ruby didn't mind that some of the petals were falling off. 'Me mum ain't had flowers for a long while.'

'Will she mind you wasting your money on things like that?' asked Elsie.

'I hadn't thought of that.' Suddenly Ruby felt guilty. She should have gone home first and given all the money to her mother. 'I don't think she'll mind. After all, this is the first wages I've ever had.'

'Didn't your mum pay you?'

Ruby had told Elsie about how they struggled. 'No, I couldn't take money off her.'

Ruby walked in the kitchen with the flowers behind her back. Right away her mother said, 'New boots?'

Ruby looked down. 'You don't mind, do you?'

A smile filled her mother's face. 'No, course not, love. You deserve 'em.'

'I've bought you something.' With a flurry Ruby brought the flowers out from behind her back. Some more of the petals had gone and there were quite a few stalks.

'Oh Ruby. This is so kind. They're lovely. I'll put 'em in water. It'll have to be in a milk jug – ain't got any fancy vases now. So, how much wages did you get then?'

'Ten shillings.'

'Ten bob? That ain't bad for a young girl.'

'I only spent one and six on me boots, and the flowers were ever so cheap.'

'Don't look so worried. I ain't gonner tell you off.'

'I did need some boots, me others were . . .'

'As I said, I don't mind.'

'You can have the rest.'

'You just give me seven shillings. That'll be like a King's ransom. What with your money and Mrs Norton's, looks as if we could be having a decent Christmas.'

Ruby felt her heart lift. She was at last contributing. She was going to keep one and fourpence for herself. She knew she would be able to help make their Christmas the best they'd had for many, many years. 'I'll be able to buy lots of Christmas presents,' she said.

'Now don't you go wasting your money,' said her mother.

'But I want to. You'll want a present, won't you, Dad?'

Her father looked at her. 'Christmas presents?'

'I will,' said Tom.

Ruby smiled at her brother, remembering her certainty a week ago that from now on things would only get better. She'd been right.

Chapter 6

For the next two weeks Ruby was as happy as she could be working in the laundry's washroom. The thing that kept her going, apart from the wages she was bringing home, was the fact that Beth Norton was now helping Tom do some of the delivering of the clean laundry, and collecting the dirty washing for her mother.

'Mum, if Beth is charging you too much to go out with Tom, I can still do it, you know.' Ruby was in the washhouse with her mother, busy sorting and peeling the potatoes she'd brought in the day before.

Her mother looked up, putting a strand of hair behind her ears. She smiled. 'D'you know, she said she didn't want paying.'

'Why?'

'Seems she's quite happy taking the baby for a walk, and she said she might as well be doing something useful at the same time.'

'Why's she doing that?'

'She said it was because she was so grateful we took her in.'

'That's nice of her.'

'I know. At least it saves you a job. And she's good with your father. He thinks the world of that baby.'

'See. I told you it would be all right her living here.'

'Yes, you did.'

Ruby smiled as she continued doing the potatoes. It was nice having Beth here. Perhaps next year, when the weather got better, they could go for a walk round the park or something. Danny was a nice little baby. But would Beth still be living there in the spring? 'Mum, has Beth said when her husband might be home?'

'No. In fact she don't say anything about him.'

That evening, Ruby was sitting at the table with Tom making paper chains. They had a bowl of flour and water paste and were busy sticking the strips of coloured paper Ruby had cut up.

'Look, Dad. Don't they look pretty?' Ruby held up the length of paper chains. 'They're for Christmas.'

He smiled and sat up. A faraway look came into his eyes. 'I remember a Christmas a long while ago. Played football with the Germans, we did . . .' There was a short silence. Then he added, 'They killed me mate the next day,' and slumped back into his chair and pulled his blanket tighter round his shoulders.

Ruby felt sad. It was the first time she'd heard him say that. She wanted to ask him more, but knew it wasn't any good. He always clammed up if they spoke about the war, and only told them things out of the blue, like just now.

'I'll make a cup of tea,' said Mary Jenkins, jumping up. 'Beth should finish feeding Danny soon.'

'I'll do it,' said Ruby.

'No, you carry on helping Tom.'

Tom sat looking at his father, then turned to Ruby and said softly, 'I miss going with you to get the washing.'

'I can't be in two places at once. 'Sides, you're all right with Beth, ain't you?'

'Yes. But . . .' He hesitated and looked at his father again, who now had his eyes closed. He then glanced at the wash-house door: his mother was out there making the tea. Beth was in the bedroom feeding her baby. 'She don't like going to the buildings.'

'I'm not surprised. I shouldn't think anyone likes going there.'

'She leaves me to go up on me own. I'm frightened. I always think that Alfie Anderson's gang's gonner be round the corner.'

Ruby looked at her brother. He was clearly worried. 'I'll have a word with her.'

'No, don't. I don't want her to think I'm a baby.'

Ruby grinned. 'She won't think that. She'll understand. I think we'd better start putting these away for tonight, Mum'll be in with the tea.' Ruby gathered up the paper chains and put them in a box. 'I think we've done enough.'

'When we gonner put 'em up?'

'I don't know. I've got to get some drawing pins.' Ruby sat back. 'Cheer up, Tom. This Christmas is going to be the best we've had in years now we've got Beth's money and me working. Mum's even made a Christmas pudding. I think she put a thrupenny bit in it as well.'

'I hope I get it.'

'So do I. I'm just going out to the lav.'

Ruby shivered when she opened the door and the cold air hit her; she pulled her cardigan tighter round her. As she walked out into the yard she banged her feet on the concrete to discourage any mice or rats that were hanging about. The usual sounds came through the night air. A couple of cats were having a scrap and somebody's dog was barking; she could hear a man shouting. The men round their way were always yelling, making the kids cry and the women shriek. Ruby pushed open the door. It was the spiders she hated most. They hung from the roof of the lav and sometimes in the dark she would walk into a cobweb. She would throw her arms about praying the spider wasn't still on her. When it was dark she couldn't even read the cut-up squares of newspaper that hung on the string. At night, when she knew Mr Cox was out, she always sat with the door wide open. She sat on her hands. It must be lovely to sit inside in a warm room that had a lav instead of having to rush in and out of the cold. She was quietly singing to herself when she heard the back door from the passage shut. Fear filled her; the family didn't come through that door, they always used the door from the washhouse. Ruby shuddered when she heard Mr Cox clear his throat and spit. He stood in front of her, silhouetted against the light from the kitchen. Ruby was terrified as she leapt up from the pan.

'You should shut the door, young lady.'

'I thought you was out.'

'I was.' He laughed. 'I'd love to be able to see your face. I bet you look like a startled rabbit. Here, let me help you.' He went to move towards Ruby. 'Your frock's all bunched up.'

'I'm all right,' she said, scurrying away.

'That Mr Cox came out,' she said to her mother as she walked into the washhouse.

'And I bet you didn't shut the door.'

'I thought he was out.'

'You're getting to be a big girl now, Ruby, you can't sit there with the door open. Tell Tom that as soon as Beth's finished feeding Danny, he'd better go to bed.'

Ruby went back into the kitchen as Beth walked in. 'Well, that's got him down for the night. They look interesting.' She peered into the box of paper chains. 'I used to love Christmas.'

'You've never told us where you used to live,' said Ruby.

'I thought you knew I was with the Manns.'

'No, before that.'

'If I told you, you wouldn't be any the wiser.'

Mrs Jenkins came into the kitchen. 'Beth, if you want to wash the baby's nappies out now, I've finished in the sink.'

'Thanks.'

Ruby watched her leave. 'Seems strange she's been here a few weeks now, but she's not had any letters from her husband. D'you think the Manns will send them on?'

'Of course. She may even go round there to pick them up. She don't have to tell us all about her private life.'

'I'd just like to know a bit more about her.'

'Why?'

Ruby shrugged.

'It's this going to work that has started to put strange ideas in your head. What sort of women work there?'

'They're all right.'

'Well, all the time Beth helps out, I'm happy. And she's good for your father, the way she sits and talks to him. I tell you I've seen a big change in him since her and Danny arrived, so don't you go upsetting the boat.'

'I ain't gonner.' Although Ruby liked Beth, it seemed the rest of the family did even more. Was she deep down getting a little jealous at Beth being so popular – and home all day?

On Christmas Eve Ruby had arranged to go with Elsie to the market when they finished work at four. The women were overjoyed at being let off early. It was a cold, dark, miserable, dreary afternoon as they wandered along the streets but when they turned the corner they found the market was alive, busy and exciting. Women were hurrying home, carrying as much produce as their money allowed them to buy. The stallholders had decorated their stalls with sprigs of holly and were shouting about their wares, all trying to make themselves heard above their competitors. The bright light from the naphtha flares swayed in the breeze. The butcher in his striped apron and boater hat stood outside with his boy selling the feathered birds that filled the front of his shop, taking them down with his long hook as he sold them to the highest bidder.

Elsie nodded towards the butcher. 'Look at the size of some of them turkeys.'

'They'd feed us for months,' laughed Ruby.

'Me dad said he'll be down later. We're gonner have a chicken, he'll be almost giving 'em away be then. Are you having a chicken?'

'No, me mum's got a bit of pork.'

'That'll be nice.'

Ruby would have liked chicken, but that was a luxury and her mother's money wouldn't stretch to that. She knew that whatever they had it would have to be the cheapest cut with Mr Cox getting the best bit. Why didn't he get them a chicken? After all, he was willing to share whatever they had. Fortunately, most days he would bring in something for her mother to cook and he'd have that upstairs on his own. Everybody knew he owned the house: he'd inherited it from his father, so the gossips said.

'Ruby, I was talking to you.'

'Sorry, I was miles away. What was you saying?'

'Let's move on to the haberdashery stall.'

'Whatever you want.'

'I love the smell of those spices,' said Elsie as they passed the grocer's.

Ruby giggled and rubbed her nose. 'They make my nose tickle.' Ruby was so happy she wanted to sing and dance along the street. She'd saved a few shillings and now she was going to spend them. She hadn't bought Christmas presents for years. Everybody was going to get something, including Milly in the dairy. Although it was cold she was like a child, warm with excitement. She pushed and elbowed her way from stall to stall picking up a handkerchief for Milly, a box of pencils and a writing book for Tom. The penny bone teething ring she bought for Danny had been well chewed by the previous owner. She even bought a pair of second-hand, black lace garters that she noticed Elsie had been admiring.

'Here, take this,' she said, thrusting them in her hand.

'I can't take these.'

Ruby's mouth turned down. 'Why not? I saw you looking at them.'

'I know. But I was only looking. Oh Ruby, I'm so sorry. I'm so thoughtless. They're lovely.'

'I would have liked to wrap them in pretty paper, but I didn't get time, and I ain't gonner see you till Boxing Day when we go back to work.'

Elsie threw her arms round Ruby, almost knocking her hat off. 'You're such a funny little thing.'

'I ain't that little. I'm as big as you.'

'But not as old or as streetwise.'

'You ain't that much older than me.'

'Ruby, don't get upset. You're a lovely person, with a big heart.'

Ruby giggled.

'I'm so lucky to have found a friend like you at the laundry,' Elsie went on. 'Can't stand some of 'em. Right big mouths, especially that Florrie James. You wonner watch her if you ever get put in the ironing room.'

'I hope I get out of the washroom one day.' Ruby pointed to the garters Elsie was holding. 'They're for putting in a good word to Mrs Watson for me. Without that I wouldn't have a

61

job and I certainly wouldn't have any money.'

Elsie tucked her arm through Ruby's. 'What say we go and have a cuppa at the café? My treat.'

'Why not?'

Ruby and Elsie made their way through the crowds, clutching all their parcels carefully. Her eyes sparkling and her cheeks flushed, Ruby looked at the mistletoe decorating some of the stalls. Her dreams would be complete if Ernie Wallis sauntered along and, after buying a sprig, came up and kissed her. She hadn't seen him since that night he was going to the pub. Whenever she left work she kept an eye out for him, but he was never around. I wonder if he ever thinks of me? she mused.

It was just beginning to get light outside. Ruby lay for a moment or two quietly taking in the silence. The baby was sleeping peacefully and Ruby could just make out Tom's head buried in the pillow. She smiled. She knew there was a stocking wedged against the end of the mattress, and she couldn't wait for him to wake and see what was in it. Ruby loved him so much and wished he could have the childhood she'd had. She couldn't hear her mother pottering about. She would wait a little longer before she got up; she didn't want to go into a cold kitchen.

Ruby must have dozed off again as she woke with a start when Danny began to cry.

'Look, Ruby! I've got some pencils and a book, and look, there's some sweets and an orange. This is the best Christmas *ever*.' Tom had scattered paper over the floor.

'Merry Christmas, Ruby,' said Beth. 'I'm sorry if Danny woke you.'

'Merry Christmas, Beth. It's all right, I should have got up ages ago. I must go and help Mum.'

'I've not heard her moving about.' Beth put Danny over her shoulder and gently patted his back.

'Did Danny get a stocking?' asked Tom.

Beth laughed. 'Not this year, he's a bit young to appreciate it.'

'I got him something.'

'Oh Ruby, that's so very kind of you.'

'It's a teething ring. I remember you said he'll be needing one soon.'

Beth put her free arm round Ruby. 'Thank you.' She kissed Ruby's cheek, then looked at her son. 'You're a very lucky little boy to have someone like Ruby to spoil you.'

Ruby quickly got dressed and went into the kitchen. It was cold. The fire hadn't been lit. Ruby stood and looked around. Everything was just as they had left it last night. She hurried through the washhouse and into the yard. She pushed open the closet door. It was empty. 'Mum,' she called softly. She rushed back through the washhouse and kitchen and gently knocked on her mother's bedroom door. 'Mum,' she called softly again.

Beth came out of their bedroom. 'What is it, Ruby? You look worried.'

'It's Mum. She ain't up yet,' Ruby whispered.

'She works very hard – perhaps she feels like sleeping in a bit longer. After all, she's got all day with no washing or ironing hanging about.'

'She's never slept in before.'

'Well, she won't be for much longer, not with all the chatter that's going on out here. Let's give her a nice surprise. We'll get the fire going, then you can take her a nice cuppa. That'll be as good as a present for her.'

Ruby smiled. 'Come on then. I hope I haven't woken her up.'

It didn't take long for the fire to take hold, and although Ruby was worried about her mother, soon she and Beth were laughing and singing, 'Away in a Manger'. Looking at Beth, Ruby realised she *was* happy to have Beth around; her stirrings of jealousy seemed to have subsided.

Tom walked in clutching his stocking. 'Where's Mum?'

'Still in bed. Here, come here and hold this toasting fork. I'm doing a piece of toast for Mum and Dad. Beth is setting out a tray. It's a sort of present.'

'Don't think much of that for a present.'

'It will be for Mum, so don't burn the toast.'

'Would be nice if we had a few flowers,' said Beth, neatly arranging the cups.

'We could put a bit of that greenery I picked up at the market on the tray,' said Ruby, going to the mantelpiece and breaking off a sprig from the evergreen that was stuck behind the mirror.

'That'll give it the finishing touch,' said Beth.

When they were ready Ruby gently knocked on her mother's bedroom door. 'I'm coming in.' She pushed open the door.

'Hello, love,' said her father. 'Your mum's still asleep.'

This was so unlike her mother. Was she ill? Fear gripped Ruby's heart. 'Is she all right?'

'Think so. She ain't said much.'

Ruby put the tray down and sat next to her mother. To her great relief she could see she was breathing. It was very slow and even. 'Mum. Mum! Are you all right?'

Mary Jenkins opened her eyes. 'Ruby!'

'I was worried about you. You looked so peaceful, hardly breathing.'

'I'm fine. Now, what time is it?'

'It doesn't matter.'

'Course it does. I've got to get up.'

'Mum, are you sure you're all right?'

Her mother appeared disorientated as she sat up. 'Yes, yes. Of course. I must do the fire.'

'It's done. Here, look, I've brought you and Dad breakfast in bed.'

'Oh Ruby. Thomas, look. Look at the way Ruby's done the tray. It looks so very pretty.'

He too sat up.

Ruby could see the tears well up in her mother's eyes.

'Beth helped,' she said, not wanting to take all the credit.

'I ain't had breakfast in bed since young Tom was born. You and Beth are such good girls. I feel as if I've two daughters and a grandson, don't you, Thomas?'

'I should say so. We've got a lovely family.'

Ruby felt as if her heart was going to burst with love. 'You don't have to get up till you're ready. Can Tom come in and show you his presents?'

'Course,' said her mother, whose mouth was full of toast. 'Sit up properly, Thomas, and I'll pass you your tea.'

Her father gave Ruby one of his grins. 'Thanks, love.'

'Is everything all right?' asked Beth as soon as Ruby walked back into the kitchen.

'Yes, she just overslept, that's all.'

'See, I told you.'

'Tom, take your presents in to show Mum.'

'Ain't she gonner get up then?'

'Yes, later on.' Ruby couldn't help wondering about her mother. Although she appeared to be her normal self, why wasn't she up and jumping about as she always did?

'If you like I'll do the potatoes,' said Beth, bringing Ruby back.

'Thanks. That'll be good. I can do the sprouts.'

It was a good hour later when Mary Jenkins walked into the kitchen. 'My, you have been busy,' she said, looking round the room.

'It's a sort of Christmas present,' said Beth.

'Thank you.' She kissed Beth's hair.

'Are you feeling all right?' asked Ruby.

'Course. Now, what's to be done?'

'The pork's in and the veg's done. I've put the Christmas pudding in that saucepan.' Beth pointed to the back of the stove.

'So it's just the stuffing then.'

'Looks like it,' said Beth. 'Now, when we've finished dinner, I've got a little treat.'

'What is it?' asked Ruby.

Beth touched the side of her nose. 'Just be patient.'

The smell of the pork roasting had filled the house all morning. The dinner was lovely; even the sound of Mr Cox, who had come down to join them, sucking on his crackling hadn't upset Ruby. Now, as they finished off the last of the dinner, the Christmas pudding was brought in.

'It would have been nice to have some flames around it,' said Mr Cox.

'Ain't got money to waste on brandy. I'm just pleased I've been able to make a pudding,' said Mary Jenkins.

They all put on the paper hats Ruby had made out of newspaper. Tom yelled with excitement when he found the silver thrupenny bit in the pudding. Beth went over to the pram and with a great flourish pulled a bottle of port from under the covers.

'Where did that come from?' asked Mary Jenkins.

'It came with the compliments of the season from Mr Thompson.'

'From the pub?' Mr Cox was sitting next to Ruby. 'He ain't known for his generosity.'

Beth smiled as she poured them all a small drop of port into cups. 'It's because I'm good at me job, and don't mind doing the odd extra bit when he asks me.'

'Ain't seen nothing of this husband of yours yet. Does he mind you working at the pub?'

'It won't be for ever, I'm just helping out.'

'So how long you stopping with your aunt then?'

'I don't know.'

'You must get very lonely without a man to keep you warm at nights. I expect your husband misses a pretty little thing like you.'

'I hope he does.'

'Still, you know what they say about sailors.'

'Yes, I do. Ruby, pass me your cup.'

'I don't think Ruby should have any,' said her mother.

'Oh go on, it is Christmas. Don't worry, I'll not give her that much.'

The laughter and noise got louder as the level in the bottle got lower. Beth began singing; Mr Cox had a flushed face; and her father, after a couple of cups of port, had Christmas pudding all down himself as he tried to find his mouth. Only Mary Jenkins was quiet.

'Your mum says you're at work now then.' Mr Cox put his face close to Ruby's; he had been at the pub in the morning and his breath smelt of beer. His hand was under the table, and he began groping her knee. 'You're getting to be quite a grown-up young lady. And a very pretty one, I might add. I expect we'll soon have all the boys knocking for your attention.'

Ruby quickly gave him a look. 'I don't think so. Mum, shall I start clearing the table?'

'No, leave it for a bit, love.'

Ruby could feel Mr Cox's hot hand slowly moving up her leg. She wanted to slap his hand but knew she couldn't do anything to upset him, as they only lived there because he let them and they could all finish up in the street, or the workhouse, if he turned them out.

She tried to catch Beth's attention, but Beth had her head back and, with her eyes closed, was softly singing.

'Tom, how are you getting on with that colouring book?' Ruby quickly pushed her chair back.

Tom looked up from the floor with a bewildered expression on his face. 'All right. Why?'

'Thought you might want some help.'

'No.'

'Ruby, do you mind if I have a lay down?'

Ruby looked at her mother. 'No, course not. Mum, are you sure you're all right?' She'd noticed how silent Mary had been.

Her mother smiled. 'Course I am. It's the port. I'm not used to drinking.'

'Don't worry about the washing up, Mrs Jenkins,' said Beth, sitting up and opening her eyes. 'We'll see to it.'

'Thanks. This is the best Christmas we've had for years. I shall be sorry when you do have to leave us.'

'You're not going away, are you?' asked Ruby, suddenly filled with gloom.

'No, course not.'

Ruby watched her mother leave the room. This wasn't like Mary at all. She always rushed about doing everything herself, yet she hadn't protested at Beth's offer. Ruby looked at her father, but now he had his eyes closed.

Beth was still singing as she began to clear the table, then she disappeared into the washhouse.

Mr Cox came over and put his arm round Ruby's shoulder.

'D'you know, you've grown into a very lovely girl.' He ran his fingers through her hair. 'This is very pretty.'

She pushed him away. 'I've got to help Beth.'

'That can wait. I'd like you to come upstairs. I've got something I'd like to show you.'

Ruby looked again at her father, who was obviously dozing. Tom was still busy drawing. Why was Beth taking so long? 'I'm sorry, Mr Cox.' She pushed him to one side and gathered up some plates. 'I must help Beth.'

'You could be sorry you've just done that,' he hissed.

Shocked, Ruby stood stock still. What had she done? She didn't want to spoil anything. Everything was going so well. Perhaps she was just being silly and seeing things that weren't there. But somehow she knew she wasn't. Would Mr Cox throw them out if she didn't do what he asked?

She stumbled into the washhouse.

'There you are,' said Beth, who was at the sink and had her back to Ruby. 'Grab that tea towel and you can . . .' She turned. 'Ruby, what is it? You look as if you've seen a ghost.' She put her wet hands round Ruby and held her close. 'Your mum's all right. She's just tired, that's all.'

'I think I've just lost us this place.'

'What? What are you saying?'

'Mr Cox wants me to go upstairs with him, and I said no.'

'What?' screamed Beth. 'The dirty old sod. Let me get at him.'

'No.' Ruby held on to her arm. 'Please don't say anything.'

'I've met men like that all me life. You mustn't give in to 'em.'

'I won't.'

'Are you sure you don't want me to thump him for you?'

Ruby half smiled. 'No, thanks all the same.'

Beth wiped her hands on the towel that hung on a nail

behind the back door. 'Now you listen to me, Ruby. I'm a few years older than you—'

'Not that many,' interrupted Ruby.

'Well, I've been around and I've seen what those sorts of blokes are like. I never got on with me mum and dad and when the chance came to get away, I took it. It was hard at first but . . .' She suddenly stopped and laughed. 'Hark at me getting all silly and sentimental. It must be the port.'

'You must miss your husband?'

'Well, yes.' Beth quickly returned to the sink to finish the washing up.

'I thought he might have sent Danny something for Christmas.'

'I expect he'll bring it when he gets home.'

Ruby was still thinking about Mr Cox. Slowly she wiped the cloth round and round the plate. Just a few hours ago life had seemed wonderful. Now she was worried about all their futures.

'Penny for them?' said Beth.

'They ain't worth a penny.' She had prayed that 1920 was going to be a new beginning, but what now?

Chapter 7

Tom angrily brushed his dull blond hair from his eyes. He glared at Beth pushing her pram in front of him. Even though he was wearing the new scarf his mother had knitted him for Christmas and the gloves Beth had given him, he was fed up and cold. Christmas had gone and all the paper chains had been taken down and everything was miserable and back to normal. Most of the clean laundry had been delivered and his pram was now full of dirty smelly washing. As usual, when they reached the street where the buildings were, Beth told him he could leave his pram with her while he went up and delivered Mrs Bell's washing. Tom was worried; he didn't want to go up on his own as he had caught sight of a gang of boys larking about in front of them when they turned the corner. They had disappeared, and he guessed they would be waiting for him as soon as he was up the first flight of stairs and out of Beth's sight.

'Please, Beth. Come with me.'

'Oh come on, Tom. You'll be all right. I'm only down here. Besides, I ain't dragging me pram all the way up there.'

Tom had been through this conversation before and knew it was no use. He picked up the neat pile of ironed clothes that were wrapped in a clean towel and made his way to the stairs.

He stopped and turned. Beth looked about, then gave him a little wave.

Slowly he peered round the corner after the first flight of stairs and was surprised to find he was alone. With his head down he quickly started to run up the stairs two at a time. Mrs Bell lived on the fourth floor.

As he went round the second bend a scruffy boy barred his way. 'Fought you'd missed us, didn't yer?'

Three more boys came and stood next to their leader. His name, Tom knew, was Alfie Anderson. Tom's legs refused to move. He was very, very frightened.

'What you got there?' asked one of the boys.

'Only some lady's washing.' His voice was very high and faint.

'Let's 'ave a look,' said Alfie, coming towards him.

'He might have some funny drawers in there,' said one of his mates.

Tom began to back away. 'Leave me alone.'

''Ave yer got some funny drawers then?' asked Alfie, grabbing the parcel.

'Give it back!' screamed Tom. He was feeling sick.

' "Give it back!" ' repeated one of the gang in a silly voice.

'Well, look at these.' Alfie held up a pair of Mrs Bell's pink satin and lace knickers. 'My mum'll like these.' He stuffed them into his pocket. 'What else yer got?'

The other members of the gang snatched the washing from Tom and began riffling through it. Loud shouts and whoops of delight filled the stairs as they held up the garments one by one, then, after a lot of arguing about who should have what, stuffed them in their pockets.

Tears filled Tom's eyes as he stood helplessly watching them. He went to back away but Alfie put his foot out and Tom stumbled over it and sat on the hard concrete floor with a bump.

They were so busy and making so much noise that they didn't see or hear Mrs Bell and a very large-built man come down the stairs.

'What's going on down here?' shouted Mrs Bell. 'And what the bloody hell d'you think you're doing? That's my washing.' She snatched back a petticoat. 'Where's the rest of it?'

Tom couldn't speak.

By now Mrs Bell's companion had slipped past the boys and was blocking their exit. They were trapped between Mrs Bell and her man.

'What's this?' she screamed, pulling at one of her garments, which was hanging from Alfie's pocket. 'It's me drawers. I'll bloody kill you. Charlie, go through their pockets.'

Charlie didn't need a second telling. He was pinning the boys down on the hard concrete floor and those he didn't catch quickly threw the garments to the ground and ran off.

'Where's your sister?' demanded Mrs Bell, looking at Tom. 'You shouldn't be up here on your own.'

'Me sister's at work. I'm ever so sorry.' Tears began to trickle down his cheek.

'You've come up here on your own? Where's the pram? You ain't left it down there, have you?'

Tom shook his head. 'Beth's looking after it for me.'

'Well, I hope she can look after herself, cos I reckon they'll be giving her a hard time. That bloody Alfie Anderson wants locking up, and his mother and her drunken old man, and all her kids along with him.'

Tom wiped his eyes with the cuff of his sleeve.

'Come on, love.' Mrs Bell put her arm round Tom's slim shoulders. Her perfume filled his nostrils. He'd never smelt anything so nice before. 'Let's go and see that this Beth's still in one piece.'

They made their way down the stairs and out into the cold air.

'About time too,' said Beth, banging her arms and stamping her feet. 'It's freezing out here.'

'This young man's been having a bit of trouble. A gang of roughnecks set on him. Thought you might be having a bit of trouble with 'em yourself, being out here on your own. Did you see 'em?' asked Mrs Bell.

'I did hear a bit of a racket, but they rushed past me quick.'

'D'you happen to know any of 'em?'

'No. I don't come from round this way.'

Mrs Bell looked quizzically at Beth.

Beth quickly looked away. 'Come on, Tom, we'd better get a move on.'

'Don't I know you from somewhere?' asked Mrs Bell.

'Shouldn't think so. As I said, I don't come from round this way.'

'Funny. You look very much like someone I used to know.'

Beth gave her a slight smile. 'I pity her then. Come on, Tom.'

They moved away. Tom looked back at Mrs Bell who stood for a moment or two looking in their direction, then she shrugged and with her arm through Charlie's, turned and walked off.

All the way home Tom worried about what his mother would say. The time she had spent ironing Mrs Bell's delicate washing, and how it was all creased. He had even forgotten to collect the money and the dirty stuff. This wouldn't have happened if Ruby had been with him. He wished he were dead.

'What d'you mean, you got set on be some boys?' His mother was very angry. 'You should stand up for yourself.'

'It was that Alfie Anderson's gang,' said Tom.

'I don't think he would have stood much of a chance. After all, there was four of them,' said Beth, walking outside to the lav.

She closed the lav door. She didn't want them to talk about it. Why did she go with Tom when she knew he was going to the buildings? What would the Jenkinses say if they really knew all about her? Would they let her stay in this house? She knew she had to keep out of that Rita Bell's way. She had a mouth on her, that one.

That night, when Tom finally managed to get Ruby on her own, he told her everything that had happened.

'And Beth didn't help you?'

'No.'

'That's not like her.'

'She's always worried when we go round the buildings. She's always looking round. Sometimes I have to leave her and the pram a couple of streets away.'

'That's funny. I didn't think she come from round that way. I wonder what she's frightened of?'

'Ruby, what about Mrs Bell's washing and Mum's money?'

'Don't worry. I'll go when I finish on Saturday.'

The next day Ruby in turn told Elsie about Beth, Tom and Mrs Bell.

'Poor little bugger. He must have been scared out of his wits. Four of 'em, you said. Did they hurt him?'

'No. I've come across that Alfie Anderson before. He saunters around with his gang as though he owns the place. He really is a nasty piece of work. D'you know I once told him and his gang off for chasing a cat. He told me to mind me own business, then said he was gonner skin it and have it for his dinner.'

Elsie looked horrified. 'No,' she said, putting her hand to her mouth. 'The horrible little bugger. But you always managed to keep him at bay.'

'Only cos I had Tom with me and we always took a big stick.'

'Good for you.' Elsie laughed. 'This Mrs Bell sounds a right old tom.'

'She's all right. She's got some lovely underwear.'

'She needs it in her profession.'

'She must make a lot of money. She always looks very nice.'

'Here, you ain't thinking of going on the game, are you?'

It was Ruby's turn to laugh. 'I wouldn't know what to do.'

'They say that you only have to lay back and think of England.'

Ruby looked very serious. 'Why do they say that?'

'I dunno. It's just something I was told.'

Ruby's mind went back to Mr Cox and Christmas night. All evening he had tried to sit near her. She gave a slight smile. It had been a bit like musical chairs without the music. She had tried not to look at him, and Beth had somehow managed to keep him at arm's length without it being too noticeable. But what would happen when Beth went? Would she be able to keep him at bay then? And should she tell her mother?

Ruby didn't take the pram on Saturday, as she was going straight from work to collect Mrs Bell's washing. She had told Elsie she wouldn't be going to the market.

'D'you want me to come with you?' asked Elsie as they met outside the laundry gate.

'Would you mind?'

'No, in fact I'd quite like to meet your Mrs Bell.'

As usual they had to pick their way through the rubbish.

'Christ. What a dump,' said Elsie as they climbed the stairs at the buildings.

The normal sounds of men shouting, kids crying and women screaming filled their ears.

'And it stinks,' said Elsie, holding her nose. 'Would have thought she could have afforded somewhere better than this to live.'

'She must like it. I think she's been here a long while.'

'How did your mum get to take in her washing?'

'Mum met her at a friend of me dad's. It was in the war. They got talking and she said she worked in a munitions factory and didn't have time to do her own washing, so Mum volunteered, and she's been doing it ever since.'

'Does your mum know what she does for a living?'

'I would think so. This is it.' They stopped outside a door that looked as scruffy as all the rest. Ruby banged on the knocker.

The door was opened very quickly.

Mrs Bell had make-up on and she looked lovely. She gave Ruby a wide smile. 'I thought you'd be round today. Come in.'

Ruby and Elsie stepped into the hall. This was the first time Ruby had been asked inside.

'How is your brother?'

'He's all right.'

'I was a bit worried about him. That girl who was with him wasn't much help. Your brother said you was at work now. Come through here,' she said over her shoulder, and held to one side a beautiful beaded curtain. Ruby had never seen anything so lovely before. She wanted to touch it, to feel the beads trickle through her fingers.

When they got inside the room, both Elsie and Ruby looked at each other. Ruby managed to suppress the gasp that came to her throat. It was the most elegant room she had ever seen. It was like stepping into wonderland. Pretty glass shades covered the gaslights either side of the mantelpiece, which was draped with a fine lace cloth. Pretty china ornaments of ladies in lovely floaty frocks were on top. There wasn't a lot of furniture, just a small table that held a couple of bottles and glasses on a tray, and a sofa, covered in a rich wine-coloured velvet. Another small table stood next to it and on it was a table lighter and matching ashtray.

'Sit down. I'll just get me washing and your mum's money.' Mrs Bell left the room.

Elsie and Ruby sat down together. Ruby was dying to say something, but couldn't.

On her return, Mrs Bell said, 'I didn't get a chance to pay your brother. Give him this extra tuppence. Poor little bugger, he looked scared stiff.'

'He was petrified. That Alfie Anderson and his gang can be very frightening.'

'Yes, I know. Some of my friends have come across them before now. But don't worry. I know some very influential people and I think your – and my – problem could be over. Now, I would ask you to stop for a cuppa, but I'm expecting company.'

'That's all right,' said Ruby, jumping to her feet. 'We mustn't stay.'

Outside Ruby hung on to Elsie's arm. 'What a place! I ain't ever been inside before. I would have loved to see her bedroom.'

'So would I. But I wonder why she lives in such a dump?'

'Could be that the rent's cheap.'

'Or free from a satisfied customer.'

Ruby giggled. 'She must be good at it.'

'I bet her so-called influential people are a couple of heavies,' said Elsie. 'And I wouldn't like to meet them on a dark night.'

'I think I met one once. He was a big man.'

On the stairs they had to step to one side as a well-dressed man, who had his head down, almost bumped into them.

'Sorry,' he said, hurrying on.

Ruby and Elsie stopped. They watched him go up the stairs, then they both laughed.

'I reckon he's this afternoon's customer,' said Elsie.

'Well, he's certainly a lot better dressed than some I've seen in there.'

'Your Mrs Bell is certainly a mystery woman.'

'She ain't mine.'

'Let's get a move on, it looks like rain again. It could even turn to snow, it's so cold.'

'Don't say that. These boots are just about hanging together and me chilblains are getting bad again.'

'Remember that Miss Cotton told you to get some waterproofs.'

'I know. I'm getting some next week. I was hoping I wouldn't be in the washroom all this time.'

'Perhaps Mrs Watson might offer you something else now she's seen that you intend to stay there.'

'I hope so. I'm fed up with being wet all day.'

'I can't understand how those women can be in there all day and every day,' said Elsie.

'Some of them have been there for years. I think that's all they know.'

'They ain't ambitious like you, then?'

'I might be ambitious, but it ain't getting me nowhere.'

'It will, you mark my words. It will.'

Ruby laughed at those words. Elsie's confidence was inspiring. Her good mood lasted all the way home. She was full of Mrs Bell's flat when she got to Hill Street.

'You should see her furniture, and the beaded curtain. I'd

like to have something like that,' said Ruby wistfully.

'Don't think you'd like to do what she does to get it,' said Beth.

'I didn't think you knew her,' said Ruby.

'I don't,' said Beth quickly. 'But I've some idea how she earns her living.'

'Anyway, it's none of our business what she does,' said Mary Jenkins. 'As long as she pays for her washing, that's all I'm interested in.'

Gradually the winter gave way to spring. With the light nights coming Ruby was hoping that sometime she would bump into Ernie again. She would love to go out with him. They couldn't afford to go anywhere but it would be nice to walk and talk with him, hand in hand as she had seen other couples do. She kept these thoughts to herself. She didn't want anyone to know her feelings for him.

Ruby was thrilled when Elsie suggested that one Saturday they should go to the picture house that showed the new silent films.

'Can you afford it?' asked Elsie.

Ruby nodded. 'I've been saving my bit of pocket money.' She didn't add that it was because if she did see Ernie she was hoping she might persuade him to go to a café with her.

At the picture house Ruby was so excited. Sitting in the dark watching moving pictures! She had never seen anything like this in her life before. She laughed and clapped at Charlie Chaplin's antics.

'We must go again,' she said to Elsie as they walked home. 'It was the best night of me life.'

Ruby couldn't wait to tell them at home; she was full of it. 'You should see that Charlie Chaplin – he's so funny and everything goes wrong for him.'

'The pictures really move?' asked Tom, his eyes full of wonderment.

'Yes, and a lady sits at the piano thumping away at the fast bits and very slowly at the sad bits. I'll have to take you one of these days.'

'Cor, would you? I'd really like that.'

'We used to see those before we was sent abroad,' said her father, joining in with the conversation. 'They were wonderful. When I feel like going out again I'll have to take you, my love.' He smiled at his wife.

'That would be very nice,' said Mary Jenkins.

Ruby was overjoyed that her father was talking about going out again. And to everyone's amusement Ruby showed them how Charlie Chaplin walked.

'You'll have to show Beth when she comes in,' said her mother.

'Where is she?'

'She had to go and do a job for Mr Thompson.'

'Where's Danny?'

'She took him with her.'

The following Wednesday Ruby and Elsie met up outside Stone's and began walking home.

Elsie tucked her arm through Ruby's. 'Ruby, I've got something to tell you.'

Ruby stiffened. She knew by the tone of her friend's voice it was going to be something she didn't want to hear.

'I shall be starting at the tea factory next week.'

Ruby stopped dead in her tracks. 'What? You're going to leave the laundry?'

'I didn't like to tell you before.'

'Does Mrs Watson know?'

'Yes.'

'What am I going to do without you?'

'You'll be all right.'

'No I won't.'

'You'll find someone else to go out with.'

'Not in the washroom, they're all old.'

'I reckon you'll be moved soon. Mrs Watson knows a good reliable worker when she sees one.'

'D'you think so?' That idea brought a little cheer to Ruby.

'We can go to the picture house again, and the market on a Saturday.'

'It won't be the same. You'll probably find a new friend at work.'

'No I won't. Come on, you old grouch. Cheer up.'

'Do they want anybody else at the tea factory?'

'I can find out. But jobs don't come up there very often, as you well know. I've been waiting a long while for this so don't make it hard for me.'

'I'm sorry. It's just that I'll miss you.'

Ruby felt as if the bottom had fallen out of her world. The laughter, going to the market and picture house had been lovely. Elsie was all she had ever wanted in a friend.

Chapter 8

At last spring was well on its way and as Ruby walked home from work the sky was a picture. Even partly obscured by the row of terraced houses, it was a blaze of colour with streaks of scarlet to gold, but Ruby wasn't looking at its beauty. Nothing could cheer her up. The thought of Elsie leaving had really upset her. She knew Elsie would soon find a new friend to go out with and she would be alone.

'All right, Dad?' Ruby asked when she walked into the kitchen.

He gave her a beaming smile. 'Yes, love. How's work?'

'Not bad.' There was something different about her father. He didn't have his blanket round his shoulders and he was sitting up. Was he getting better?

'Ruby, can you come with me tonight? I've got to collect some washing and I don't want to go on me own.'

Ruby ruffled the top of her brother's head. 'All right, just let me have me tea first. Where's Mum?'

'I'm out here.' Mary Jenkins walked into the kitchen.

Some evenings Ruby went out with Tom. It was nice just to be with him, catching up on all that had happened through the day. 'Beth feeding Danny?' she asked her mother.

'No, she's popped back to the pub. Seems that Mr Thompson wants her to do a bit of serving tonight,' said her mother.

'She got Danny with her?' asked Ruby.

'No, he's in the bedroom. She's left a bottle for me to give him later on.'

'What?'

'I don't mind. He's a good enough little lad.'

Ruby looked at her mother: she seemed weary. 'Are you all right?'

Mary smiled. 'A bit tired, that's all. That ironing seemed to take it out of me today. Must be to do with the weather.'

Ruby was concerned. 'Beth shouldn't have left Danny with you. You've got enough to do without looking after him while she's out working. I hope she's not going to make a habit of it.' Although Beth's cleaning was hard work, she always seemed very cheerful about it. She didn't have to stand on a cold concrete floor with water swirling round her feet all day.

'It might only be for tonight. I think the young man he's got there is away sick.'

When Ruby finished her tea she put on her hat and coat and went out with Tom. As she pushed the heavy pram she couldn't stop thinking about Beth. It seemed she could do no wrong in her mother's eyes.

'You ain't listened to a word I've said,' said her brother.

'Sorry, Tom. I was miles away. What was you saying?'

'I met that Ernie Wallis and he said he wanted to see you.'

Ruby stopped. 'What?'

'Ernie Wallis said he wanted to see you.'

'When did he say that?'

'Yesterday. That's why I wanted you to come out with me, so I could tell you without Mum knowing.'

'Was Beth with you?'

'No.'

'What else did he say?'

'Just that he got you the job at the laundry and he reckons you should take him out.'

'Bloody cheek. He didn't get me the job, I got that meself.' Ruby smiled to herself. He had been thinking of her. He wanted her to take him out.

'I'm only telling you what he said.'

'I know. Did he say anything else?'

'No.'

'If you see that Ernie Wallis again, tell him I got the job meself.' Ruby bumped the pram down the kerb.

'All right.'

'We'll have to get a bit of dripping on that wheel. Don't the squeak get on your nerves?'

'No, but it gets on Beth's. She said she was going to get her boss to put a drop of oil on it.'

Ruby now knew Beth would be working at the pub for many weeks to come as they'd heard that the break in Mrs Moss's arm had developed complications and was taking a long while to heal.

Ruby looked about her. She was sure this was near to where Ernie lived. Would she bump into him? She wanted to hang about, but knew that wasn't possible. Perhaps she would ask some of the girls in the laundry if anyone had seen him, but she had to be careful, she didn't want to upset Mrs Watson. Although the washroom wasn't the best job in the laundry, it was better than no work at all.

It was late and dark when Ruby suddenly woke. She sat up. She could hear shouting.

'What I do is me own business.'

Tom sat up.

'What's that racket?'

'It's Beth. But I don't know who she's shouting at, I can't

85

make out the voice. Go back to sleep.' Ruby began to pull her coat on. 'I hope she ain't brought nobody back here.'

'Ruby, where're you going?'

'To tell her to shut up. I don't want Danny disturbed when he hears her voice – it might take a while to get him settled again.' Ruby was also thinking about her father; he hated people shouting.

Ruby stepped into the passage. The gaslight was popping; she would have to get a new mantle for it.

'Beth,' she hissed, 'keep your voice down.' Mr Cox peered round the banister. 'Mr Cox, what're you doing?'

Mr Cox had great difficulty getting to his feet. When he managed it, he swayed about. 'This cousin of yours, that's if she *is* your cousin, is a trollop.' His face was very red and he held on to the banisters for support.

Beth laughed.

Mary Jenkins came out of her bedroom pulling her shawl round her shoulders. 'What's all this noise?'

Mr Cox drew himself up to his full five feet four and said, very seriously, 'You might not be aware, but your sister's daughter is a trollop.'

Ruby was trying hard to keep a straight face.

'What are you talking about, Mr Cox?' her mother asked with a serious look on her face.

'She was behind the bar tonight in the Royal Albert.'

'I know that,' said Mary Jenkins.

He wagged his finger. 'Ah, but you didn't see the way she looked and flirted with all the men.'

'I was only being polite,' said Beth, grinning.

'Polite? Is that what they call it now?'

'Please, Mr Cox. It's very late.' Mary Jenkins looked nervously towards her bedroom door.

Beth took off her hat and tossed her head back; her blonde

hair fell round her face. 'You're only jealous because I didn't pussyfoot up to you.'

'You mind your tongue, young woman.'

From being amused at Mr Cox's condition, Ruby was suddenly filled with horror. How could Beth talk to him like that? Beth knew how important it was to keep Mr Cox happy.

'That's it. I'm not having her take that tone with me. You can all go. I want you out of this house by the end of the week.'

Ruby could see the tears filling her mother's eyes. 'You can't do that,' she cried out.

'I can and I will.'

Ruby went and put her arm round her mother's shoulder, then she turned on Beth. 'Thank you. You have just lost us this place.'

Beth shrugged. 'Well, I ain't having him telling me what I can and can't do.'

'You will all the time you live here.' Ruby was desperately worried. She didn't want any more trouble for her mother. She quickly turned back to Mr Cox. 'It's her you should be throwing out, not me mum and dad.'

Mr Cox was having a job keeping his balance. 'What, a mother and her baby? Dear me. You ain't got a lot of respect for your cousin, now have you?'

Mary Jenkins dabbed at her eyes with her shawl. 'Don't say any more, Ruby, please.'

'Beth, how could you be so stupid?'

'You know what a dirty old bugger he'd be, given half a chance! Look how he wanted you to go upstairs with him at Christmas!'

'What?' said Mary Jenkins.

Mr Cox looked alarmed. 'I only wanted to show her some drawing I'd done. There ain't nothing wrong in that.'

'It depends. I've met a lot of dirty old men like you,' said Beth. 'I'm going to bed. I've got work to do in the morning.' With that she went into the bedroom.

Mr Cox was trying to find the bottom stair. 'You should keep that girl in check,' he said over his shoulder.

'I'm sure she didn't mean it,' said Mrs Jenkins.

'I'll talk to you in the morning. Goodnight, madam.'

Ruby and her mother stood in the passage watching their landlord slowly make his way up the stairs. The popping of the gaslight was filling her ears. In her heart, Ruby was almost wishing he would fall and break his neck, then all their worries would be over.

When he shut his door, Mary Jenkins turned to her daughter. 'Ruby, did he really touch you?'

'He tried.'

'I'm sorry. Why didn't you tell me?'

'Didn't think you'd believe me.'

'I don't know what we can do. We can't upset him. This place is all we can afford. It's going to be hard when Beth moves on.'

'Is she moving on?'

'She will one day and it might be sooner than we thought, and us along with her.' Her mother sat on the stairs. 'Where will we finish up?' She looked up at Ruby and the tears ran down her face. 'If we get thrown out they could take your dad away. We could finish up in the workhouse.'

Ruby sat next to her mother and put her arm round Mary's thin shoulders. 'Mum, don't say that. I'm sure we'll be able to manage. What was Beth thinking about?'

'I'm sure it wasn't really her fault. She's such a nice girl. Perhaps tomorrow she'll go up and tell Mr Cox she's sorry.'

'I'll have a word with her and see if she'll do that.'

'I'm sure she will. Ruby, if anything happens to me,

promise me you'll look after your dad and Tom. You will, won't you?'

'For goodness sake, Mum, nothing's going to happen to you.'

Mary Jenkins clutched her daughter's hand. 'Promise me, Ruby, promise me, please.'

'Now honestly, do you have to ask?'

Her mother slowly shook her head.

'Well, come on then. Let's stop all this silly talk and get to bed. We'll worry about Mr Cox tomorrow.'

Her mother held Ruby's face in her thin red hands and kissed her cheek. 'You're a good girl, Ruby.'

Ruby watched her mother go into her bedroom. She was looking old and very thin. Many times Ruby had told her that now money was a little easier she didn't have to work so hard, but she worried it might not last, and if she lost her customers now she wouldn't get them back.

Beth was flat out on her back snoring. Ruby lay next to Tom. His steady breathing told her he knew nothing of the drama that had been unfolding. Danny was making funny little snuffles. Beth was lucky to have such a lovely son. Ruby knew sleep wasn't going to come easily. Her mind was going over and over all that had happened. Why wasn't Beth more diplomatic? She had known how they got these rooms and knew what was at stake. Perhaps tomorrow she would go up and tell Mr Cox she was sorry.

Beth was feeding Danny when Ruby opened her eyes.

'I bet you're really angry with me, ain't you?'

Ruby sat up. 'What do you think? I'm worried we might get chucked out.'

'It won't come to that.'

'How do you know?'

'It was the drink talking. 'Sides, he ain't that daft. He won't throw you out; he knows he's on to a good thing. Who else would do his washing and cooking?'

Ruby didn't reply as she pulled her frock over her head.

'And I earn my own living, so he can't hurt me,' said Beth.

'What happens when Mrs Moss gets back and you're out of work?'

'I'll cross that bridge if and when I get to it. Something always turns up.'

'Ruby, what's the shouting about?' asked Tom, sitting up.

'Nothing. Come on, it's time to get up.' Ruby gathered up the bedclothes and put them in a pile away from the door.

'What's wrong?' asked Tom looking bewildered. He could see Ruby was angry.

'I had a little drink last night and me and Mr Cox had words.' Beth was smiling. 'Don't worry about it.'

'Is Dad all right, Mum?' Ruby asked when she went into the kitchen.

Her mother gave her a slight smile and nodded. 'I don't think he heard the rumpus.'

'That's good.'

'Is she awake?' Her mother inclined her head towards the door.

'Yes. I've told her to go up and apologise.'

'D'you think she will? I don't know what we'll do if we have to move out.'

'I told you. I don't think it'll come to that.'

'I hope not. I didn't sleep a wink last night.'

Ruby looked round the tidy room. On top of the range, which had been black-leaded, the kettle was singing softly, and the hearth had been whitened. 'What time did you get up?'

'I couldn't get back to sleep, so I got up and carried on with me chores. The first lot of washing's on the line.'

'Mum, this ain't going to do you any good, working like this and not getting any sleep.'

Mary Jenkins patted the back of her daughter's hand. 'I'll be all right. Don't you go worrying about me. You find yourself a nice rich young man then we'll all be in clover.'

Despite feeling down, Ruby gave a little chuckle. 'Chance'd be a fine thing.' The only person she really liked was Ernie Wallis, and he was far from rich.

Chapter 9

The following morning, as soon as Ruby caught sight of Elsie outside the laundry, she ran up to her and without giving Elsie time to take a breath, poured out all her problems. 'I'm ever so worried, I just had to tell someone.'

Elsie had listened in silence. When Ruby finished, her first words were: 'The silly little cow. Why did she do that?'

'I don't know.'

'Was she drunk?'

'Didn't look like it, but she did stink of beer.'

'I expect working in a pub you must get a few drinks spilt on you. How old is she?'

'She's never said, but I reckon she must be about eighteen.'

'That all? Eighteen and married with a kid, she must be mad. So what are you going to do?'

'I don't know. I'm hoping she's going to go up and apologise. That Mr Cox can be nasty. But it's Mum I'm worried about. She didn't get any sleep last night.'

'You didn't tell me about Christmas and him wanting to take you up to his place. What's he like?'

'Short, fat, smelly and needs a shave.'

'Nice.'

'I tried not to think about it. The thought of it makes me shudder.'

'Me too.'

They slowly walked towards the door, standing to one side when a horse pulling a delivery van trotted past them very close.

'Watch it,' shouted Elsie.

'Sorry, girls,' yelled the driver, peering round his cab.

'That's Ben Stone. He's a bit of all right. I went out with him once.'

'You didn't say. What's he like?'

'Very nice.'

'So why did you stop seeing him? He married as well?'

'Na. He's a bit shy and quiet, not like his brother. There's a few of 'em in there that'd like to get their hands on him though, but he's not my type. Let's hope there's some good-looking blokes at the tea factory.'

Ruby was a little shocked at Elsie's revelations. All the time they had known each other she had never told her she had been out with both of the boss's sons. The cobbles felt hard under Ruby's feet as they got nearer the door and the hooter blew for them to start work.

Ruby held on to Elsie's arm. 'I wish you wasn't leaving on Saturday. I don't know what I'll do when you go.'

'Now come on, don't go upsetting yourself. I'll see you later,' said Elsie, taking Ruby's arm from hers. 'I'm sure everything will work out.'

Although Ruby smiled, her heart was heavy. Who would she be able to talk to when Elsie left? All through the day she thought about home. She had told Elsie she would be going home as soon as she could get away. The day dragged; even the women she worked with couldn't bring a smile to her face with their tales of what they'd be doing over the weekend. Doris would tell them about her husband and how she'd put salt and even pepper in his tea when he was drunk, but

93

according to her he always drank it before falling asleep. Then there was Mrs Ramsey; she would carry on about her two sons who had been caught pinching. As they were only six and seven they got away with just a clip round the ear from the copper, but she knew they would finish up in prison just like their father and two older brothers. They were lovely down-to-earth ladies and she enjoyed being with them. They didn't mind being up to their ankles in water every day, just as long as they earned enough money to put food in their children's mouths.

Ruby was fed up and couldn't wait for the end of the day, and then she would know if she still had a home to go to next week.

Ruby rushed down the passage and threw open the kitchen door. 'Well?' she shouted.

Tom was sitting at the table and her father in his usual chair. They both looked up.

'Where's Mum?' Ruby asked.

'I'm here, what on earth are you shouting about?' Her mother came into the kitchen from the washhouse wiping her hands on her sacking apron. She pushed her hair behind her ears.

Ruby stood and looked at them all in surprise. 'Did she go up?'

'Yes,' said her mother.

'And?'

'Don't worry, it was all a misunderstanding.'

Ruby could have cried with relief, but also with frustration. All day she had been worried sick, and now it was all over and no one else seemed at all concerned. 'What did she tell him?'

'I don't know. I think she took him a bottle of something. Anyway, she said we had nothing to fear.'

'He didn't say anything when you took his dinner up to him then?'

'No, but he'd had a shave.'

'So how do we know she's telling the truth?'

Her mother was signalling with her eyes, but it was too late.

'You don't,' said a voice.

Ruby turned. Beth was right behind her.

'As I told your mother, it's all right.'

Ruby sank into the chair. 'I'm sorry. But I was so scared.' Was it really going to be OK?

'Ruby, I know you ain't best pleased with me,' said Beth that night as she got undressed ready for bed. 'But I'd had a couple of drinks and me tongue ran away with me.'

Ruby eased herself up on her elbow. 'You know me mum didn't get a wink of sleep last night through worrying?'

'I know, and I'm really sorry about that. I think the world of your mum. You're very lucky.'

'Well, it's a pity you didn't think about that last night. That's why we try to keep him upstairs happy.'

'It won't happen again, I promise. Ruby, please don't be cross with me. I've said I'm sorry. You're much too young to worry so much. Look, why don't we go out one Sunday afternoon now the weather's getting better?'

'I'd like that. We could show Danny the ducks.'

'I might even buy you an ice cream.'

Ruby smiled. 'That would be really nice. Could we take Tom?'

'Why not. We can make it a family outing.'

Ruby hadn't got used to the idea of Elsie leaving and when Saturday arrived she didn't want to go to the market as they usually did.

'Now come on, cheer up,' said Elsie. 'We'll go to the café and have a nice cuppa, and then we can make arrangements to go to one of those picture houses again.'

Ruby's face lit up. 'D'you mean that?'

Elsie nodded.

'I really enjoyed meself last time.'

'Well then, come on, we can talk about it.' Elsie tucked her arm through Ruby's and almost marched her down the road.

As they sat drinking tea Ruby's thoughts were miles away. The very idea of going to see moving pictures again was filling her mind.

'Ruby,' said Elsie. 'I was saying I can come to the laundry next Friday if you like, then I can tell you all about me new job and we can sort out about going to the picture house on Saturday.'

'Yes, yes. Friday will be fine. Will you have any money? Don't you have to work a week in hand?'

'Yes, but me dad'll see me all right. If any week I can't come out with you, why don't you ask that Beth to go with you? She should have more than enough money if she does the odd night in the pub as well as the cleaning.'

'It wouldn't be the same as going with you.'

'I know. But we all have to move on.'

Ruby fiddled with the spoon in the saucer. 'I suppose I could ask her if you couldn't make it. Me mum don't mind looking after Danny. He's sitting up now. He's certainly made a difference to me dad; he sits and talks to him. Danny's such a happy little soul.'

'Well then, that's settled.'

But although Ruby liked Beth, it was Elsie who was her best friend. Things wouldn't be the same.

Ruby spent the whole of the following week looking forward

to Friday when hopefully they would be planning to go out together. Ruby rushed through the arch and grinned when she saw Elsie waiting for her.

Ruby listened to Elsie excitedly telling her how much she liked the women she worked with. What with the extra money she would be getting, it was a lot better all round. 'And there's some good-looking blokes there as well.'

Ruby had to try hard to conceal her disappointment as she listened to Elsie telling her they wouldn't be going to the pictures the next day.

'Now don't get angry, but me sister wants us all to go tomorrow as it's me dad's birthday. We can go another time.'

As they walked along Elsie took Ruby's arm. Somehow Ruby felt this was a sign she wouldn't be seeing so much of Elsie now.

On Saturday, despite her disappointment about Elsie, she was almost pleased to be out with Tom.

'I saw that Alfie Anderson the other day.'

'You didn't say. Did he hurt you?'

'No.'

'What happened?'

'Nothing.'

'Was he on his own?'

'No. I was very frightened when I saw him and his mates hanging about at the bottom of the stairs in the buildings.'

'Was Beth with you?'

'No, I was on me own. I really thought they was going to beat me up.'

'So what happened?'

'He just stood to one side and told his mates to step back. I tell you, Ruby, I was up those stairs like a shot and I was terrified to come down, but they just stood and looked at me.'

'I wonder if any of Mrs Bell's men friends have warned them off?'

'I dunno, but it was very strange.'

Ruby ruffled his hair. 'How d'you fancy coming to the picture house one of these Saturdays?'

'What? Go with you? D'you really mean it?' Tom's eyes were filled with amazement.

'Why not?'

'I'd really like that.'

'That's settled. Tell you what, it could be your birthday treat.'

'Can we go next Saturday, on me birthday?'

'Maybe, or perhaps the week after.'

'Ruby Jenkins, I want a word with you.'

Ruby's heart missed a beat when she heard that voice. She turned.

'I reckon you owe me. I got you that job at Stone's.'

'Did you now?'

'I had a word with that Mrs Watson.'

'Why? After what you told her?'

He hung his head. 'D'you think you could walk on, son,' he said to Tom. 'I want to talk to your sister.'

'Go on, Tom. I'll catch up with you.'

Tom turned his mouth down. 'Don't be long.'

'I won't. So you reckon you got me this job?'

'No, but I had to say something. I'm sorry about telling Mrs Watson that, but I was jealous of you getting a job and me still trying.'

'You've tried to get a job at Stone's?'

'Yer. Taking the van out. I'm good with horses, but they didn't want to know. They only take on girls. That's why I butter up Mrs Watson when I can. You never know, one day there might be a job for me.'

Ruby's heart went out to him.

He ground his cigarette into the ground with the heel of his scruffy boot. 'After, I was sorry for what I said. I realised we're all hard up and need all the money we can get.'

'In that case, thank you.' She went to move on but he put his hand out to stop her.

'Look, I know you don't like me and I don't blame you.'

Ruby could have died. How could she tell him she almost worshipped him? 'You're all right, I suppose,' she said nonchalantly.

'In that case, if you can stand being with me, I'd like us to be friends. You know I can't afford to take you out, but I was wondering now the better weather's here if we could perhaps go for a walk somewhere. I could meet you in the park.'

'Why?'

'I like you, Ruby.'

'You've got a funny way of showing it.'

When he grinned at her and his blue eyes sparkled, she found she was having trouble keeping her feelings under control.

'I think I'm beginning to grow up,' said Ernie.

'Come on, Ruby,' shouted Tom.

'I'd better be off.'

'Can I see you at the park gates tomorrow evening about eight?'

'I'll be there. Bye!'

As Ruby ran to catch Tom up she was so happy, she had a wide grin on her face to prove it.

'Ruby, would you go over to the dairy and get a couple of rashers of streaky for Mr Cox's breakfast,' said her mother when they walked in.

'Hello, Ruby love,' said Milly. 'Don't see a lot of you these days.'

'No, I know. Mum wants a couple of rashers for Mr C's breakfast.'

'How are things?'

'Not too bad now. Even Dad's beginning to look better. He's even talking about going out.'

'That's wonderful news. Still enjoying being out at work?'

'It's OK. I was hoping I'd be moved into a better job when me mate left, but that's not to be.'

'That that Elsie you're always talking about?'

'Yes, she's gone to work in the tea factory. I've asked her to try and get me a job there. Anything's got to be better than standing about all day lifting heavy washing from the boilers and being up to your ankles in water.'

'You wonner be careful you don't finish up with rheumatics. I see that Mrs Moss has got the plaster off her arm – I reckon that Beth Norton will be looking for another job soon.'

Ruby looked up in alarm. 'How will she pay me mum?'

'She must get some sort of allotment from the Navy.'

'Don't know.'

'Let's hope she's put a bit by for a rainy day,' said Milly.

'I hope so,' said Ruby again.

As Ruby crossed the road her good mood had evaporated. Although she sometimes got upset with Beth, her money was more than useful. If she left then Ruby would have to give her mother all of her money. What about Tom? It was his tenth birthday on Saturday and although she had promised to take him to the new picture house sometime, spending all that money on bus fares and the pictures would be an expensive luxury. Should she think of something else to make him happy as the good times might not last for ever? He would be very disappointed. Despite the upset over Mr Cox, she wanted Beth to stay. Perhaps she could find another cleaning job?

From the shop window Milly watched Ruby slowly cross the road, the spring quite gone from her step. Ruby had grown into such a lovely girl. She was so willing to work to help the family. She deserved so much more.

The following evening Ruby set off to meet Ernie. She couldn't believe that he wanted to take her out. She walked slowly round the park. Would he be here?

'You came then.' Suddenly he appeared behind her.

'Yes.' As he fell into step beside her, she was tongue-tied. For the first time they weren't hurling insults at one another.

'So, how is it at Stone's?'

'All right.'

'I told you I wanted a job there as a driver. That's when I first saw Mrs Watson. I was fondling the horse. I'm good with horses, but she told me that his sons do all the collecting and delivering.'

'I've only seen the one horse and cart.'

'He's got two sons, they take it in turns. When they're not out they spend time in the office, or out trying to drum up extra clients.'

'You know a lot about them.'

'Made it me business.' He stopped and looked at her. 'Ruby, I'm sorry I was in a hurry that night.'

'When? The night you was rushing to the pub?'

'Yes. You see I had to get me sister a drop of brandy, she's got this terrible cough and that's all Mum could think of to settle it and help her sleep. She's tried everything: mustard poultices, steaming her over a bowl of boiling water. The poor little thing's exhausted through not getting any sleep, and it ain't doing me mum a lot of good either.'

'I'm sorry. What sister's that?'

'Little Eve.' A smile lit up his eyes. 'She's a funny little thing.'

'How old is she?'

'Four, going on forty.'

'Is she better now?'

'For the time being.'

'Has your mum taken her to see a doctor?'

'No, can't afford it.' He kicked a stone. 'I wish I could get a proper job.'

Ruby was amazed, and full of sympathy. He'd always been so sure of himself, yet now he was letting his guard down, standing here confiding his innermost secrets. 'Why are you telling me all this, Ernie?'

'I need someone to talk to. Me sisters are all right, but I need a friend. Ruby, will you be my friend?'

She couldn't believe this. 'What about your mates?'

'Ain't really got any. Trouble is I've always been a bit of a show off. But things are different now.' He looked at his feet. 'I've always liked you, you're sensible.'

Oh, how very lonely he must be. But he wanted to be her friend. She didn't want to be thought of as sensible, she wanted to be a laugh and make him happy, but being his friend was the next best thing that could happen to her. She swallowed hard. 'I'd love to be your friend.'

He smiled. 'I can't afford to take you out, but it would be nice if some evenings when I'm not busy, and you can make it, we can go for a stroll.'

'I'd like that very much.' Ruby was suddenly walking on air.

He smiled at her. 'That's good.'

'They found a bench, sat down and talked. Ruby was no

longer tongue-tied now she knew he really liked her. He told her how devastated he'd been when his dad got killed.

'I thought the world of me dad. We was more like mates. Me mum was in a terrible state. Suddenly she had me and three girls to bring up on her own. His parents live up north, Scotland somewhere, but they didn't want to know about me mum looking after us lot. She did get a note from his brother once. Dad talked about him sometimes.'

Ruby wanted to hold him, he looked so sad, but knew that wouldn't be right. What a wicked war it had been.

'Things should get a bit better when our Daisy starts work next year. She ain't old enough yet – just thirteen. Mum's hoping to get her into service.'

'Will she like that?'

He was staring at the ducks playing on the pond. 'She ain't got a lot of choice. At least she'll get some decent clobber and food. And it'll be a mouth less for Mum to feed.'

'Ernie, I'm really sorry things are so hard for you.'

He sat up. 'Sorry. I didn't ask you out to hear all about my problems. I shouldn't be going on about me and mine. You ain't exactly had things going your way, have you?'

'No. But with a bit of luck everything will turn out fine one of these days for all of us.'

'I hope so. I've got to be going. It's been really nice talking to you.' He stood up. 'P'r'aps we can do this again. See you around.'

'Yes.' She watched him walk away, disappointed. There were so many things she wanted to ask him, like the washing he delivered to the laundry: where did he get it from? Did his mother work? But Ruby knew she had to take one step at a time; she had to gain his confidence. She went in the opposite direction to Ernie, but she had a smile on her face. Like the weather, she had a spring in her step once more. She didn't notice that Ernie had stopped and was looking after her with a grin on his face. When he set off again, he too had a spring in his step. He liked Ruby very much and hoped this would lead to something more.

Chapter 10

Beth smiled at Mr Thompson when he walked into the bar.

'You make a good job of that floor, Beth.'

'Thank you.' She sat back on her haunches. 'I'm very grateful for you letting me work those few nights behind the bar.'

'You're a very bright young lady, and the customers liked you.'

'I have to start looking after the pennies now. I was very worried that Mrs Jenkins might throw me out after that rumpus I caused with Mr Cox.'

'Heard about that. From what I know of the old goat he deserves taking down a peg or two – always boasting about that house he owns.'

Beth wrung out the floor cloth. 'I didn't know that. Does he own many houses?'

'Na. Right old skinflint. Always moaning that I don't give him a full pint, says there's too much froth on it.'

'I'm surprised we don't see any relations hanging about waiting to pounce when he croaks it.'

'Don't think it's worth much.'

'He must be getting on.'

'All of sixty.'

'And he's never married?'

'No. They say his father won the house in a card game years ago, before my time here. He must have all the papers cos when his father died a few years back he just stayed there.'

'It's strange he only lives in the upstairs rooms. And he must have some money to live on cos he doesn't work, does he?'

'His father was a gambler, so perhaps he left him a few bob. He stays upstairs cos he likes to be waited on. Had a Mrs Potter there before the Jenkinses; she went to live with her son. Cox was an only child as far as we could make out.' Mr Thompson pulled himself a pint. 'Been coming in here for years, and his father before him. Funny pair.'

'Still, I shouldn't have said what I did, about him and Ruby.'

'Oh, what was that?' He held up the beer to the light.

'I think he was trying to get her into his room.'

'The dirty old sod.'

'That's what I called him.'

'Good for you.'

'I was very worried. He threatened to throw the Jenkinses out.'

'Did he now? That sounds like him. From what I gather that Mrs Jenkins looks after him very well.'

'She does.'

'I feel sorry for old Jenkins. He was such a lively bloke, used to come in here, always liked a laugh. That was a bloody awful war, and the government should do more to help the likes of them.'

'Yes, he is a nice man. D'you know they were saying they've seen a difference in him since I moved in? He thinks the world of Danny.'

'That's good.'

'I don't know what I'm going to do when Mrs Moss comes back here to work.'

'Yes, I expect that will be a worry for you.'

Beth liked Mr Thompson. She guessed he was in his fifties; a fair and straight man who didn't stand any nonsense from his customers. He was tall and upright with deep brown eyes and a big moustache. His brown hair was getting a little thin on top, but he was very muscular and could lift the heavy barrels of beer without too much effort.

He wiped the beer froth from his moustache. 'You're very young to be left a widow with a young baby.'

Beth hung her head. 'Yes. It was heartbreaking when I got the news. My Danny never got to see his son.'

'That was a wicked shame. But it can be very hazardous working in the docks. You were very brave the way you carried on. Mind you, he's a dear little chap and no trouble.' He looked towards the pram.

'You didn't have any children then?'

'No, the wife was always too poorly. Pity really. Would have liked someone now to look after me in me old age.'

Beth smiled. 'Come on. You're not that old. You've still got time to marry again.'

'Na. Too set in me ways.'

'I must get on. It's young Tom's tenth birthday today and when Ruby finishes work we're taking him out for a treat. We're going to a café for tea and cake. She's hoping to take him to one of these new picture houses next week.'

'That'll be nice.'

'I promised I'd help Tom today so he can finish early and I don't mind especially now the better weather's here.'

'You're a very hard-working young lady. I shall be sorry to lose you, but I must look after Mrs Moss, she's been with me for years.'

'I know, and I'm very grateful to you for giving me the chance to earn a few bob.' Beth stood up and ran her hands down the front of her sacking apron. 'Is there anything else you'd like me to do today?'

Mr Thompson looked round the bar. 'I don't think so. You've done a grand job as usual.'

Beth pushed her blonde hair from her face. 'Thank you,' she beamed. 'I'll see you tomorrow.'

'I hope so.'

As Beth pushed Danny back to number thirteen her mind was full of Mr Thompson. Had she been silly telling him she was a widow? He didn't go into Milly's who might tell him that her so-called husband was in the Navy and away. Only Mr Cox would tell him a different story, but would Mr Thompson believe him? Besides, she wouldn't be working there for much longer; pity, she enjoyed his company and the money he paid her.

The following week Ruby took Tom to the picture house. He was overjoyed. Ruby laughed with him and at him when he showed the family how the Keystone Cops raced about. She knew she had given Tom a treat he would remember for the rest of his life.

Although Ruby was missing Elsie, who was busy going out with her sisters and her new friends, it wasn't upsetting Ruby as much as she had thought it would, as she now had something to look forward to. Seeing Ernie was the best thing that had happened to her for years. Once a week she would meet him in the park and they would sit and talk or watch the ducks.

'I wish I'd learnt to play the trumpet or something,' Ernie mused.

'Why?'

'You get a free uniform when you join the Boy's Brigade.'

Ruby laughed. 'I hadn't thought of that. Perhaps we should learn together.'

'They don't take girls in the Boys' Brigade.' He laughed with her.

Ruby also went out with Beth some Sundays now Mrs Moss was back at work and she wasn't doing the cleaning any more. So far Beth was still paying her way as Mr Thompson had asked her to work behind the bar on a Saturday and Sunday morning. Ruby did worry about how they would manage when they stopped getting her money. Ruby's mother always looked after Danny while Beth worked now. He was getting to be a bonny baby, sitting up and taking notice. He always welcomed Ruby with a beaming smile, which cheered her up when she came home from work. Ruby found, like her father, she was getting very fond of him. But what would happen when Beth's husband came home. Would they move away?

As it was Saturday, Ruby had finished at four. She didn't want to go to the market on her own, but knew if she went home there would be a pile of ironing to do. Although she knew she should help her mother, she wanted time with her own thoughts so she dawdled home.

Beth had told them how much she enjoyed working in the pub, but she never said what pay she was getting. However, she was forever getting something different to wear, so she had to be doing all right. Even if the clothes weren't new, Ruby couldn't help the jealousy that filled her when she saw Beth go to work in decent shoes and not waterproofs.

Today Ruby noted the pram wasn't in the passage when she walked in. 'Beth out?' she asked when she went into the kitchen.

'Yes. She's gone with Tom,' said her mother, who was doing the ironing.

'D'you want me to do a bit of that?'

'Thanks. I'll make a cuppa. Thomas. Thomas.' She shook her husband's arm. 'Wake up. You won't sleep tonight.'

'I'm all right. Hello, Ruby.' He grinned at her.

'Dad, it's a lovely day out, why don't me and you go for a little walk later on?'

'No, not today.'

'What about tomorrow?'

'Yes. I'd like that.'

'I'll ask Tom to come with us.' Ruby took the iron from her mother, amazed, hardly believing her ears. Did her father really mean it?

'Could we take Danny?'

'I don't see why not.'

'That would be really lovely for you, Thomas,' said Mary Jenkins, patting her husband's shoulder. 'It's a while since you ventured out and pushing the pram will help you walk.'

The thought of that outing really cheered Ruby up. Hopefully tomorrow could be the start of many days out with her father. They could be like a proper family again. Lately he had seemed to be a bit more alive, taking an interest in what they said and did, but it was a long while since her father had been out. Would he cope?

'You mean me, you and Dad're going for a walk tomorrow?' said Tom, equally amazed as they settled down for the night.

'Yes!' said Ruby.

'How long is it since he's been out?' asked Beth.

'Must be months. Mum managed to get him to the cottage hospital when his chest was very bad, but that was before you came to stay. But she had such a job with him at the hospital, she said she'd never do it again.'

'He walks a lot more upright now – he was very bent over when I first came here.'

'I know, that's why I reckon a little walk will do him the world of good,' said Ruby.

'That's if he don't change his mind,' said Tom.

'We shall see.'

'It might rain,' said Tom.

'I'm sorry I can't go with you, but as I said I've got an errand to run,' said Beth, tucking a sheet round Danny's waving legs.

'We could take him,' said Ruby.

'No, thanks all the same, but I don't know how long I'll be. Mr Thompson don't mind me taking him in the back now while I'm serving as he sleeps most of the time.'

Ruby was pleased to see the sun shining when she opened her eyes. It was very quiet save for the sound of church bells in the distance. 'Come on, Tom, get up,' she whispered.

'Why've we got ter go so early?'

'It won't be that early be the time we get ready.' Ruby was too excited at the thought of the day ahead, to stay in bed. 'Pity you can't come with us, Beth,' she added.

'I know, perhaps next time. D'you know where you're going?'

'Not yet. I'd like to get to the docks. Dad always liked to look at the ships, but I think that's a bit far.'

'It is really. Still, I might see you around.'

When Ruby went into the kitchen she was half expecting her father to have changed his mind. She liked Sunday; it was the only day the washing wasn't boiling away and hanging to dry in front of the fire. Although her mother didn't go to church, it had been instilled in her as a child that Sunday was the Lord's day and, despite everything, you mustn't work on Sunday.

'Your dad's really looking forward to this little outing. Just don't take him too far, will you? I don't want him tired out and fighting for his breath half the night.'

'No, of course not. I'll just have me toast then we can be off.'

Outside, the sun was warm and, with her father leaning heavily on her arm, Ruby took a gentle stroll up Hill Street.

'How far shall we go, Dad?'

'Don't mind.'

Ruby wanted to cry, she was so happy. She was out walking with her father and brother. This was how families should be.

'Could we go to the docks?' asked Tom.

'No, I think that's a bit too far for Dad's first outing.'

'We should have brought the old pram, then you could have a ride when you get tired.'

Thomas laughed and ruffled Tom's hair. 'You cheeky young bugger. I don't mind going as far as the park.'

'Are you sure?' asked Ruby. 'I don't want Mum telling me off.'

'I can always have a sit down and watch the ducks. I've missed that.'

'OK then. The park it is.'

Slowly they made their way towards the park. Many times they had to stop, but Ruby didn't mind. They had just turned into the gate when, although Ruby had the sun in her eyes, she thought she caught sight of Beth in the distance.

'That looks like Beth,' she said, pointing.

'Where?' asked Tom.

'Over there. I'll ask her to come over.'

'I can't see her,' said Tom holding his hand to his eyes, shielding them from the bright sunlight.

'No, she's gone behind the bandstand. Dad, can I leave you here while I wander over to her? We'll bring her and Danny back.'

'I'd like that. I'll be all right.'

Suddenly a horse and rider came full pelt towards them. Ruby screamed out. 'Watch where you're going!' She dragged her father to one side. He fell to the ground crying.

'Dad. *Dad*! What is it?'

'The horses. The horses.'

'It's all right. They've gone.'

He touched his forehead and looked at his hand. 'Blood. Blood!' he screamed out.

'It's not that bad.'

He was shaking. 'Blood. I want to go home.'

Ruby took hold of her father's arm. 'It's all right, Dad. I won't let anybody hurt you.' She looked along the path. She wanted to kill that rider. It had taken them months to get their father out, now this had to happen. She also wanted to see who Beth was talking to. Although it was a long way away it looked very much like Alfie Anderson. What was she doing talking to him? That was odd. Did she know him?

Chapter 11

Getting their father home was proving to be very traumatic for Ruby and Tom. He was crying and every few steps he held on to the railings and refused to move.

'Come on, Dad. Let's get you home. Hold on to me. I won't let anyone hurt you.' Ruby was still very angry with the horserider. Who did he think he was?

'The horses. The horses. Make them go away. Make the Germans go away.' He fell to the ground and looked up at Ruby. His eyes full of fear. 'The blood.'

'Ruby, what's wrong with Dad? He ain't bleeding that much. Did the horse hit him?'

Ruby looked about her for help. 'No. I think it must be something that happened in the war.'

'Come on, Dad,' said Tom, trying to help his father. He was clearly very upset. 'Shall I run home and ask Mum to come and help?'

'That might not be a bad idea. He'll listen to her.'

As they slowly moved on Ruby could only wonder what had happened to their father to make him so afraid of horses and the sight of blood?

Ruby gave a sigh of relief when she caught sight of her mother hurrying along the road. Her coat was wide open showing her overall. She wasn't wearing her hat and her hair was flying all over the place.

She came up to them and held her husband tight. 'There, there, love.' She patted her husband's back like she would a child's. 'It's all right, I'm here.'

It upset Ruby to see this tall man holding on tightly to this fragile woman and crying like a baby.

'I'm sorry, Mum. I'm so sorry,' said Ruby.

Her mother continued patting her husband's back and over his shoulder said, 'It's all right, love. Tom told me all what happened. It wasn't your fault. Now come on, Thomas, let's get you home.'

Ruby marvelled at her mother's patience with her father as the sorry bunch slowly made their way back to Hill Street. She knew she would never possess such understanding.

Milly was sweeping the pavement outside her shop when she caught sight of them. She threw her broom to the ground and rushed across the road. 'What's happened? Can I help?'

'Would you mind opening our front door, Milly?' asked Ruby.

'No, of course not. Has he had an accident?' She reached up and took the key from the ledge above the front door and held it open for them to file through.

'Sort of,' said Ruby, hovering round her father and mother.

'Sit him in his chair,' said Mary Jenkins. 'Ruby, pop up the pub and get a small drop of brandy.'

Ruby was breathless when she got to the pub and, bursting inside called out, 'Please, could I have a small drop of brandy?'

'You're in a bit of a hurry, gel,' said a customer who was standing at the bar.

Ruby ignored him and asked again, 'Could I have a small brandy please?'

'Sorry, love,' said Mr Thompson, 'but you're too young.'

'It ain't for me, it's for me dad. Mr Jenkins.'

'What, Thomas Jenkins?'

Ruby nodded.

'He been taken bad again?'

'Yes. A horse almost knocked him down.'

'No.' Mr Thompson handed Ruby a glass with the brandy in. 'You can give the glass to Beth to bring back. What happened?'

Ruby very quickly told him. 'I'm sorry. I forgot to pick up any money.'

He smiled. 'That's all right, love. Have this one on me.'

Milly was still at the house when Ruby returned.

'Here, Thomas, drink this.' His wife held out the glass. His hands were shaking and he had to steady it with both hands.

Milly moved closer to Ruby and in a loud whisper asked, 'Your mum told me what happened. D'you think you should call the doctor?' She directed her question to Mary Jenkins.

'Can't afford it. He'll be all right in a day or two. He's just a bit shook up, that's all.' Mary Jenkins looked very worried. 'The cut ain't very deep. I've washed it and put a bit of iodine on it.'

'Your mum said the horse didn't actually hit him.' Ruby could see Milly was very concerned.

'No, but it came very close and was very fast.'

'I wonder what made him so frightened?'

'It was something to do with the war. He ain't told us a lot about what happened,' said Mary Jenkins.

'Shame,' said Milly.

'Yes. He's been doing so well since Beth's been here, she's been a Godsend the way she cheers him up.'

'I'd better get back,' said Milly.

'How's your dad these days?' asked Mary Jenkins.

'Much better, thanks. But he can't stand for too long.'

'He must be grateful to you and your mum.'

'He gets a bit fed up at times.'

Ruby sat looking at her father. 'I'm so sorry, Dad.'

'I told you, Ruby, it wasn't your fault,' said her mother.

Milly touched Ruby's shoulder. 'People like that want locking up, Ruby. Pop over later and let me know how he is.'

She nodded. 'Thanks, Milly.'

Milly left and Mrs Jenkins looked a little calmer. 'I'll make a cup of tea,' she said.

'I'll do it, you sit with Dad. By the way, Mr Thompson said to give the glass back to Beth.'

'Did you tell her?'

'No. She wasn't in the pub.'

'That's funny, she said she was going up there this morning.'

'I think I saw her in the park.'

'Oh yes. That's right. She had to go somewhere for him.'

Ruby didn't mention that she thought she'd seen her with Alfie Anderson; she would see what Beth had to say about it first.

It upset Ruby to see her father, who in these past weeks had been getting more like the man he used to be, slip back into his old ways. He was sitting once more with his blanket round his hunched shoulders rocking back and forth. If only he would tell them what had happened during the war. If he talked about it, it might help him, and them, to understand.

It was now well past their usual dinnertime and Mr Cox came striding into the kitchen. He sat himself at the table. 'Dinner's late.'

'Yes, I'm sorry. We've had a bit of an upset this morning.' Mrs Jenkins lifted the steaming saucepan off the range and took it out into the washhouse.

'Didn't I see your daughter in the pub?' he shouted.

'Yes, you did,' said Ruby. 'I was buying me dad a drop of brandy.'

'This laundry lark must pay well if you can afford to buy brandy.'

'It was medicinal.'

He laughed. 'I've heard that one before.'

Ruby was finding it hard to keep her patience with this man. 'Me dad was in a accident.'

'Don't give me that. He never goes out.'

'We went for a walk this morning.' Why did she have to tell him all this?

'Ruby. Take these plates in.'

She jumped up, pleased to be able to get away from Mr Cox.

When they were sitting down Mr Cox asked, 'Where's the girl?'

'She's doing something for Mr Thompson,' said Mary Jenkins.

He grinned. 'I bet she is. It's well past closing time, so what's she up to?'

'It's none of my business,' said Mary.

'She wasn't behind the bar this lunchtime.'

'As I said, it's none of my business. Would you like some apple pie?'

Ruby wanted to smile. He hadn't seen the size of the maggots that had been in the apples when she picked them up from behind the barrow. If she had her way she would have dished him up a couple.

It was evening when Beth came in.

'Sorry I'm late, but I had to go over Jamaica Road way and hang about waiting to see someone.'

'Did you manage to get some dinner?' asked Mrs Jenkins.

'Yes, thanks. Mr Thompson gave me some money to get meself a sandwich. Good job I took Danny's bottle with me.'

'Ruby thought she saw you in the park,' said Tom.

'Is that where you went?'

'Yes. But we had to come home cos someone nearly knocked Dad over.'

'No! Where is he? He didn't have to go to hospital, did he?'

'No, he's gone to bed,' said Mary Jenkins, and she told Beth what had happened.

'I've seen those blokes on horseback. They think they own the park.'

'I was going to come and ask you to walk with us,' said Ruby.

'It wasn't me. I told you, I was over Jamaica Road.'

But Ruby knew that part of Southwark Park ran along Jamaica Road, so she could have been in there.

That night when they were in bed, Ruby decided she had to find out more about Beth. She sat up and, hugging her knees, said, 'Beth, I know it was you in the park and you was talking to Alfie Anderson.'

'Who's he?'

'One of the boys at the buildings.'

'Never heard of him.'

'It was his gang that set about Tom.'

'I said at the time I didn't see who it was and I certainly don't know who this boy is.'

Ruby lay down and looked up at the ceiling. She knew it had been Beth, the pram was unmistakable. What did Beth have to hide? Ruby wanted to be friends with Beth, but how could she be if she wouldn't tell her the truth?

But then she had to think of her father. He thought the world of Danny and the little lad's presence had helped him so much. His face lit up whenever Danny was around. Now he was sitting up and crawling about Thomas was even more interested; he had even offered to feed him. So despite any of her own misgivings, she had to think of her father – even more so after today. He'd need all the love and help they could give him.

Beth too lay wakeful. She was getting worried. She should have been more careful. She knew they would hate her if they knew the truth about her.

One Monday morning a couple of weeks after the horse incident, Mrs Watson called Ruby and told her she was taking her out of the washroom and putting her in the pressing room, as one of the women was ill. There she would have to lift the huge, heavy lids on the pressing machines, then help fold the sheets making sure there weren't any wrinkles. Although it was hot and hard work, the pay would be the same if she could keep up. At least in this room she had dry feet and legs and it was only her arms that ached, manhandling those lids. A week later Ruby was filled with dread when Mrs Watson called her out and told her she was moving her again. She couldn't bear the thought of going back into the washroom.

'You're going in the ironing room, but first I want to see if you can iron a shirt. If you're any good you can start in the collar room then go on to the finishing room.'

Ruby had been told that everybody hated the collar room. You couldn't earn good money in there because the collars were so shiny and slippery, as fast as you piled them up so they would fall about, and you seemed to spend most of your time picking them up off the floor.

'You want to think yourself lucky, you're getting to know all the various stages of the work here,' said Mrs Watson. 'Most of the finishers start in the collar room.'

Ruby smiled.

'You'll be on piecework in there, so you have to make sure you work hard to earn your money. No chatting or larking about and you have to do it again if it isn't up to scratch.'

In the ironing room the heavy gas irons were joined to the gas supply by a long pipe that ran overhead. The long tables they sat at were attached to the concrete floor and every so often they would work loose. The girls were younger than those in the washroom, but they were very loud, laughed a lot and were very bitchy. As soon as someone went out of the room they would talk about them. Ruby tried very hard to keep herself to herself. She didn't laugh at their coarse dirty jokes – some of which she didn't understand anyway – and after the first week earned herself the nickname of Miss Stuck-up.

When she was moved into the finishing room, the girls were worse.

One older girl looked Ruby up and down when she walked in.

'Guess what? They called her Miss Stuck-up in there,' she said, pointing towards the ironing room. 'I'm Florrie, by the way. Don't know why you've got your nose in the air, you're only a bit of a kid, a laundry girl like the rest of us.'

'I ain't stuck-up. It's just that I don't like some of the things they said and did.'

'See what I mean, gels? She don't like what we say and do.'

Ruby didn't like Florrie at all; she was flashy and crude. She was always telling everyone how good she was at her job and deserved something better. She was very proud of the fact that she didn't wear drawers in the summer and thought it was great fun when the tables worked loose and the young maintenance lad had to crawl under the table to fix them. She told the rest of the girls she'd sit with her skirt up and her legs open and shout out: 'All right, lad! Got yer eyeful?'

The poor young men used to come out all red-faced and embarrassed.

'One of these days someone's gonner grab hold of that if yer keep flashing it about,' said another of the girls.

'I'd like to see 'em try,' said Florrie.

Although the job was better Ruby missed the women in the washroom with their jolly tales of their homes and families. She knew she would never find a friend in here, not like Elsie. One Saturday, when Ruby was out with Elsie, she told her about her latest move and Florrie.

'That Florrie can be a right cow. I've had a couple of bust-ups with her in the past meself. She's only doing it to make you feel small.'

'She succeeds in doing that. I don't know where to put me face sometimes.'

Elsie laughed. 'You are a funny little thing. That's a good job in the winter, and a dirty joke helps the time pass. At least you won't get those horrible chilblains on your feet and hands in there.'

Some Saturdays Elsie brought Mary, one of the girls from the tea factory, with her. Since Elsie and Mary worked together they seemed to have much more in common than Ruby did with Elsie, now they had the same things to talk about, and sometimes Ruby felt like a stranger when they invited her along. Ruby hadn't told Elsie she was sometimes seeing Ernie, she didn't think she would approve of that.

Although the long warm nights meant Ruby could help her mother and Tom, she felt like life was slipping past her. She would be fifteen next month. She wanted something exciting in her life, but knew she'd never find it at the laundry or round Rotherhithe. If only she and Ernie could go somewhere interesting. It must be lovely to get away. Some evenings they would walk to the docks and stand and marvel at the big ships.

'If it wasn't for me mum I'd go to sea,' said Ernie, leaning against the wall.

'Would you?'

'Yer.' He threw the butt end of his cigarette over the wall and watched it float away.

'I wish I could do something better with my life.'

Ernie looked at her. He held her hands and she thought she would die with pleasure. She liked him so much, but did he like her in the same way, or did he just need someone to talk to?

'You've got plenty of time to do something more with your life. You're . . . what? Still only fourteen?'

Ruby pulled herself up to her full five feet four and straightened her beret. 'I'll be fifteen in a month's time.'

He smiled and Ruby thought her heart would burst.

'You've got plenty of time then.'

Her mother had laughed at her when she told her she wanted to be more like Beth.

'She's always so full of life and enjoying meeting people at the pub.'

'It's your age. You're getting restless,' said her mother.

'I wish I could work in a pub and meet different people.'

Beth, who had overheard, laughed. 'You don't see a lot of different people, it's mostly drunks who ain't interested in you, only what you're serving, and making sure they've got a full measure.'

Ruby hadn't been into Mrs Bell's flat again, but every time she knocked on the door she could visualise that lovely room. However, she certainly didn't want to go down that road.

Throughout the long hot summer, gradually Thomas Jenkins seemed to be getting a little better. It thrilled Ruby to see her father laugh at Danny's little antics and go after him when he tried to crawl away. It was her mother that was causing Ruby the most worry. She appeared to be getting thinner than ever.

'Why don't you have a bit more dinner?' asked Ruby when she looked at the meagre amount on her mother's plate.

'That's more than enough for me. Always had a small appetite.'

One Sunday afternoon, after the washing up was done, they took the chairs out into the back yard and sat catching the last rays of the sun before it disappeared behind the houses.

'I'm glad we're all out here together,' said Beth. 'I've got something to tell you.'

Ruby opened her eyes and sat up.

'Oh Beth. Is it your husband? Is he coming home?' Mrs Jenkins looked very happy.

Beth was taken aback. 'No, it's not that. I'm afraid I shall be moving out next Sunday.'

'Where're you going?' asked Ruby.

'Ruby, don't be nosy. Beth will tell us if she wants to.'

'I only asked, Mum.'

'It's all right. It ain't no secret. I'm going to live at the pub.'

'You're going to live at the pub?' repeated Ruby.

Beth nodded. 'Mr Thompson said he wanted a live-in housekeeper, so I volunteered.'

'We're all going to miss you, Beth,' said Mrs Jenkins sadly.

'And I'm going to miss you. But I'm only up the road. You must pop in and see me sometime.'

'Dad'll miss Danny,' Ruby said softly.

'Yes, I know. But I can bring him back to see him – that's if you don't mind?'

'We'd be pleased to see you,' said Mrs Jenkins quickly.

Tom looked at Ruby. 'Who'll help me with the washing?'

'I'll have to,' said Ruby.

'I'm sure you'll be able to manage,' said Beth, ruffling his hair. 'You're getting to be a big boy now.'

He kicked one foot against the other. 'It won't be as much fun.'

'When are you going?' asked Mary Jenkins.

'Sunday afternoon. Mr Thompson normally has a sleep then, so I'll be able to move in without disturbing him too much.'

'We're really going to miss you, Beth.'

'I'm sorry. You have all made me so welcome, I feel I'm part of this family.'

'You are,' said Mary Jenkins.

'When I get settled you'll all have to come along to tea one Sunday.'

'Cor, I'd like that,' said Tom. 'Going in a pub.'

'We'll see, young man,' said his mother. 'Beth will have enough to do looking after Danny as well as Mr Thompson.'

Beth smiled. 'I'll always be grateful for you putting me up. But it will be nice to have my own room.'

'Course it will,' said Mrs Jenkins. 'But we are going to miss you, ain't we, Ruby?'

Ruby half smiled. 'Yes, we are.'

Chapter 12

'It's only me,' said Beth as she made her way up the stairs.

'That's all right. Thought I heard the door go. I was just having a little doze.' Len Thompson stood at the bottom of the stairs and looked up at her. 'I've put the kettle on, or do you fancy something a bit stronger?' He gave her a warm smile.

'No, tea will be fine. We can have a drink when we close tonight. Are you sure the pram won't be in your way left there?'

'No, it's no problem. I'm really glad you've come. I was a bit worried in case you changed your mind.'

'You didn't have to be. I told you I'd be here.'

'I know. But what about your reputation?'

'As far as everyone knows, I'm just your housekeeper and have me own room. I'm glad I *will* have me own room, but where I sleep is me own business.'

'That's what I like about you, Beth. You don't let anybody walk over you.'

'After the life I've had, I've found out it don't pay. Now, where's this tea?'

Len Thompson smiled. 'I can't believe me luck,' he said, shaking his head as he walked away.

Beth was singing softly as she began to carry the few bits

and pieces she possessed up to the room Len had given her. It was a small compact room with a bed and dressing table. It had been his wife's room. Mr Thompson told her he had long since moved her stuff out. She opened the wardrobe door; it was empty and smelt musty. She put her few clothes on the floor and went down to collect her coat and hat.

She looked in the pram and smiled down at Danny who was fast asleep. She bent her head closer. 'Looks like we've landed on our feet this time, my love,' she whispered and, kissing her finger gently, touched his forehead.

Len Thompson came from the room at the back of the stairs carrying a tray. 'Wasn't sure where you wanted this tea.'

'We can have it in your living room if you like. Danny shouldn't wake for a while.'

Len turned round and walked along the passage. He gently pushed open the door with his foot and set the tray down on the table, which was covered with a thick brown oilcloth tablecloth. The roses had been washed away long ago.

'Everything all right?'

'Lovely. Thank you.'

'Sit yourself down.'

Beth had been in this room many times; it was a dark manly room with a table and four matching chairs. As she pulled the chair out from under the table she did wonder if they came out very often. A very old large dark sideboard took up the whole of one wall; a photograph of the late Mrs Thompson smiled at her. She had been a very beautiful woman, but had eyes that looked sad and wistful. There were pictures of old hunting scenes on two other walls. A window hung with thick heavy brown brocade curtains looked out on to the back yard full of wooden crates and beer barrels. A brown leather armchair stood next to the fireplace. The range hadn't been black-leaded for years. The whole place smelt of the tobacco Mr Thompson used in his pipe. Now as his housekeeper she would keep it tidy and perhaps add a few knick-knacks. He had told her he had let things slide after his wife died ten years ago. But as he was in the bar mornings and every night it didn't matter. Beth had other ideas.

That evening when the pub opened, Beth kept out of the way. She didn't want everyone to know right away she was living there, but knew it would soon get out.

As she sat in his living room, Beth looked around. The first thing that'll have to go is this pile of old papers and books, she said to herself as she thumbed through them. Unlike Ruby, she couldn't read properly, but she had kept that secret to herself. Beth had envied Ruby when she sat with Tom teaching him. She would listen very carefully, trying silently to learn along with Tom. Beth was very quick and somehow she had managed to bluff her way round that failing. She picked up things fast, and she could count. Her mother hadn't taught her much, but she was a shrewd old bird, streetwise, and knew how to make the money go round. When her father – Beth shuddered at the thought of him – came home from the pub three sheets to the wind, her mother would go through his pockets and take just enough to make sure her kids were fed, but no so much that it would be noticed. They all learned very early on never to take it all as that would be far too obvious.

Sitting in the armchair, Beth cast her mind back over these past months. She thought she had done well when she moved in with the Jenkinses, but now, this time, she really had come up trumps. She would miss the Jenkinses; although they had nothing they were a loving family and she was very fond of them. Mr Cox was a bit of a pain. She smiled to herself. After she had found out he had property she had thought about going after him, but quickly decided against that when she saw what he owned. Ruby was the one she had been wary of.

Ruby was a clever girl, and very watchful. Beth had worried about those alert eyes seeing more than Beth wanted. But despite the age difference, Beth would have liked to have been more friendly with Ruby: she was kind and thoughtful, always worrying about her parents, and certainly not afraid of hard work; she should go far. Beth felt guilty about the fibs she'd told to people, especially the Jenkinses, but it was for the best. She didn't want to finish up in the workhouse. She smiled to herself. Wouldn't they all be surprised if they knew the half of it?

She settled back in the armchair and looked about her. It was going to be lovely to be the mistress of this place. Soon everybody would know she was living at the pub as Mrs Moss would still do his cleaning and would tell everybody. Of course they'd all want to know their sleeping arrangements. Beth was going to help in the bar and cook his meals. Later on, who knew, things could change. She grinned. She might even get him to marry her.

Ruby looked round the bedroom as she settled down for the night. Without the pram and Beth's mattress, the room looked very empty. She knew they would all miss Beth and Danny, but none more so than her father. The little boy had certainly brought a lot of happiness into his life. How would her mother manage without Beth's money? Ruby knew that now she would have to work a lot harder and try to bring in more money as well as help Tom with the collecting and delivering. She liked Beth and had grown very fond of Danny. Beth was lucky – but was it luck, or just her?

'Ruby?' Tom's voice came from out of the darkness.

'What do you want?'

'I really will miss Beth coming out with me.'

'I know you will.'

'It made the journeys go ever so much quicker when we played games and I didn't have to push the pram up some of the alleyways.'

Ruby was upset. Tom had never said that about her. Perhaps she had always been too busy and serious to have fun.

'Go to sleep.'

'Will you come out with me more now?'

'I should think so.'

It wouldn't be so bad at the moment; it was the winter Ruby always dreaded, the long, dark, cold nights and mornings. She would have to get up very early if she had to collect washing before she went to work. If only her mother didn't have to work so hard. Ruby was certain her mother wasn't in good health even though she quickly dismissed it when Ruby caught her with her head in her hands, looking worn out.

'Will I ever get to see those moving pictures again?' asked Tom.

'Of course you will. These times won't last for ever.'

Some of Beth Norton's luck had fallen on her once before when she got her job at Stone's. Could it happen again? She prayed it would. Ruby fell into an uneasy sleep as she dreamed of being buried under piles of dirty washing.

As the winter began to close in, Mary Jenkins found it increasingly hard to manage without Beth's money coming in. Extra money was needed for coal to dry the washing and Mr Cox was complaining about his windows steaming up.

'He's asked for more rent money as well.' Mary Jenkins slumped in the chair, running her thin red hands through her hair. 'I don't know what I'm going to do.'

Ruby glanced at her mother. 'Would you like me to go and have a word with him?'

'No, what good will that do?'

'I could explain things.'

'He won't listen. You know what he's like. Sometimes I just feel like running away from it all.'

Tom looked up from his writing. 'I could get a job now if you like.'

'I need you here.'

'When I get a bit older I'll go out to work – that'll help, won't it?'

His mother gave him a faint smile. 'Of course it will, love.'

Ruby looked over at her father. He was definitely a lot better now, although he hadn't been out. Perhaps she could find him some home work to do, anything that would bring in a few more pennies every week and keep him occupied. Perhaps she could have a word with Beth? Although Ruby hadn't seen much of Beth since she left, Ruby knew she had been to the house a few times while Ruby herself was at work.

Ruby recalled the conversation that had taken place in the dairy only a few days ago.

'They say she's more than just a housekeeper. Some of the old dears told me she sits up at the bar most nights like Lady Muck. They reckon old Thompson wants his head examined, getting involved with a flighty young bit like that. She's only a kid; he's old enough to be her father.' The large woman pulled her floral overall round her.

Mrs Moss was sitting on the stool. 'She has got her own room, mind, but it makes you think.'

'Well, I reckon his wife must be turning in her grave. And what about her husband? I reckon there'll be some trouble there when he returns,' said the large woman.

Ruby had been upset to hear people talk about Beth like that, but didn't know how to stop them.

There were a few women in the shop and they were all laughing about the situation.

'Nobody knows about this so-called husband of hers, do they?' said Mrs Moss.

'What about you, Ruby, do you know if one exists?' asked another of Milly's customers.

'Only what she's told me.' Ruby had had to get out. She had to tell Beth what they were saying.

She decided she would go tonight and ask Beth if she could help her father. Ruby knew Beth was streetwise and she might know of something he could do at home. That was it. She had made up her mind. And if Beth wasn't sitting in the bar Mr Thompson would get her, then she could tell her what was being said.

It was almost nine o'clock when Ruby finally had the chance to go out.

'Mum, I've got to go out for a little while.'

'What, in this weather? Where're you going?'

'Just out.'

Her mother smiled. 'Have you got a boyfriend?'

'No.'

Tom looked up from the sums he'd been doing with his sister. 'I bet you're going to meet that Ernie Wallis.'

Ruby blushed. She hadn't told them she had been seeing him. But now the weather was on the turn it was getting too cold to sit in the park. 'No I'm not,' she said abruptly. She couldn't tell them she was going to the pub to try and get her father some work.

Tom grinned. 'I bet you are.'

'No, I'm *not*.' Ruby was getting angry.

'Leave it out, son,' said his mother. 'Our Ruby will tell us if she wants to.'

'Honest, Mum, I ain't going out with Ernie Wallis.'

'I believe you. But don't be too late.'

Ruby grabbed her coat from the nail behind the kitchen door and, pushing her flyaway hair under her black felt hat, left. As she walked up the road she thought it would have been nice if she had been going to meet Ernie. She hadn't seen him for a few weeks; it would be lovely if they had somewhere warm to go to.

She pushed open the pub door. Ruby had never been inside a pub at night and the smell of beer and tobacco almost took her breath away. She stood for a moment or two in the doorway, looking around. Out of the corner of her eye she noticed a group of men had stopped talking and were looking in her direction. After a cursory glance, they ignored her and resumed their conversation. Through the crowd Ruby caught sight of Beth sitting on a high stool at the bar. She was wearing a tight black frock and smoking a cigarette; she looked very grown up.

'Ruby,' she screamed when she saw her and, jumping down from the stool, rushed over to her and, holding her close, kissed her cheek. She stood back and, still holding Ruby's arms, said, 'What you doing in here?' She gently began to push Ruby to the side of the room. 'Let's go out to the kitchen.'

Ruby followed Beth behind the bar. Mr Thompson gave her a nod. She was pleased to be getting away from all the eyes that were now following her.

'What you doing here? Is it your dad?'

'In a way.'

'Oh my God.' Beth put her hand to her mouth. 'He's not ill, is he?'

'No.'

'Thank God. I'm very fond of him, you know.'

Ruby nodded. 'And he thinks the world of you and Danny. How is he, by the way?'

'He's fine. You should see his pram; Mr Thompson has paid to have the hood repaired, it looks very grand. Now, you haven't come up here to hear me whittling on, so what is it?'

'I know this may sound daft, but d'you think you could find out if there is any work Dad could do at home?'

Beth sat in the armchair. 'Pull out a chair.'

Ruby did as she was told and sat down.

'I don't know of anything, but I can always ask Mr Thompson. He knows a lot of people and he might be able to think of who wants a job done. What can he do?'

'I don't know. But it would have to be at home, he couldn't go out.'

'That's a tall order.'

'I wouldn't ask, but he misses Danny and I don't want him to slip back again like he did over that horse thing.'

'Course you don't. That was very sad. He was doing so well before that.'

'I know. Beth . . .' Ruby blushed. 'People are saying . . .' She fiddled with her fingers. 'It ain't any of me business what you do, but . . .'

'I know. They wonner know if I'm sleeping with him.' She inclined her head towards the door. 'Tell 'em to mind their own business, but for their and that Mrs Moss's ears: I ain't.'

'I'm sorry.'

'Come here, it ain't your fault.' Beth clasped Ruby to her again.

'Can I have a peep at Danny?' Ruby asked, freeing herself from Beth.

'Course.'

They went up to the bedroom and Ruby looked at Danny lying peacefully in his cot.

'This is one up from his old pram,' said Beth, tenderly touching her son's cheek.

'He looks so content.'

Beth smiled. 'I love him so much. I don't know what I'd do if anything ever happened to him.'

Ruby looked at her. 'Nothing will.'

'Mind you, I'm worried what'll happen to him if anything ever happened to me—'

'Don't talk like that,' interrupted Ruby. 'Why are you saying such things? Is that man hitting you or something?'

Beth laughed softly. 'No, course not. He's very kind to me and Danny. It's just that everything is going so well for me and I always worry that you have to pay for your good fortune.'

'You mustn't think like that.'

'Come on, let's go downstairs.'

Ruby had noted that Beth's bed was very ruffled. It had been slept in.

'Look, I'd best be off,' said Ruby when they reached the bottom of the stairs. 'You won't tell me mum or dad I've been here, will you?'

'No, course not. Where do they think you've gone?'

Ruby looked down; she could feel her cheeks getting red. 'Out with a boy.'

Beth laughed. 'I hope it goes well for you.' She took Ruby through the bar. At the door, she said, 'Ruby, I'd like you and me to be really good friends.'

Ruby smiled. 'Well, we can.'

'Come up here again and we'll see about going out to the market or somewhere.'

'I'd like that.'

'I'd better be going. Sometimes if they get busy I have to help out.' She kissed Ruby's cheek again and went back inside.

Ruby stood for a moment or two on the step. She tenderly touched her cheek. Beth was so nice, and she seemed such a happy person: she infected others with that happiness. Ruby thought that quality far outweighed the niggles of doubt she had harboured about their lodger, and resolved to put them behind her. But why did Beth have these morbid fears? Was it to do with her past?

Ruby went to walk away from the pub when a hand on her arm stopped her.

'Thought it was you. What you doing here?'

'Mr Cox!'

'You're a bit young to be in the pub.'

'I had to give Beth a message.'

'That husband of hers will be in for a shock when he finds out she's moved in with old Thompson.'

'She's his housekeeper.'

He took her arm and moved her along the road. 'That's what she tells you. But I know different.'

Ruby wanted to get away from this man but he was holding her arm very tightly. 'Please, Mr Cox. I must go. I must hurry home.'

'That's all right. We can walk home together.'

Ruby looked about her. She was frightened of this man. 'Please let me go.'

'Stop being such a silly girl. I only want to be friends with you.'

'I don't want to be friends with you.'

'Why not? I'm very good to your family.'

'You're going to put the rent up and me mum's worried sick.'

'Is that all that's upsetting you?'

'Where will we go if you throw us out?'

'I'm sure we can sort this little problem out.'

The sound of someone running behind them made him quickly let go of Ruby's arm.

'Ruby! Ruby, I forgot to— Hello, Mr Cox,' Beth came up to them and put her arm round Ruby's shoulder. 'I forgot to give you something. Could you come back for a minute?'

Ruby was puzzled. What was Beth going to give her? 'Yes, of course.'

They turned and walked along the road together.

'Goodnight, Mr Cox,' shouted Beth over her shoulder.

When they thought he was well out of earshot, Ruby stopped. 'What are you going to give me?'

'Nothing. It was the only thing I could think of to get you away from him.'

'I'm so glad you did. But how did you know he came after me?'

'I saw him make a beeline for the door when you left. I guessed what he was up to. I've told you before, you've got to be very careful of that man.'

'I try to keep out of his way as much as I can, but it's a bit awkward sometimes.'

'I know.' Beth looked up the road. 'I think he's gone home. Now remember what I told you.' She laughed. 'This is the second time I've saved your honour, Ruby Jenkins.'

Ruby laughed too. 'I know. Thanks, Beth.'

'That's all right. And I'll see what I can do for your dad.'

Ruby walked away. She was so deep in thought as she pushed open the front door and stepped into the passage, that she jumped when the kitchen door flew open.

'And where have you been, young lady?'

Ruby had never seen her mother look so angry.

Confused, she stammered, 'What is it? What's the matter?'

'You've been to the pub.'

'What?' screamed Ruby. 'Who told you?'

Mr Cox stepped out from behind her mother. 'I told your mother all about how you have been flaunting yourself in front of the men.'

'What?' she said again. Ruby couldn't believe what this man was saying. 'I wasn't. It wasn't like that.'

'But you was in the pub?' said her mother.

'Yes. But . . .' She wanted this wicked old man to go away. She didn't want him to hear why she had been there.

'So what was you doing there?'

'I went to see Beth.'

Mary Jenkins gave a sigh of relief. 'Why didn't you tell me that's where you were going?'

'I didn't think you'd like me going to the pub. But we was in the back room and Beth's bedroom.' She glared at Mr Cox. 'I wasn't in the bar, honestly, Mum.'

'I saw you.'

Ruby wanted to kill this man who was trying to make trouble between her and her mother.

'I believe you, Ruby. Now if you don't mind, Mr Cox, I've got to get to bed. I have to get up very early in the morning.'

Mr Cox looked angry. 'So you take her word against mine. Well, you listen to me: you'll remember my words when she brings a bundle of trouble home. Goodnight.' He slammed the door as he walked out of the kitchen.

Ruby began to cry. 'I'm so sorry, Mum. I wasn't doing anything bad.'

Her mother put her arm round her shoulder. 'I know. Do you want to tell me why you went to see Beth?'

'I just wanted someone to talk to. We're going to go to the market together one Saturday. Is that all right?'

'Of course. Now off to bed with you.'

'I hope all this racket didn't wake Dad.'

'I don't think so.'

'Goodnight, Mum.'

Mary Jenkins smiled. 'Goodnight, love.'

Ruby smiled back but she couldn't stop fretting about Mr Cox. Why did people have to be so mean?

'Ruby?'

'You should be asleep, Tom.'

'I heard you shouting. What's wrong?'

'Nothing.'

'I heard Mr Cox. Is something wrong?' he repeated.

'Nothing for you to worry about.'

She lay down next to Tom. But despite her brave words, she knew once again Mr Cox had given her plenty to worry about.

Chapter 13

Ruby stood looking at the mess someone had made of her pile of finished work. 'Who did that?' she screamed.

Florrie looked up. 'What's upset our little gel then?'

'I've just been out for a pee and someone's gone and chucked me finished ironing about.'

'Now who would do a fing like that? It must'a fell on the floor and someone picked it up. I must say they wasn't very careful, was they?'

Ruby looked along the line at the others, but they had their heads down, working away.

'Still,' said Florrie, 'the way you work, yer'll soon make up yer money.'

As Ruby sorted out her work she knew why they were jealous. She was a lot younger than they were, but she could keep up, and even at the beginning when her work was being heavily scrutinised by Mrs Watson, she'd been able to earn nearly as much as they did – after all she had had many years of practice. But it still didn't get her over that ten-shilling barrier.

She sat down and got on with her work. She kept her head down, to hide the fact that her eyes were smarting with unshed tears. She wasn't going to let them see.

It was dark by the time Ruby left the building; she had hung about waiting for the others to leave. If only Ernie were around to talk to her, but she knew if he had passed by today he was long gone and she couldn't blame him for not hanging around, not in this weather. Ruby stood close to the corner of the building; she didn't want to bump into Florrie.

'You're late,' said a voice behind her.

Ruby turned and under the gaslight recognised Frank Stone. 'I got a bit behind the others.' She started to move on.

'That's all right. We don't mind you working hard as long as you ain't hanging about waiting for some bloke. We don't like that. Been working for us long?' He had fallen in step beside her.

'A little while.' She felt terribly alone. Elsie had told her to beware of Frank, he had a reputation as a ladies' man, and she knew some of the workers had been out with him. She didn't want any scandal.

'You're quite a pretty little thing, and a frightened one by the look of it. I don't bite.'

Ruby gave a nervous laugh. 'I hope not.'

'I'll have to find out more about you. I like the thought that you stay behind to work. I expect I'll see you around. Bye.' He walked away, disappearing as suddenly as he had appeared, leaving Ruby more alone than ever.

Things in the Jenkins household were getting very hard. Ruby blamed herself for Mr Cox putting the rent up, but the miners' strike had added to their problems as coal was in very short supply and getting more expensive. Ruby's birthday had come and long gone. She hadn't reminded the family of the date, she didn't want them to feel bad about not being able to get her something. Beth had come up with a few ideas for Thomas Jenkins, but none of them had been practical.

'How's your mum managing to get coal?' asked Beth as she and Ruby were taking a stroll round the market. Ruby was looking for anything that had been thrown away behind the barrows, even the old newspapers after she had read them were useful when cut into squares for the lav.

'Not good. She sends Tom out looking for any bits that might have fallen off the cart, but there's always someone walking behind with a dust pan and brush sweeping up any that's been dropped. And he said he's seen fights break out round the coal carts. The biggest trouble is trying to get the washing dry to pay the extra for coal and rent.'

'I feel really bad about that,' said Beth.

'Why should you? It's not your fault that old man put our rent up.'

'I feel I'm a bit to blame.'

'Well, you mustn't. No news about anything for Dad then?'

'No, but I'm trying to persuade Mr Thompson to get someone to wash the glasses. Do you think you could get your dad to come to the pub? I'd make sure he got home safe.'

'I don't know. Would he have to be out late at night?'

'No. They could be left till the morning.'

'I could ask Mum. Thanks, Beth.'

'Don't thank me till it's settled.'

'It's a bit cold, I think we'd better make our way back, and I've got to deliver Mrs Bell's washing.'

'I hate those buildings. Let me treat you to a couple of apples then your mum can make one of her lovely pies.'

'You don't have to.'

'I'm not taking no for an answer.' She was rummaging in her purse. 'Tuppence, you say?' She handed the man the money. 'There, take them home. I'm sure your mother will work wonders with those.' She gave the apples to Ruby.

'Thanks, Beth.'

★　★　★

Christmas was almost on them and at last they had managed to get Thomas Jenkins to go to the pub and wash glasses.

'I hope that man's not doing this out of charity,' said Mary Jenkins when Beth first approached her about it.

'No. It's near Christmas and we're getting very busy and we're too tired at night to stand washing glasses.'

'Well, just as long as you're sure.'

'If you like I'll come along in the morning and take him back with me. Don't worry, I'll make sure he's all right.'

'This is very kind of you, Beth.'

For Ruby, on Saturday, the time seemed to go on for ever. She was desperate to get home and find out how her dad had got on with his first morning at the pub. Oh, please let it have gone well! If it worked she'd be eternally grateful to Beth. Now she didn't see so much of Elsie it was nice to wander round the market with Beth, pushing the pram and exchanging chatter; it was almost like having a sister.

All morning Florrie had been her usual crude self. She was telling them all about the bloke she'd met in the pub the night before. She said they were banging away behind some houses when one of his kids came up and said, 'Dad, yer dinner's ready.'

Everybody screamed with laughter.

'So what did he say to that?' asked one of her friends.

'He told 'em he'd be in when he'd finished his afters.'

Again everybody thought that was hilarious, but Ruby didn't. She felt sorry for the wife who probably had loads of kids to feed.

'Did he pay yer?'

'Course. Yer don't think I stand there with me frock round me neck and me drawers round me ankles fer nothing, do yer? It's too bloody cold.'

'How much d'yer get?'

'Enough.'

Ruby tried to ignore the filthy chatter and concentrate on her work.

As soon as she'd finished, she hurried home. 'Well?' she burst out on opening the kitchen door. 'How did you get on, Dad?'

'Not bad.' He looked different; he was sitting up and smiling. 'Didn't break any. He's a nice bloke, that Mr Thompson. Always liked him.'

Ruby thought her heart would burst. Her father was at last, after all these years, going out to work.

'Beth came and collected him and brought him home,' said Mary Jenkins, standing next to him with a proud smile on her face.

'And he gave me a bottle of beer to have with me dinner.'

'Don't let old Cox see that,' said Ruby. 'He'll want half.'

'I'm taking his tea up to him. I don't want him down here putting a damper on things.'

All evening her father sat and told them what he'd done. 'That baby's a dear little chap.'

Ruby couldn't believe it. This was the first time in years they had heard him hold a conversation. He sounded so happy. 'Are you going tomorrow, Dad?' she asked.

'Yes, love. But only on Saturday, Sunday and Monday mornings and it'll only be till Christmas.'

Ruby smiled. 'It's a start, Dad. I can take you up on Sundays.'

'Thanks.'

For the first time in months, when Ruby went to bed, she knew she would sleep soundly. Even though this job was only temporary, it could be the start of her father living again and, who knew, he might be able to start providing for his family.

Then her mother wouldn't have to take in washing, and she wouldn't be permanently exhausted.

Ruby's thoughts went onto Ernie. What sort of a Christmas would he have?

It was Christmas Eve morning; Mary Jenkins had been up since five finishing off the last of the ironing. She hadn't got any washing today. Thomas was at the pub, like Ruby, working, and Tom was out delivering washing. Mary prayed her customers would have enough money to pay her so she could do some shopping. She was now standing at the kitchen table wrapping up a pair of socks she had knitted for Tom from a jumper she'd unpicked. Ruby had bought two jumpers from a jumble sale, they were only a few pence, they weren't fit enough to wear but the wool had come in useful. Ruby had gloves and Tom had socks; she had even knitted her husband a nice scarf he could wear to work. She smiled to herself. What a lovely phrase that was, her husband at work. She knew it wouldn't last as Mr Thompson had told him it was only up till Christmas, but that didn't matter. It was a start. She held up the socks. She hoped they would like their presents, but she really couldn't see Tom wearing them outside the house. When she'd told Milly what she had done, Milly had given her some greaseproof paper to wrap them in. It would have been better if the wool had been a more neutral shade, but they wouldn't mind everything in bright red, at least they would be warm.

The banging from above made her jump. She raised her eyes to the ceiling. What was he doing? The banging started again; this time it was louder and more intense. Was he ill? Mary Jenkins realised she hadn't heard her landlord moving about. He hadn't looked that good when she took his breakfast up to him. The banging started again and she left her parcel-wrapping and went upstairs.

She gently knocked on his door. He didn't yell at her to come in as he always did. She slowly pushed the door open and to her surprise found him lying on the floor.

'What is it? What's wrong?'

He groaned. 'I feel ill.'

'Do you want me to get you a doctor?'

'No. Just help me get into bed.'

With a struggle Mary Jenkins helped him to his feet and into his bedroom. She knew every part of this sparsely furnished room, as every week she had to clean it and change his sheets.

He fell onto the bed. Mary could see he was very pale and the sweat was glistening on his brow.

'Can I get you a drink?'

'Water.'

'I really think you should have a doctor.'

'I said no, woman. Just get me a drink.'

Mary rushed to his tiny scullery and filled a glass. She noted that the glass had the pub's name on it. 'Is there anything else?'

He closed his eyes and shook his head. 'I'll bang on the floor if I want anything.'

As Mary slowly made her way down the stairs it was with mixed feelings. Part of her wanted to sing and dance: if he didn't get up tomorrow they could be on their own at Christmas. That was a lovely thought. But she also knew he could have her up and down those stairs day and night. What if he died? What would happen to them? Could they be thrown out of their home? As far as she knew he didn't have any relations, but in those sort of cases, there was always someone who could come out of the woodwork. Mary also knew that even if he were ill she couldn't let Ruby go up to him. For a while she had been worried about his attentions towards her daughter. Ruby had grown into a lovely young woman and Mary knew he watched her every move. She would kill him if he ever touched her.

When Mary stood at the table downstairs she found herself remembering last Christmas when they had had Beth staying, and how much difference her money had made. She also remembered how ill she had felt. It had taken all her strength to get out of bed that Christmas morning. Thank goodness she had managed to let it slip past everybody by saying she just wanted a rest.

Ruby was worried to see her mother running up and down stairs every time Mr Cox banged on the floor. 'I'll go up next time.'

'No, it's all right,' she said quickly. 'He don't want you to.'

'I'll go,' said Tom. 'I'll find out what he wants then you can take it up.'

Ruby looked at her mother. She looked harassed.

'Ain't he got a relation or something?' asked her father. 'If he needs waiting on hand and foot it should be one of his own.'

'I asked him that, he said there ain't no one. Felt a bit sorry for him really. Must be awful to be on your own with no friends or family.'

'None at all?' asked Thomas.

Mary shook her head.

'He ain't the sort of man you'd like to meet on a dark night,' said Ruby.

'He ain't the sort of bloke I'd like to run into in the light,' said Tom.

'Now, young man, don't be so cheeky.'

'Sorry, Mum,' he said with a big grin.

★ ★ ★

Christmas was very quiet without Beth and Danny. The paper chains they had made last year were hanging from the ceiling, although many of them were squashed and looked bedraggled. The four of them sat quietly round the table and finished off their dinner that this year consisted of a small piece of bacon that had been boiling all morning. Ruby sat thinking about the previous year and all the happiness and the laughter.

Fortunately Mr Cox settled down and was quiet for most of the evening. The beer Thomas had brought him might have helped.

'We should play a game or something,' said Ruby after they had cleared away the tea things.

'Wish Beth and Danny still lived here,' said Tom.

'So do I, son,' said her father. 'She always had a smile and that boy of hers is a little cracker. D'you know he gives me a big smile whenever I walk in the pub.'

At that moment Ruby desperately wanted to be like Beth, smiling and happy. 'I don't think she's working tonight, would you like me to go and ask her to come here this evening?'

'That would be very nice,' said her mother. 'But I can't see her leaving that Mr Thompson on his own.'

'No, I suppose not.' Ruby sat and gazed into the fire; unconsciously she rubbed her heels.

'Stop scratching those chilblains,' said her mother. 'You'll have 'em turn septic.'

'They ain't nearly as bad this year. It's very warm in the ironing room.'

At last it was time for bed. As Ruby lay down she thought: That's another year nearly over. She closed her eyes tight. If there is a God above, please make things go right for us during 1921.

'Ruby?'

'Yes, Tom.'

'It wasn't a very nice Christmas, was it?'

'No, love.'

'I hope Mr Cox gets up soon.'

'Why is that?'

He sniffed. 'I don't like to see Mum running up and down the stairs.'

'Neither do I. But it won't be for ever. Besides, you've been helping her.'

'I know.' He turned over. 'I hate that man.'

After the New Year, to everyone's relief Mr Cox was up and about. He said he'd caught a chill.

The weather had turned bitterly cold and as Ruby hurried back and forth to work she hoped it wouldn't snow. Every evening on her way home she longed to go into the kitchen and see the cosy fire and not have it hidden behind draped washing. If only her mother would let a bit of warmth come into the room. The weekend over the New Year her father had been washing glasses, but now he was almost back to his old ways. He hadn't been out and spent his time just sitting in the chair. The damp air had started his cough again, and the rasping sound worried Ruby. She hadn't seen anything of Ernie for weeks. She guessed he'd been at the laundry as some of the girls had seen him. It would have been nice if she'd had a Christmas card from him, or something, but like her, he wouldn't waste money on things like that.

It was Monday morning and as the girls settled down to a day's work Molly, who sat along from Ruby, yelled, ''Ere, you'll never guess who I saw on Sat'day night! That Ernie Wallis, and guess what? He was with that Mrs Watson!'

'What?' screamed Florrie. 'You seen him out with old Mrs Watson? Where was that?'

'They was going to that music hall. I was there with me feller. We was up in the gods and they was waiting to go in. I didn't see what seats they had, they didn't come up with us, but they was all dressed up. She had a smashing fur coat on.'

That statement surprised Ruby. How could Ernie be all dressed up?

'All fur coat and no drawers I bet. Did she see you?' asked Florrie, obviously very interested in this.

'Na, as I said we went up in the gods. Bloody good show it was.'

'You'll have to ask her if she enjoyed it,' said Florrie.

'Yer, could do,' said Molly.

Ruby just listened. Ernie must be very well in if he was going out with Mrs Watson. Why had she taken him? He certainly couldn't afford to take her; besides, she was old enough to be his mother.

Everybody was eagerly waiting for Mrs Watson to come and collect their work.

'Did you enjoy the show on Sat'day?' asked Molly.

She looked up in surprise from the items she was counting. 'Yes, thank you. How d'you know where I was?'

'I saw yer. You was with that Ernie Wallis.'

'Yes, I was. He's a nice lad.'

They waited for some more information, but it didn't come.

As soon as she left the room Florrie called out, 'The old cow. Why didn't she tell us why she was with him?'

'Might be cos you didn't ask her,' said another woman further up the table.

Ruby was also intrigued. She gave a little grin; she knew

150

that when she saw Ernie he would tell her. But why hadn't he made an effort to see her? He knew what hours she worked. She missed their walks and talks. She would love to see him again.

Chapter 14

It was a week after Ruby had heard about the incident with Ernie and Mrs Watson. As she left the laundry on Saturday, she was surprised to see Ernie coming towards her.

'Hello there, Ruby. All right?'

'Yes, thanks.' She tried not to look too happy at seeing him. She glanced round, knowing the women from the finishing room were watching her.

He fell in step beside her. 'Just took a bit of washing into Mrs Watson. I knew this was the time you finished, so I thought I'd wait for you, seeing as I ain't seen you for quite a while. You going home?'

'Yes.'

'I can walk a bit of the way with you. That's if you don't mind?'

'No.' She didn't want them to see her making conversation.

'Bye, Ernie,' shouted Molly.

'Bye,' he replied.

'Ta ta, Ruby,' said Florrie. 'See yer boyfriend's waiting fer yer. Yer wonner watch him, remember he only likes older women. So is there a chance fer me then, Ernie love?'

Ruby wanted the ground to open and swallow her.

'Come on,' he said hurrying along. 'Let's get away from this lot.'

When they were well away he slowed down. 'What was all that about back there?'

'Molly saw you at the music hall with Mrs Watson.'

He threw his head back and laughed.

'Well. Was it you?'

'Yes.'

'How could you go out with a woman who's old enough to be your mother?'

He laughed again.

Ruby was beginning to get angry. 'I don't think it's funny.'

'I'm sorry. I guessed that one way or another you'd get to hear about it.'

'Would you have told me?'

'Yes. You wouldn't have turned down a free night out at the music hall, would you?'

'No. Suppose not.'

'Well then.'

'She paid for you?'

'Yes, and she lent me a couple of bob to get a suit from the pawnbroker's. I had to take it back the next day.'

'Molly said you was all dressed up.'

'I was, and I tell you it felt great to look like a toff. Mind you, it stunk of mothballs. I was surprised she didn't make me sit on me own.'

She giggled. 'But why you? Ain't she got a husband?'

'No, he was killed in the war.'

'I didn't know that.'

'She don't talk about it. It seems she got these tickets but was let down be some bloke, she didn't say who, so she asked me along as her escort.'

'Ain't she got no kids?'

'She never said.'

'So that's a bit of luck then.'

'Yer. Who knows, I reckon I could make a living doing this escort thing.' He grinned at her and with both hands smoothed his dark straight hair down. 'Well, what d'yer think? Will I do?'

Ruby nodded and laughed again to hide her feelings. She wanted to hold him and kiss him. If only he felt the same way about her.

'What's so funny?'

'Them back there. They're dying to find out what you was doing with her.'

'I bet they are. Here, you wonner tell them I'm her long-lost son, that'll get them going.'

Ruby looked stunned. 'I couldn't say a thing like that. What if it got back to Mrs Watson? I'd lose me job.'

'Yer, you could be right. Just tell them I couldn't tell you, as it's a secret.'

'You are daft. What was the music hall like?'

'Girls dancing, blokes eating fire and juggling, and some woman singing, and there was an old man telling jokes and singing very naughty songs. You wait till I get enough money. I'll take you there. Ruby, it's magic. I only wish me mum and sisters could see it. Young Eve would love it.'

'It sounds lovely.'

He wanted to take her out, to somewhere special: Ruby almost hugged herself with delight. She looked at him wistfully. It was a shame that they had to live like this when there was so much out there to see.

'When the weather starts to get a bit warmer I hope we can see each other again and have our little talks and walks.'

'Don't see why not. That's of course if you ain't off out with your older woman.'

He laughed. 'One of these days, Ruby Jenkins, I will take you to the music hall, you wait and see.'

'I'd like that.' Ruby was thrilled beyond words. 'I've been to the picture house.'

'Have you? Lucky you.'

'It was smashing. Me and Elsie went. We saw that Charlie Chaplin. Then I took Tom, but that was when Beth was living with us. Things were a bit easier then.'

'I've never met this Beth.'

They stopped when they reached the road Ernie went down.

'I'd better go.'

'How's your little sister?'

'Much better, thanks.' He moved away. 'Can we go for a walk soon?'

'Yes. I'd like that.'

'When?'

'Tomorrow?'

'Why not? I'll meet you in the park. They should be starting to play on the bandstand soon.'

'That'd be great.'

'OK, see you tomorrow.'

'All right.' She stood and watched him go. She did like him. He was nice: fun and funny yet dependable. If only their lives could be like those in the storybooks. She would love to get married and live happily ever after. But life round Rotherhithe wasn't like that.

On Monday Ruby was dreading going to work; she knew she would be pounced on to answer questions about Ernie and Mrs Watson.

'So,' said Florrie as soon as she walked in, 'what did lover boy tell yer about him and old Watson then?'

'He didn't say anything, and I didn't ask.'

'I don't believe that for one minute. Does he reckon he'll get a good job if he pussy foots round her?'

'I don't know.'

'I reckon yer not telling us everything.'

'Well then, ask him yourself.'

'D'yer know, I might do that.'

Ruby smiled to herself. Wouldn't Florrie have loved to have seen them walking in the park? And wouldn't Elsie love to hear all this latest gossip about Ernie going out with Mrs Watson? She saw even less of Elsie now as she had a boyfriend. The way she sat and drooled over him the last time Ruby saw her had made Ruby laugh. Finding Charlie had been another bonus for Elsie when she started work at the tea factory. Life was pretty good all round for her old friend. Perhaps Ernie's reappearance meant things would soon get better for Ruby?

It was two weeks later, Thursday 14 April. That date was going to be one Ruby would never forget.

Mrs Watson walked into the ironing room and straight up to Ruby and whispered, 'Follow me.'

'But what about me work?'

'Leave that.'

Ruby looked round at Florrie and began piling her work up neatly. Although there hadn't been a repeat of the problem she'd had before, now she was always on her guard and waited till her work had been collected before she left the room.

'I said leave that.'

She wanted to tell Mrs Watson that it would be a mess when she got back – that's if she was coming back. She could feel herself getting hot as she stood up. What had she done wrong?

'What you been up to then, young Ruby?' shouted Florrie as they made their way towards the door. 'Is it your boyfriend? He been saying naughty things about what you and him get up to?'

Mrs Watson turned and looked at Florrie. 'I've no doubt that you'll find out soon enough.'

Ruby's knees shook as she was led up to the office. She had only been in there once before, that was when she first came here to work.

When Mrs Watson pushed open the door, Ruby couldn't believe her eyes. Tom was standing there.

She rushed over to him. 'Tom? Tom! What're you doing here?' She looked at Mrs Watson with a bewildered look in her eyes. 'What's happened?'

He threw his arms round Ruby's neck and cried, 'It's Mum.'

'Mum?' repeated Ruby. 'What's happened to her?'

'She's dead, Ruby. She's dead.'

Ruby felt numb and her jelly-like knees buckled. Words wouldn't come.

'I'm very sorry, Ruby,' said Mrs Watson.

'What we gonner do?' asked Tom.

'I don't know,' said Ruby, finding her voice. 'How's Dad?'

'Crying.'

'How did it happen?'

'I don't know. Milly said I should come and get you.'

She turned to Mrs Watson. 'I've gotter go home.'

'Of course.'

'I don't know when I can get back.'

'Don't worry about that at the moment.'

'Will I lose me job?'

For the first time Mrs Watson smiled at her. 'Don't worry about that.'

Ruby collected her hat and coat from the cloakroom and left the laundry with her brother. They were running as fast as they could. There were so many questions she wanted to ask Tom, but she could see he wasn't in any fit state to answer her.

She threw open the front door and ran down the passage.

Her father was sitting in his chair crying. She fell to her knees beside him. 'Dad, what happened?'

He looked at her and grabbed her hand. 'What am I gonner do, Ruby?'

'Hello, Ruby.' Milly stood in the washhouse doorway.

'Milly, please tell me what's happened.'

'I'm so sorry, love. It's your mum. It was her heart.'

'But when? How?'

'It must have been this morning.'

'She was all right when I left.' Ruby stood up. 'She looked a bit tired, that's all. But she's looked tired for a long while, and every time I asked if she was all right she always said yes.' Slowly tears trickled down Ruby's cheeks.

Milly came up to her and held her. 'Tom came back from delivering and found her sitting at the table.'

'I thought it was funny, she was just sitting there,' said her father. 'I asked for a cup of tea, but she didn't answer me. I didn't know, Ruby. I didn't know.'

'Course you didn't, Dad.'

'It was Tom who realised something was wrong,' said Milly. 'And he had the good sense to come over for me.'

'What happened then?'

'I got a doctor and he said she was worn out, her heart couldn't take any more.'

Ruby looked towards the door. 'Is she in the bedroom?'

Milly nodded.

'I want to see her.'

'Course you do. I'll get Mrs Riddle to lay her out for you if you like.'

Ruby nodded. 'What happens then?'

'You'll have to arrange the funeral.'

'I never said goodbye properly.' She put her head in her hands and wept.

Milly gently touched her shoulder. 'I'm sorry. Look, if you need anything just send Tom over. I'll come back a bit later on.' She closed the kitchen door quietly behind her.

Ruby went into the darkened bedroom and sat on the bed next to her mother. She took her hand and kissed it, letting the tears trickle down her cheeks as she sat there. 'Mum, why have you left us?' Suddenly all kinds of emotion swept through Ruby. Love. Sadness. Regret at what hadn't been said, and anger. Anger that her mother had left her.

Ruby could feel someone standing in the doorway. She turned and gave her brother a watery smile.

'Ruby, what we gonner do?'

'I don't know.' Ruby gently patted the bed. 'Come and sit down.'

He hesitated. 'Will it be all right?'

She took his hand. 'Course. Come on, Mum won't hurt you.'

Very gently he lowered himself down on the bed. He was terrified he would disturb her.

'We must do what we can for Dad. That's what she'd want us to do.'

'Why did she have to die?'

'We all have to die sometime.'

'I know. But I didn't want it to be Mum. I loved her, you know?'

'Course I do. We all loved her.'

A knock on the bedroom door startled them.

The door was pushed open slowly. 'It's all right, Ruby. It's only me. I won't stop. I've just brought Mrs Riddle over.'

'Thanks, Milly.'

Tom jumped off the bed.

Mrs Riddle, a short stout woman, came quietly into the bedroom. 'I've very sorry, Ruby. Milly said you'd like me to lay your mum out.'

Ruby brushed the tears from her cheeks with her hand and nodded.

Mrs Riddle took off her coat but left her black felt hat on. Despite everything Ruby couldn't take her eyes off the enormous pearl hatpin that was stuffed into it. Mrs Riddle rolled up her sleeves. 'I'll need some hot water and a cloth.' She looked down at Mary Jenkins. 'She was a lovely woman. It's a bloody shame.' She turned to Ruby. 'Is this what you'd like her to be buried in, love?'

'She ain't got much else. Can you take her overall off?'

'Course, love.' She patted Ruby's hand. 'Now, go and get me the water and I can start to make your mum look pretty. Mind you, it ain't gonner be a hard job.' She put her head on one side as she looked at Mary Jenkins. 'A really lovely lass, and don't she look peaceful?'

'What's she gonner do to Mum?' asked Tom when they were outside the bedroom.

'She's gonner comb her hair and make her look nice.'

'But why? She looks nice now.'

Ruby put her arm round Tom's slight shoulders and gently moved him along the narrow passage. 'I know she does.'

'Ruby, can I have a cup of tea? I ain't had one all day,' said her father as she walked back into the kitchen. He ran his hand under his running nose.

Ruby turned on her father. 'What?' Her anger was now directed at her father. 'Have you been sitting there all this time?'

'Don't shout at me, Ruby. It ain't my fault.'

She was angry. Although she could see how upset he was

she couldn't stop herself. She needed someone to vent her feelings on.

'I'll see to the tea,' said Tom.

'Thanks, son,' he sniffed.

Tom went into the washhouse to fill the kettle.

'So, have you just been sitting there all this time?' asked Ruby.

'I didn't know what else to do.'

'You could have done something. You could have put a bit more coal on the fire for a start. How you gonner have a cup of tea if we can't boil the water? And Mrs Riddle wants hot water to lay Mum out.'

'Ruby, don't shout at me. It ain't my fault.'

'No. It's the bloody Germans. Well, the war's been over for years now and it's about time you got off your arse and did something useful.'

Tom stood in the doorway with the big black kettle in his hand. 'Ruby,' he shouted. 'Don't blame Dad. It ain't his fault, and don't swear, Mum wouldn't like it.'

Ruby didn't know what to do. Everything was closing in on her. She didn't want to hurt her father. She stood in the middle of the room moaning. Then she fell to her knees and hugged herself. 'I want my mum,' she said over and over again, her voice heart-rending.

Tom looked at his sister, bewildered. 'Ruby. Ruby. What can I do?'

She looked up at him. 'I don't know,' she whispered.

The kitchen door opened. 'Come on now, Ruby,' said Mrs Riddle, bending down and cuddling Ruby to her ample bosom. 'All this shouting ain't gonner help your mum, or your dad come to that. Remember he's in shock too.'

Ruby slowly scrambled to her feet.

'You go in your bedroom and have a good cry. Tom, you

see to the tea, and Thomas, put some coal on the fire.'

Everybody knew Mrs Riddle; she was one of those kindly women who was a tower of strength at times like these. She laid people out and brought others into the world. It was rumoured that if a baby was born with some sort of deformity she would leave it and see to the mother. It was also suspected that she helped those that didn't need another mouth to feed. She was a forceful woman, and to Ruby's surprise her father got up and did as he was told.

Ruby went into her room, lay on her back and looked up at the patterns that had been formed on the bedroom ceiling through years of neglect. She couldn't cry any more. She knew she had to think about the future without her mother. What was going to happen to them? How would they manage? Her wages wouldn't cover the rent and food. And what about Mr Cox? He would still want his washing, cleaning and cooking done. How would she manage to do everything if she didn't finish work till seven? She would have to find Tom a job, but what about her father? Ruby felt guilty about shouting at him, but now he *had* to contribute. He'd been happy enough at the pub washing glasses. She would ask Beth if she could talk Mr Thompson into letting him work there again.

A gentle tapping on the door brought her to her feet.

'Ruby, I've finished.'

'Thank you, Mrs Riddle. What do I do now?'

'I'll go along and see Mr Cooper. He'll come and talk to you about what sort of funeral you want.'

Ruby took a sharp intake of breath. 'We ain't got any money for a funeral.'

'I'm afraid it'll have to be done. It don't have to be a fancy affair with horses and the like, but Mr Cooper's a fair man and I'm sure he'll sort something out for you. And, Ruby, have a bit of patience with your dad. He's a very sad man.'

'I know and I'm very sorry I shouted at him.'

'I understand. You were in shock and needed to take your anger out on someone.'

Ruby gave her a slight smile. 'Thank you. What do we owe you, Mrs Riddle?'

'See me when you're back on your feet.'

'But I don't know when that'll be.'

She touched Ruby's arm. 'Don't worry, love. I can see better times for you.'

When she moved away from the doorway Ruby followed her to the front door. 'Thank you.'

'That's all right, love. And as I said, things will get better for you, I can see it.'

Chapter 15

It was only an hour or so later that Beth arrived at number thirteen.

She threw her arms round Ruby when the door was opened. Tears were streaming down her face. 'I've just heard. How did it happen?'

'Seems her heart just wore out. Come in the kitchen.'

In the passage, Beth hesitated outside the bedroom door, then asked over her shoulder before going into the kitchen. 'How's your dad taking it?'

'He's in shock. He's just sitting in his chair.'

'Hello there, Mr Jenkins,' said Beth, opening the kitchen door. She went over to him and kissed his cheek.

'Hello, Beth. Have you got the little feller with you?'

'No.' She patted his hand. 'I'm so sorry.'

He looked at her and tears began slowly to trickle down his face. 'What am I gonner do without her? She's always been there for me. I let her down.'

'I should finish this ironing,' said Ruby, sitting at the table and pushing a pile of clean washing to one side. 'But I don't think I can, not with Mum in the bedroom.'

'Don't worry about that. Bundle it up and I'll do it tonight.'

'I can't let you.'

'Course you can. Besides, you'll want the money. Tom can

164

deliver it tomorrow. Does up there know?' She raised her eyes to the ceiling.

'I don't know. He ain't been down for his dinner. He must have heard all what's been going on.'

'Ruby, how you gonner manage?'

'I don't know.' She began to cry. 'I didn't even have two pennies for Mrs Riddle to put on me mum's eyes.'

'What did Mrs Riddle want two pennies for?' asked Tom. His question was ignored.

'Have you got them now?' asked Beth.

Ruby nodded. 'Mrs Riddle lent them to me.'

'Can I go and see her?' asked Beth.

'Yes.'

In the darkened room Beth gazed down on Mary Jenkins. 'She looks very peaceful.'

'Yes, she does,' sniffed Ruby. 'Beth, I'm dreading Mr Cooper coming and telling us how much it'll cost to bury Mum. We ain't got nothing left to sell.' Ruby sat on the bed and looked down at her mother.

Beth didn't have an answer, so she pulled Ruby to her chest and let her cry.

It was much later that afternoon when Mr Cooper arrived. He was a short dapper man with a thin black moustache and kind eyes. He sat at the table and went through the proceedings with them. When he'd finished there was silence.

Ruby looked at her father, but he clearly wasn't going to say anything.

'Mr Cooper, we ain't got any money,' said Ruby.

'You're not the first, young lady. Don't worry, we can sort something out. You don't have to buy a plot and you don't have to have a big affair. And a loan can be paid off a little at a time.'

Ruby couldn't see any way that a loan could be paid at all.

'I don't earn a lot, Mr Cooper.'

'Now don't you worry, just leave it all to me. I'll let you know when it'll be.' He took a little black book from his jacket pocket along with a pencil. He licked the point. 'Would next Monday be fine for you?'

Ruby nodded.

'I'll call in tomorrow and let you know the time.' He rose and picked his hat up off the table. 'Goodbye, Mr Jenkins.' He held out his hand and Thomas Jenkins stood up too.

'This is all my fault, you know.'

'These things happen.' Mr Cooper smiled at him. 'Unfortunately a lot of women have a very hard life.'

'But I should have been out working. I should have been looking after her.'

'Excuse me, but I must go.' Mr Cooper, his eyes full of sympathy, left the kitchen with Ruby following behind.

He stopped at the open door and touched his trilby. 'Try not to worry too much, young lady. These things have a way of working themselves out. Bye.'

Ruby stood in the doorway and watched him go. How will they work themselves out? What will happen to us now? she thought.

That evening they simply sat in the kitchen. Hardly a word had passed her father's or her lips. She had just sent Tom out to collect the ironing from Beth when a tap on the kitchen door startled her. She jumped up and was surprised to see Mr Cox standing there. He didn't normally knock. He always barged in.

'I was sorry to hear about Mrs Jenkins.'

This was the first time she had seen him all day. 'Thank you. I'm sorry I ain't got any dinner for you.'

'That's all right. I understand. Young Beth up the pub gave me a bit of dinner.'

'That was very kind of her.'

'Don't worry about me for the moment, we can sort something out. Just thought I'd pop in to give you my condolences.'

'Thanks,' said Thomas Jenkins.

When Cox had left, Thomas looked at his daughter. She had every right to be angry with him. The strain was already telling on her. She was far too young to have to carry this burden alone. If only his pain and fear would leave him. His nightmares had got better over the years, but would they return now Mary wasn't at his side to comfort him? He had to do something. For the first time since he had returned from the Front he forced himself to think about other people. If only Mary had been firm with him. She had been a good wife but too soft with him. Well, now she had gone, and he knew that it was his duty to try to help Ruby. But how?

All weekend people came and paid their last respects to Mary Jenkins. Ruby was surprised how many knew her mother and the kind words they had for her. It was mostly people she had done washing for. Sometimes Ruby would find a few pence left in the bedroom after they had gone.

On Monday morning Ruby woke with a terrible feeling of foreboding. She had been sleeping in the kitchen in the hard armchair. She had made her father sleep in with Tom, as she couldn't let him stay in the bedroom with her mother lying peacefully in her cheap coffin at the foot of the bed. There weren't any brass handles or nameplate on the lid that was standing to one side.

Every part of her body ached. She was dreading today.

Mr Cooper had arranged for a small handcart to carry her mother to the cemetery and a priest was going to bless her at the graveside. Mr Cooper said he wouldn't charge them very much. There were no flowers.

Ruby looked out of the window. It was a grey day, which matched her grey mood. It was seven o'clock. Mr Cooper was coming at eleven. Ruby quickly dressed and, after seeing to the fire, went into her mother.

'I don't want you to go. I wish you could stay here for ever.' Ruby kissed her mother's cold forehead and left the house.

She quickly made her way to the market. She had to buy some flowers. She knew her mother would be cross at the waste of money, but it was something Ruby just had to do.

When she returned home her father was making toast. 'Where've you been?'

The atmosphere was very hostile between them. Although Ruby knew she should be civil to her father she had to blame someone for her mother's untimely death, so she'd turned her anger on her father.

'I had to go out.'

'Where?'

'To get some flowers.'

'But I didn't think we was going to get flowers.'

'I had to.'

He smiled. 'I'm glad you did. Ruby, please don't hate me.'

'I don't hate you, Dad.'

'I'm gonner change. I promise you.'

'It's a bit late for Mum, ain't it?'

'Don't you think I feel bad about that?'

She shrugged.

The banging on the front door sent her hurrying along the passage.

'Milly, come in.'

'Hello, Mr Jenkins. Ruby, Mr Jenkins, is it all right if I come along this morning?'

'Of course,' said Ruby.

'I thought a lot of Mrs Jenkins, she was a lovely lady. And this is for you.' She held out one of the blue paper bags that she used for sugar and dried goods. 'It's from the neighbours. We thought the money would be better than flowers. I collected two pounds; put it towards the funeral expenses.'

Ruby gasped. 'Two pounds! But . . . how? Most people round here ain't got two ha'pennies to rub together.'

'You're a very much liked family, and, well, people want to help. Some come from the pub as well.'

Ruby held Milly close. 'Thank you. Thank you so much.' Ruby guessed that quite a bit of the money had also come from Milly's parents.

'Milly, can you thank everybody for us?' Thomas Jenkins was on his feet holding her hand.

'Course, Mr Jenkins, but if you like you can put a little note in the shop window.'

'That's a good idea. I'll do that.'

Milly moved towards the door. 'I'll be over at eleven.'

Ruby looked down at the coffin being gently lowered into the grave. Her mother was in that box. She wanted to stop them; she didn't want them to throw dirt all over her. It wasn't right. She had placed the small bunch of flowers next to her mother before Mr Cooper had come to put the lid on. She wanted her mother to hold them, to let her know she would be part of her for ever. Everything was becoming a blur as tears streamed down her face. This was the unhappiest day of Ruby's life.

Little Danny was gurgling. Ruby glanced over at Beth who was trying to keep her son happy and distract him. He was such a lovely little boy. Her mother would never see him grow up. Her mother would never see Tom grow up. Ruby looked at her brother. His ashen face told of all his pent-up feelings. He had been so quiet since last Thursday that she had almost neglected him. She should hold him and tell him how much they all loved him, how much his mother had loved him. Mary would never see either of them get married and have children. This was a wicked world.

When they got into Hill Street Milly left the sad party and went into the shop. Beth walked along to the house with them, but she said she wasn't coming in. In many ways Ruby was pleased; she didn't really want anybody there; she didn't want to have to make small talk. This was their grief. She didn't want to share it.

Outside the house Beth rummaged around in the bottom of Danny's pram. 'Ruby, Mr Thompson sent this along.' She handed Ruby a small bottle of whisky.

'I can't take this.'

'Why not?'

'I don't know.'

'Look, give your dad a drop, and then put the rest away for when things get bad. It might help him sleep.'

'You've been very good to us.'

'I shall never forget that you took me in.'

'We wanted your money.'

'I know. In some ways I feel I should move back to help you out, but I don't want to leave Mr Thompson, or my lovely room.'

'I can understand that. You've very lucky.'

'I know. I'd better go, I always help with the lunchtime trade. It gives Mr Thompson time to bottle up for the evening. That way he gets a bit of rest and I can give him dinner before he starts in the evening.' She smiled. 'Please, I know it's going to be hard for you and you have a lot on your young shoulders. But look after your dad.'

'I will.'

Beth tucked a blanket round her son's legs. 'Why is it the good always go first? I know a few I'd like to see the back of. I worry at times that my Danny might be left alone if anything ever happened to me.'

'Don't say things like that.'

'I'm afraid these things do happen.'

'But not to you. You'll live a very long and happy life now you're with Mr Thompson.'

'I hope so, Ruby. I really do. But that don't stop me worrying.'

Ruby gave a weak smile. 'I'll look after Danny. There, does that make you feel any better?'

'Thanks.' Beth kissed Ruby's cheek. 'Bye and thank you.'

Ruby stood for a while watching her push the pram along the road. Then she turned and went inside. Life would have to go on just the same for her and the family. Tomorrow she would have to go back to work. But how would she be able to clean Mr Cox's place and feed him? His washing shouldn't be too much of a problem as she could do that with theirs. She would have to break her mother's rule about not washing on Sunday. That would be the only day she could fit everything in. It was a bleak prospect.

Chapter 16

The following morning Ruby walked to work with a heavy heart. She had made herself and Tom a black armband to wear. It was a sad reminder of what had happened since she last came through these gates just a few days ago, but did she want to wear it to work? Did she want the likes of Florrie and her friends gloating?

'All right then, Ruby?' shouted Molly, catching sight of her. 'You coming back to work with us?'

'Yes.'

Molly caught up with Ruby. 'Thought you'd got the sack. You're gonner be a couple of days short in yer wage packet this week, taking – what? – three days orf. You'd better have a good excuse when old Watson comes round.'

'Mrs Watson knows why I was away.'

'Does she now? You'd better tell Florrie, she's dying ter know.'

Ruby walked on. Florrie was the last person she wanted to talk to. In the cloakroom she took off her coat and carefully put the left sleeve out of sight.

Florrie came up behind her as they entered the building and, with her bony finger, prodded Ruby in her back. 'I hope you know, Miss Snotty Nose, that we had to do your work what you left. And a bloody state it was in as well.'

'Was that before or after you messed it up?'

'You saucy cow. Who d'you think you're talking to?'

Ruby ignored her and sat in her seat.

Mrs Watson followed them into the ironing room. 'It's starched collars this morning.'

A groan went up.

'We can't earn our money on those,' shouted Florrie.

'I can't help that. The irons are all out of order in the collar room.' Her voice softened. 'Everything all right, Ruby?'

'Yes, thank you.'

As soon as she left the room Florrie was on her feet and standing behind Ruby. 'What you after then?'

'I don't know what you mean.'

'Why's she being nice to you and letting you stay on after taking time off? You and your boyfriend up to something?'

'If you're talking about Ernie Wallis, he ain't me boyfriend. We was at school together.'

'Don't give me that. First we find out he's been taking you out.' She pointed towards the door. 'Then the next thing we see is him waiting for you outside and the both of you talking and walking orf together, then you're orf for days. And on top of that, you have the bleeding cheek to walk yer arse back in here as if nothing's 'appened. You got something on her? That why you took three days orf and didn't get a rollicking?'

'Leave me alone.'

The bony finger prodded her again. 'I won't leave you alone. I wonner find out what you've got on her.'

'Nothing.' Ruby wasn't going to tell them about her mother. Unshed tears stung her eyes. She knew she wouldn't get any sympathy. She very much doubted that they would even believe her.

Wicker baskets were pushed into the room filled with the stiff starched collars. Everybody hated ironing collars, they

173

were horrible. Ruby had been in that room for a few days so she knew what it was like. They curled up and as soon as you piled a few up they slipped and fell to the floor.

'Ruby, looks like even you ain't gonner earn your money today,' shouted Molly.

But Ruby was desperate to earn as much as she could. She was now the breadwinner. At least thanks to the neighbours' generosity she had almost paid for her mother's sad and paltry funeral. She would always be more than grateful to everybody who had made it possible. This morning before coming to work she had lit the fire and had given Tom money to get some coal and bread. At least the fire under the boiler didn't have to be lit every day now, but how would they manage without her mother's money? And the rent still had to be paid.

As soon as it was time to leave she hurried home. What could they have to eat?

She pushed the front door open and the smell of something wonderful wafted along the narrow passage and filled her nostrils. Who had been cooking?

'Dad?' she called out on opening the kitchen door. The table had a piece of oilcloth on it. Ruby hadn't ever seen that before, they normally used newspaper and a sheet was taken off the bed at Christmas. 'Where's that come from?'

'Hello, love. All right?'

She nodded.

'Beth came along and brought a veg pie. It's finishing off in the oven. Smells good, don't it? Oh, and she brought along this piece of oilcloth, she said she's bought a new bit for Mr Thompson.'

Ruby looked at the faded brown material. The roses had almost been scrubbed away. 'That's very nice of her.'

'Pie smells good, don't it?' said Tom, who was sitting at the table, his knife and fork at the ready.

'Take your hat and coat off, love, then sit yourself down. I've made a cuppa. I expect you're ready for one.'

Ruby did as she was told. She knew her mouth had dropped open. Her father was waiting on her. This had never happened before. 'What's been going on?' she asked.

'After you left, I took a gentle stroll over to Milly to ask her what I should get to eat tonight. It had to be something simple and cheap, something that I could manage. She suggested egg and a bit of streaky. I thought, I reckon, with young Tom here helping, we could manage that.'

Tom just grinned at his sister.

'I want to do my bit, love.'

Ruby couldn't believe that her father had been out to get the shopping.

'I was just coming back across the road when I caught sight of young Beth. She's a nice girl. She came running up and was pleased to see I was out. Well, when I told her what I'd bought, she said, "Put that away for tomorrow, I'll bring along a pie I've just made you." '

'D'you know, she even made one for old misery guts upstairs,' said Tom.

At first, Ruby was speechless. She knew her mother would be cross at this. 'That's very kind of her, but what about Mum? She wouldn't like us accepting charity.' As soon as the words had left her mouth, she regretted it. The look on her father's face filled her with remorse. 'I'm sorry, Dad. I didn't mean to upset you. It was very kind of her.'

'No, you're right. Your mother wouldn't like it. Will you pour out the tea while I get the pie out of the oven?'

Ruby stood up and reached over for the teapot. 'I'll go up and see her later on to thank her.'

'Yes, and you can take the pie dish back.'

The pie tasted as delicious as it smelt, but Ruby knew she had put a damper on the meal.

Ruby was pleased to see that there weren't many men in the Royal Albert. She looked around for Mr Cox; she didn't want him following her home again. Perhaps he'd nodded off after that wonderful pie. Beth wasn't in the bar so Ruby went over to Mr Thompson.

He gave her a warm smile. 'Hello there. I was very sorry to hear about your mother.'

'Thank you, and thank you for the money. Is Beth around?'

'Yes, she's in the back room, come through this way.' He held up the flap of the bar and Ruby went through.

'Beth?' she called softly. She didn't want to shout out in case Danny was asleep.

The door opened and Beth appeared, looking surprised. She asked, 'What are you doing here?'

'I've brought your pie dish back.'

'You didn't have to come out tonight. I could have collected it in the morning. Was it all right?'

'It was lovely. Thank you very much. Beth, I think I've upset Dad.'

'How?'

'Well, I wasn't thinking. I want us to stand on our own two feet. I want Dad to try to be a bit more responsible.'

'Yes, I can understand that.'

'Well, I told him Mum wouldn't like us accepting charity.'

Beth suddenly looked very angry. 'Is that what you think it was, charity?'

'No, I'm sorry. I didn't mean—'

'I didn't make you a pie out of charity. Your mother and father, and young Tom, have always been good to me and I thought I'd like to give a little kindness back.'

'Beth, what can I say?'

'This time I'll put it down to grief. But I'm telling you, Ruby, if you carry on behaving like this when people want to help, you might find they turn their backs on you.'

Ruby let her tears fall. She turned and went to walk away, but Beth stopped her.

'Come here.' Beth held out her arms.

Ruby nestled into them. She needed a shoulder to cry on. 'Am I forgiven?'

'I would think so.'

'I'm so unhappy,' sniffed Ruby.

'Of course you are.'

After a while Ruby dried her eyes. 'I've got to find Tom and me dad a job. They can't stay home all the time. I don't earn enough to feed them and pay the rent.'

'I'll ask around, but it ain't easy.'

'I know.' Ruby blew her nose on a piece of old pillowcase she'd cut up and had carefully sewn round the edges.

'Now, Ruby, remember: don't get upset if people want to help.'

Ruby gave Beth a slight smile. 'I won't, and thank you for making me see sense.'

Beth kissed her cheek. 'Now go on home.'

As Ruby walked through the bar she was pleased to see Mr Cox still hadn't arrived at the pub. He was the last person she wanted to see. He'd be down soon enough with his dirty washing and for the rent money.

On Saturday Ruby was very pleased to see Ernie leaning against the wall outside the laundry.

'Mrs Watson told me.' He nodded towards her black armband.

After that first day back at work Ruby decided to let

Florrie and the others know what had happened. A few had mumbled their condolences, and after that the matter was quickly dropped.

'I was sorry to hear it.'

'Thanks.' They began walking along together.

'I was wondering if you fancied coming out on Sunday?'

'I can't. I've got too much to do at home.'

'That's a pity.'

'Things should get better when I've worked out me routine.'

'Yes. I'm sure they will.'

'P'r'aps we could do something then?'

'Yer. Why not?'

The conversation was very subdued. Ruby was worried. They had almost reached the point where he turned off. Would she lose him? Would he find someone else to talk to if they didn't meet?

'Ernie, I *will* try and come out one day.'

He smiled. 'I know that. Anyway, I'll see you around.' He left her to walk home.

Ruby was near to tears again. She wanted to be with him so much. She was hurting wanting his love and comfort. Could that kind of happiness ever be for them? She didn't realise that as he walked away Ernie was going over and over the words *he* had wanted to say. He really liked Ruby. He wanted to be with her all the time. Were they too young to have feelings like this? What could he offer her? Would love be enough for her? He would wait till things got better for them. But would she want him?

Two weeks had passed and Beth hadn't come up with any work for Ruby's father. He was so different these days; he was doing things Ruby had never seen him do before. He swept and washed up, and although he couldn't get the range as shiny as her mother had, he tried. One thing he wouldn't be seen doing, however, was whitening the step. He seemed prepared to look for a job, but with so many men out of work Ruby knew it was going to be hard for him to find one after all these years.

It was Friday, and as she walked home she tried to work out how this week's money would pay the rent and food. She had just about earned eight shillings. One shilling had to be put aside for the week's gas, two and six for the rent, then there was at least two shillings for coal, that left two and six for food. Perhaps they could sit in the dark a bit longer to save the gas. Ruby felt miserable, her arms ached and today she had burnt her arm.

'Hello, love. All right?' asked her father.

How could she tell him that money was so short that she didn't know where the rent was coming from? 'Mustn't grumble.'

'Been down the docks today.' He was sitting making some toast. 'Got some eggs boiling. Not a lot of work to be had down there.'

He was a different man; was it guilt that had brought him out of his shell? 'I'm sure something will turn up one day.'

'Dunno.'

'Where's Tom?'

'He's running an errand for Milly. Taking someone a few groceries they couldn't carry. She gives him a penny for it.'

Ruby knew the neighbours were all trying to help the Jenkinses as much as they could; it was charity but she had to accept it.

'Dad. Dad!' Tom came racing into the kitchen. 'Guess what? I've gone and got meself a job.'

Ruby saw a flash of disappointment cross her father's face, but he hid it at once.

'That's nice. Doing what, son?'

'That lady I had to take those bits to, she wants me to collect some wooden boxes from the market and chop them up for her. I can manage a lot; I can take the pram to the market. She reckons I could sell little bundles.'

'Tom, I'm really pleased for you,' said Ruby.

'I'll only get tuppence from that lady, but it'll help, won't it, Ruby?'

'Course it will.'

'I could give you a hand. Come on, have this toast,' said her father.

'You'll get something soon, Dad,' said Tom. 'I know you will.' He didn't actually want his father helping him. He wanted to show them that he could do something on his own.

'Course I will.'

Ruby looked at her father's sad face. After all these years he was really concerned about getting a job. If only her mother were here to see the dramatic change.

Ruby was hurrying round the market when to her delight she caught sight of Elsie. It was ages since she had seen her. 'Elsie!' she called.

Elsie turned and a huge grin spread across her face. She ran to Ruby and hugged her. 'How are you?' She held her at arm's length and suddenly caught sight of Ruby's black armband. 'Oh no. Is it your dad?'

'No, it was me mum.'

'Your mum? I'm so sorry. What happened?'

'It seemed her heart just gave out.'

'You poor thing. I know what it's like to lose your mum. How're you managing?' Elsie tucked her arm through Ruby's as they walked slowly along.

'It's very difficult.'

'How's your dad taking it?'

Ruby let a slight smile lift her troubled face. 'It somehow seems to have brought him out of his shell. In fact, he's even trying to get a job.'

'No!'

'He's not having a lot of luck though.'

'It ain't easy. But I'll keep me ear to the ground and if I hear of anything I'll let you know.'

'Thanks, Elsie.'

'It seems such a long time since I saw you. I've got a lot to tell you. What's your news about work? You still in the ironing room? That Florrie giving you trouble?'

'We have had a few clashes.'

'Look, I'm dying to find out all about it. Let's go and have a cuppa.'

'I can't, I've got too much to do.'

'Oh, come on.'

'I can't afford it.'

'Did I ask you to pay?'

Ruby shook her head.

'Well then.' With her arm through Ruby's, they made their way to the café.

As soon as they sat down Elsie took off her gloves and flashed her left hand under Ruby's nose. 'D'you like it?'

'Elsie! It's lovely.'

'So's the chap what gave it to me.'

'You gonner get married?'

Elsie nodded. Her eyes bright as buttons. 'Christmas. We've got to save a bit, as I want a posh wedding and I can't expect me dad to pay for it all.'

'Oh Elsie. I'm so happy for you. Where're you gonner live?'

'With his mum. She's a lovely lady. She makes me ever so welcome. Charlie, who's an only child, ain't got a dad, so we're gonner live at his house. That way his mum won't lose my Charlie's money, and I can still go to work till we start a family. I'm so happy.'

'And I'm so pleased for you.'

'Look, I've been rabbiting on, anything exciting happened in your life? What about Ernie?'

Ruby took a mouthful of tea, looked down into her cup and said softly, 'I see him sometimes.'

'You dark old horse. So, is it for real?'

'I don't think so. We just used to go for walks and sit in the park. But it's difficult now, without Mum. I have to do so much at home.'

'Ruby, what can I say?'

Ruby began to grin.

'What's so funny?'

'You'll never guess. Ernie went out with Mrs Watson one night.'

'What?' exploded Elsie.

Ruby laughed. 'I thought you might like to hear about it?'

'I should say so.'

Ruby went into great detail of what had happened and how Florrie and her lot had been trying to prise it out of her ever since.

Elsie sat back, still laughing. 'Well I never. I wouldn't have liked to sit next to him if he stank of mothballs.'

'He said he didn't care, she was paying.'

'So she's not a bad old stick after all? I would have loved to have seen him.'

'So would I. It must be nice to get all dressed up.'

'That's why I want a white wedding with all the trimmings.'

'I bet you'll look lovely.'

'You'll be able to see for yourself.'

'What? Don't worry, I'll try to be there outside the church.'

'Not outside. Inside with me family.'

'I've never been to a wedding.'

Elsie laughed. 'Well, you're coming to mine. As soon as the date's settled, I'll come and tell you.'

'Me going to a wedding. What do I wear?'

'Don't worry, we'll sort something out. It's so good to see you again. Here, what's happened about all the washing your mum used to do?'

'Had to let it go. I couldn't do it, not with going to work. When Tom took all the stuff back a lot of Mum's customers was very upset.' Ruby shrugged. 'But it couldn't be helped.'

'So you don't see that Mrs Bell then?'

'No. I don't know who does her washing now.'

'I often think of her smashing place. I'd like things like that in my home.'

'It was the buildings that I didn't like.'

'It was a bit rough round there.'

They talked a bit longer, then Ruby stood up. 'I'm really sorry, but I must be off. Let's try and get together again.'

'I'd like that.'

Ruby hugged Elsie.

'I'm really sorry about your mum.'

'Thanks.'

Elsie kissed Ruby's cheek and wandered away. Ruby waited till her friend was well out of sight before she began scrambling round the back of the stalls for tomorrow's veg.

A week later Ruby was surprised to see Elsie waiting for her outside the laundry.

'This is just a quick visit, I can't stop. Here, take this.' She shoved a piece of paper into Ruby's hand.

Ruby turned it over. 'What is it?'

'Does your dad still want a job?'

'Yes.'

'That's an address.'

'Where, where is it?'

'The Green Man off Lurcher Street. Me dad said George wants a pot man as his old boy had dropped dead. What d'you say?'

'Well, there's no harm in him going to see him.'

'Must go.' Elsie quickly kissed Ruby's cheek and hurried away.

'Bye,' Ruby called after her. 'And thanks.' She looked at the paper. Although in many ways Ruby was pleased her friend had thought of her, the problem was she knew where the Green Man was: it was near the docks and not a very nice area. Would he take it, or was it all just a front on his part?

Ruby was surprised at her father's reaction when she told him her news.

'I'll have a walk round there tomorrow and have a word with this George.'

'Just be careful, Dad.'

'Ruby, I keep telling you. Things are different now.'

'Yes, I know, Dad.' She kissed the top of his head.

Ruby was having mixed feelings. Lurcher Street was also a short walk from the buildings. Should she have told him about the job? She could have kept it to herself, but she knew she had to help her father get back out into the world. But what if when he walked home late at night someone set on him? If anything happened to him she'd never forgive herself. She could still remember the state he was in after the incident with the horse. Had she done the right thing?

The following morning Thomas went to the Green Man. He knew where the pub was and as he passed the docks and slums he barely glanced at the men lolling against the wall; he knew it didn't do to look them in the eye. This wasn't what he wanted, but he had to do something. Ruby had been trying hard to get him a job, but with the work situation as it was, he had to take anything. It was going to be hard after all these years but he wanted to show Ruby he was capable of helping to look after his family. She was too young to shoulder such responsibilities alone.

'So you're Thomas,' said the landlord when he walked over to him.

This place was very different to the Royal Albert; the sawdust on the floor was sparse and the place stank of stale beer.

'I only want you Friday and Sat'day nights. Me missus helps out at other times. The name's George by the way.' He threw his dog end to the floor to add to the others.

'What time do you want me?'

'After seven.'

'Does it get a bit rough round here?'

'A bit. Can you handle it?'

'Yes. Yes, of course.' He wanted to ask how the other pot man had died, but thought that was a little unwise at the moment.

'Me wife don't like coming down here on those nights; being pay day it tends to get a bit boisterous.'

Thomas gave him a half-smile. 'I can understand that. So I'll see you on Friday.'

'OK.'

As Thomas walked home his head was pounding. Would he be able to stand the noise and the people? He had to for Ruby and Tom's sake. But he knew it was going to be very hard.

That evening her father told Ruby he was starting work Friday night. 'He only wants me Fridays and Sat'day nights. He seems a decent enough bloke.'

'Are you sure you'll be all right, Dad, walking home on your own?'

'I ain't a kid.'

'I know, but you ain't used to walking about in the dark.'

His voice rose. 'Stop fussing. I'll be fine.'

But would he? Ruby knew that was the worst time to be round that way.

Friday was his first night, and he had left by the time Ruby got home from work.

'Dad said to make sure you wash up the pot when you finish that bit of stew. Look at me hands. I've got blisters from chopping up all that wood. Mr Cox gave me tuppence for a bundle.'

'Did he now?'

'I should have pulled a few sticks out, but I didn't have time.'

Ruby tutted as she took her dirty plate into the washhouse.

'I hope I'll be able to get more boxes. Some of the other kids do it as well.'

'Well, just make sure you keep out of trouble,' said Ruby over her shoulder. 'I don't want you coming home with a busted nose.'

Tom laughed. 'I ain't that daft.'

After Ruby had finished the washing up she set about doing the bit of ironing that had been hanging around all week. She looked at the pile on the chair and knew there would certainly be some sewing in that lot. Tom was very good at losing buttons. Her mother had taught her well; Ruby had been sewing and knitting for years.

'Tom, can you take this upstairs when I've finished his bits?'

'I don't like going up there.'

'Why not? You just said he gave you tuppence.'

'That was in the yard.'

'I heard him go out a while ago.'

'I don't care. I don't like going up there.'

Ruby finished the ironing and took it up herself. She pushed open the door and put his ironing on the table. She looked around. Every Saturday afternoon after she had been to the market, she had to come up here and clean this place. She was pleased he didn't have a lot of furniture to polish and was out of there as quick as she could be. She was also on her guard every time she went up. She told her father to ask him down for a chat. Her excuse was that she didn't want him getting in her way, and so far it had worked.

Ruby couldn't rest all evening and kept looking at the clock. She knew the pub closed at eleven and it should take him about twenty minutes to walk home. She knew if she went to bed she wouldn't be able to sleep, so she decided to go and meet him. As she was putting on her hat and coat, Tom asked, 'You going out?'

'I'm just going to meet Dad. I'm not happy about him walking home on his own.'

'He ain't gonner thank you. He reckons all his demons have gone now.'

Ruby looked shocked. 'Is that what he told you?'

Tom nodded. 'We was sitting here one day after Mum died and he blamed the Kaiser for Mum and he reckoned he shouldn't let him stop him any more.'

'Well, I must admit he has changed. I only wish he'd helped Mum out.'

'He said he'd never forgive himself.'

Ruby was overjoyed that her mother's death hadn't had the opposite reaction that she had been dreading, and he had not gone deeper into his shell. 'I'm glad you and Dad can sit and talk.'

'He had a terrible time in that war, you know.'

'I gathered that.' She looked at the clock. She wanted to hear more, but she had to go. 'You must tell me about it sometime.'

'He don't say much, but some of the things he saw must have been nasty.' Tom stopped.

Ruby hoped her father hadn't been too graphic; Tom was young and at an impressionable age. 'Now off to bed.'

'You still going out?'

'Yes.'

'Dad won't like it.'

'He don't know what it's really like down there now. I'll just tell him I fancied a stroll.'

Tom laughed. 'What, at this time of night?'

She kissed the top of his head. 'Off to bed. Now.'

Ruby left the house at once. She was truly concerned. Everybody – except probably Thomas – knew it was very rough round that way, especially when some of the foreign ships were in dock. And just what had the previous pot man died of? She pulled her coat round her and hurried along just as a spring shower started.

Chapter 17

By the time Ruby arrived at the Green Man the rain was falling steadily and men were spilling out of the door. She stood on the far side of the road and well back in the shadows; she didn't want to be seen. The laughter and shouting was very loud and filled the air. She saw some enormous men with bushy beards wearing navy blue jackets. A couple of men were holding up another, very drunk, whose boots dragged along the ground as they moved on. When he started to be sick they let him go and he fell to his knees. Ruby realised that the shouting was in a foreign language and it was getting louder and more aggressive. One man pushed the other and suddenly they were fighting and rolling on the ground. Ruby squeezed herself into a dark doorway. She was very frightened. She hoped her father was busy and wouldn't come out till this was all over. As more men spilt out of the pub they formed a jeering crowd round the men who were fighting, egging them on. Suddenly, in the light from the pub, Ruby saw the flash of a knife. A man slipped to the ground holding his stomach. The crowd disappeared at once, leaving the man groaning in the wet gutter.

She put her hand to her mouth to suppress her scream. What should she do? Why had she let her father come and work here? For a few moments she stood and watched the man writhing on the ground. Should she help him? Had his attacker gone? The rain was coming down more heavily now, she could feel it trickling down her neck then on down inside her coat. She heard the bolts going on the door of the pub and realised she had to go in there. She had to get help. She ran across the road and banged hard on the door.

'Bugger off, we're closed,' came a voice from inside.

She banged harder this time, hurting her hands. 'Dad. Dad. It's me, Ruby. Please open up.'

The bolts were pulled and the door was swiftly opened and Ruby fell in. She looked up at the man who was holding onto the door. He was a tall, thickset man with wild salt-and-pepper-coloured hair and a bushy moustache to match.

'Ruby?' said her father.

She looked over at her father, he was standing next to the bar. He put the glass he was wiping on the bar and hurried over to his daughter. 'What're you doing here?' he asked, helping her to her feet. 'You're soaking wet.'

'Dad. Dad.' She held on to her father.

'What's happened? You all right?'

She shook her head. 'I come to see if *you* was all right,' she sobbed, brushing sawdust from her coat. 'There's a man out there.'

'I'll kill him. What's he done?'

She pointed to the door. 'The man out there. Someone's stuck a knife in him. He's lying in the gutter.'

'Is he dead?' asked the man who had opened the door.

Ruby shook her head. 'No, he's groaning.'

'Get this wet thing off,' said her father as he helped her remove her coat. 'This is George, my boss.' He nodded towards the big man.

Ruby brushed her tears from her eyes and gave him a weak

smile. She could see that he wouldn't stand any nonsense from his customers.

George went outside and half carried, half dragged the man back inside the pub. He sat him on a seat then quickly locked and bolted the door. 'I'll see how bad he is.'

'Do you want a doctor?' asked Thomas.

'No. If he ain't too bad I'll get someone to take him back to his ship.'

Ruby sat on the rough wooden bench that ran round the wall of the bar and looked about her. She was shaking with cold and shock. The pub was very stark. The air was smoky and the smell of tobacco very strong. The long wooden bar had a brass rail running round the bottom; it hadn't been polished in years and was black with scuffmarks. The wooden floor was wet with beer and the tables covered with burn marks and beer stains.

'Give your daughter a drink,' said the owner over his shoulder as he removed the man's jacket.

'She's under age, George.'

'That don't matter. The poor girl's in shock.'

'What are you doing here anyway? You should be at home, not running after me,' said her father in a loud angry whisper.

'I was worried about you.'

'I ain't a child,' he said, giving her a withering look. He went behind the bar and poured out a drink and with a steady hand silently held out the glass.

Ruby looked up at her father. 'Thanks.' She knew now that he was in control.

Ruby sat watching George remove the sailor's jacket. His shirt was covered with blood. Thomas gave out a gasp.

George looked up. 'Don't just stand there looking, give us a hand – get some water, then I can see how bad he is. You, girl, go through his coat pockets and see what ship he's on.' He threw the coat to Ruby.

She looked at the blood then looked at her father. He had turned very pale.

The man was still groaning.

Ruby frantically went through the pockets. She brought out a pipe, a tobacco pouch. And a wallet. 'Shall I look in his wallet?'

'That's the way to find out the name of his ship. This ain't too bad. Just a flesh wound.'

'I am from Russia,' said the man in very broken English. He tried to struggle to his feet.

'Thought as much,' said George, looking down on him. 'He's on one of the ships that brings in timber. That's one of the *Surrey*'s main cargoes. Is there any English money in that wallet?'

Ruby gasped. 'A ten-bob note.'

Thomas was holding on to the bar. His head hurt. The noise in his head was pounding. Blood was all around him. He couldn't see.

'Dad. Dad.' His daughter's voice was coming through the mist. 'Are you all right?'

'Yes, love.' He gave her a smile.

'You've gone ever so white.'

'I'll be all right.'

'Thomas, give this bloke a drink and take the money for it and for your daughter's out of that ten bob – oh, and get me and yourself one while you're at it. I'll put the change back in his pocket.'

Ruby was amazed that this man would take money for a drink that could be called medicinal. There was a photo of a very young man and a woman; was this the man in the photo? The woman was pretty and laughing.

George washed and tied a cloth from behind the bar around the man's wound. The cloth didn't look very clean. 'That'll do you for now. It ain't deep, and you won't bleed to death. D'yer think you'll be all right to get back to yer ship?'

The man nodded. 'Thank you so much.'

'Don't thank me, thank this girl here. If she hadn't seen you, you would have stayed there all night.'

The sailor gave Ruby a beaming smile.

'Right, on your feet.' George put his arm under the man and helped him to his feet. He got him to the door and after removing all the bolts sent him on his way.

'Does that sort of thing happen very often?' asked Thomas.

'Yer, at least once a month. It's mostly the toms they fight over. You get used to it. He's a lot luckier than some. I've come out on a couple of Sunday mornings to find a stiff in the gutter. But that's mostly in winter,' he said, completely unruffled.

Ruby sat with her eyes wide open. Did she want her father working in such a place?

George must have sensed her anxiety. 'You don't have to worry about your dad, you know. By the time he's finished they've long gone.'

Thomas Jenkins put his arm round Ruby. 'This is my little Ruby. She's a rare little gem and can't help looking after her dad, can you, love?'

Ruby shook her head. What could she say?

As they walked home it pleased Ruby to see her father was more like the man she remembered before that terrible war. She wanted to know what had happened to him. She had so many questions to ask him, but knew she had to take it one step at a time.

'Do you think you'll be happy working there, Dad?'

'Yes. That George seems a decent enough bloke.'

'Pity you couldn't work in the day.'

'His wife gives him a hand then.'

'Where was she tonight?'

'She sits with her mother. Her mother don't like to be on her own at night.'

'That's a shame. It would be nice if you could do something in the day.'

'You never know, when I get known someone might want a bit doing. George reckons there's a few widder women round that way that sometimes want a shelf put up, so that would be a bit extra.'

Ruby laughed. 'Don't you go getting yourself mixed up with any widder women!'

Thomas stopped, his expression suddenly serious. 'Ruby, I've got to look after you and Tom as much as I can. I've been a terrible father. I'm responsible for your mother's death.'

'No you wasn't, Dad.'

'Yes I was. I should have tried to pull myself together, not rely on your mother all the time. The trouble was she let me sit around so long that I got so I didn't want to get out. But I mustn't blame her, she was a good woman.' He began to move on slowly.

'But we know you had a bad time in the war.'

'Yes I did, but so did a lot of other men. I was just very weak.'

Ruby tucked her arm through her father's. 'Come on. Let's get home.'

He grinned. 'Yes, let's. It's been a long evening.'

But Thomas Jenkins was putting on a brave face. When he had seen the blood on that man tonight he'd almost gone to pieces. Blood seemed to fill him with terror. Yet he had to keep his demons at bay. He must never let them rule him again.

★ ★ ★

Tom was out of the bedroom as soon as he heard his father and Ruby come in.

'Thought you wasn't gonner come home.'

'And where else would we go then, young man?'

'It's about time you was asleep,' said Ruby.

'I'll be able to now.' He left the room.

'He's a good lad,' said Thomas Jenkins.

'Yes, I know.' Ruby had a lot of affection for her brother. 'He's trying so hard to help out.'

'I know, and that only makes me feel worse. I am doing my best, you know.'

'Course I do, Dad.' She watched him as he sat wearily in his chair. This must be very hard for him after all these years.

The following week Ruby couldn't believe Elsie was waiting for her again.

'Thank you so much for getting Dad the job.'

'That's why I'm here. I had to come and see you.'

'I can't stay long as I have to clean Mr Cox's place.'

'Ruby, I'm ever so sorry, but I didn't find out till after your dad had started that the bloke what worked there before got beaten up and they reckon that's what killed him.'

Ruby smiled. 'Dad knows. That George told him.'

'And he don't mind?'

'No. I was there the other Friday, when they chucked everybody out, and this bloke got knifed.'

Elsie's eyes opened like saucers. 'No! What happened?'

'It was a couple of sailors fighting.'

'My dad only ever goes in there straight from work for a quick one. Is it very rough?'

'A bit. But Dad seems happy enough.'

'I'll tell you I was dead worried when me dad told me. I

remember when you had that trouble with the horse.'

'Don't worry. Dad's fine.'

'I'm so glad. By the way, a lot of toms get in there as well . . .'

'So Dad said.'

Elsie grinned. 'I don't know how me dad knows that, and I ain't gonner ask.'

Milly had told Beth about Thomas's new job and she came round on Sunday to see them. She took Ruby to one side.

'I nearly died when Milly told me what pub your dad was working at. And on Friday and Sat'day nights as well.'

Ruby could see she was concerned.

'You know it then?'

'No, Mr Thompson told me about it. It's got a dreadful reputation.'

'Don't worry. Dad seems fine. So how're things with you and Mr Thompson?' Ruby asked.

'Lovely. He's a really nice man. I'm very happy there.'

Ruby looked out of the window at her father playing in the yard with Danny.

'He just gets happier and happier, that little chap, doesn't he? I'm really glad you manage to find time to come and see Dad during the day.'

Beth smiled. 'He's like a father to me. It was certainly my lucky day when I moved into Thirteen Hill Street. By the way, how's him upstairs behaving?'

'Fortunately I don't see a lot of him. I just do his washing and clean his place out on Saturday. I somehow manage to get Dad to entertain him down here while I'm upstairs.'

'I worry about blokes like that.'

'You don't have to worry about me. Like Dad, I seem to have got a lot stronger since losing Mum.'

'I saw young Tom pushing his pram loaded with wooden boxes. I told him I'll have a couple of bundles of wood off him every week.'

'He's a good lad, and he's building up quite a round, but you should see his hands – they're red raw and he's always getting splinters. I don't know what he'll do in the winter. I hope his chilblains don't come back again or he won't be able to hold the axe.'

'Have to see about getting him some mittens.'

'I wish he could go to school. He knows we really can't afford the penny a week for his slate.'

'Is that all that's stopping him?'

'That and the fact he don't wonner go.'

'That's a shame, he's like you, bright.'

Ruby smiled. 'I ain't that bright.'

'Yes you are. Now I'd better be off as it'll be opening time soon.'

Ruby watched her father hand over Danny to Beth. So much had changed in such a short while. Her mother's death had had a dramatic effect on her father. He should have gone back to work years ago. If only he could find more work, then things might be less of a struggle for them. But they weren't alone. Her thoughts went to Ernie. She hadn't seen him for a while. She knew he was always at the laundry, but didn't have time to stop as he was very busy collecting and delivering. Surely the weather was good enough now for them to go out again? It would be lovely if they had a front room they could sit in. If they were older they could sit in a pub, but drink cost money they didn't have. There was really nowhere for them to go except the park. How could they build a future like that? Did he even want to? Would she ever get married and have children? Or was that just another pipe dream like the one she had had about having her own business all that time ago?

Chapter 18

Although life was a struggle the Jenkinses were just about managing to keep their heads above water. As long as Ruby had the rent everything else depended on how much she could take home from the laundry. Mrs Watson often stood over her, watching her work, which made Ruby very nervous.

'Ruby Jenkins,' called Mrs Watson one morning just as they walked in.

Ruby looked about her. Whenever Mrs Watson called her name it worried her; she was always sure it was because she had done something wrong. But instead: 'You've got very nimble fingers,' Mrs Watson commented. 'Some days, when the women can't keep up, I'd like you to do some specialist ironing. You will be ironing delicate things and gentlemen's shirts. It could mean extra money.'

Ruby breathed out a sigh of relief. But she knew this would upset Florrie even more and that she'd have to be on her guard at all times.

The odd days Ruby did the specialist work, she enjoyed it very much, especially as the women in that room were much nicer.

A week later, when Ruby left the laundry on Saturday afternoon, she was pleased to catch sight of Ernie walking towards her, despite the comments from Florrie and Molly as they walked past.

'Hello, this is a surprise,' said Ruby when he came up to her.

'I was hoping you'd still be here.'

'Been busy?' she asked, as that was the first thing that came into her head as they walked along.

'Yer. I'm sorry I ain't been around but I've been trying to build up me customers, and it ain't easy.'

'I know. I thought I'd try and do that once, but it didn't work out.'

'You did? I'll say that for you, you're a worker. No wonder Mrs Watson has always got nothing but praise for you.'

Ruby stopped and beamed at him. 'Did she say that?'

'Yer. She reckons you'll know the workings inside and out of this laundry be the time she's ready to retire.'

'She said that? Well, when I'm in charge you'll have a job here.'

Ernie laughed out loud, crinkling his lovely blue eyes. 'Thanks. I'll look forward to that. Good job you and me have got dreams.'

'And a sense of humour.' But deep down Ruby hoped it would be more than just a dream.

'So what made you look for more work?'

'Sorry, Ruby, but it was one of your mum's customers, she came and asked if I'd take their washing to the laundry. It seems she can't find anybody to do it.'

'I bet it costs her a lot more than what Mum charged.'

'I bet it does.'

'What about *your* mum, don't she take in washing?'

'She does a bit, but she ain't very strong and she couldn't manage any more. Mrs Porter said your dad was working at the Green Man. That right?'

'Can't keep nothing quiet round here, can we?'

'Didn't think he ever went out.'

'He's a lot better now.'

'You do know it's a very rough pub?'

'So everybody keeps telling me. But as you know jobs ain't that easy to get. I was there one night when a sailor got stabbed.'

'No! Was he killed?'

'It was just a flesh wound, so George the owner said. The bloke went off on his own, I don't know if he ever made it back to his ship or not.'

'Ruby, if there's anything I can do . . .'

She stopped again. 'Thanks, Ernie, but we're all a bit in the same boat.'

'Suppose we are – more so with this bloody miners' strike.'

'That's a big problem, trying to get coal. My brother is always out looking for a coalman.'

'You should see the state of my sisters after they've been chasing the coalie.'

'One day, when we make our fortune, we'll laugh at these times.'

'Do you honestly think that?' he asked as, with his cloth cap perched on the back of his head and his hands in his trousers pockets, he sauntered along.

'No. Not really. But I think we should have heart.'

He stopped and kicked the wall. Then he pulled out the empty pockets from his trousers. 'I hate all this poverty. Sometimes I wish there was another war, then I could go and fight.'

'Ernie! That's a dreadful thing to say. Especially as your dad got killed and mine was, well, shell-shocked.'

'I know. But I feel there should be more to life than just pushing a bloody pram loaded with other people's dirty washing.'

Ruby wanted to hold him and comfort him, he was so down. 'I know, that's how I feel.'

'I'm sorry.'

'That's all right. We all have to let off steam now and again.'

'That's what I like about you, Ruby. You're so good to talk to. Most of the girls I know just laugh and act silly, but you're different.'

Ruby didn't want to act different. She wanted to laugh and giggle with him, but he didn't see her in that way. In fact, she wanted him to hold and kiss her – and she blushed at that thought.

'Will you meet me in the park on Sunday? The band's always good in the afternoon.'

'It'll have to be after I've done the washing up.'

'OK. See you about three?'

'I'll look forward to it,' she said lightly, trying to keep her emotions under control. She would have loved to know what Ernie really thought about her.

She would have been surprised if she knew he too was thinking how much he wanted to hold her and kiss her. But he was frightened of showing his feelings; after all, he had nothing to offer. Would she be happy with just his love? He didn't want to spoil her chance of finding someone else who could offer her much more.

They continued walking and talking about neutral topics like his family till he left her to go home and Ruby continued on to the market.

As usual, after Ruby had been to the market, she had to set about cleaning Mr Cox's rooms.

She went into the washhouse. 'Dad, if he's upstairs shall I tell him to come down?'

'If you like.'

As he had never said anything about her going up there, as far as Ruby knew her mother had never told him about Mr Cox.

'These carrots look a bit ropy,' he said, sorting them over.

'I know. That's all I could find,' she replied defensively.

He turned and smiled at her. 'I know things are hard, love, but I am trying to get more work.'

'I know you are. Leave those.' Ruby pointed to the carrots lying on the wooden draining board. 'I'll see to them. Don't let him upstairs see you doing woman's work.'

'All right. I'll leave 'em for now. Tell him I'll have a cuppa ready, and one for you when you finish.'

Ruby gently knocked on Mr Cox's door. 'It's me, Ruby.'

'Come in, girl.' He was sitting in his armchair reading a newspaper. He peered at her over his glasses.

'Dad said would you like a cuppa. He's got one ready.'

'No. I'd rather stay up here and talk to you. I like you, you're sensible.'

Ruby froze. She had to think quickly. She didn't want to be up here alone with him. 'I'd really like to get on, if you don't mind,' she said, putting the dustpan and brush on the floor.

'I don't mind at all. D'you know, you've grown into a pretty little thing.'

Ruby visibly shuddered. She moved back against the door. She knew she had to tread carefully: after all, he was their landlord and she could make them homeless if she wasn't careful.

'How old are you now?'

'I'll be sixteen next month.'

'Old enough to get married then.'

'I don't think so.' Ruby looked around the sparsely furnished room. If she had as much money as everybody said he had she'd have a few more home comforts.

'How's your dad getting on working at the Green Man?'

'All right.'

'I was very surprised he was going out to work again after all this time.'

'A lot of things had to change after Mum died.'

'I expect they did. You want to find yourself a rich husband, then you wouldn't have to go out to work.'

'I don't think that will ever happen.'

'You never know. As I said, you're a very pretty young lady and we'll soon have the young men banging on the door. But take a word of advice from me.' He stood up and came towards her. 'You don't want to worry about young men. You should think of yourself and find someone who has a bit of money.'

'I don't know anyone who has money.'

He folded his newspaper. 'As I said. You never know.'

Ruby took a dishcloth from her overall pocket. 'I'll start in the scullery.'

He laughed. 'Well, that won't take long.' He had a tiny scullery; it was very sparse, with only a deep butler sink, a wooden draining board and a tin bath that stood on its side against the wall.

He stood in the doorway watching her clean the sink. 'I've been thinking about getting one of those new gas stoves.'

'That'll be nice. I read that they're a lot quicker at boiling a kettle than the range.' Although he didn't cook his main meal he still had tea to make.

She moved back into the kitchen, which was just as simply furnished. There was only a very old dresser in one alcove and a table that was pushed under the window covered with a brown chenille tablecloth. Two odd upright chairs were pushed under it, and one hard uncomfortable-looking tapestry-covered armchair stood in front of the fire. She knew that his bedroom wasn't any better, containing just a bed, a chair and a small table at the side that always had a glass on it. A cupboard that served as a wardrobe held his few meagre clothes.

Ruby picked up the dustpan and brush. She was trembling as she went down on her knees and began feverishly brushing the small coloured mat that was in front of the fire, trying to create as much dust as she could.

'I'll have to get some black-lead so's you can bring that stove back to its former glory, and the hearth could do with a whitening. Your mother never did make a good job of that.'

Ruby angrily sat back on her haunches. 'That's because we couldn't afford the whitening and black-lead. So if you want it done you'll have to buy it. We ain't got the money to afford things like that.'

He laughed again. 'I know. I'll give you the money to get what you want. But I'll need a bill, mind. I want to make sure you don't cheat me.'

It took all Ruby's self-control not to throw the brush at him and walk out, but she knew that was more than she dared do. 'If you don't mind I've got to get on. I've got to put the washing in to soak yet.'

'I've left my dirty stuff in the bedroom. I think my bottom sheet could do with mending. I put me foot through it last night.'

Ruby wanted to cry. She didn't want to repair his rotten sheet. She knew as soon as she repaired one hole there would be another next week; his sheets were thin and well worn. 'I'll see what I can do with it. But you could really do with some new ones.'

'New ones? I must say, you're very good at spending my money one way and another. And I suppose if I buy new ones, you'll have me old ones?'

Ruby couldn't answer that, as the thought had flitted through her mind. She could make herself a chemise and some drawers and perhaps new hankies with any part that wasn't too worn.

The banging on the door startled her.

'Mr Cox? It's me, Tom.'

He went and opened the door. 'Well?'

'Dad said the tea's ready.'

'All right. I'll be down in a jiffy.' He closed the door on Tom.

Ruby almost gave a sigh of relief out loud when he picked up his jacket and left.

Ruby went into the bedroom; it smelt of tobacco and beer. She opened the window and began pulling the bedclothes off and throwing them on the floor. She knew he never made his bed. The bottom sheet was all in a heap and when she saw the large rip in it her heart sank. It would take for ever to repair that. She put the top sheet to the bottom and pulled the clean top sheet as hard as she could and tucked it under the huge feather mattress. She did the same to the blankets. When she put the flat eiderdown on top she stood back and smiled. 'He's gonner have a right old job getting into that tonight,' she said out loud. 'Especially if he comes back three sheets to the wind.' She gave a little giggle.

Ruby's birthday had come and gone without celebration and preparations for Christmas were in the air. It was Elsie's forthcoming wedding, however, that filled her mind. What could she buy them for a present and, more important than that, what could she wear?

Ruby was in the dairy telling Milly about the problem.

'Why don't you ask Beth if you could borrow something of

hers? She always looks smart these days, and you're about the same size.'

'I couldn't.'

'Why not? She's always grateful she fell on her feet after staying with you.'

'And what about a present?'

'I don't reckon this Elsie will expect a present. She knows how hard things are for you.'

'I was talking to Ernie Wallis a while back; he was saying how fed up he was with all this poverty.'

'You been out with Ernie Wallis?'

'Not been out with him, we just walked home from the laundry together. He's had it pretty hard.'

Milly rested her elbows on the counter. 'I know things ain't that good for me mum and dad when people ain't got the money to spend, but we're still pretty lucky.'

'This ain't helping me get a new frock.'

'I'd let you have one of mine, but nobody'd find you in it.' Milly laughed. 'You'd disappear never to be seen again. It'd fit you like a tent.'

Ruby laughed with her. 'You ain't that big and I'm good with a needle.'

'It wouldn't look right. No, as I told you, have a word with Beth.'

'I'll see.'

As Ruby hurried back across the road her mind was churning, as ever, trying to think of ways of making extra money. Would George in the Green Man want help behind the bar? She could add up and pour out drinks. Her father had told her how busy it was when a lot of ships were in the docks, and it was getting near to Christmas. She pushed open the kitchen door.

'Dad. I've been thinking. I want to earn a bit extra.'

'Don't we all, love.'

She sat at the table. 'Does your boss George want any help over Christmas?'

'I'm going to ask him if he wants me in for any more nights. I don't even mind going in at lunchtime. It's started to get really busy.' He laughed. 'A lot of the toms come in for a warm. I sometimes do a stint behind the bar.'

Ruby knew her father had settled down despite her anxiety about him working there. He had told her that George was pleased with him as he was reliable and worked well.

'Dad, would George want me to work as a barmaid, like Beth does sometimes up at the Royal Albert?'

'What? No, I wouldn't hear of it.'

'But, Dad—'

'No, Ruby. The Royal Albert is much posher than the Green Man and they don't get so many unsavoury customers as we do.'

'But I want to help out.'

'I said no, and I mean no. I know times are hard, but they will get better, I promise you.'

Ruby was suddenly reminded of what Mrs Riddle had told her after her mother died. She had told her things would get better. But when?

Ruby didn't pursue that line of conversation with her father as she could see his mind was made up.

It was two weeks before Christmas and Ruby was overjoyed to see Elsie waiting for her on Saturday.

'You took your time coming out,' she said, kissing Ruby's cheek.

'I had to finish off a couple of shirts Mrs Watson was waiting to parcel up.'

'So you're still doing the specials then?'

Ruby nodded. 'Till the next move.'

'It's bloody cold out here.' Elsie pulled her large scarf tighter round her neck. 'I suppose that's the one good thing about working in a laundry, it is warm.'

'Not if you're in the washroom. I couldn't bear it if I ever had to go back in there. Is your place warm?'

'Not too bad. It's very dusty and you should see the state of me hair when I wash it.' She laughed. 'Talk about a tea rinse.'

Ruby had noted that when she saw Elsie now, she never said a lot about her job: was it all she had expected?

'So how are things?' asked Elsie.

'Not too bad.'

'How's the money situation?'

'I can just about keep me head above water, but it's hard. I'm hoping Dad's gonner be able to do a few more hours over Christmas, so that'll help.'

'He's settled in at the pub then?'

'Yes, thanks to your dad.'

'Is it as bad as they say?'

'No. Not really.'

'You off to the market?'

'Yes. Got to pick up the veg.'

Elsie tucked her arm through Ruby's. 'Ruby, I don't want you to buy us a wedding present.'

'But why?'

'I know how hard things are for you and my Charlie said you shouldn't. We both earn a decent wage and we ain't got a home to get so we don't need it.'

'I can't walk in without a present.'

'Charlie said to tell you that if you do walk in with a present, you'll be sent straight home again.'

'He sounds really nice. I'm looking forward to meeting him and all your sisters.'

'He's a smashing bloke. And my sisters are all looking forward to meeting you. Now, you know the date?'

'Sat'day December the thirty-first 1921 at two o'clock. What a lovely way to round off the year. I'm hoping they'll let us go a bit earlier that day.'

'They might let you go at two.'

'I hope so. I'd love to see you in the church.'

'Let's keep our fingers crossed. I only live round the corner from the church so we can all walk back afterwards. I wish we could have got married sooner, but it's cost a bit for me wedding frock and the bridesmaids. I was determined to have what I wanted, even if it did mean waiting a few more months.'

'I bet you'll look really lovely.'

'I hope so. Have you got something to wear?'

'Not yet.'

'I'm so excited. I can hardly wait. And I know my Charlie's having a bit of trouble keeping his feelings under control.'

'You are very lucky, Elsie.'

'I know. I know.'

They continued walking and talking but all the while Ruby was getting more and more disheartened. What could she wear for this wedding? She had nothing that would do. If only Elsie had asked her to be bridesmaid: that would have solved all her problems. She was still considering what Milly had suggested about asking Beth. Would she mind?

Elsie stopped at the haberdashery stall. 'I remember when you bought me those black lace garters, that was the Christmas before last. You were so happy at having money.'

'That was the best Christmas we'd had in years. Then it all went wrong.'

'But you kept working. I admire you.'

Ruby stopped and, with her hands on her hips, announced,

'I was young and full of ambition.'

They laughed together.

'You are daft.'

'I know. Elsie, I ain't got nothing to wear for your wedding.'

'I guessed that. That's why I'm really here. You see, I want to give you an early Christmas present.'

Tears filled Ruby's eyes. 'But I can't give you—'

Elsie held up her hand. 'Me and Charlie want to treat you to a frock. It can only come from the second-hand stall, but I'm sure she's got something that'll do you.'

'I can't take that.'

'Why not?'

'I don't know.'

'Let's go and look. She might not have anything that's any good.'

Elsie began rummaging through the pile of clothes. She picked up a lovely pink frock that had floaty sleeves. 'This looks good.' She held it against Ruby. 'It suits you. What do you think?'

'It's lovely.'

'How much?' asked Elsie.

'Five bob,' came back the answer.

'What?' cried Elsie and Ruby together.

'You heard.'

Ruby threw the frock back down. 'I ain't paying that much for something that stinks of scent.'

'It don't,' said the stallholder, picking it up and sniffing it. 'Well, it ain't that bad. It'll soon go off if you hang it on the line for a bit.'

'You got something cheaper?' asked Elsie.

'Not as pretty as that.'

Ruby looked at the frock, which was lying forlornly on the stall. She would have given anything to have a frock like that, but five shillings was half a week's wages.

'What about this?' The stall lady held up a brown woolly frock.

'No thanks.'

'Come back next week. I might have some more.'

As they walked away, Elsie said, 'Don't get disheartened. My sister's got a frock that's a bit like that and it's too small for her now. I'll see if I can get her to part with it.'

'I'll pay for it,' said Ruby quickly.

'As I said before, this'll be a Christmas present from me and Charlie. I'll come to the laundry next Sat'day, but I won't be able to come to the market as we're going out to get me wedding ring.' Elsie squeezed Ruby's arm. 'I can't wait!'

Ruby smiled at her. 'I can see that!'

'Seen anything of Ernie lately?'

Ruby nodded.

'We gonner hear wedding bells one day?'

'What? I ain't old enough.'

'You will be one day.' Elsie kissed Ruby's cheek. 'Bye for now.'

Ruby watched her walk away. What a lovely thought. Wedding bells for her and Ernie.

When Ruby got home she was taken back by a nasty smell.

'What's that smell?' she asked her father.

'Ask him.' Her father pointed to Tom who was sitting in the corner crying.

'What's happened?'

'I was only trying to help,' sniffed Tom.

Ruby stood looking from one to the other. 'What's he done?'

'He's been stealing.'

'What?' Despite all their poverty they had been taught

211

never to steal. 'What's he been pinching?'

Tom looked up, his eyes red from crying. 'Coal.'

'Coal?' repeated Ruby. 'Where did you get it from?'

'The railway yard.'

Ruby sat down. What could she say? Although it was wrong, it'd been done with the best intentions.

'There was a lot of other boys doing it, so I thought it was all right.'

'So what's the smell?'

'I hid it in one of the wooden boxes then put horse muck on top. I thought that way nobody would see it. But when I told Dad, he walloped me.'

Ruby could have cried for him. He was sitting on the floor looking so sad and vulnerable.

'I had to teach him that no matter how bad things are, the Bible says: "Thou shalt not steal." '

Ruby looked at her father. Although she knew he was right, she really didn't agree with him. Tom had only been trying to help, and after all, he was burning the coal.

'Right, now Ruby's home you can go to bed.'

Tom looked up. 'What about me tea?'

'You'll get nothing tonight, young man. Now, off with you.'

Ruby thought her father was being harsh, but didn't interfere.

Tom clambered to his feet. 'I bet if Mum was here, she wouldn't send me to bed, or give me a hiding.'

'Your mother was too soft with you.'

Tom stood by the door. 'And she was bloody soft with you an' all. It's your fault she's dead.'

Ruby gasped. 'Tom!'

Tom ran out of the kitchen, slamming the door behind him.

Ruby stared at the closed door. The crashing of the front door sent her hurrying along the passage.

Mr Cox had been going up the stairs. He looked down at Ruby. 'You want to tell that brother of yours not to slam the door like that, you'll have it falling off its hinges – then that'll cost yer.'

'Yes, I will tell him.'

'Are you coming up to clean?'

'I'll be up in a minute. I've just got to catch Tom.'

'Here's me tea.' He handed her a parcel wrapped in newspaper. 'It's a nice piece of haddock and I want it poached with a bit of butter. It's all there.'

Ruby put the parcel on the stair. 'I'll collect it on me way back.'

Outside Ruby looked up and down the street. There wasn't any sign of Tom. Where could she go? It was freezing cold and he wasn't wearing a coat.

She went across the road to Milly. 'You haven't seen our Tom, have you?'

'No. Why?'

'It's nothing.' Ruby didn't want her to know the reason. All this while Tom had had this resentment towards his father locked inside him, and she hadn't realised. Please don't let him do anything silly. 'Please, Tom. Come home,' she said out loud as she walked back to the house.

Chapter 19

Ruby pushed open the kitchen door.

'Did you find him?' asked her father. A look of worry haunted his eyes.

'No.' She looked at the clock. 'Shouldn't you be getting off to work?'

'I suppose so. Ruby, I'm so sorry. I was wrong.'

'He did it for us all, you know.'

'Yes, I know.' He buried his head in his hands. 'I'm not sure I can go off leaving it like this.'

'You must. He'll be back soon.'

'Will he? He hates me.'

'No, he don't. He was just upset, that's all.'

'He's such a good little lad.' He looked up at Ruby; tears were now filling his eyes.

'Come on, Dad.' Fear grabbed her. At the back of her mind was always the worry that he might go back to his old ways. 'Come on now. You must go to work. I'll go out and look for him. He won't have gone far.'

'I can't.'

'Dad.' Her voice was forceful. 'You mustn't lose your job.'

'Is my job more important than Tom?'

'You know it's not, but it won't help for you to sit here

worrying. Besides, we can't be your money short just before Christmas.'

'Christmas. What sort of Christmas will it be without your mother?'

'It won't be easy, but we've got to make the best of it.'

He stood up and brushed a tear from his cheek. 'You're good kids. I don't deserve you.'

To Ruby he suddenly looked old. His face was grey with worry. She threw her arms round his neck. 'We've got to stick this out together.'

'I know, love. I know.' He kissed the top of her dark unruly hair.

'Now be off with you.'

'Just as long as you're sure?'

'Wrap up, Dad, it's bitter out there.'

He was winding his scarf round his neck when he realised. 'He ain't got a coat on.'

'I know. That's why I'm sure he'll be back soon.' But Ruby was finding it hard to keep a smile on her face.

As Thomas walked to work he went over and over in his mind what had happened. He should never have hit Tom; after all, he was only trying to help, even though stealing was wrong. He remembered when he was in the trenches, he would have stolen food, clothes, anything to help keep him alive. He stopped and sat on a wall; he held his head as the sound of guns filled his ears. He was back there. The sky at night, with shells from an unseen enemy falling all around them. The days when you had to march through mud. The blood. The warm sticky blood; you were never sure if it was yours or the poor devil you were trying to get to safety. Falling over parts of men. And the smell of cordite and rotting bodies. 'Please make them go away,' he said out loud.

'You all right, mate?' asked a man who was walking past.

Thomas smiled. 'Yes, thanks. Just got a bit of a head.'

'Been on the beer last night?'

'Something like that.'

The man moved on and Thomas closed his eyes. There were times when he wanted nothing so much as to creep back into his comfortable shell with the comfort of his blanket around him. But in doing that, he had let his wife down, and that was something he would never forgive himself for. He forced himself to stand up and continue on his way to work. He had to stay strong for his children.

Ruby put her hat and coat on and left the house as soon as she knew her father would be out of sight. She would go to see Beth. She knew that if there was one person Tom would go to, it was her.

She felt she could have cut the smoky air with a knife when she pushed open the pub's door. It was very busy and the men were laughing and talking loudly; it took a while for her to weave her way through the crowd, trying to ignore their remarks and groping hands.

Beth, who was behind the bar serving, caught sight of her and waved.

When Ruby reached the bar she leaned over and said, 'Beth, has Tom been in here?'

'No. Why should he?'

'Can you spare a minute?'

'Not really. As you can see we're run off our feet. Yes, sir,' she said to a man who was standing with an empty glass in his hand.

'Pint o' bitter, love.'

As Beth stood holding the glass under the tap while she expertly pumped with the other hand she said to Ruby, 'So what's happened?'

Ruby looked about her. 'Tom's gone off somewhere and we don't know where.'

'You mean run away?' She handed the man his brimming glass and took the money he held out. 'Thanks.'

'We don't know.'

'What's he done that for?'

'It's a bit of a long story.'

'So where's your dad?'

'He's had to go to work.'

Beth considered. 'Well, Ruby, Tom won't have gone far. I'm sorry I can't be of any help, but if he does come in here I'll send him straight home.'

'Thanks. He ain't got a coat on and it's bitter out there.'

'Don't worry too much. He's not a silly boy. He might even be at home already. He probably just wanted to give you a fright.'

'I hope so.' As Beth's attention was claimed by another customer, Ruby left the pub disappointed.

She walked home quickly, her mind going over all the places he might be hiding if he weren't at home. As they didn't have any friends, she had covered the only person who might have been able to help. There was no point in going to see Milly because he wouldn't have gone there.

'Tom. Tom!' she shouted when she pushed open the front door.

Mr Cox stood at the top of the stairs. 'Where's my tea? And you ain't been up to do my cleaning yet.'

'I'm sorry, but I've been out looking for Tom.'

'Why?'

'I think he's run away.'

'What d'you mean, think?'

'Him and Dad had a row, and he run off.' Tears were slowly running down her cheek.

Mr Cox came down the stairs. He put his arm round Ruby; for once she didn't shy away.

'There. There.' Mr Cox gently patted her shoulder. 'He can't have gone far. Have you looked in the lav?'

Ruby shook her head.

'Well, why don't you go and take a look now? I've just made a pot of tea and then the both of you can come up for a cup.'

'Thank you.' Ruby walked away.

Ruby wiped her nose and went through the washhouse and into the yard. She didn't notice Mr Cox watching her, before he went upstairs. 'Tom. Tom,' Ruby called. But the lav was empty.

She sat on the wooden lid of the seat for a moment or two wondering what to do next. Slowly she went into the house. She quickly turned when Mr Cox pushed open the kitchen door.

'Was he there?'

Ruby shook her head. 'No.'

'Come up and have this cuppa. Perhaps we can sort out what to do next.'

Without thinking, Ruby was slowly led upstairs.

At the back of the pub, Tom weaved his way between the crates of empty beer bottles and the large wooden barrels. He sat on the ground and leant against one of the barrels, shivering. He had been going to see Beth, but he had caught sight of Ruby going into the bar and he didn't want her shouting at him. He should go home. He knew Ruby would be worried sick, but he wanted to teach them a lesson. He wasn't just a kid who did as he was told. He ran with a gang now: they decided where they were going to go and what they were going to do. Now he didn't have to spend all his day collecting and delivering washing he had time on his hands, even after he'd run a few errands for Milly and chopped up the boxes. Ruby had talked about school, but he didn't want to go, not now. When he'd first met Freddie Porter he'd been frightened of him. Freddie wanted the wooden boxes Tom collected. He wanted to chop them up into bundles and sell them, but after a few days he changed his mind because he got blisters and splinters. Freddie Porter told him there were easier ways of making money and he would teach him, but it would cost him thrupence to join his gang. He showed Tom how to take things and not pay for them. Ruby hadn't had any nice chocolate for years, but he had. And it was easy to hide things under the feather mattress; she didn't lift that up very often. He didn't know where Freddie lived, so he couldn't go there. He only ever met him at the railway yard. Tom tried to wrap his arms round himself. He'd have to go home soon. He could freeze to death out here and nobody would find him for days. When he was dead everybody would be sorry.

He stood up and stamped his feet. He tried to lift open the huge wooden cellar doors, but they were locked on the inside. He sat down again; he was getting hungry and began to feel sleepy. A cat came and snuggled up to him. 'You can help to keep me warm.' He pulled it on to his lap and began to fondle its ears. 'I bet you always find enough to eat. There's always plenty of rats and mice round here.'

Fear suddenly gripped him. What if he fell asleep and the rats attacked him? They would bite him and start to eat him. He jumped up and the cat ran off screeching.

Ruby sat at Mr Cox's table drinking tea.

'You've had to grow up very quickly. One way and another your family seems to cause you a great deal of trouble. You're a good girl to take on so much responsibility.'

'Dad couldn't help getting shell-shocked.'

Mr Cox patted her hand. 'I know, love. I know. But I do think he could have made a bit more of an effort to look after you all.'

'He's a lot better now he's going to work.'

'I'm surprised he finished up working at the Green Man.'

'Jobs are very hard to get and George is very good to him.'

'George?'

'The owner.'

Mr Cox smiled. 'Would you like another cup of tea? I have some very nice biscuits if you fancy one.'

'No thank you. I must be going. I must try to find Tom.'

'Where will you start?'

'I don't know.'

'Have you thought of telling the police?'

She shook her head. 'No. Dad wouldn't like that.'

'Wait till your father gets home, and if young Tom ain't back be then, then I think you should.'

'Tom will be back before then.'

Mr Cox stood up. 'Ruby, as I said before, you should think about letting someone else look after you for a change.'

Suddenly Ruby realised she was alone in the house with this man, and she was vulnerable. She must be mad. What was she doing sitting at his table drinking his tea and letting him touch her? She jumped up. 'I must go.'

He went to move round to her side of the table. He laughed. 'You look like a frightened little rabbit. Come here.' He stood in front of the kitchen door and held out his arms. 'I'm not going to harm you. I would never do that.'

Panic filled her. She had to get away.

The front door slammed.

'Who's that?'

'It might be Tom, or Beth with some news.' She pushed him

to one side and ran out of the room.

Tom was standing at the bottom of the stairs. 'Don't shout at me, Ruby.'

She raced down the stairs and threw her arms round his neck. 'I ain't gonner shout at you. Where have you been?'

'I've been sitting behind the pub.'

'Phew, you smell like a brewery. What was you doing there?'

'I was frightened of Dad.'

'Why didn't you go in to Beth?'

'I was going to, then I saw *you* go in.'

'Everything all right down there?'

Ruby looked up the stairs. 'Yes thank you, Mr Cox.'

'Well, can you cook my haddock now?'

'I'll do it right away.'

'And what about this cleaning?'

Ruby could see he was angry. 'I'll do it in the morning.'

'Well, not too early. I might have a hangover.' He went into his kitchen, slamming the door behind him.

Ruby pushed her brother along the passage. 'You're shivering. Come and get warm.'

Tom sat on the floor in front of the fire.

'Well, what have you got to say for yourself?'

'I'm sorry. But I didn't like it when Dad hit me.'

'I know. But he was only trying to make you see that it doesn't matter how bad things are, you mustn't steal.'

'I know. But it didn't stop him from burning the coal, did it?'

'I'm not going to argue. I've got to cook this bit o' fish for Mr Cox. We'll have a cup of tea and a bit of toast, then I'll have to go to the pub to tell Dad you're safe and sound.'

'Will he hit me again?'

'I shouldn't think so for one minute.'

Ruby shoved her wayward flyaway hair under her hat and pulled it down hard as she hurried along to the Green Man. It was getting late; she would have to leave it until tomorrow to go and tell Beth that Tom was back. As she got nearer the pub she gave up a silent prayer that there wouldn't be another incident like before.

Nervously Ruby pushed open the door. The bar was full of men singing loud songs and holding each other up; the floor was wet and sticky with beer. She could see her father. He was laughing and talking to two women at the bar. They had their backs to Ruby, but she could hear their screeching laughter above all the other noise around her. She was jostled as she went towards her father and was pushed against a big man.

He quickly turned on her. ''Ere, what's your game?'

'Sorry.'

'Yer will be, yer've just spilt some of me beer.'

Fear gripped her. 'I'm sorry.'

He put his arm round her shoulder. 'What's a pretty little thing like you doing in a place like this?'

'I've come to see me dad.'

'Have yer now? And who might that be?'

'Thomas.'

He laughed. 'Thomas. And where might we find him?'

'Behind the bar.'

''Ere, Thomas me old mate,' he shouted. 'Yer missus's gone and sent yer daughter ter come and get yer, so yer'd better stop giving those toms the glad eye.' He put his face close to Ruby's. 'I bet he thought he was gonner get lucky ternight.'

Ruby wanted to die. She looked towards her father, but thankfully he hadn't heard the man above all the noise.

The man shoved Ruby towards the bar. 'Out the way, you lot. This little gel's come ter see 'er daddy.'

Thomas, who was at the other end of the bar, turned when

he heard the commotion from the men being pushed aside. 'Ruby! What're you doing here? Is it Tom? What's happened to him?'

'It's all right. I've just come to tell you that he's home.'

'Thank God for that.' He began filling a glass that had been handed to him. 'Didn't think he'd stay away for long, he ain't that silly.' Her father looked around nervously.

Ruby could tell he was pleased about Tom and didn't want these people to see his true feelings.

'Hello there,' said George, coming up to Ruby. 'Everything all right?'

She nodded. 'Yes thanks.'

'Not a nice night for a youngster like you to be out.' He leaned forward. 'And this ain't the right area to walk about at night.'

'I was just going. I just had to tell Dad something.' As her father continued filling glasses she felt uncomfortable. 'I best be going, Dad.'

'See you when I get home. I might be a bit late – as you can see, we're busy.'

'Bye.'

One of the women she had seen her father talking and laughing with turned. 'Thought I recognised that voice.'

'Mrs Bell!' said Ruby in amazement.

'You know this lady?' said her father.

'Mum used to do her washing.'

'Thomas, you're this young lady's father?'

He grinned and nodded. 'This is my Ruby.'

'You dark horse,' said Mrs Bell. 'You didn't tell me your name was Jenkins.'

'You never asked.'

Ruby looked at her father.

'Now you go on home. As I said, I might be late back.'

Mrs Bell smiled at Ruby. 'I wish you was still doing my washing. Me frillies don't look the same now. How's that young brother of yours?'

'He's all right, thank you.'

She turned to Thomas. 'You should be very proud of your kids. They've got lovely manners. Can I buy you a drink, love?' she asked Ruby.

'No thank you. I'd better be getting back home.'

'That's a pity, we could have had a little chat.'

Ruby smiled, then said, 'See you later, Dad.' He didn't answer, as he was too busy serving.

Ruby had guessed Mrs Bell used that pub. As she pushed her way through the crowd, Ruby thought about her lovely flat. Her father had told her about some of the women that frequented the Green Man. Did Mrs Bell pick up her men friends in there? She shuddered when she got out into the cold night air and, putting her head down against the biting wind, quickly made her way home. Her thoughts went to Tom. She was tired of running after her family, making sure everybody was all right. A lot of the trouble was because Tom didn't have enough to do. She had to find something to keep him busy. She knew some schools didn't charge and although when she had mentioned it before, Tom had been against it, she had made up her mind that he must go to school.

Chapter 20

As Ruby hurried home her mind was going over and over what had happened this evening. Thank goodness Tom was home and her father was pleased she'd made the effort to tell him. Then fancy seeing Mrs Bell; she looked even nicer than before. It must be wonderful to have lovely clothes and make-up like that and sit in a pub laughing and talking. A bit like Beth does, but Beth's working. Ruby grinned to herself. So's Mrs Bell, in a way. Ruby pulled her scarf tighter. 'I hope Dad's not getting over friendly with her,' she said out loud. But then she thought again of Beth. After all, it was part of the job, being friendly with the customers. Perhaps she should have waited till Thomas had finished and then they could have walked home together. But she had to let him live his life freely; after all, in his mind he'd been trapped for years.

'What did Dad say?' asked Tom as soon as she opened the kitchen door.

'He was all right.'

'Was he mad?'

'No. He was too busy to say much. Now you go on to bed. You just tell him you're sorry in the morning and that you won't do it again.'

'All right.' Tom put his book away. How could he tell Ruby that he wasn't going to stop pinching things? If people left them lying about then that was their fault. He smiled to himself when he thought of his loot under the mattress. There were some sweets and five Woodbines; he hadn't had the nerve to smoke any of them yet, but he knew he would have to soon, just to show he wasn't a cissy. He didn't feel guilty at taking things. As his mate Freddie said, 'They must have plenty otherwise they'd look after what they've got.'

Freddie, who was on the plump side, had told Tom about his two brothers and father, who were rough villains and had been in prison a few times. But they were never short of anything and he was very proud of the fact that his mother had more rings than fingers. Freddie was determined to be like the rest of the family.

When she was alone Ruby sat staring at the fire thinking about her father. He was so different now. It was a shame he hadn't been more like this when her mother was alive. Had it been her mother's fault? Had she fussed over him too much? Since he had been at work these last few months he had become much more self-assured. But the Green Man was that kind of place; you would quickly go under if you couldn't hold your own. Thank goodness George liked him and had helped give him confidence again. At the beginning Ruby had been very worried that Thomas would simply run away; now she could see he enjoyed working there. Her thoughts went to Mrs Bell. He must know what she did for a living, surely? Ruby knew he would be paid tonight. She smiled. Would he ever let a woman like that take him home and take all his money? No. She couldn't see him being led astray like that.

The front door closing woke Ruby who had been dozing in the chair. She looked up at the clock: it was midnight.

'You still up, love?'

'Thought I'd wait up for you.' Ruby could see her father's

eyes were a bit glazed. 'D'you want a cuppa? The kettle's boiling.'

'If you like. Sorry I couldn't talk much tonight.'

'That's all right. I could see how busy the place was.'

'So, where was Tom?'

'At the back of the Royal Albert. He went to see Beth but he caught sight of me going in there.' Ruby stood at the table and put a spoonful of tea into the teapot; she added the water and covered it with the multicoloured tea cosy her mother had knitted years ago.

'Did you tell Beth I'd walloped him?'

'No. I just said you'd had words. He stayed round the back for a bit, then came home. He was freezing.' She put the tea strainer over the cup and poured out the tea. 'Dad. Does Mrs Bell go in the pub very often?'

'Not too many times. She's a very nice woman. Very generous. Always buys me a drink.'

'You didn't know Mum used to do her washing?'

'Not till tonight. She said she was very sorry to hear about her passing away. She missed young Tom collecting and bringing back her washing. She said nobody does her clothes as nice as your mother.'

'You know she lives in the buildings?'

'She did tell me that.'

'You do know . . .' Ruby hesitated. '. . . she's a woman of the night?'

Her father threw his head back and laughed. 'Of course I know that. Most of the women who come into that pub are looking for punters.'

'You will be careful, won't you, Dad? I don't want you spending all your money on women like that.'

He smiled and shook his head. Picking up his cup, he finished his tea. 'Chance'd be a fine thing. 'Sides, she's only interested in those what's got a few bob. Got very expensive tastes, has that lady. I'll be off to bed now.'

The following morning Tom was already sitting up when Ruby opened her eyes.

'Tom. What is it? What's the matter?'

'I was frightened to get up in case Dad was still mad at me.'

'No, don't worry. Everything's all right. Now turn round while I get dressed.' She was getting embarrassed with him watching her. 'I've got to get that fire going then and clean upstairs. And later on you'd better go and tell Beth you're home. She was very worried about you.'

It was cold in the kitchen. As Ruby raked the ash out from the grate she thought about sharing the room with Tom. She would ask her father whether, if she split the feather mattress in half, Tom could sleep on the floor in his room so she could have a bit of privacy now she was getting older and becoming a woman. She knew Tom wouldn't like to sleep in the bed with his father, so that could be the solution. After checking there weren't any bits of coal amongst the ashes that she could use again, Ruby laid the fire and took the ashes out to the yard. It would take a while for the coal to burn and heat the kettle, so she could clean the lav and put the washing into soak while she was waiting. It was still very dark out. She stood for a moment or two looking up at the stars. They were very bright. Her thoughts went to her mother. 'I miss you so much,' she whispered. 'Why did you leave us?'

After they had had their toast Ruby sent Tom along to Beth and then she told her father her plan.

'That sounds all right. You sure you can manage to divide that mattress?'

'It'll be a bit hard, and I won't be able to do it all at once as I've got to put two rows of stitching right down the middle before I can cut through it, otherwise we'll have feathers everywhere. It ain't gonner be that easy.'

'Have you got enough covers for Tom to come in my room?' he asked.

'I think we can manage. It's mostly our coats on the bed as it is.'

'Well, that's all right with me.'

'Good. I'll start sewing tomorrow night. I'll have to do it in the bedroom to keep the feathers in one room.'

'I'll give you a hand, love. Otherwise you'll end up with blisters. I don't think those scissors are all that sharp.'

That night as soon as her head hit the pillow Ruby was asleep. She had been working all day and had forgotten to tell Tom her plan.

On Monday, after he had finished his jobs and errands for Milly, Tom hurried to meet his gang.

'Well,' said Freddie to the three boys sitting on the coal at the back of the railway. 'What shall we do today?'

Tom wasn't listening, however. He was thinking about yesterday, when he had sheepishly told Beth why he had run out of the house. She'd been angry with him and had given him a telling off.

'Now you listen to me, young man. Your sister and father are good people, so don't you go bringing home any trouble. I know how easy it is to get in with the wrong sort and even if it seems simple to steal, it ain't right to take something that belongs to someone else. They might have worked bloody hard to get it.' Then she had relented and kissed the top of his head.

He smiled. He liked Beth. He could talk to her. But it was all very well saying things like that: she was living in a pub and had her own room, and she had a husband who must send her money sometimes. He had nothing.

'Can we git some Christmas presents?' asked Ginger, breaking into Tom's thoughts. Ginger was the youngest of the gang.

'Could do. What d'yer want, Ginge?'

'Don't know. Me sister wants a doll and me mum wants—' He stopped. 'Me mum said she wants everyfing, including a man.'

Freddie laughed. 'Can't git her that, she'll have ter find one of those 'erself. What about you, 'Arry?'

'Dunno.' Harry was tall and skinny. He always looked as if he was going to fall asleep. 'S'pose we could do with a chicken.'

'We'll get them on Christmas Eve. What about you, young Tom?'

'Dunno. I got a wallop for giving 'em coal on Sat'day.'

'If yer daft enough ter tell 'em yer pinched it, what d'yer expect? Yer could 'ave said yer found it after the coal cart went past. I can see yer've got a lot ter learn. Where d'yer keep yer loot then?'

Tom sat up and looked very pleased with himself. 'Under me mattress. Me sister don't lift that up. It's on the floor and it's heavy.'

'Good ter see yer learning then, me old son.' Freddie, at thirteen, was all of two years older than Tom and very streetwise. 'So what d'yer want fer Christmas then?'

'Dunno.'

'I'll tell yer what. We'll go down the market and pinch a couple of handbags. Then with a bit o' luck we'll find enough money ter share out. OK?'

'OK,' said Tom, Harry and Ginger together.

'Right, give the sign.'

All four boys put their hands on top of one another's. 'To us,' they yelled.

They worked out a plan. Two of them would start fighting as a diversion when they saw a bag that was easy to run off with; one would keep guard and, if need be, barge into and trip up anyone who looked as if they might run after them; the other one would pinch the bag and they'd have a share out in the park round by the bandstand.

Tom was so excited, he was worried he might wet himself when the crucial moment came.

They ambled round looking as if they didn't know each other, then Freddie gave Tom and Ginger a nod. They began pushing and shouting. Ginger threw Tom to the ground. He hurt his knee and he wanted to cry, but he knew he had to be brave.

'Don't hit me so hard,' said Tom. But Ginger wasn't listening. He was enjoying giving Tom a thumping.

''Ere, stop it, you two,' yelled an old lady. She pulled Ginger off Tom. 'What's your game, young man, hitting this little lad? He's half your size.'

'He said my sister was stupid.'

'Well, that don't give you an excuse to bash him like that. Now say you're sorry.'

'Sorry.' Ginger had his head down.

'And you, young man, say you're sorry for saying nasty things about his sister.'

Tears were welling in Tom's eyes. 'Sorry.'

'Now run along, the pair of you.'

They both ran away as fast as their legs could carry them. They raced over to the bandstand where Harry and Freddie were sitting on the floor.

'That was a good show you two put up,' said Freddie.

'He didn't have to hit me so hard,' said Tom. 'Next time I'm gonner be the one that does the bashing.'

'Yer too small,' said Ginger, grinning. 'What'd yer get, Fred?'

'We did all right. Got two pounds.'

'Two pounds,' said Tom, his eyes wide with disbelief. 'Does that mean we get ten bob each?'

'No, it don't. Yer quick with yer sums,' said Freddie.

Tom smiled proudly.

'What it does mean, my son, is that I get a pound, you get five bob and Ginge and 'Arry get seven and six each.'

'But that ain't fair. I was the one what got beaten up.'

'I know. But you're the last to join, so you get less. It's called the name of the game.'

Tom would have liked to thump Freddie, but he knew the other two would be on him before he could run away. Besides, he had to stay; this was a good way of earning money. Five bob. It took Ruby all week to earn ten. Perhaps later on he could do it on his own, then he'd be able to keep all the money.

As soon as he got home he went into the bedroom and sat on the mattress. He took the money from his pocket. He had never seen so much. Very carefully he counted it out; this was the tenth time he'd done so. He couldn't believe all this was his. What could he spend it on?

'Tom. Tom,' shouted his father.

He quickly stashed his loot under the mattress. He had to be very careful otherwise Ruby would guess, then he really would be in trouble.

'Yes, Dad,' he said when he went into the kitchen.

'Did you manage to get any veg from the market?'

Tom shook his head. 'No. It was a bit early, they ain't started throwing stuff away.'

'Well, you can go later on.'

'All right.' Tom wasn't going to start moaning about it. All he hoped was that someone didn't recognise him as one of Freddie's gang.

★ ★ ★

That night Ruby didn't feel like sitting in the cold bedroom sewing; besides, she had the ironing to finish.

'Dad, do you think you'll be able to help me bring the mattress in here tomorrow? It's so cold in the bedroom I reckon me fingers'll drop off if I have to sit in there for too long.'

'Why don't you leave it till Sunday, then you'll have better light.'

'I mustn't sew on a Sunday, it ain't right.'

Thomas Jenkins laughed. 'That's one of your mother's ideas. She'd work herself to death all week—' He stopped. 'Sorry, I shouldn't have said that, but you know what I mean?'

Ruby nodded. 'It was just her way. It was the way she was brought up.'

'I know, love.' He sat back in his chair. 'I should have helped her more. I'll never ever forgive myself for being so selfish.'

Ruby noted that he quietly wiped his eyes with his sleeve. 'That bit of liver I got from the butcher's wasn't too tough, was it?'

'Would have been better if young Tom had managed to get some onions to go with it. I don't know what he's been doing with himself all day. I made him go back to the market as the first time he came back with nothing.'

Ruby was thoughtful. Tom *was* acting a bit strange. He was so eager to go to bed, which wasn't like him at all. She gave a little smile. Perhaps he was trying to make something for Christmas and didn't want them to see.

Chapter 21

On Sunday Tom was filled with horror when Ruby told him why she was going to take the mattress into the kitchen to sew and cut it in half.

'But I don't want to sleep in Dad's room.'

'Well, I want you to. I don't want you looking at me getting undressed.'

'I don't look at you – honest.'

'Well, I'm sorry. I'm dividing it in half, so don't start arguing.'

Fear was making Tom sweat. Where could he hide his money? Freddie had told him they would get plenty more money now that people were getting their Christmas clubs out. Yesterday he'd spent so much on sweets and cakes that he'd thought he was going to be sick. He had to be very wary where he spent his money. He couldn't go into any of the shops where Ruby was known. Perhaps sometimes he could buy fresh veg at the market instead of scrabbling around the back like a lot of others, pushing and shoving them out of the way when there was anything worth having. Ruby was always pleased when he brought home decent stuff, but he had to be careful, she would soon guess it wasn't all rubbish that had been thrown away.

Ruby smiled. 'What you got hiding in that room?'

'Nothing. Nothing,' he shouted.

'All right. Keep your hair on,' said his father, laughing. 'If it's something you've got us for Christmas we don't want to see it anyway.'

Tom almost breathed a sigh of relief. 'Is it all right if I go and get it then?'

Ruby ruffled his hair. 'Course.'

Tom ran into the bedroom. He quickly fished around for the money.

He jumped when Ruby knocked on the door. 'D'you want a big bag to put it in?' she called out.

'No. Go away.'

When Tom came back into the kitchen he looked very guilty.

Ruby laughed. 'Well, whatever you've got us, it can't be very big. Where is it?'

'I ain't telling.'

'Stop teasing the lad. Now come on. Let's go and get this thing out of the bedroom.'

Tom watched them walk away. He ran into the lav. He had to find a hiding place. What about the yard? There wasn't any earth he could dig up, but what about the pile of ashes? No, they were hot when Ruby threw them out and they might melt the money. He shut the door and sat on the lid of the pan. He looked around. Above the door was a ledge. Surely that would be one place nobody looked at. That would be the perfect hiding place. Could he reach it? He peered outside. There was one of his boxes waiting to be chopped up. He quickly dragged it into the lav and with a lot of difficulty managed to shut the door and stand on the box. He ran his hand along the shelf. It was very dirty and he shuddered as a big spider ran away from him. He would put the money up there for now, but he would have to find a bag to keep it in, and a stone to put on top, especially if he ever got a ten-bob or a pound note; they might blow away.

He looked out of the door again, just to make sure nobody was waiting and would wonder what he was doing taking a wooden box in the lav. The coast was clear and he walked back into the kitchen.

'While I'm doing this,' said Ruby to Tom, 'you can make some tea. Dad's seeing to the veg. They were certainly very nice this week. You're a clever boy. I even wondered if they had been thrown away they look so good.'

'Well, they was. D'you think I pinched them?'

'No, course not. I only said they looked too good.'

Tom put the hot water in the teapot and went into the washhouse to empty it. 'I'll have to be careful,' he said under his breath. 'I don't want her to get suspicious.'

All morning Ruby sewed and didn't seem to be getting anywhere. It was hard work, her fingers were sore and in many ways she wished she hadn't started.

'What you doing there, girl?' asked Mr Cox when he came down for his dinner. 'There ain't room to swing a cat round in here with that thing stuck in the middle of the room.'

She explained.

'So you want to be on your own in the bedroom then?'

'She is growing up,' said her father. 'And, after all, a girl needs a bit of privacy.'

'Course she does. You never know who she's gonner bring home.'

'That ain't the reason,' said Ruby quickly.

'I should hope not,' said her father.

'I'll finish this another evening,' she said, putting her needle and cotton away. How dare that man suggest that sort of thing. 'Dad, give me a hand to drag it back into the bedroom.'

★　★　★

As the week went on Tom kept adding to his money in the lav, although the mattress was still in its original place in the bedroom. Every evening when Ruby got home from work, it was dark and she was too tired to sew.

Although deep down Tom knew it was wrong, he became more and more excited as his money grew. The boys stole handbags from women at the market or as they waited for a tram. Anywhere where a crowd gathered they'd push and shove people and at the right time one of them would run off with the goods. Sometimes they would peer into a pram when the woman went into a shop and see a bag just sitting there, waiting to be taken. Those were the ones Tom liked grabbing the most, as it didn't cause so much fuss. They didn't always strike lucky, as some of the bags were empty, but the excitement for Tom was exhilarating. At the end of every day he would spend a long while in the lav counting his money. He now had fifteen shillings. He was terrified when one afternoon Mr Cox knocked on the lav door and told him to hurry up. How could he get the wooden box out without him seeing it? Tears filled his eyes. He had to think quick. He was so frightened. 'Mr Cox,' he called through the door. 'I ain't got no newspaper. Could you ask Dad for some?'

'I ain't your bloody servant, you should have seen that before you started.'

Tom listened to Mr Cox coughing and spitting as he went back to the house. He quickly opened the door and threw the box out. He sat back down and took all the paper off the string and shoved it up his jumper. He heard Mr Cox coming back. A newspaper was pushed under the door. Tom tore off a piece, then pulled the chain.

'I hope you ain't made it stink in there?' said Mr Cox.

'It's not too bad,' said Tom, pulling his holey jumper down. He put his hand in his trouser pocket and let his fingers wrap round the coins that were nestling there. He gave a little smile as he walked back into the kitchen.

On Saturday Ruby was thrilled to see Elsie waiting for her outside the laundry.

'I've got a frock for you to wear at my wedding.' Elsie held out a paper bag. 'Go on, have a look. You're a bit thinner than our Jenny, but you're clever with a needle and you can make it fit.'

'Would she mind me altering it?'

'No. She can't get into it now anyway.'

Ruby took the frock out of the bag and held it up. She gasped. 'It's lovely.' The green silk slipped through her fingers. 'Are you sure she won't mind me altering it?'

'I told you, she said go ahead.'

Just then Florrie walked past.

'What's that you got there then?' she asked, coming up to them.

'Nothing,' said Ruby, quickly putting it back in the bag. She was taken by surprise when Florrie suddenly snatched the bag from her. 'Give that back to me,' she shouted.

Florrie laughed. 'Here Molly, take a look at this old tat.' She held the frock up. 'Where d'yer get this from?'

Elsie went to grab it back. 'Give it to me.'

Florrie put it high above her head out of Elsie's reach. 'Is this yours?' she asked.

'What business is it of yours?'

'Just want ter find out what dustbin yer raided ter get it.'

Ruby wanted to cry for Elsie and herself.

'Why are you doing this?' asked Ruby.

'Just nosy, that's all.'

'Everything all right, Ruby?'

She turned to see Ernie standing behind her. 'Yes thanks.'

' "Yes thanks," ' mimicked Florrie. 'Here y'are, yer can have this back. I've got enough rags fer dusters anyway.'

'What's she on about?' asked Ernie.

'She's just trying to be clever,' said Elsie. 'How are you, Ernie, ain't seen you for a while.'

'No, you upped and went out of me life before I had time to whisk you away. I hear you're gonner get married as well. Me poor heart's broken.' He put his hand on his heart and grinned, making his blue eyes crinkle.

Elsie giggled. 'Go on with you. You'll be having Ruby think there was something going on between us.'

He put his arm round Ruby's waist. Ruby thought she would die. This was the first time he had ever done anything so romantic in front of someone.

'She knows me better than that.'

'I'll tell you what,' said Elsie. 'Why don't you come to me wedding? We're gonner have a bit of a do after the church at my house. You'll be more than welcome, and I'm sure Ruby will be pleased to see you. What do you say?'

'I'd really like that. When is it?'

'New Year's Eve. Ruby knows where it is.'

'That'll be really nice. Thanks, Elsie. Ruby, I'll come to your house and pick you up, if that's all right with you?'

'No. I'll meet you at the church.'

'It's St Mary's, and it's at two o'clock,' said Elsie. 'I'll be looking out for you both. I must go, got lots to do.' She kissed Ruby's cheek. 'Don't take any notice of that silly cow Florrie. She's only jealous. Bye.' She hurried away leaving Ruby and Ernie alone.

'Can we walk along together?' asked Ernie.

'Course.'

'That was real nice of Elsie inviting me to her wedding. She's a bit of all right.'

'Yes, she is.'

'What was all that about with Florrie?'

'She was trying to take this frock away from me.' Ruby showed him the paper bag.

'Is it nice?'

'I think so. It's one of Elsie's sister's, she's letting me wear it for the wedding.'

'I bet you'll look a little smasher.'

In many ways Ruby was pleased it was getting dark so that he couldn't see her blushing.

'D'you know, I reckon 1922 could see a new beginning for all of us.'

'Why? What makes you say that?'

'Dunno. I just feel it. Me mum had a letter from me dad's brother, he's coming down to see her. Dad's family lived up north somewhere, in Scotland. They didn't approve of me mum and when Dad got killed they didn't have any more to do with her.' He laughed. 'I dunno whether to be angry or pleased about it, but Mum thinks it'll be all right.'

'Have you ever seen him?'

'No, but me mum has. He came to her and dad's wedding, be all accounts.'

'Did he say why he was coming to see your mum?'

'No.'

'When does your Daisy start work?'

'She's going after Christmas. Mum's a bit upset about it, but Daisy reckons it'll be all right. It's a big house over the back of the park and they've got other servants; she'll start in the kitchen. I shall go sometimes and keep me eye on her. If any of the blokes try anything, I'll kill 'em.'

'It must be lovely to have a big brother to look after you.'

Ernie stopped. 'Ruby, has anyone ever tried to hurt you?'

'No, course not.'

'You would tell me if they did?'

'Would you be my knight in shining armour?'

'Dunno about that, but I wouldn't want anything to happen to you.'

Ruby felt her inside do somersaults. He must love her to say that. 'Thanks,' she said weakly.

They reached the point where they parted company.

'If I don't see you before I'll see you at the church. Bye – and Happy Christmas!'

'Bye.' Ruby stood and watched him walk away. They were going to meet at the church. She gave a sigh. Wouldn't it be wonderful if it could have been their wedding. Perhaps one day it might happen.

Ernie was whistling when he left Ruby. They were going out on a proper date. Everybody would see them together. He wasn't so sure about going to a church but if it meant seeing Ruby and being with her, then he would do anything. If only he could get a decent job. He would love it if one day he could ask her to be his wife. He stopped whistling and took a deep breath. That sort of thing didn't happen to the likes of them; it only happened in books.

It was almost eight o'clock when Ruby got home on Friday as she'd been wandering through the market. Tomorrow would be Christmas Eve. Everybody was hoping Mrs Watson would let them finish a bit earlier than their usual time. Some of the women had a great deal to do, but Ruby didn't have a lot of money for shopping or presents. She had managed to get Tom a book and her father a packet of cigarettes. She desperately wanted to buy Danny something.

She remembered the Christmas when Beth was living with them, how thrilled she'd been with the teething ring Ruby had bought him. He was still the loveliest, happiest little chap. Now he was running about, Beth told her how worried she was every time she went behind the bar and had to strap him in his pram, he certainly wasn't happy about that. Ruby picked up a fluffy teddy bear. It was old and almost bald. 'How much?' she asked the stallholder.

'Tanner.'

'Sixpence!' Ruby put it back. Everything was well out of her price range. To Ruby the most important thing they had to spend their money on was the rent. The idea of them being homeless wasn't even to be contemplated. She would be glad when Christmas was all over; at least she had the wedding to look forward to.

She began to walk home, and then suddenly on a mad impulse she rushed back and picked up the teddy bear. 'I'll give you thrupence.'

'Make it fourpence and it's yours.'

As Ruby walked home with the teddy in her bag, her step was light.

'I didn't think you'd still be home,' Ruby said to her father as she took off her hat and coat.

'I'm just off and I'll be late. Don't worry about getting me anything to eat, George said I can have a sandwich with him and his missus.'

Ruby had never seen George's wife; she always stayed upstairs with her mother. 'Is his wife nice?'

'Yes, and she's a handsome woman. I can see why he don't like letting her loose with the rough toerags we get in at the weekends.'

'Where's Tom?'

'Dunno. He went out after bringing in that load of veg. It

242

looks real good. He musta been lucky.'

Ruby sat at the table. 'I'm worried about him. Since Mum died and he only has a few errands to do for Milly, I wonder what he gets up to all day. I thought he should go to school but he absolutely refused. I was hoping he would go next year. He should have some schooling and discipline.'

'You mustn't worry about him. He seems to be doing very well with this wood lark.'

'He does seem to have a few bob to put in the kitty.'

'So what you worried about then? What with the extra hours I'm putting in, it'll all help.'

'I know it will, but yours is only till after Christmas.'

'There's the New Year.'

'I know. But after that, what?'

'We'll worry about that when it comes, but I'll still have me two nights a week. By the way, I met the bloke who got me the job today, he comes in lunchtime.'

'What, Elsie's father?'

'He's a nice bloke. He was telling me all about this wedding next week. I think it's gonner be a right old do, so you should enjoy yourself.'

'I know I am.' She would have liked to add: More so now that Ernie will be there. 'And I've got Elsie's sister's frock to wear as well. Look, I've nearly finished altering it.' She held up the dress.

'It will look lovely. You'll look like a princess.'

'I hope so.'

'I wish your mother was here to see it.'

'So do I.' Ruby put the frock on the back of the chair, running her hand over the material. 'It was so good of Elsie's sister.'

'Now I really must go.' He put on his trilby at a jaunty

angle. He smiled and, kissing Ruby's cheek, said, 'Mustn't be late for work.'

'Bye, Dad.' She watched him leave the room, walking upright like he used to years ago. Ruby closed her eyes. 'Mum,' she whispered, 'I wish you could see the difference in Dad. But why wasn't he like this when you were here?'

Chapter 22

Ruby must have dozed off as she woke with a start when the kitchen door was pushed back with a bang. She looked at the clock; it was nine o'clock. 'What time do you call this?' she asked Tom.

'Sorry, but everything at the market is so exciting! I didn't know how late it was. Where's Dad?'

'Gone to work. What you been up to?'

'Nothing. Why?'

'You look very flushed.'

'Been running.'

'Who from?'

'Nobody.' Tom wasn't going to tell her it was from a couple of men from the market. Ginger had nearly got caught and they had had to leg it quick. 'What's for tea?'

'It's too late for that.'

'What? I'm starving.'

'Then you should have come home earlier. I can do you a bit of toast.'

'That all?'

'It's that or nothing.'

'We always have toast.'

'That's cos it's easy and cheap, and uses up the stale bread. When I feel a bit rich you can have jam on it, if not, it's dripping.'

'All right.' Tom looked at his sister; she looked sad and tired. He wanted to tell her about the lovely cream bun he'd had this afternoon. He would love to give her a big box of chocolates for Christmas, but he'd settled on a very small box that held just five chocolates: that way he wouldn't arouse too much suspicion. He felt very guilty that he couldn't share his wealth with her. He had been busy trying to work out how he could tell her where this chicken, which Freddie reckoned they would all get tomorrow, came from.

'You finished sewing this?' he asked, picking up the frock that was hanging over the back of the chair.

Ruby smiled. 'Yes. I hope it'll look all right.' She stood up and held it against her. 'What d'you think? It's very pretty, ain't it?'

'Yes. Yes it is,' said Tom.

'I love these pretty bows and flouncy bottom.' Ruby twirled round. 'I hope it ain't too short. Don't want to show off.'

Tom looked at his sister. He had enough money to buy her a new frock. All her life, like him, she had had to wear second-hand clothes and cut-downs. Should he go and buy a nice frock for her? She was so excited about this wedding; he wanted her to look like a queen. Who could he ask to help him? Beth came to mind, but he knew she wouldn't approve, since she was bound to guess where the money had come from. Although he felt guilty he couldn't help but feel good when he had money to spend.

'It's Christmas Eve tomorrow. Are we gonner put the decorations up?' asked Tom.

'I don't know. They're a bit squashed. And it don't seem right somehow.'

'Mum would have wanted us to.'

'I'll wait and ask Dad when he gets home.'

'I think I might be able to get us a chicken for dinner.'

Ruby laughed. 'And where d'you reckon you'll get one of those from?'

'The market.'

'The market? In case you didn't know, young man, they cost money.'

'I know that. I ain't daft. But my mate reckons they almost give 'em away at the end. Especially those that have got a leg missing, or look a bit battered.'

Ruby laughed. 'So who's this clever mate of yours then?'

'Just a mate.'

'I hope he ain't leading you into any trouble?'

'No.'

'You wouldn't do anything wrong . . . would you?'

Tom looked away. 'Course not.'

'You know what happened with the coal?'

Tom couldn't look at his sister. 'I'm just going out to the lav.'

'Tom. You all right?'

'Yes, why?'

'Nothing. I'll try and make it a nice Christmas for you.'

He smiled and left the room.

Outside he kicked the wall. 'If only I could tell her I could give her the best Christmas she'd ever had. She could have anything she wanted,' he mumbled as he dragged a box into the lav. In the dark he stood on it and felt for the blue sugar bag that held his money. He had another five shillings to add to it. He ran his fingers along the ledge. Panic overtook him. Where was it? Desperately he moved the box further along. It was there yesterday. Had it moved? Ruby never cleaned up there. Who could have taken it? Tears filled his eyes. He climbed down and sat on the box. What could he do? He climbed up again. Perhaps he'd missed it. 'I must do it very slowly,' he said to himself as carefully he felt every inch of the ledge.

★ ★ ★

Thomas Jenkins was finding the build-up to Christmas very busy. The pub was full and people were shouting their orders. At times he worried that all of his demons might return and he wouldn't be able to cope, but he knew he had to for his children's sake. Since working he had managed to keep them at bay, but he knew they were never far away.

George was up one end of the bar serving drinks as fast as he could. This pub didn't have a snug where old ladies could sit on their own; if any came in they had to share the bar with all the others. The thought of trouble like the first night he'd started work was never far from Thomas's mind, but fortunately only a few times since then had they had any bother. Usually it was all over by the time he was ready to go home. He was pleased with himself at being able to hold down this job. At first he had felt so insecure, but he had Beth to thank for getting him started. Working at the Royal Albert had been a big step for him.

Thomas's face lit up when he caught sight of Mrs Bell and her lady friend walking in. Mrs Bell certainly was a handsome woman.

He smiled at her and the woman she was with; he hoped she hadn't told her friend what had happened on last Saturday afternoon. George had asked him to work the lunchtime shift and Thomas'd been pleased to see Mrs Bell walk in. After he'd finished work he'd offered to walk her home. He remembered what Ruby had told them about her lovely flat but was still taken aback by the beautiful things she had.

'Sit down, Thomas,' she said, smiling.

He sat on the velvet-covered sofa.

'There's an ashtray there if you fancy a smoke. I'll just get us a drink.'

He had watched the way she moved when she left the room. He knew she would have long slim legs under that hobble skirt. He did wonder why she lived in these terrible buildings, but she must have a reason.

She came back and sat next to him. 'Here's your drink. You're a very handsome man, Thomas Jenkins.'

'You have a lovely place here,' he said, sheepishly looking around. 'I can remember our Ruby telling us about it. She said it was like a palace, and she's right.'

'Why thank you. I do rather a lot of entertaining.'

'Thomas! For Christ's sake, wake up.' One of the customers was waving a glass under his nose. 'Twice I've asked you for a pint.'

'Sorry, Bill. I was carried away.'

'You will be if I don't get me beer.'

Tom was trembling. Tears were stinging his eyes. He had run his fingers along the rough concrete ledge a dozen times till they were sore, but his money had gone. Who could have taken it? Mr Cox was the only name that came into his head. 'I'll kill him. I will.' But how could he accuse him of pinching his money when it wasn't really his? 'But I need it more than him,' said Tom to himself. He suddenly felt sick as he began to realise how those poor women must have felt when they found their purses missing. Did any of 'em get a beating from their old men? But the moment of insight didn't last long. Tom was soon thinking about the money, again. He couldn't give it back. He had to get it off Cox. Tom knew he was up the pub as he had seen him go out earlier. He would have to wait till tomorrow to ask him. But what if he wouldn't give it back? And what if it wasn't him? If it had been his dad or Ruby, they would have been full of it; no, it had to be old man Cox. Anger filled him. He must have seen me bring the box in here, he thought.

The banging on the door frightened him. 'Tom? Tom, are you all right?' Ruby was outside the door.

'Yes. I'll be out in a minute.'

'You'll freeze to death out here. So hurry up.'

'All right.' He heard Ruby running back indoors and shutting the washhouse door. He took his box outside and threw it in the corner of the yard.

Towards the end of the evening Thomas's heart sank when he saw Mrs Bell and her friend walk out with two strapping blokes, who, with their docker's hooks in their wide belts, looked very frightening. The women were laughing and giggling like a couple of schoolgirls.

She hadn't even bothered to say goodnight.

He began collecting the glasses.

'Cheer up, Thomas,' said George.

'I'm a bit tired, that's all.'

'It has been a bit of a night. Still, next week you'll be with your family round a cosy fire.' George began wiping down the tables.

'Won't be much of a Christmas this year, not without Mary.'

'Yer, it'll be hard for you. Chuck me another cloth, this one's soaked.'

As he washed the glasses, Thomas's thoughts drifted back once more to that Saturday afternoon. After Mrs Bell had given him his drink she had asked him if he was comfortable. He had just nodded.

'Thomas. If you feel the need for a woman, I will always be of service, that's my job.'

He laughed. 'I couldn't afford you.'

'No, I don't suppose you could, but sometimes I can be,

shall we say, very accommodating.'

It was then he suddenly realised he didn't want to rush things. He stood up. 'I think you are a very handsome woman, and I could get very fond of you.'

That was when she had laughed at him and made him feel a fool. 'Oh, come off it. I ain't the type you take home to your family, now am I?'

He picked up his hat. 'I'm sorry. I only wanted to see you home, just to make sure you got here safe.'

She lit a cigarette and blew the smoke high in the air. 'Thomas, I've been looking after meself since I was nine years old. I know all the wrinkles and how to get what you want out of life. The reason that I live in this block, this glory hole' – she pointed to the front door – 'is because I get it free from a punter. That way all the money I earn goes on the things I want and not on rent.'

'I'm sorry,' said Thomas.

'No, it's me that should be sorry. I should have guessed that you would still be in mourning. But you see, I like you, and I thought I could help cheer you up.'

He smiled. 'Perhaps some other time.'

'Yes,' she said, opening the door.

As he walked home he thought of Ruby. What would she say if she knew her father had been to Mrs Bell's place? This was something he would have to keep to himself.

Tom tossed and turned all night.

'I shan't be sorry when you're in Dad's room,' said Ruby the following morning. 'You've been a right fidget all night. What's the matter with you?'

'Nothing. A bit excited, I suppose. It's Christmas Eve!'

Ruby felt her heart sink. 'Tom, I'm so sorry. I don't think there's anything to get excited about. We've only got the pork chops Mr Cox gave us for Christmas. We ain't got a pudding or anything fancy.'

'It's all right. I've got you a little present.'

She couldn't bear to puncture his enthusiasm. 'Look, I've got to get ready for work. Make Dad a cuppa, will you?'

As soon as he'd finished chopping the wood and doing the errands for Milly, Tom raced to the coal yard. The thought of bringing home a chicken was uppermost in his mind and he didn't want to miss the gang. He was relieved to see they were still sitting talking.

'Yer late,' said Freddie.

'I had some other things to do.'

'Are they more important than the gang?'

Tom looked at his boots and shook his head.

'Right,' said Freddie. 'After last night I think we'd better move on ter new territory. I thought we might give the market round by the Blue Anchor a go.'

Ginger took a quick intake of breath. 'That's Alfie Anderson's patch.'

'So what?' said Freddie.

'He can be very nasty,' said Ginger.

'I know. So can I when I need to.'

Tom knew he must be visibly shaking. He couldn't tell them that he didn't want to go. He was terrified of Alfie Anderson.

Freddie stood up. 'OK. It'll be the same as we always work.'

'When we gonner get these chickens?' asked Tom.

'Not till ternight. We've got ter wait till the blokes come out the pub stoned out their minds and all the old dears are hanging about waiting fer their old men and somefink cheap. That way the butcher and his boy will be so busy pulling the birds down 'e won't notice when a few of 'em go missing.'

'Is it safe?' asked Harry.

Freddie grinned. ''As been all the years me and me dad's been doing it. Now 'e's inside I told me mum I'd take over.'

Tom felt sick. He didn't want to be here. All the money he'd had had gone. He knew now that it wasn't worth it. He felt guilty. He had let Ruby and his dad down. He had to get away from Freddie Porter and his gang, but how? Would they beat him up now he knew about their gang? How could he get away?

As they were marching out of the coal yard somebody called to them, 'Oi, you lot. What you up to?'

Tom looked round and then realised the others were running away.

'Come back 'ere, yer little buggers.'

Tom took this opportunity to run in the opposite direction to the gang.

'Look where you're going, Tom!' said Beth as he rounded the corner and almost fell over the pram. 'What's wrong, you're as white as a ghost.'

He burst into tears.

Beth quickly put her arm round his shoulders and pulled him close to her. 'What is it?'

He couldn't speak. All the exhilaration at his exploits over the last weeks left him. He was angry, upset and full of guilt.

'I'd better walk home with you. Is your dad home?'

Tom shook his head.

'In that case you'd better come back to the pub with me. It'll be opening time soon.'

Slowly they walked along. Beth was wondering what had happened to upset him like this. She wouldn't question him in the street, but his sobs were pitiful to hear.

When they reached the pub she went from the back out to

the bar. 'Can you manage for a while without me?' she asked Mr Thompson.

'What's up?'

'I'll tell you later.'

'Don't be too long.'

'No, I won't.'

Beth hurried back to Tom who was sitting playing with Danny.

'Now, young man. I want you to tell me what's the matter. I haven't got a lot of time as I've got to go into the bar.'

'I'm sorry.' Tom stood up.

'Sit down.' Beth's voice was forceful.

Tom did as he was told.

'Well?'

Tears sprang to his eyes as he told her everything that had happened. Beth didn't interrupt till he had finished. Tom blew his nose. 'I wanted to give the money to Ruby. I wanted her to have nice things. I wanted to buy her a frock so she can go to her mate's wedding in something nice, not always wearing other people's left-offs. And I wanted us to have a nice Christmas even though we ain't got Mum.'

Beth thought her heart would break. She went to him and held him close against her.

'Beth. Beth! Hurry up!' Mr Thompson was shouting from the bar.

'Look, I've got to go. Stay here and look after Danny for me. We'll try and sort this out, don't worry. We'll find out who took your money, but remember, you stole it in the first place, so . . .' Beth shrugged. 'Don't worry,' she repeated. She kissed the top of his head and left the room.

Tom sat on the floor and looked round the room. They had decorations, plenty of them. He looked at Danny's toys. 'You're a lucky little boy, you've got lots of nice things. I was gonner buy you a bar of chocolate for Christmas.'

Danny toddled over to Tom and gave him a small horse. 'Horse. Horse,' he said, and fell on his bottom.

'Have you got a cart we can fill up?'

He gave Tom a cart but said, 'Horse. Horse.'

'This is a cart. Say "cart".'

'Horse. Horse.'

Tom laughed, then stopped. He hadn't laughed in a long, long while.

Chapter 23

Beth had told Mr Thompson that Tom was looking after Danny, as she knew he worried about him when she was behind the bar. The thing that had been uppermost in her mind lately was that soon she wouldn't be able to leave her son in his pram, he was getting too big. Although he was just in the passage, she spent a lot of time looking out of the door to make sure he was all right. He was usually very noisy and restless, and although he was strapped in he could tip the pram over. She needed someone to keep an eye on him; she didn't know what she'd do if anything happened to him. He was more than the apple of her eye, he was her life. She had nobody but him. Her family was something she would rather forget. When she and Len sat quietly together in the afternoons she had gradually told him the truth about her past and her fears. She'd admitted that she'd run away from home when she was very young, and that she hadn't been married to Danny's father.

'So you're not a widow,' Len had said.

'No,' she'd whispered. She'd been worried he would hold it against her, but he'd told her he wasn't interested in her past. Perhaps on New Year's Eve she could get Tom to come and look after him during the lunchtime shift. Evenings weren't a problem as Danny was in bed and fast asleep before she went down. In fact she could do with Tom every Saturday and Sundays: they were the only lunchtimes she was in the bar. She would ask Tom. She knew he could do with the money.

Beth's thoughts went back to Tom and why he was here. She was confident he had told her everything and suspected he was right that Mr Cox had taken his money. It was going to be difficult to accuse him though, with the money being stolen in the first place; Mr Cox was no fool and was probably aware of that. Tom must have been desperate to do a thing like that. She knew how easy it was to get in with the wrong crowd; she had been born into it, and she didn't want her son to finish up the same way. Would Mr Cox go to the police? When he walked into the bar, it took Beth all her energy to be polite to him. Her smile was fixed on her face like a mask.

'Looking forward to Christmas?' she asked him.

'Not really,' he said, taking the froth off the top of his glass and wiping his mouth with the back of his hand. 'Young Ruby does her best but it ain't the same since her mother went. I told her she should find herself a rich bloke, then we would all have decent meals.'

'If she found herself a rich bloke she wouldn't stay in that house looking after you.'

He gave her a smarmy grin and walked away to the seat next to the fire; it was the one he always sat in.

Beth was pleased when Mr Thompson called time and, as he ushered the last customer out, she said, 'I'll just pop out back and put the kettle on, then I'll come and give you a hand with the glasses.'

'You're a good 'en, Beth, and no mistake.'

She smiled at him. She was so happy here. She knew that if he ever asked her to marry him, she would. It might come as a shock to those who thought she was already married, but she could live with that. He was good to her and he loved Danny and she knew he would look after her and her son.

'Is your dad at home, Tom?' she asked when she walked into the back room.

'No, he's working.'

'Well, it is Christmas Eve and one of the busiest times. Tonight we'll be rushed off our feet. Would you like me to come home with you and try to find out if Mr Cox has taken that money?'

'It's got to be him. Ruby and Dad would think they'd found a gold mine and they'd be full of it.'

'Yes, you're right. When I've made this tea I've got to help with the glasses so that Mr Thompson can bottle up for tonight. You keep your eye on Danny, then when I've finished we'll go and see him.'

'Thanks, Beth.'

'Would you like to look after my son next Saturday when I have to go behind the bar at lunchtime?'

'I don't know. What if he cries?'

'I'll only be in the bar. I'll pay you.'

Tom smiled. 'All right.'

'How's the little lad?' asked Mr Thompson when Beth returned to the bar.

'He's all right.'

'Now, you've made sure that guard is firm in front of the fire?'

'Course.'

'Would never forgive meself if anything happened to him.'

Beth kissed his cheek. 'I know. When I've finished here I've got to pop along with Tom. He's had a bit of trouble.'

'Nothing serious, I hope?'

'No. I can handle it. But can I leave Danny here with you?'

'Course.'

'I'll put him down for his afternoon nap. You can have a little rest when I get back.'

'As I said, Beth, you're a good 'en, and the best thing that ever happened to me.'

Tom was shaking when they went into the house. It was with fear and anger. Beth had warned him that Mr Cox might deny it, and he might even threaten Tom with the police. 'After all, it wasn't really your money, was it?'

Tom shook his head. 'Shall I come up with you?' he asked as he stood at the bottom of the stairs watching Beth go up.

'Perhaps you'd better. Just in case he thinks I'm making it up.'

Beth knocked on his kitchen door. 'Mr Cox,' she called softly. 'It's me, Beth.'

There was no answer.

'I don't want to knock too loud in case he's asleep,' she said over her shoulder. 'I don't want him to have a heart attack. Mr Cox,' she called again.

'He must be out,' said Tom, almost relieved. 'Let's leave it, shall we?'

'No. I think he should know how you feel.'

'But what if he's gone to the police? He could be there now.' Tom was full of dread. He ran down the stairs.

'Tom. Tom. Come back.'

'I don't want to go to prison. Freddie's dad and brothers are in prison,' he shouted from the bottom of the stairs.

'You won't go to prison,' said Beth, hurrying down to join him.

'How do you know?'

'I'm sure it won't come to that. We can talk to Mr Cox.'

'We might be too late.' Tom's voice was high and emotional. 'He can keep the money.'

'Make a pot of tea. Your dad should be home soon. Is Ruby finishing early today?'

'I don't know.'

'You'd better put a bit of coal on that fire, they'll be frozen when they get home. I'm just going out to the lav.'

Tom took the big black kettle that sat on the range and poured some water into the teapot. He took the pot into the washhouse to empty. He looked through the washhouse window and through the late afternoon gloom he saw Beth – she was arguing with Mr Cox. He must have been in the lav.

'Thomas, I'm very sorry about last Saturday,' said Mrs Bell as they walked along.

Thomas had been very surprised to see her waiting for him outside the pub. 'What are you doing here? And why are you waiting for me?'

'I want to apologise.'

'Apologise! What for?'

'Last Saturday. I didn't mean to hurt you. You are a very warm and sensitive man.' She touched his arm. 'I didn't like to say anything in there.' She looked behind her towards the pub. 'I've brought you a Christmas present.'

'What?'

She delved into her handbag.

'Mrs Bell—'

'Please, call me Rita.'

'Rita. I can't . . .'

'Merry Christmas,' she said, handing him a small package. 'I won't be in tomorrow lunchtime as I'm going away with a gentleman friend. I hope you have a nice Christmas.' She pulled the luxurious black fur collar of her coat closer to her face, leaned forward and kissed his cheek.

She turned and hurried away, leaving Thomas Jenkins

bewildered. At the corner of the street she turned and waved. He smiled, waved back and touched his cheek. He really didn't know what to make of that woman.

Tom rushed out into the yard.

'Ah, here's our little thief. You thought you was being clever, hiding your ill-gotten gains on the ledge in there, didn't you?'

'How d'you know it was stolen?'

'Come off it. I wasn't born yesterday. When I saw you drag that box in the lav I wondered what you was up to.'

'But . . . How . . .?'

Mr Cox pointed up to his kitchen window. 'Saw you from up there. Thought it was a bit odd, so I decided to come down and see what it was all about.'

Tom felt deflated. He had never thought to check up there. Mr Cox's kitchen window overlooked the yard. He often looked down on what they did. Tom had to think quickly. 'How d'you know I wasn't saving it for Christmas?'

'What? Where would you get twenty-five bob from?'

Tom heard Beth take a quick breath. He hadn't told her how much there had been.

'It ain't from chopping up wood,' continued Mr Cox.

'I think you should give it back to Tom,' said Beth. 'After all, his needs are greater than yours.'

Mr Cox laughed in her face. 'So you're encouraging this little sod to steal?'

'Course I'm not.' Beth's voice was full of anger.

'You lot are all tarred with the same brush.' He poked her shoulder with his finger. 'You ain't a relation, you're just a trollop, you ain't married neither. I've made it me business to find out all about you. I know where you've come from. Right old lot they are an' all.'

Tom looked from one to the other.

Beth was seething. 'Don't you poke me. How dare you talk to me like this? You're barred from the pub.'

'You can't do that, it ain't yours. I know what your little game is – you've set your sights on poor old Thompson. Wait till he knows all about you.' He went to walk away. 'And you wait till I tell his father and that stuck-up sister of his about this. Then, when I've spent half of it, I'll go to the police.' He laughed. 'I'm really going to enjoy this.'

'You can't, you can't,' yelled Tom.

'And who's gonner stop me?'

'Me.' Tom lunged at Mr Cox and knocked him against the wall.

He quickly regained his breath and balance. 'You little sod, come here. I'll kill you.'

'No you won't!' said Beth, hitting him with her clenched fists.

'You cow.' He threw his hands across Beth's face and she fell heavily to the ground.

Tom and Mr Cox stood and looked at her lying still on the damp concrete.

'You've killed her,' said Tom softly.

'Course I ain't. Get up, you silly cow.' He touched her with the toe of his boot.

Beth didn't move.

'You've killed her!' repeated Tom, his voice rising.

'Shut up.'

'You've killed her!' shouted Tom, falling to the ground beside Beth. He put his hand under her head. He slowly brought it out and looked at it. It was covered with blood. He sat on his haunches for a moment or two then leapt to his feet. 'You've killed her. You've killed her,' he yelled, pummelling Mr Cox's chest with his fists.

'I said shut up!' Mr Cox was trying to get hold of Tom's hands.

The last thing Tom felt was a blow to the side of his head.

Ruby looked across at Florrie and Molly. They had been laughing and singing all morning. They were full of what they were going to do tonight and over Christmas.

'Why don't yer come ter the pub with us?' shouted Florrie. 'It might help ter put a smile on that miserable face of yours.'

'I can't. I've got to get home,' said Ruby.

'Why's that, yer gonner see yer lover boy? I've heard he only likes older women. I bet he's giving Mrs W. a present.'

'I wonder what it'll be, Florrie,' shouted her friend.

'I've gotter good idea,' she said, laughing. 'She must like 'em young and with a bit of go in 'em. She'll certainly get that with that Ernie Wallis, won't she, Rube?'

Ruby ignored her.

'Thought the miserable cow would have let us go a bit early today seeing as how it's Christmas Eve,' said Molly, standing up and moving towards Ruby.

The door opened and Mrs Watson walked in. Molly quickly pretended to straighten her frock and sat down again.

'You'll be pleased to know that the management is going to let you go at two today, instead of making you work till four. I think that's very generous of them, don't you?'

Ruby heard Florrie comment very low that she thought a Christmas box wouldn't come amiss; fortunately Mrs Watson didn't hear that.

Soon after Mrs Watson had left the room the hooter went for them to leave.

'Right, I'm off,' said Florrie, gathering up her belongings. 'See yer ternight in the Beak,' she yelled to Molly.

Ruby let them rush out. As she left she decided to go to the market. She gave a little smile. She had to admit that the thought of Tom getting a legless chicken had worried her a bit. He had been acting very secretively lately and she couldn't be sure that he hadn't got himself in with a wrong lot. There were plenty of kids running about who didn't go to school or work, and they could be a problem; she hoped Tom wasn't mixed up with any like that. He was definitely going to school after Christmas; they would find the penny a week from somewhere.

She loved the market at Christmas. There was always an air of excitement and lots of colour and decorations. The stall-holders always seemed cheerful despite the cold wind that had come up. She hoped it didn't rain, or it could turn to snow it was so cold. Her boots always wore out quicker in the wet, and her chilblains would come back again. Since she'd been in the ironing room she hadn't had them nearly so badly.

She had a few pence to spend and wandered from stall to stall gazing at all the many delights that were on display. She stopped at the fruit and veg stall. I hope Tom managed to get some decent veg, she said to herself. On impulse she bought two oranges that were wrapped in silver paper. They looked so very pretty. One could go inside Tom's Christmas stocking. The other one she would give to her father. What wouldn't she give to be able to buy things she wanted? Even though her father was bringing in a few extra shillings at the moment, the rent was the most important thing, and she always had to make sure it was put to one side. It was a dark cloudy day and with the fog that was always hanging in the air, it never really seemed to get light. After an hour or two she decided it was time to go home. I hope Tom's kept that fire in, I'm frozen, she thought.

Thomas Jenkins hurried home. He had to be back at the pub

later on, but George had told him not to come in till just after seven, which gave him just a short while to get Ruby and Tom a present. George had been very good; he had given him two shillings extra. What could he get them? He felt like a kid again, it was years since he'd been able to buy something. It was before the war; he and Mary would go out on Christmas Eve to buy the children's presents. That was a lifetime ago. He missed Mary so much. With his hands thrust into his pockets, he could feel the small packet Mrs Bell had given him. He hadn't opened it. Should he? Did he want Ruby to see it? He could tell her a customer had given it to him, which was the truth, but what if it were something very personal? He stood on the street corner and tore away the paper. He opened the small box and was taken aback. It was a pair of mother-of-pearl cufflinks. He stood looking at them. Why should that woman give him something as expensive looking as this? What were they worth? He looked up the road. He could see the three brass balls of the pawnshop. He grinned. This could be the best Christmas present she could have given him. He put them into his pocket and went along to the shop.

'Tom, Tom,' shouted Ruby, lighting the mantle in the passage. 'I hope you've kept that fire in, I'm frozen.'

She walked into the dark kitchen. 'Where the hell have you got to?' She threw her handbag and the oranges on the table and lit the gaslight. 'Oh no, the fire's nearly out.' Without taking off her hat and coat she fell to her knees and, holding up a sheet of paper in front of the fire, gently blew on the dying embers trying to bring a bit of life back into them.

The kitchen door opened.

'Hello, Dad.'

'What you doing, love?'

'Trying to get a bit of life into this. You wait till I see Tom. I told him to keep an eye on the fire.'

'Where is he?'

'I don't know. I've just got in meself.'

'I've had a good day.'

Ruby smiled up at her father. 'That's good.'

'Is that kettle hot?'

'No, we'll have to wait a bit. What time have you got to go back to work?'

'Just after seven.'

Ruby looked up at the clock. 'You'll just about have time for a cuppa and a sandwich.'

'That's all right. It'll suit me fine. I wonder where Tom is?'

'I don't know, but I'll give him a piece of me mind when he does walk himself in here.'

'What's this?' Thomas picked up the paper bag.

'Leave that. Don't touch that.'

He laughed.

'I'll take 'em in the bedroom,' said Ruby, jumping up and scooping the oranges off the table.

'I've got a surprise as well.'

'You have?'

'Yes. But you ain't seeing it till the morning. So no peeping tonight when I'm at work.'

'I wouldn't do that. It'll spoil the fun.'

The loud knocking on the door startled them.

'Who can that be?' asked her father.

'Don't know.' Ruby knew that Tom would use the key on the ledge at the side of the door.

'I'll go,' said Thomas.

As her father left the kitchen Ruby found herself feeling happier than she had done for a very long while. She was pleased he'd made an effort to get them something for

266

Christmas. Perhaps now was the moment things were going to get better for them.

The kitchen door opened and Ruby was taken aback to see Mr Thompson standing behind her father. He was holding Danny.

'What is it? What's wrong with Beth?' asked Ruby.

'I don't know. She came down here with Tom to sort out something, and she didn't come back.'

'What time was that?' asked Thomas.

'I dunno, after closing time. Must have been about half two – three.'

'It's nearly five now. Where could she be?' asked Ruby.

'Don't know. Look, is it all right if I leave the boy here? I've got to open up.'

'Course,' said Ruby, taking Danny from him.

'You don't think anything's happened, do you?'

'Course not.'

'Would young Tom know where she could be?'

'Tom ain't in yet. I think he's hanging round the market trying to get a cheap chicken,' said Ruby. She laughed. 'He's hoping to get one without legs.'

'D'you think she might be with him?' asked Mr Thompson. He was clearly concerned.

'Could be. Don't worry, as soon as they come back I'll send her home.'

'Thanks.'

'I'll see you out,' said Thomas.

'I bet you want your tea, young man,' said Ruby to Danny. 'Now, I wonder where that naughty mummy of yours has got to?'

'He's a nice bloke, that Mr Thompson,' said Thomas, coming back into the kitchen. 'I'll always be grateful to him for getting me back to work.'

'Beth thinks the world of him.'

'I know.'

'Dad, keep your eye on Danny while I pop out to the lav. I've been dying to go for ages.'

'Course. Come here, little feller.'

'I bet it's freezing out there, I wish we had a lav indoors,' called Ruby as she went into the washhouse then on through into the yard.

Chapter 24

It was pitch black when Ruby went outside. Although she knew this yard well, it still took a moment or two for her eyes to adjust to the gloom. She groped her way towards the lavatory. Her foot touched something soft and she almost tripped over. She stood stock still. Fear lanced through her. What was it? It felt like a bundle of old clothes. Slowly she bent down and ran her hands over the mound, then jerked quickly back upright. It was a body.

'Dad! *Dad!*' she screamed as she rushed into the house.

'My God, girl, whatever's the matter with you? You look like you've just seen a ghost. And shut that washhouse door, you're letting all the cold air in.'

Ruby was trembling from head to foot; she was also aware that she had wet herself. She looked over her shoulder, almost expecting someone to be following her. Her voice was high. 'Dad, I think I just fell over a body.'

'What?'

Ruby was nearly hysterical. 'Come and look!'

'Don't talk so daft. It was probably some old rags somebody's given to Tom.'

'I don't think so.' She pulled on his arm. 'Please, Dad, please, come and look.'

'All right. All right. Anything for a quiet life. You'd better put a coat on, you're shivering.'

'Dad, we ain't got *time!*'

'Ruby, just calm down. I'll put little 'en on the floor.' He stood Danny against the chair. 'Won't be long, son.'

In the flickering gaslight from the washhouse, Ruby stood and watched her father go into the yard. He stopped.

'Oh my God,' he yelled. 'Quick, Ruby, give me a hand.'

'Who is it, Dad?'

'I think it's Beth.'

'Beth?' screamed Ruby.

'Give me a hand to lift her. Go round to her feet.'

Ruby rushed round and fell over. 'Oh, Dad,' she cried out. As her eyes became accustomed to the dark she saw another bundle on the ground. 'Tom? *Tom.* Dad, it's Tom as well.' Tears began to pour down her face.

Thomas let Beth slip from his grasp and, falling to his knees, let out a blood-curdling scream and cradled Tom's head to his chest.

For a few moments Ruby froze, unable to take in the scene. Then she bent down and gently touched Beth's face; it was very cold and damp. 'Dad. We've got to get them inside.'

Her father was still sitting on the cold hard ground rocking Tom back and forth and wailing.

'Dad.' She touched his arm and he recoiled.

'Leave me be.'

'Dad. We've got to get them in the warm. They'll freeze to death out here.'

'We mustn't let the Germans get 'em.'

'The Germans won't get them. We must get them inside.'

A little voice interrupted them. 'Mummy. Mummy.' Danny was standing in the doorway.

'Danny,' shouted Ruby.

He began to cry.

'I'm sorry. I didn't mean to shout at you.' She was beside herself. She didn't know where to turn. What could she do? She had to get help. Very slowly flakes of snow drifted down. Out of the blue, she said, 'Looks like we're going to have a white Christmas.'

'On your own tonight?' one of the regulars asked Mr Thompson as he opened the pub door.

'For the moment. Pint of the usual?'

The customer nodded. 'Beth out the back?'

Mr Thompson began pulling the pint. 'No. She went out this afternoon and ain't come back yet. Must have been held up at the market. You know what these women are like when they start shopping.'

'Don't tell me. The wife went to buy a hat the other week. I thought she'd run orf, but no such luck, she come back and I was half a bleeding crown lighter.'

'I hope Beth won't be too long. Don't know what I'll do when I start getting busy.'

'She got the little 'en with her?'

'No. He's up at the Jenkinses. He'll be screaming blue murder for his tea, and so will I before long.'

The customer laughed. 'Don't worry. If we know our Beth, she'll be back soon and she may have a lovely present for you.'

'I hope so. I've got something good for her.'

'Have you now. What is it?'

Mr Thompson touched the side of his nose. 'Not telling you. But I daresay you'll know soon enough.'

'That sounds interesting.'

'It is. Very.' He grinned and moved along the bar to serve another customer.

'Thomas is late coming in,' said George's wife as she poured a drink for herself and her mother.

George looked at the clock. 'Something must have cropped up. He'll be here soon. He won't let me down, not tonight of all nights.'

'I hope not. Can't say I fancy coming down here on Christmas Eve. Hey, you don't reckon he's gone off with that Rita Bell, do you?'

George laughed. It was deep a throaty sound. 'I shouldn't think so for one minute. Anyway, what makes you say that?'

'I've seen the way she looks at him.'

'That's the way she looks at all her potential customers. But for one thing, he couldn't afford her and for another, he thinks too much of his kids to start playing around with the likes of her. You go on up, love.'

She put the drinks on a tray and left him.

But George was worried. This wasn't like Thomas. He was always early and willing. George had been pleased with him; he was a good worker. He knew Thomas always found time to have a word with Rita, and she seemed to like him, but he couldn't see him going off with her. Still, you never knew. That sort of woman could have a very funny effect on a man.

Ruby was crying with cold, fear, anxiety and anger as she pulled and pushed Beth into the washhouse. She was angry with her father who was still cuddling Tom and not making any move to help her. When Ruby got Beth into the light she gasped at the state of her. Beth's eyes were closed and her face a deathly white; her blonde hair was stuck to her head with blood. Danny looked down at his mother.

'Mummy.' He squatted beside her and shook her, trying to wake her.

Ruby left him and went out to her father. 'Dad, you've got

to help me get Tom inside.' She began to pull her father away from her brother, but he hung on to him. Ruby didn't know what to do. She started shouting, 'Dad. Let go. Tom's cold.'

Tom started moaning and her father at last released him.

'Tom,' yelled Ruby, falling to her knees. 'Oh Tom. You're alive.'

He groaned.

'Dad, give me a hand.'

Between them they managed to get him in the house. Tom had blood all over his hair and clothes too, but at least he was drifting in and out of consciousness.

Ruby settled Tom in front of the fire. Danny thought this was a game and tried to crawl over him. Thomas sat on the floor with his son and held him close. He didn't speak.

The washhouse was as far as Ruby had been able to drag Beth. She gently tapped Beth's pale cheek. 'Wake up. Please, Beth. Wake up.' There was no response.

'Dad. I've got to get help. They need a doctor. Look after Danny while I go over to Milly's.'

There was no reply.

Ruby wanted to scream at him. This was the last thing she needed. How could he just sit there? 'Dad.' She began shaking him. 'For God's sake help me.' But he just held Tom. 'I've got to get help,' she cried as she ran out of the kitchen.

'All right. All right. I'm coming.' Ruby could hear Milly's voice as she came down the stairs. 'We're shut, so what's your bloody game. Give us . . .' She stopped when she saw Ruby standing on the doorstep. 'Ruby? What is it?'

Ruby, with tears streaming down her face, gasped, 'It's Beth and Tom. I don't know. They're ill, something's happened, they've been hit. I don't know.'

'Come in.'

Ruby shook her head. 'I can't. I've got to go back.'

'You're not making a lot of sense. I'd better come with you. Mum,' she called out. 'I'm just going over with Ruby.'

'Well, don't be too long,' came the voice from upstairs. 'Remember you're in the bath first tonight.'

Ruby ran across the road and into the kitchen. Everything was just as she had left it.

'My God,' said Milly, who was right behind her. 'What's happened to Tom?'

'We don't know. We've got Beth out here.' Ruby pushed Milly into the washhouse.

For a second or two Milly stood in the doorway. 'Who did this?'

'We don't know,' Ruby repeated.

Milly fell to her knees. 'Is she dead?'

'I'm not sure.'

'Feel her pulse. It's in her neck.'

'I can't find it.'

'Here, let me.' Milly pushed Ruby roughly to one side. 'I can't find it. We've got to get a doctor. I'll run over to me dad, he'll go and fetch him.'

'Milly, don't leave me.' Ruby clung to her. 'Please don't leave me.'

'I must get help.' She unwound Ruby's arm. 'I'll only be a minute. Come on, Mr Jenkins, try to help Ruby.'

Danny was now looking bewildered and began to cry. Ruby swept him up in her arms. 'It's all right.' She kissed his head. 'I'm here. I'll look after you.'

'I'll be right back.' Milly left the room at a run.

Although they were being taken to the hospital in one of the new automobiles, Ruby couldn't be thrilled at the wonder and excitement of it. Her mind was full of worry for Beth and Tom. When they arrived at the hospital it took two nurses to get Thomas away from his son.

They were told to wait in the corridor. Milly was with them, comforting Danny. Always the practical one, she said to Ruby, 'Someone will have to tell Mr Thompson.'

Danny began to cry. 'I think he's hungry. I'll ask a nurse if she can help,' said Milly. 'He's soaking wet.'

Ruby turned to her father. 'Dad. Dad. Talk to me. Don't go back to your old ways, please.'

His shirt was covered with Tom's blood. He looked at her with a vacant look on his face.

When Beth and Tom had been taken away, Ruby put her head in her hands and cried. What was she going to do? She had Tom in hospital with concussion. Beth was barely alive. She had Danny to look after and her father had retreated into his shell-shock where she couldn't reach him. She sobbed. Her world had fallen apart. What could she do? She needed a shoulder to cry on. She needed strong arms round her, holding her close. She needed Ernie at her side. Through the quiet stark white-tiled corridor came the echoing sound of the Salvation Army singing outside in the street: 'Hark the Herald Angels Sing'. Ruby looked up. How could God be so cruel at Christmastime?

'Miss. Miss.'

A hand was shaking Ruby's arm. She quickly sat up. Her back was aching. It seemed she had been sitting on this hard chair for hours. She had been exhausted and must have dropped off. It took a moment or two for her to adjust to her surroundings. 'What is it? What's happened?'

'Your brother's asking for you,' said a nurse.

Ruby leapt to her feet.

'Follow me.'

When they first came into the hospital she and Milly had pleaded with the Matron to let them stay. It was only because it was Christmas she had agreed. A nurse had taken Danny, fed him, changed him and put him in a cot. The nurse had given her father a sedative and he was sleeping in a armchair. Milly had gone home, but promised to return as soon as she could.

'Has he told you what happened?' Ruby asked the nurse.

She shook her head. 'No. Don't ask him too many questions. He's had a nasty bang on the head.'

The nurse showed Ruby which bed her brother was in and pulled the screen round them. Ruby had to keep smiling as she looked at her brother. She wouldn't let him see her reaction to his bruised face and head that was swathed in bandages. 'How're you feeling?'

Tom clutched Ruby's hand. 'Is Beth dead?'

'No.' Ruby couldn't tell him that she was very near to it, and the hospital didn't hold out much hope for her. 'Don't you worry about Beth. You just get yourself better.'

'It was all my fault.'

Ruby looked round the ward. 'How could it be?'

Tom lay back. His face was ashen.

Ruby bent her head closer. 'Who did this?'

'Mr Cox.'

Ruby felt every part of her body tense. *Mr Cox.* She was finding it difficult to contain her anger. She wanted to go and kill him, but all she quietly asked was, 'Why did he do it?'

'Dad won't hit me, will he?'

Ruby smiled. 'No, course not.'

Tom struggled to sit up. 'You see I stole some money and Mr Cox found it. He said he'd tell the police and Beth started hitting him.' He stopped. 'Then he hit her. I thought he'd killed her so I hit him. That's all I remember.' Tom lay back down again, exhausted.

A nurse came to the bedside. 'You'd better go outside for a moment.'

Ruby did as she was told.

Her thoughts were tumbling over and over trying to make sense of it all. Who did Tom steal the money from? And Mr Cox – where had he gone? It suddenly struck her that he hadn't been around when all this had been discovered. Perhaps he had been in the pub. Most of the neighbours had come out into the street when the ambulance arrived. It was something they didn't see very often; not everybody could afford a doctor. That was another thing that came to her. How could they pay for all this? But Ruby knew that was the least of their worries. Tom had to get better and Beth . . . 'Beth,' she silently moaned, 'please get well. Don't die.' She wanted to run away from this horror. She was at her wits' end. It wasn't fair. Mr Cox would have to pay for what he'd done. Tears ran down her cheeks yet again. What if Beth dies? Who is her family? Who will look after Danny? Ruby sat back and put her head against the cold tiled wall. If Beth does die, it'll be murder. I have to go and see the police. He mustn't be allowed to get away with it.

Chapter 25

Milly couldn't face being cheerful even when her parents wished her a merry Christmas.

'D'you mind if I don't open my presents till this afternoon? We might have some news be then.'

'Course not, love.' Her mother had been very shocked when she heard what had happened. 'We understand.'

Milly had tried – and failed – to make sense of it all. Who would do such a thing and for what? She hadn't slept very well. Every time she closed her eyes, Beth's pale face came into her mind. Although she really didn't know Mr Thompson, Ruby had asked her to go and see him and tell him what had happened. Some people thought he and Beth were living as man and wife. Mrs Moss, who still did his cleaning, had once told Milly and those that had been in earshot that they had a very close, cosy relationship.

It had been very late last night when Milly had got home from the hospital and she had felt too drained to go out again. Besides, the pub on a Christmas Eve was the last place she wanted to go to, and she'd been afraid Mr Thompson would be angry that Beth hadn't turned up for work. 'Mum, I must go up and tell Mr Thompson what's happened.'

'Course, love. Oh, I hope Ruby's home soon with some

more news. What a dreadful thing to happen, and at Christmas as well.'

'Well, I hope they find the bugger what did it,' said her father, wiping egg from his moustache. 'They want stringing up.'

'They will be if Beth dies.'

'Oh love, don't say things like that. It's very worrying that somebody could do such a thing – they might even be walking about round here. He might even come into the shop. It just don't bear thinking of.'

Milly shuddered at her mother's words. 'I'll be off now.'

Milly banged hard on the door at the back of the pub. It took a while before she heard bolts being pulled. She was taken aback at the sight of Mr Thompson. When he passed the shop he always looked so smart, but this morning he looked tired and dishevelled.

'Yes. What is it?' There was anger in his voice.

'Mr Thompson, I'm Milly from the dairy, I live opposite the Jenkinses.'

'Oh yes? Beth has spoken about you. You don't happen to know where she is, be any chance?'

'Can I come in?'

'The place is in a bit of a state.'

'That's all right.'

'By the way, merry Christmas,' he said over his shoulder as they walked into the parlour. 'Although it don't seem very merry to me.'

'Mr Thompson, I think you'd better sit down.'

'Why?' Horror filled his face as he did as he was told. 'Is it Beth?'

Milly nodded.

'Has she got someone else? A younger man?'

'No. She's in hospital. Ruby asked me to tell you.'

His face drained of colour. 'Why? What happened?'

As Milly told him all she knew she watched the colour return. By the time she had finished he was scarlet with rage.

'I've got to go to her.'

'I'm sure they'll let you see her. As it's Christmas Day they seemed to be bending the rules. She may be a little better today.'

'And you say you don't know who did it to her and young Tom?'

Milly shook her head.

'Danny! Where's the boy?'

'Ruby took him to the hospital with her. When I left he was asleep.'

'I've got to get to them.'

Milly stood up. 'I'll leave you to it. I hope everything's all right. If you get back before Ruby, will you call in and let us know how they are?'

'Yes, yes, of course. And, Milly, thanks. Thanks for everything.'

'That's all right.' Milly could see how devastated he was. He really must love Beth. Whoever did this terrible thing was going to have to answer to a lot of folk round here; Beth and Tom were both very well liked.

The ward was full of people. The vicar was coming round shaking everybody's hand and wishing them a merry Christmas. Tom was sitting up and Ruby was helping him with his breakfast, but Ruby couldn't take her eyes off the tide mark that washing the blood off Tom's head had left. Her mother would go mad if she were here now looking at his dirty neck. Ruby vowed silently to herself that in future she would take more care of Tom and make sure she knew what he was up to.

If she had been more interested in him this situation would not have arisen, and Beth wouldn't be facing death. A lump came to Ruby's throat as she looked at Danny toddling round the ward and enjoying all the fuss that was being made of him. He had chocolate round his mouth. Beth too would go mad if she could see him eating all these sweets. Ruby swallowed hard. If only she *could* see him.

Thomas Jenkins sat looking at his son; he hadn't had a shave and his lack of sleep was telling: he looked dreadful.

'Why don't you take your father home?' said a nurse to Ruby.

'I can't get him to leave Tom. How's Beth this morning?'

'There isn't any change. You can go and see her if you like.'

'Can I go?' mumbled Tom.

'Not yet, young man. Not till the doctor says you can.'

'I'll tell her you want to see her,' said Ruby, giving him a weak smile. They hadn't told him how bad she was.

In the women's ward Beth had the screens drawn round her bed. Ruby gazed down at her. She had also been washed and most of the blood had been removed from her hair. Her body was still and her face waxen; her gentle breathing was the only movement. Ruby let her tears fall. 'I'm so sorry, Beth. Promise me you'll get better soon,' she whispered. She sat on the chair and held Beth's hand; it was cold. 'You stepped in to save Tom and it has almost cost you your life.'

She jumped when the screen was pulled aside. 'Mr Thompson! Milly told you?'

He nodded. He looked down on Beth. 'Who did this?'

Ruby didn't answer.

He took Beth's hand and kissed it. 'Beth. My Beth.'

Ruby walked away.

'How's Beth?' asked Tom softly when she returned to his bedside.

'About the same.'

'Did she say anything?'

Ruby shook her head. 'Mr Thompson's in with her.'

A tall older-looking doctor with wild white hair came striding up to the bedside. 'You can take Tom home if you like. I'll give you a letter to take to the cottage hospital; he'll have to have his bandages changed in a day or two.'

'Thank you,' said Ruby. 'Come on, Dad, we're going home.'

'Excuse me,' said the doctor to Ruby. 'Can I have a word with you?'

'Yes.' She followed him to the door.

'You will have to keep an eye on your young brother. Any sign of vomiting or falling asleep must be reported to the cottage hospital.'

'Thank you.'

'Now, your father, is he always this way?'

'No. It was the shock of finding Tom.'

'I see.'

'He was shell-shocked in the war, and sometimes . . .' Ruby couldn't keep her feelings pent up any more and she burst into tears.

'My dear child, come along to my office.' He took her arm and propelled her along the corridor.

'Please. Sit down.' The doctor ran his fingers through his wild hair, then continued kindly. 'I was in the war and I saw many men like your father. He needs help.'

'He was better after me mum died. He even went back to work.'

'I see. When did your mother die?'

'April,' sniffed Ruby.

'The nurse said he hasn't spoken since he came here with your brother.'

'No. I don't know what I'm gonner do. What if Beth dies – who'll look after Danny?'

'What about her family? They'll have to be told.'

'She ain't got no family.'

'I see.' The doctor came round his desk and put his arm round her shoulders. 'Do you know who did this dreadful thing to your brother and Mrs Norton?'

She nodded. 'Tom said it was Mr Cox, our landlord.'

'I see. D'you know why?'

Ruby quickly shook her head. Till she could find out more about Tom and this stealing, she had decided not to tell anyone.

For a few moments the doctor stood over Ruby then moved round to sit behind his desk again. 'Young lady, I'm going to see if I can get your father into a sort of convalescent home.'

Ruby jumped to her feet. 'What? No. I ain't having him put in a loony bin. He ain't mad – he's just had a shock. He'll be all right in a couple of days.'

'It won't be that sort of place. He'll be supervised and given things to make him better. He must have had a terrible time in the war, and any little thing will start bringing back all his bad memories. I've seen this so many times.'

'No. I ain't letting him go.'

'Please, sit down. How are you going to manage?'

'I don't know, but I'll think of something.'

'You're a very gallant young lady. You deserve to go far in this world. I have to inform the police of what's happened, and if Mrs Norton dies . . .'

'She won't, will she?'

The doctor picked up his pen. 'I'm afraid things don't look very good for her. And if she dies, that's murder.'

Ruby took a sharp intake of breath. 'Will Mr Cox go to prison?'

'Yes. If he did do it, and if he's found guilty, he could hang.'

Ruby felt the breath leave her body and a blackness came over her.

When Ruby opened her eyes, a nurse was standing over her tapping the back of her hand. She smiled at Ruby. 'Welcome back. How are you feeling?'

'I'm all right.'

'It must be the lack of food.'

So many thoughts came flooding into Ruby's mind. 'They want to take me dad away.'

The nurse busied herself. 'It could be for the best.'

'No. No. I won't let him go.'

'Think it over. Tom's ready to go.'

Ruby stood up. 'He wants to see Beth.'

'I know. The nurse is taking him in there now.'

'The doctor said she might die.'

'We are doing our best, but she did have a very nasty bang on the head.'

At one side of Beth's bedside sat Mr Thompson holding a very fidgety Danny. Her father and Tom sat on the other.

Ruby looked at the scene. If it weren't for the dreadful circumstances, it would have been a heart-warming scene: all the people she cared about gathered together. She wished with all her might that Beth would wake up.

Tom was crying. 'I love Beth,' he whispered.

'I know,' said Ruby.

Her father sat, ever motionless.

Danny began crying. 'Mummy. Mummy.'

Mr Thompson put Danny's face close to Beth's. Danny tried to touch her eyes, then he grinned. 'Mummy sleep.'

'Yes,' said Mr Thompson. 'Mummy's asleep.'

Ruby let her tears fall too. What would happen to this dear little boy? 'The doctor said we can take you home now, Tom,' she sniffed.

Tom's head shot up. 'I don't want to go back to that house. He might be there. He might try to hurt me again.'

'You don't have to worry about him, lad. He'll be taken care of,' said Mr Thompson.

Ruby was filled with horror. 'Who told you?'

'Tom, and the doctor. He'll have to tell the police. I just want to know why Cox did it.' Mr Thompson looked back at Beth. 'And if anything happens to her, he'll have me to answer to.'

Tom was still crying. Ruby put her arm round his shoulders. 'Come on. Let me get you home. Mr Thompson, shall I take Danny?'

He nodded. 'As soon as things improve I'll be along with his stuff.'

Ruby took Beth's son in her arms. 'You're such a big boy now. Say goodbye to Mummy.' Ruby bent down so that Danny could kiss his mother's cheek.

'Bye, son.' Mr Thompson kissed him. Turning to Ruby, he added, 'Thanks. You're a good girl. A rare jewel.'

'Come on, Dad,' she said, trying very hard to keep her feelings under control.

The four of them left Beth's bedside. Would this be the last time Ruby saw Beth alive? How could so many things go wrong? Ruby let Danny walk as they slowly made their way along the corridor and out into the cold. It had stopped snowing and the early-morning sunshine had melted the snow, but it was now a grey, gloomy, miserable day. Although the weather matched her mood, Ruby was grateful that for the moment at least they would stay dry as they started the long walk home.

★ ★ ★

It was dark and the streets were empty when they turned into Hill Street. Ruby could picture the happiness and laughter behind the closed doors. Everybody would have finished their dinner by now and be settled in front of a cosy fire. Those that had a piano would be singing round it and in many houses the beer would be flowing. It didn't matter how hard up people were, every week most of them somehow managed to put in a few pence in a Christmas club for the big day. Tomorrow everybody had to go back to work, but a hangover would keep some away, even if half the home was in the pawnshop and it would take them till spring to recover their possessions.

As they got closer to number thirteen, Ruby could feel the atmosphere grow ever more tense. Would Mr Cox be there? Would he say it wasn't him? She had been carrying Danny for well over an hour. He was a big boy and she was tired.

'Ruby. I'm frightened,' said Tom.

'Don't worry. Nothing's gonner happen. I'm here now.'

But despite her brave words, her mind was churning over and over. Her father had remained silent throughout the long journey home. Would he snap out of it again? Should she let that doctor send him away? Could she cope with all that was in front of her? Danny began to wriggle to get down. Who was there to look after Danny? Did Beth actually have a husband? In all the time they'd known her he had never appeared, not even a letter, as far as Ruby knew. Would Mr Thompson know who her family was and where she'd come from? How would she be able to look after her father, Tom – and Danny if need be – and go to work? This wasn't how Christmas should be.

Milly must have been looking out of the window because as

soon as Ruby had collected the front-door key from the ledge she was at her side.

'That's a smashing hat you're wearing,' she said to Tom.

He gave her a watery smile and touched his bandage.

'At least it's keeping your brains in. How're things with Beth?'

Ruby didn't answer at once. In the narrow passage she put Danny down. 'He's a ton weight.'

Her father, Tom and Danny moved on to the kitchen. Milly went to follow them but Ruby put out her hand to stop her.

'Milly, they think Beth will die.'

Milly put her hand to her mouth. 'No! Do they know who did it?'

Ruby nodded. 'Mr Cox.'

'What?' Milly screamed out.

'Shhh, keep your voice down. He might be upstairs.'

They both looked up at the stairs to the door of his kitchen – it was closed.

'Have the police been here?' asked Ruby.

'No. I would have seen them from the front-room window.'

'Ruby, it's freezing in there,' said Tom, poking his head out of the kitchen door.

'I expect it is. I'll get the fire going as fast as I can.'

Milly waited till Tom went back into the kitchen, then asked, 'Why did he do a thing like that?'

Ruby didn't answer and, as they moved on, Milly asked, 'What you gonner do about it?'

'That's up to the police.'

'Look, it'll take a while for the fire to take hold and the oven to get hot, so I'll just pop home and get you a few bits.'

Milly was back and forth to the shop fetching a pot of tea and food for Danny and the Jenkinses. She wanted to stay a while to help, but Ruby told her she had to get back to her own family. After all, it was Christmas night. All the while the only time Thomas Jenkins moved was to pick up Danny and sit silently with him on his lap.

After a while Danny fell fast asleep. Ruby took him and put him on the floor in her and Tom's room. She sat next to him. If only she had finished sewing that mattress. Tom would be in with her father and she wouldn't have any fear of touching his head in the night. She gazed down at Danny sleeping peacefully. Thank goodness he was too young to know what had happened. This was all wrong. He should be playing with new toys. He didn't know he could be all alone. Who was his father? Was there any way of finding out? She gently kissed his forehead. 'This is a wicked world you have been born into, but I'll do my best for you. Your mother's bravery in looking after my brother may have cost her her life, and I'll never ever forget that.' Ruby lay next to her charge hoping she wouldn't roll on him in the night. Soon she was sound asleep.

Chapter 26

It was Danny crawling all over her that woke Ruby up. She screwed up her nose. 'You smell.'

He gave a little chuckle.

'Ruby. Is Mr Cox home?' Tom's voice came through the darkness.

Ruby gave a start. 'I don't know.' She hadn't really thought about him.

'Don't let him get me.'

'He won't. How are you feeling?'

'Me head hurts.'

'I expect it does, you've got a nasty bump.'

'Can I stay here for a bit? It's nice and warm in bed.'

'Course. Now, I've got to get this young man changed and fed.'

With Danny over her shoulder Ruby went into the kitchen. It was cold and she was taken aback to see her father sitting in front of the empty fireplace. 'Dad. *Dad.*'

He looked up. 'I'm sorry, Ruby.'

'Ain't you been to bed?'

He shook his head.

Ruby stared at her father. 'You should have kept the fire in.'

'Wasn't thinking.'

She sat Danny on the floor and began clearing out the

grate. 'Keep your eye on Danny while I get some wood and coal.' Outside it was just beginning to get light. Although the snow had kept away it was still freezing. She collected the wood and as she made her way back to the house she suddenly stopped. There on the ground was a large dark patch of blood. She felt sick at the thought of what must have happened here such a short while ago. She carefully stepped over it. 'Please let it rain and wash it all away.' Ruby knew that if she had to scrub it away, she would feel she was scrubbing Beth away.

Deep in thought she laid the fire and soon it was blazing and the kettle in place.

'Dad, I'll take a drop of water to wash Danny with. When the rest boils, make the tea.'

'I can't.'

'Why not?'

'The voices.'

Ruby couldn't help herself as she shouted, 'Tell them to go away.'

'They won't. I've tried.'

Her shouting made Danny cry.

'Now see what you've done.' Tears filled her eyes.

'It was the blood.'

'Oh Dad, please don't give up. We've got to get through this together.'

'It was seeing young Tom and Beth lying there. I haven't slept worrying about her. She was there because of our Tom.'

'I didn't think you was listening.'

'I was listening, but the voices in my head were getting louder.'

'Look, I've got to get Danny changed. I'll have to go down the ragbag to make him some sort of nappy. Later on you can go up to Mr Thompson and collect some of his things.'

'I can't.'

'You've got to help.'

'I don't know if . . .'

'That doctor said you could go to some sort of home. They can help you.' As soon as the words left her lips Ruby regretted them. A look of horror filled her father's face.

'I'm sorry,' she said immediately.

'The doctor wants to put me away?'

'No. No, course not. They can help war victims. Look, I've got to get Danny cleaned up.' Ruby took the kettle into the washhouse and poured the water into the large butler sink. She sat Danny in it and gently let the warm water trickle over him, making him splash and laugh. She laughed with him but her thoughts were with her father. He must be having a terrible time fighting his demons. She should be more tolerant. Then there was Mr Cox – where was he? He hadn't come down, nor had she heard him moving about upstairs. Does he know what he's done? she wondered.

A knock on the front door startled her, then she heard Milly's voice calling from the passage. 'It's me, may I come in?'

Milly walked into the washhouse. 'Mum's in the shop and Dad's doing the books. I don't think we'll be very busy today. I've brought you over a couple of eggs and a bit of bacon. The bread ain't that fresh, but it'll do for toast.'

'But we can't—' began Ruby.

'Call it a late Christmas present. Besides, we've all got to help.'

'You're so good to us. I don't know what we'd do without you.'

Milly shrugged her shoulders. 'How's Tom this morning?'

'Got a headache and a bruise on his face, but other than that, he seems fine. He's worried about seeing Mr Cox though.'

'Where is he? Is he upstairs?'

'I don't think so. I ain't heard him.'

'D'you want me to go and look?'

'I don't know. If he knew what's happened wouldn't he run away?'

Again Milly shrugged. 'Knowing him, I wouldn't have thought so. D'you know why he did it?'

Once again Ruby ignored the question as she lifted Danny from the sink and wrapped him in a towel.

'He's a lovely kid,' said Milly, holding his hand. 'What's gonner happen to him, if anything . . .' She couldn't finish the sentence.

'I don't know. But we mustn't give up. Beth is still alive and you hear of wonderful things happening these days.'

'Yes, that's true. Are you going to work?'

Ruby shook her head. 'I can't go and leave all this.'

'Perhaps it will sort itself out.'

'I wonder if Mr Thompson's home? I need clean clothes for Danny and nappies. And I could do with his pram and high chair.'

'It sounds as if you're taking over.'

'Who else is there?'

'I don't know. I'll tell you what, I bet when this gets out all sorts of people will come and tell us about Beth. We might even find out if she really is married and who Danny's father is. How's your dad taking this?'

'Not well. It looks like he's slipping back to the way he was before Mum died.'

'Look, I'll go up and see if he's home.' Milly raised her eyes to the ceiling.

'Give me a minute to dress Danny, then I'll come up with you.'

Milly followed Ruby up the stairs. Ruby could feel her

heart racing. What would she say to him? Not that she wanted to talk to him: she wanted to hit him.

Ruby knocked on the door. Silence.

'Let's go in,' said Milly, grabbing the handle and attempting to turn it. 'It's locked.'

'He always keeps his door locked.'

'So how we gonner get in?'

'I don't know.'

'What happens when you do his cleaning?'

'He leaves it open.'

They stood for a moment or two looking at the door.

'I've got an idea,' said Milly, rushing down the stairs.

'What you gonner do?' yelled Ruby over the banister.

'Get a chopper.'

The gentle tapping on his shoulder woke Mr Thompson. 'What is it? What's happened?' He quickly regained his senses and sat up. 'Is she all right?'

The nurse was standing over him. 'Nothing's changed. I'm afraid you have to leave.'

'But why?'

'The hospital has to get back into its routine.'

Mr Thompson was stiff from sitting in the chair all night. He hadn't had a lot of sleep, as the corridor was a constant hive of activity. 'Please let me stay, just in case she wakes up.'

'I'm sorry. You have been very lucky to be here all this time. It was only because it was Christmas that Matron was so generous.'

He stood up. 'Can I say goodbye?'

The nurse smiled. 'Yes, but you must be quick. The doctor will be doing his round shortly.'

He arched his back. Every bone in his body ached, but he would have climbed Everest if it meant seeing Beth well.

Behind the screens he gazed down on her lovely face. 'You have been like a breath of fresh air into my life. I'll be back with the ring I bought you for Christmas. Beth, will you be my wife? I promise to take care of you and Danny till the end of my days.'

The screen was pulled to one side. 'Please. You must go now.'

He bent down and kissed her pale lips. 'I love you.' With tears stinging his eyes he quickly walked away. It wouldn't do for anyone to see what a stupid old fool he was. After all, she was years younger than him.

Outside he stood and blew his nose. The first thing he had to do was find Cox. He didn't know what would happen after that.

The crashing of the chopper hitting the door brought Tom and his father to the foot of the stairs.

'What are you doing?' shouted Tom.

'Trying to get in,' said Milly with the chopper above her head, ready to give the door another blow. 'Who knows what we'll find.'

'You can't do that,' said Thomas.

'I can,' Milly said defiantly.

'We've got to get in,' said Ruby.

'Why?' asked her father.

'He might not be at home,' said Tom from the safety of the bottom of the stairs.

'If he's not in, then he's deaf, or dead,' said Milly.

Ruby took in a quick breath. 'You don't think . . .? He wouldn't . . .?'

'You never know.' The chopper crashed against the door again and Milly put her hand through the hole and opened the door. 'Welcome,' she said with a grand gesture, standing to one side.

Ruby wanted to giggle at the mess. Her father and Tom remained at the bottom of the stairs; both had a worried look on their faces.

Ruby went into the kitchen. It looked just the same as always. On the table was a dirty cup and saucer, a teapot and a milk jug. Ruby picked up the jug and smelt it.

'Phew, this is off.'

The sugar in the bowl was caked and brown with tea.

Ruby walked into the tiny scullery and looked about her. There was nothing different.

Milly went out of the room and Ruby followed her.

'This the bedroom?' asked Milly, pointing to another closed door.

Ruby nodded.

Milly stood to one side and let Ruby go first.

'Do I need me chopper?'

'Might do. It is normally locked.' Ruby took hold of the handle and turned it. The door opened and as she slowly pushed it open a little wider and moved in, it squeaked in protest. Ruby was very frightened at what she might find, but the room was empty. 'He's gone.' Relief sounded in her voice. 'He's not here.'

'Let's see if he's taken his things,' said Milly, opening the cupboard.

Ruby stood and watched her.

'There ain't much here.'

'Never did have a lot. Come on, let's get downstairs, it's freezing up here.'

In the cosy kitchen Milly asked, 'What happens now?'

'Don't know,' said Ruby.

'He ain't gonner be pleased at that mess,' said Tom.

'I know. I wonder where he's gone,' said Ruby.

'D'you think the police have got him?' asked Milly.

'They don't have a reason,' said Thomas Jenkins.

Milly looked at Tom and his father. 'Not yet they don't. After all, a lot of men knock women about,' she said with displeasure in her voice.

Tom said nothing.

'D'you think Mr Thompson is still at the hospital?' asked Ruby.

'He seems a nice man.'

'I think he is.'

'He should be back soon to open the pub,' said Milly.

'Unless . . .' Ruby shook her head. 'I mustn't think like that.'

It was later that morning when Mr Thompson finally knocked on the front door.

'Come in. How's Beth?' asked Ruby.

'About the same. Is Cox upstairs?'

'No.'

'Where is he?'

'We don't know. Would you like a cup of tea?'

'Yes please. Then I must get back to open up for the lunchtime trade.' He bent down and picked up Danny. He turned to Ruby. 'I wish I could take him with me, but I expect I'll be busy. You do understand?'

'He'll be all right here. Could I possibly have some of Danny's things?'

'Yes, of course. You can walk back with me. I'll give you some money too, so that you don't go short.'

'That's very kind of you.'

'How are you feeling, young man?' he asked Tom.

'Not too bad. I'm ever so sorry about what happened to Beth.'

'Not nearly as sorry as Cox will be when I catch up with

him. Do you know what made him do it?'

Ruby and Tom looked at each other.

'I'd rather not say,' said Tom.

Mr Thompson put Danny on the floor. 'If it's what I think you're trying to say, then he should be strung up. If there's something I can't stand, it's dirty old sods what . . . I bet you're livid, ain't yer, Thomas?'

Thomas looked at him. 'I don't know why it happened.'

'Never mind. My Beth's a good girl and she wouldn't let anybody do anything like that.'

Ruby could see Tom was about to speak. 'Is it all right if we go soon? I don't have any more rags to make Danny a nappy.'

'Course, love. I've finished me tea. Can't say I'm looking forward to the mess up there. Just went off and left it.'

'Dad, Tom, let's all go and give Mr Thompson a hand.'

'I can't let you do that.'

'Why not? It was Beth who helped us.'

For the first time in two days Mr Thompson smiled. 'Thanks.'

'I ain't going,' said her father.

'But, Dad, why not?'

'I'll wait here for Mary.'

Ruby slumped into the chair. 'Mum's dead.'

'No, she's at the hospital.'

Ruby looked up at her father. 'No, Dad. It's Beth. Oh, what am I gonner do?'

'Give him time,' said Mr Thompson. 'You stay here and look after your father. Tom can come with me and bring Danny's things back.'

Ruby stood up. 'No. I'm coming with you.'

'Are you sure?'

'Yes.' Ruby was putting on her hat and coat. She knew if she stayed with her father she would say things she might in later life regret. She had to keep herself busy. She knew she should be scrubbing the yard, but she couldn't bring herself to do that, not just yet. 'Ready.'

Outside, Mr Thompson put Danny high on his shoulders and they walked up the road.

'He's getting to be a ton weight. You'd better take his pram.'

Ruby knew then that she was going to be expected to take care of Danny till his mother came out of hospital. But what if . . .? That didn't bear thinking about. And she had to get her father back to work, and soon – that's if he hadn't lost the job already.

Chapter 27

All morning, as Ruby and Tom worked helping Mr Thompson, Beth filled Ruby's thoughts. As she washed glasses, swept and, in between, fed and changed Danny, she knew these were Beth's jobs. She should be here, not lying in hospital unaware of what was happening all around her. As soon as they had arrived at the pub, Mr Thompson had told Ruby to find something for them all to eat at closing time.

At first Ruby had protested, but when he pointed out that was the only way he was going to have a meal today, she relented. Even though she'd never used a gas oven, after Mr Thompson gave her a quick lesson Ruby soon got the idea of it. She marvelled at getting heat so quickly and promised herself that one day she would have one of these. As they worked, the delicious smell of a chicken she had found in the outside meat safe gently cooking filled the pub. Before the terrible events that had taken place on Christmas Eve, Beth had been well organised and had plucked and cleaned the chicken ready to pop into the oven. Mr Thompson had shown Ruby where to find things and Beth's well-filled larder, to Ruby, was almost like an Aladdin's cave. As she busied herself doing the potatoes and veg Beth had bought for Christmas dinner, it upset her to think that through Beth's misfortune they were going to have the best dinner they'd had in years; and a few times the odd tear spilt out and trickled down her cheek.

Ruby looked through the window at Tom struggling with a crate full of bottles. With his bandage round his head he looked like an Indian prince she had seen in a book. Ruby was still furious with her father. He should have come with them. He should be here helping Mr Thompson when he opened the pub. Fear suddenly struck her. What if he wouldn't go to work again? Danny, who had been fast asleep, woke with a cry. Ruby rushed over to him.

'Don't worry, little 'en. I'm here. I expect you're wet and hungry.' As Ruby set about seeing to Danny, she resolved to ask Mr Thompson if he knew whether Beth had any relations. He might even know if Beth came from round this way. And who was Danny's father? Had she told him? Would his father come to claim the little boy? Ruby knew she didn't want to part with him. If he went away she might never see him again. Could she look after him? Would her father look after Danny while she was at work? She knew it was silly, but she was simply trying to see if there was a light at the end of this very long, long tunnel.

At opening time Tom stayed in the back room with Danny as Mr Thompson had asked Ruby to help him. She couldn't serve behind the bar as she hadn't any idea what to do, but he was pleased when she offered to collect the empty glasses and wash them.

'Could do with your dad out here,' he'd said when he had unlocked the door.

'So where's our Beth then?' asked the first man to walk in. 'She done a runner?'

'I'm afraid she's in hospital.'

'No! What's up?'

Ruby held her breath. What was he going to tell his customers?

Mr Thompson was very discreet. He told them that she had had an accident.

'How did that happen?'

'She's had a nasty fall.'

'Will she be all right?'

'I hope so.'

'Thought it was funny she wasn't here yesterday. Not like her to leave you on your own.'

All morning, everybody who came in asked after Beth and got the same answer. Ruby could see she was very popular. Mr Thompson never mentioned Mr Cox at all. What would happen if he walked in?

It was getting near to closing time and Mr Thompson said that perhaps Ruby should go and see to the dinner. The smell was making her stomach turn over. She was so hungry; she hadn't eaten for a long while. As she was dishing up she couldn't resist the odd sprout. She gazed at the chicken; Mr Thompson would soon be carving it. She couldn't remember what chicken tasted like. It had been before the war, when her father was working, that they'd last had one at Christmas.

'That was delicious,' said Mr Thompson, sitting back in his chair. 'I needed that. I was starving – and so was you, young man, be the way you've emptied your plate.'

'We ain't had a good dinner like that for a long time,' said Tom. 'I ain't ever had chicken before.'

'Would it be all right if I took a plateful along to me dad?' asked Ruby.

'Course. Now, what are we gonner do about Beth?'

'I don't know.'

'I might not open the pub tonight.' He lit a cigar.

'But you must,' said Ruby.

'I'll go along to the hospital first, then I can make up me mind.'

'You must like her very much,' said Ruby.

'I do. I want her to marry me.'

Ruby took a breath. Did he know she was married? *Was* she in fact married at all?

He gently tapped the end of his cigar into the ashtray. He didn't drop it on the floor like most men.

Ruby had noted that he was indeed a gentleman and she could understand Beth being so happy living here.

'But she's—' Ruby stopped herself just in time. If and when Beth was well, what she did with her life was her business. 'Mr Thompson, would you like me to look after Danny till things get sorted out?'

'I was hoping you'd say that. I don't know how long it'll be for. Will you be able to manage?'

'Tom here will help.'

'I'll give you money. You won't go short. But what about your job?'

'I'm sure Tom and Dad will be able to manage while I'm at the laundry.'

'Well, only if you're sure. Your dad don't seem that good.'

'He'll be all right. It was the shock of seeing Tom covered with blood and in hospital.'

'Will he be going back to the Green Man?'

'I hope so.' As Ruby was saying it, she wasn't sure if he would. But he had to.

It had gone six o'clock. Thomas had finished the dinner Ruby had brought down for him. 'That was really delicious, love,' he said, wiping his chin. He looked at Ruby's sad face. He knew he had to make an effort to help his daughter. He should be thinking of going to work, but the thought of walking about in the dark filled him with horror. What if Cox were waiting for him? Danny began to scramble on to his lap.

'Hello, son,' he said, affectionately kissing the top of his head. 'And what's going to happen to you?'

'He's going to bed. He's getting too big for his pram so d'you think you could get me his cot from the pub tomorrow?'

To Ruby's surprise, her father replied, 'I should think so.'

Ruby was still thinking about this as she pushed the pram into the bedroom. Had her father realised that she needed his help?

She had to get the mattress finished now Danny was going to be in with her. Ruby looked at her frock hanging behind the door. How would she be able to enjoy herself at the wedding at the end of the week with Beth so ill? Beth would want her to enjoy herself; she had been thrilled when Ruby had been given Jenny's frock to alter. Her thoughts went to Ernie. What sort of Christmas had he had? Perhaps at Elsie's wedding they would be able to enjoy themselves and not think about what had happened. But she had Danny to think of now, how would Ernie feel about that?

Back in the kitchen Ruby glanced up at the clock. Mr Thompson should have been back to open the pub hours ago. He had promised to tell them if there was any news, but he hadn't returned from the hospital. What was wrong? Earlier that evening Ruby had begged her father to go to work, but he'd refused, saying he couldn't walk about in the dark. Danny was asleep and Tom had gone to bed.

'Dad. I'm going to bed. I've got to go to work in the morning. You'll have to look after Danny.'

'I know, so don't keep on.'

Ruby walked away. She felt too tired to argue.

303

The following morning Ruby got up, cleaned out the grate and lit the fire. Black-leading and whitening would all have to wait till the weekend when she had more time. She sat for a moment or two with her ears alert. She still hadn't heard Mr Cox walking about. Surely if he was home he would have been down shouting about the state of his kitchen door. A slight smile lifted her sad face. He's gonner be in for a bit of a shock when he does find it. I only hope I'm here to see it. Ruby got Danny cleaned up and told Tom to get up and see to the toast. She was trying to slice the bread but it was as hard as a bullet.

'I'll get home as fast as I can. I've left some of yesterday's dinner for all of you. You've got to see to Danny for me.'

'Have I got to change his nappy?'

'Afraid so.'

Tom held his nose. 'He don't half stink sometimes.'

'I know, but it might only be for a few days. Let's see what happens.' She left the house and hurried to work.

The last thing Ruby wanted was Florrie's comments, but as usual, the minute she sauntered into the room, she made a beeline for Ruby.

'Where was yer yesterday? I reckon yer'll get the sack taking time orf again like that.'

As soon as Ruby arrived at the laundry she went straight up to Mrs Watson and explained that her brother had been in hospital over Christmas. She didn't mention Beth. Mrs Watson had been very sympathetic and told her not to worry, although she would be a day's money short at the end of the week.

'Yer look bloody awful,' said Florrie, continuing to needle Ruby. 'Yer bin nursing a hangover? Yer bin on the tiles? And what did that boyfriend of yours buy yer fer Christmas then?'

'What, our Ernie?' shouted Molly. 'I bet what he give her she couldn't wrap up. No wonder she couldn't get inter work yesterday. Don't reckon she could walk. No wonder she looks like that.'

Ruby was having difficulty keeping the tears back. She picked up her iron; she wanted to throw it at Florrie, but knew that wouldn't do any good.

'Here, take a gander at this,' yelled Florrie. She held out her arm and flashed a gold-coloured bracelet.

'Cor, that's lovely. Is it real?' asked her mate.

'Course it is. I don't go out with no cheapskate.'

'What d'yer have ter do ter get that?'

'I ain't telling.'

'I bet yer didn't keep yer drawers on,' screamed another friend from up the line.

'Well, it ain't no good sitting on a fortune. Make the most of it, I say, while it's still in good working order.'

That brought forth shrieks of laughter.

'You wonner make use of yours, young Ruby. Find somebody that can give yer a few bob. It might put a smile on that bloody miserable face of yours.'

With a smug look, Florrie sat down the instant Mrs Watson walked in.

'Now come on, girls, settle down. The merrymaking's over and you've got a lot of work to catch up on.'

Merrymaking was the last thing on Ruby's mind.

Ruby hurried home as fast as she could. Seeing Mr Thompson sitting at the kitchen table with such a sad expression on his face, somehow she knew the worst had happened.

'When?' was the only word she could say.

'Early this morning. Last night her breathing became very

bad. They let me stay till the end. I couldn't leave her.' He blew his nose. 'I'm sorry.'

Danny clambered up onto Ruby's lap and Ruby held him close, letting her tears fall onto his back. 'I don't know what to say,' she sobbed.

'I understand. I feel that there ain't no words . . .' He stopped.

Ruby wiped her eyes with the back of her hand. 'Where's Tom? How's he taking this?'

'Leave him. He's outside,' said her father.

'I've been busy all day arranging her funeral. Do you happen to know who her mother was?'

Ruby put Danny on the floor. 'No. I was hoping Beth might have told you.'

'The little lad might even be an orphan.'

'Mr Thompson, I don't know how to say this.' Ruby wiped her eyes. 'I don't think Beth *was* married. Nobody knows who Danny's father is. She would never talk about her past.'

'I know.'

'You're not angry at that?'

'No. I loved Beth for what she was, not for what she'd been.'

Ruby was amazed. This man had been ready to accept Beth whatever her past held.

'Did she ever have any letters while she was living here?'

Ruby shook her head. 'Would you like me to go through her things?'

'Thanks all the same, but I can do that. I don't think it'll do much good, though.'

'Did you know where she came from?' asked Ruby.

'She never said a lot.'

'Are you going to open the pub tonight?'

He shook his head. 'No. I can't. The customers will

understand. She's going to have the best funeral money can buy. Horses, carriages and flowers, plenty of flowers.'

'She would have liked that,' said Thomas Jenkins quietly. 'She loved pretty things.'

'Does Milly know Beth's . . .' Ruby couldn't say the word.

'I'm afraid I came straight here. I wanted to see the boy.'

'I think they do their stock-taking after Christmas so she wouldn't have seen you arrive. I'll go over later. Tom's a long while outside, he'll freeze to death.'

'He feels very bad about Beth.'

Ruby stood up. 'I'd better go and get him.'

'No, leave him be,' said her father.

'Has Mr Cox come back?'

'No,' said her father again, with more force than Ruby could believe he was capable of. 'This is all his fault.'

'We know, Dad.'

Suddenly there was a loud knocking on the front door.

'I'll go,' said Ruby.

She was taken aback to see two large policemen standing on her doorstep.

'I understand a Mr Cox lives here,' said the one who stood at the front.

'Yes, but he's not here.'

'Do you know where we can find him?'

'No.'

'Can we come in?'

'Yes.' Ruby stood to one side. As they pushed past her in the narrow passage, a feeling of guilt fell over her, although she hadn't done anything wrong. What if they found out about Tom's stealing? Would he go to prison? 'Mr Cox lives upstairs,' she said as they reached the bottom of the stairs.

'Who lives there?' The one who had been doing the talking pointed at the kitchen door.

'Me, my dad and my brother.'

'Would that be Tom Jenkins, the lad that was injured?'

'Yes.'

'We'll just go up and look in Mr Cox's room, then we'll have a word with the lad.'

'Shall I come up with you?'

'No, it isn't necessary.'

Ruby watched them go up the stairs.

'Who did this?' called one of the policemen over the banisters.

'We was worried about him when we didn't see him. At first we wondered if he'd been taken ill. Then we tried to find out where he might have gone to,' said Ruby.

'You could be had up for criminal damage, you know?'

Ruby was shaking. 'We didn't know what else to do.'

Mr Thompson came out of the kitchen. 'Ruby? Everything all right?'

'Yes. The police are here.'

'Are they? I'll go up and have a word with them.'

Ruby went in to her father. 'That was the police. Dad, I must go out to Tom. I'm very worried about him.'

'He won't come in. I don't know why, but he thinks this is all his fault, you know?'

'I know. But he might have to answer some questions.'

'He won't like that.'

It was very dark outside and Ruby made her way to the lav carefully. She knew she was stepping on the dried blood. If only it would rain and wash it away. She gently knocked on the door. 'Come on, Tom. You've got to come in. You'll freeze to death out here.'

Tom opened the door and rushed into Ruby's arms. 'It was my fault. It was me what made him kill her. I loved Beth.'

Ruby held him close. 'I know. Now come on. There's a

policeman inside, and he might want to ask you some questions. Don't say anything about the money.'

'I don't want to talk to him.'

'You must.'

'But—'

'Come on.' She rubbed his hands. 'You're freezing, you're gonner end up with bad chilblains again.'

As they walked back Tom stood still for a moment at the place where they had found Beth. 'I was gonner wash the blood away, but I couldn't. It would be like washing Beth away.'

Ruby held her brother tight. 'We'll never ever forget Beth. She was part of our lives, and with Danny to look after, in a way, she'll still be here with us. Now come, let's get in the warm.'

Chapter 28

Tom, with fear written all over his pale face, sat at the table and looked from one policeman to the other as they sat opposite him. Mr Thompson stood behind Tom with his hands gently resting on the boy's shoulders.

'Now, young man, don't be nervous,' said the policeman who had been doing all the talking. 'It's not you that's in trouble, unless you've got something to hide? The doctor told me you came to the hospital the same time as the young lady. Is that correct?'

Tom nodded.

'You told the doctor a Mr Cox hit you and Mrs Norton. Can you tell me why?'

Tom bent his head and shook it furiously, making his bandage wobble.

'Don't worry, son,' said Mr Thompson. 'I've told them what happened. They just want to make sure it was Cox what did it.'

'It was. It was.' Tom looked up, his face full of despair.

Ruby looked at her father. It should be him standing beside his son giving him support. Danny began to whimper and tried to climb on Ruby's lap.

'I'll take him,' said her father.

'It's time for his drink and bed,' said Ruby, but she didn't want to leave Tom. 'I don't think my brother can tell you much more.'

'No, perhaps not at this stage. When we find Mr Cox, he may well have to give evidence in court.'

Tom let out a little cry. 'I can't. I don't know what to say.'

'Just tell the truth, son. That's all.' The policeman looked at Ruby and her father. 'We've taken a few papers from upstairs. When he comes back would you tell him we wish to talk to him at the police station?'

'Course,' said Thomas Jenkins.

'Now we must be off.' The policemen stood up and put on their helmets. Ruby went with them to the front door.

'Remember: Mr Cox is innocent until proved guilty, so I don't want any of the family, or friends, taking the law into their own hands.'

'We won't.'

'I hope not, but after looking at that door . . .'

'As I said, we was worried he might have been taken ill or something.'

'I see.'

As soon as they left the room Tom let his tears fall.

When Ruby returned to the kitchen, she was pleased to see that Tom was being comforted in his father's arms.

'I'll get Danny's things down to you later on,' said Mr Thompson, gathering his overcoat and trilby.

'You didn't tell us what day and time Beth's funeral will be,' said Ruby softly.

'No. It's at two o'clock on Saturday.'

'Saturday,' repeated Ruby.

'Yes. I expect a lot of the regulars will want to attend. I thought that was the best day and time. Now I must go. I'll be along in the morning. I shall be asking the young lady in the dairy if she and her mother would do a bit of food for everybody. And, Thomas, I'd like you to give me a hand.'

Thomas didn't answer.

Mr Thompson stopped at the kitchen door. 'I'm having Beth brought home tomorrow afternoon, so please, come and say goodbye to her.'

'Thank you for asking Dad to help,' said Ruby as they reached the front door.

'I want to help him to get his head round all this.'

'Thank you. You're a very kind man.'

'I don't suppose I'll see you till Saturday, with you working all day, and me working all evening, but if you wish to come and see Beth, please do. We have a very nice room we don't often use.'

'I'll come and bring Danny to see his mother.' Ruby swallowed hard. 'I promise I'll look after him.'

'Thank you. I really do admire you, young lady. Goodnight.'

Ruby tried hard to smile. 'Goodnight.' She looked out on the cold night air. It was raining at last, a steady even downpour. Soon all traces of Beth would be washed away. Ruby closed the door and, leaning against it, cried. After a few desolate minutes, she wiped her eyes and returned to the kitchen door.

'I don't know if I can go to the funeral,' said her father as soon as she walked into the room.

'You will. And what's more you'll give Mr Thompson a hand with the drinks and stuff.'

Tom looked at his sister. 'You can't make Dad go.'

'I can. Do any of you realise that I should be going to Elsie's wedding on that day and at that time?'

'Ruby. I'm so sorry,' said Tom.

She looked at Tom's sad face. What words of comfort could she give him? Ruby sat heavily in the chair. She wanted to cry again, but didn't have any tears left.

★ ★ ★

The following evening, after Ruby had put Danny to bed and done his bit of washing, she turned her attention to her brother. Tom was reading; he had hardly spoken a word since they'd been told Beth had died. Their father sat staring into the fire and played with the poker. Someone banging on the door sent Ruby scurrying along to open it.

'Milly,' said Ruby on opening the door.

'Look, it's in the newspapers.' Milly waved the paper at Ruby.

'What does it say?'

'It ain't much, what with the trouble in Ireland, Christmas and everything else.' Milly followed Ruby down the passage. 'Everybody's talking about it. I tell yer, if and when Cox gets back, he'll be lucky to get to prison, the way some of 'em round here feel.' In the kitchen Milly gave Thomas a nod. 'Sad do, this. You all right, Tom?'

'Yes,' he said softly, watching Milly spreading the newspaper on the table.

'What's it say?' asked Ruby.

'This is it. Look, it says that Mrs Elizabeth Norton died from head wounds inflicted by a person or persons unknown.'

'This means everybody will know about Beth,' said Ruby, reading the few lines, which were almost hidden away on an inside page.

'Only those that can afford a paper and knew her name was Elizabeth Norton.'

'That's true.'

'The rest of us have to wait till we buy something and have it wrapped in the paper and be then it's all over and out of date. I'm glad they ain't said anything about Tom.'

'No, they ain't even said where Beth lived. I wonder if old Cox will see it?'

'Might do. He often bought a paper.'

'Let me see,' said her father.

Ruby handed it to him. 'Milly, did Mr Thompson ask you about doing the food?'

'Yes,' she said, sitting at the table.

Ruby sat next to her.

'Mrs Moss said she looks ever so nice,' Milly added.

'You've not been to see her?'

'No. Didn't like to. I'll pay me respects when I see him about the food. I tell you, what he's asked for is gonner cost him a few bob.'

'Is he opening the pub?' asked Thomas.

'Think so. Well, it is for the best. It don't do any good just sitting looking at her, does it?'

'No, suppose not.'

'You could go up there and give him a hand, Dad,' said Ruby.

'He'd certainly appreciate that,' said Milly, giving Ruby a sly wink.

'No. No. I couldn't.'

'Ain't you going up to say goodbye to Beth?' asked Milly.

'Give me time.'

Ruby turned her back on her father.

'We've started a collection in the shop. I reckon everybody will turn out on Saturday. Mr Thompson's a nice man and this will be quite a sight.'

Ruby looked at her fingers. 'I should be at Elsie's wedding at that time.'

'Oh Ruby. What can I say? Have you told Mr Thompson?'

Ruby shook her head.

'What you gonner do?'

Ruby's head shot up. 'Go to Beth's funeral. I've got Danny to think of now.'

314

'What's gonner happen to Danny?'

Ruby shrugged. 'Someone's got to look after him. Mr Thompson can't and we don't want him put in care.'

'Heaven forbid. Will it be just for now?'

'I don't know.'

'You're much too young to have to take on so much responsibility.'

'Who else is there?'

'She must have a family somewhere.'

'But where?'

'They might see that in the paper.'

'But would they know she had a son?'

'Dunno.' Milly leant across the table and gently patted Ruby's hand. She stood up. 'D'you know you've got a rare one here, Mr Jenkins. I'd better go. Goodnight.'

Milly left the kitchen with Ruby walking behind to see her out. After she'd said goodbye she closed the front door. Shouting was coming from the kitchen. She rushed in and quickly shut the door behind her. 'What's all the noise about? Don't you wake Danny. I need me sleep. Remember, I've got to go to work in the morning.'

'I'm sorry,' said Tom. 'But Dad started blaming me.'

Ruby went to her brother and held him close. 'Dad, please help me. I can't look after Danny, Tom *and* you.' There was no response. She looked round the kitchen as if seeking inspiration, but there was none. She had to get away in case she said something she would regret. She turned and left the room.

In the dark bedroom Ruby lay listening to Danny's steady breathing. 'There's such a lot you will have to know about your mother,' she whispered.

The door opened and Tom came and sat next to her. 'Dad don't look very happy.'

'I should try to be like Mum and have a bit of understanding, but everything is getting on top of me.'

'I'm so sorry, Ruby. This is all my fault.'

'Come here.' She held Tom close. 'We'll manage somehow.'

'What will happen to us if Mr Cox don't come back?'

'I don't know.'

'Will we have to move?'

'I don't know. I can't answer that.'

Tom's words sent her thoughts racing. With all that had happened she hadn't given that any thought. Who was his next of kin? Who would own the house if he were found guilty and went to prison? And if he weren't, would they be thrown out for smashing his door?

For the rest of the week Ruby felt she was in a daze. She had no way of telling Elsie she wouldn't be going to the wedding. Even if she'd had time she didn't know where Elsie lived. Every night she had to hurry home to see to Danny and cook. And what about Ernie? She was hoping she would see him at the laundry to explain why she couldn't go to the church. Would he think she didn't want to go with him? She seemed to spend her life running from one thing to another. This was all Mr Cox's fault, but he hadn't been seen, nobody knew where he was. And what about the house? That was another worry constantly on her mind.

On Thursday night it was late before she left the laundry. Mrs Watson had asked her to iron some lord's beautiful frilly evening shirt. Although it was a great honour and she couldn't refuse, it delayed her leaving. It was dark and drizzling and as she was hurrying over the wet cobbles, Stone's horse and laundry van came round the corner and she slipped. She sat on the ground and cried.

'You all right?'

It was Ben, the younger of Mr Stone's sons. She had often seen him attending to his horse. 'No. No I ain't.'

'Here. Let me help you up.'

'Leave me be.' She pushed his arm away.

'Are you hurt?'

'No.' It was Ruby's pride that had been hurt the most. She was only relieved that Florrie and her friends had left the premises and hadn't had the pleasure of seeing her sitting on the wet ground with her skirt well above her knees. She quickly pulled her skirt down and struggled to her feet.

'You're all wet.'

'It's raining, in case you didn't know.'

Ben Stone took her arm. 'Come under the canopy.'

'Leave me be. I've got to get home.'

'You're Ruby Jenkins, aren't you?'

Ruby looked surprised. 'How d'you know my name?'

'I know a lot about you.'

'Do you now? Who told you?'

'Mrs Watson.'

'What's she been telling you?'

'She said you're one of the best workers we've got.'

Ruby couldn't believe her ears. 'She said that?'

'Yes. And she reckons, with a bit of time, you could almost take over running the place.'

Ruby was glad he couldn't see her blushing. 'Don't talk daft.'

'No. It's true.'

Ruby was suddenly aware this was all flattery. 'I've got to go.'

'What's your hurry? I reckon I should take you out to make up for knocking you over.'

'Thanks all the same, but you didn't knock me over, I fell. These cobbles are slippery when they get wet.'

He stood in front of her. 'She reckons you've got a lot to put up with, with some of the others here.'

'She said that? Is that all you've got to talk about: me?'

'Don't flatter yourself. We sometimes talk about the staff.'

'Now, please let me get home.'

'I'd like to take you out one night.'

Ruby remembered what Elsie had told her when she went out with Ben's brother. 'You only want to take me out for one thing.'

He laughed. 'And what's that?'

'I can't say. I've got to get home, I've got a lot to do.'

He stood to one side. 'Goodnight, Ruby Jenkins.'

She ran all the way home. Her mind was full, but it wasn't Ben Stone that filled it, even though he was nice looking and seemed kind.

Milly was sitting at the kitchen table when Ruby walked in.

'What is it? What's wrong?'

'A lot of people have been in the shop today. Stories about this murder are spreading like wildfire. Mrs Mann come in this morning. She reckons she could find out who Danny's dad is.'

'How can she? She said she didn't know anything about Beth before.'

'That's as may be. But it seems she's changed her tune.'

'I bet that's cos there ain't anybody to deny it. Where's Dad?'

'He's gone up to Mr Thompson,' said Tom, who was feeding Danny.

'What?' Ruby looked at Danny. 'Tom, what are you giving him?'

'A bit of soup me mum made,' said Milly.

Danny grinned and let the soup run out of his mouth.

Ruby sat at the table and mopped his face. 'You're a mucky little boy. Thank your mum, Milly. So what's Dad up to?'

'Well,' said Tom, 'he's been helping Mr Thompson.'

For the first time in days, Ruby let a smile lift her sad face. She turned to Milly. 'What else did Mrs Mann have to say?'

'She's gonner pray for Beth and she's gonner try and find out a bit more from her people.'

'Do we really want to know?'

'Well, I think we owe it to Danny.'

'Suppose so.'

'We're closing the shop Sat'day afternoon as a mark of respect,' said Milly.

'Beth would be tickled pink if she knew all what was going on for her.' Ruby looked at her brother. He sat silently putting food into Danny's open mouth.

'I wonder where Cox is?' said Milly.

'I don't know. Any day I expect him to come back and throw us out.'

Thomas Jenkins looked down at Beth's pale face.

'She was lovely,' said Mr Thompson, who was standing beside him.

'Yes, she was.'

'Don't have a lot of luck with our women, do we?'

'Don't seem to. But I blame meself for Mary's death.'

'Well, I can't say anything about that, but, Thomas, I think you should look after that daughter of yours. She's a good girl and works hard.'

'I know. I'm definitely going to try. I'm glad you've asked me to help you.'

'Good for you.' He put his arm round Thomas's shoulder. 'Come on. Beth wouldn't want us to stand here moping.'

They left the darkened room together.

'By the way, call me Len.'

'Thanks, Len.'

Thomas Jenkins had resolved to push his demons to the back of his mind for ever. It wasn't easy: no one could appreciate how hard it was for him to defeat the voices and images that were the war's dreadful legacy. But he would succeed. He had to, otherwise he might lose his precious Ruby.

Chapter 29

It was dark when on Saturday morning Ruby opened her eyes. A feeling of dread swept over her. Yesterday she had asked Mrs Watson if she could have the day off. She was angry and had at first said no, but when Ruby explained why, for a moment or two she was speechless.

'So that young lady I read about in the newspapers was a friend of yours?'

Ruby nodded.

'Well, I can't let you go to the funeral as she's only a friend, and you've already taken one day off this week. I'm sorry she died.'

'Till we find out who her mum and dad was I'm looking after her little boy.'

'You are? What about her husband?'

'We don't know where he is.'

'I see. How old is the boy?'

'Two.'

'You poor child. How are you managing?'

'Me dad and brother look after Danny during the day.'

Mrs Watson smiled. 'I'll talk to Mr Stone. I'll see if I can get you the day off. Perhaps we can get up some sort of collection for you.'

Ruby cringed. She didn't want Florrie to know. But would

she have seen the papers anyway? Could she read? Even if she could, as Mrs Watson had said, you didn't think that sort of thing happened to people you knew.

As it *had* been in the papers and all the locals were talking about it, had the news reached Ernie? She hoped it had, then he would understand why she wasn't at the wedding. The wedding: how Ruby would have loved to be there. To be wearing that lovely frock and laughing and seeing people happy.

Danny stirred and began clambering over her. 'Come on, young man. Let me get you sorted out.' With Danny on her hip, Ruby padded into the kitchen. She was surprised to see the fire alight and the kettle's lid gently bobbing up and down.

'Dad?' called Ruby.

He poked his head round the door. 'I'm just seeing to the tea. At least it ain't raining,' he said, collecting the kettle. 'I'll fill it up again, then you can wash the little feller.'

'I hope it stays dry for Elsie.'

'That's a shame you couldn't go to her wedding. What about after?'

Ruby shrugged. 'Wouldn't seem right somehow.' The frock was now in a paper bag ready to give back to Elsie's sister. Ruby knew that she would never wear anything so beautiful now.

'I know Beth would love you to go and enjoy yourself. She wouldn't want you sitting around and moping. Besides, you deserve it.'

'Thanks, Dad. I'll see.' Ruby knew she desperately wanted to go. To be with Ernie all evening.

'Ruby. I'm really trying to get things sorted out.'

Ruby smiled and touched his hand. 'I know, Dad. I know.' But at the back of her mind was always the fear of what the doctor had told her, that anything could trigger him off and send him back to his old ways.

All morning Ruby busied herself.

'Len asked us to be at the pub be one o'clock,' said her father, standing in front of the mirror and checking the knot in his black tie.

The black armbands Ruby had made after her mother had died were brought out again.

Just before one, the sad group slowly made their way up the street to the Royal Albert. When they reached the pub, Len Thompson took Danny from the pram. Mrs Moss was busy helping Milly and her mother put the food on plates.

''Ello, Ruby, Mr Jenkins,' said Mrs Moss softly, giving them a nod. ''Ave yer seen the flowers? They're lovely. I ain't seen anythink like them before. Must 'ave cost a pretty penny. 'Ow's the head, son?' she asked Tom.

'A bit better. I had to go to the cottage hospital to have a clean bandage. It hurt a bit when they took the old one off.'

Ruby had made sure his neck was clean this time.

'A terrible thing. Terrible,' muttered Mrs Moss as she continued with her chores.

A few of the regulars had gathered in the bar and were having a quiet drink.

Someone at the door announced the cortège was here.

Ruby stood holding Danny as they watched the flowers being placed around and on Beth's expensive-looking wooden coffin with shiny brass handles. They were beautiful; she didn't know how they could grow them at this time of the year. Yet the thought that was filling Ruby's mind was: Beth is in that box.

Danny was squirming to get down and see the black horses with their black feathered plumes, snorting and shaking their heads.

Finally it was time to leave. Mr Thompson took Ruby's

arm and helped her and Danny into the carriage.

As they made their way to the cemetery, Ruby was astonished to see so many people had come out to watch them passing. Ruby looked at the back of the crowds. She was searching for Mr Cox. Would he be here? Had he seen it in the newspapers?

At last it was all over and they were back at the Royal Albert. It had been so bitterly cold as they stood at the graveside. The wind had gone through Ruby's thin coat and her thoughts had gone to Elsie: I hope she's wearing something warm under her long frock.

The lounge bar's welcoming fire roared in the grate, sending out plenty of warmth.

'That vicar gave her a nice send-off,' said one of the customers, warming his behind.

'Yes,' said Mr Thompson. 'Now we've got to find the bastard who put her there.'

His customers now knew why Beth hadn't been behind the bar on Christmas Eve and they were very angry.

'Not heard nothing from the police then?' said the man who was standing with his back to the fire.

'No. But give 'em time.'

Ruby was taken aback at the cold fury in Mr Thompson's voice.

People milled about saying nice things about Beth. Ruby couldn't believe that she had gone for ever. And in a way it was her brother's fault. She looked at him sitting in the far corner. He had cried a lot and Ruby knew he would have to carry this burden for the rest of his life.

A commotion at the door caused all the heads to look up.

'I tell yer we should be 'ere,' someone was shouting.

Ruby couldn't see who it was because of the crowd, but she

did see Mr Thompson, who was the other side of the room and a good head taller than most, stride over to where the person was shouting.

Ruby heard her brother make a funny sound in his throat. She quickly looked round. Tom had gone a pasty white.

'Tom? Tom! What is it?' Ruby looked back towards the door. The crowd had parted. 'Alfie Anderson,' she said, barely above a whisper. 'What's he doing here?'

'I tell you the pub ain't open.' One of the customers was trying to push him out.

'I've got every right to be here.' Elbowing the man to one side, he strutted into the bar.

Len Thompson quickly went over to him. 'Out.' He took hold of Alfie's collar and began manhandling him towards the door.

A silence fell over everybody save for a quiet muttering from Mrs Moss. 'Ought ter be ashamed of hisself, coming barging in like that, on terday of all days. Got no manners, that's the trouble with some people.'

Alfie was struggling to get away, but he was no match for Len Thompson. 'Get your hands off me,' he yelled out.

'If you don't get out I'll have to do something I might regret.'

'I don't think you will when you find out who I am.'

'So, who are you then?'

'Lizzie Anderson's brother,' he said softly.

Mr Thompson quickly glanced round the bar and let go of him as if he were a hot coal.

'That's better.' Alfie shook himself and brushed himself down. After retrieving his cap from the floor, he put it on at a jaunty angle. 'Thought that'd git your attention.'

'What do you know about my Beth?' hissed Mr Thompson.

Alfie smirked.

Once again Len Thompson was filled with anger. 'If you've just come here for a free drink and food you can think again.' He swiftly moved towards Alfie, who hastily stepped back.

Alfie knew he had this bloke where he wanted him and said out loud, 'Lizzie was me sister. When she got up the spout me dad chucked 'er out. Wouldn't say who did it.'

The silence in the bar was complete.

'It took a while to put two and two together at first. But when everybody started ter say who she was and where she lived, and then about the boy, well, we got there in the end.' A look of triumph filled Alfie's face.

Ruby's heart went out to Mr Thompson, whose face had turned ashen. He stood looking at this intruder.

'How can I believe you?' he said in a hushed tone.

'Come and see me mum. She's ever so upset. She would have liked to come and see Lizzie but Lizzie wouldn't have anythink to do with us. I tried once to make her come and see Mum, but she wasn't 'aving any of it.'

'How do I know you're telling the truth?'

Alfie picked up a sandwich. 'You don't. Me brother and sisters will tell you all about our Lizzie. Thought she was better than us. Especially when she landed you.'

Ruby wanted to hit him. How could he say things like that?

Mrs Moss suddenly jumped to her feet. 'Look, go out in the back room,' she said, ushering Mr Thompson and Alfie through the bar.

Milly also jumped up. 'Mr Jenkins,' she said. 'Get everybody a drink.'

The mumbling became very loud and Ruby followed Alfie and Mr Thompson through the back of the bar. Why hadn't he thrown Alfie out? Did he know something about Beth's past? What had Beth told him?

★ ★ ★

Outside the church Elsie was looking anxiously around for Ruby when she suddenly caught sight of Ernie. She gave him a wave. Why wasn't Ruby with him? Perhaps she'd missed her, after all there were a lot of people there. When they got back to the house she tried to look again but it was very crowded. Elsie was about to check upstairs, when: 'All right, my love?' asked Charlie, following her.

'I've been looking for Ruby and Ernie.'

'I expect they're around somewhere. You look so lovely. I can't wait to get you home.'

Elsie giggled. 'I am home.'

'Not any more.' He sat on the bottom step and patted the stairs, Elsie sat down with him.

'I do love you, Charlie.'

'And I love you. You're all mine now, you belong to me.' He nuzzled his lips against her neck.

'Charlie, don't. You're making me come over all unnecessary.'

'Good.'

'I've been looking for me frock,' said Jenny, Elsie's older sister, as she leaned over the banister. 'I can't see it. Ain't your mate turned up?'

'I've not seen her, but she must be here, I saw her boyfriend outside the church.'

'P'r'aps they've run off together. Pity, I'd like to see what sort of job she made of me frock. If she was any good I might get her to do some alterations for me. And, Charlie, you'll have to wait till you get home before you start having your wicked way with my little sister.' Jenny walked off laughing.

Charlie put his arm round Elsie's waist. 'Don't look so worried, she must be here somewhere.'

'I'm surprised at Ruby. I would have thought she would have come and seen me.'

'Could she get time off from work?'

Elsie clapped her hand to her mouth. 'I've been so stupid. I thought they might have got today off, seeing as how it was New Year's Eve. I thought at least old Watson would have let them go early. Poor Ruby. She's been so looking forward to this.'

'Don't worry. She'll turn up.'

'She don't know where I live.'

'With all this racket going on, somebody will tell her. Now come on, give us a kiss.'

Elsie laughed. 'Well, only one.'

Charlie kissed her eager lips.

'Come on, let's go and join the others.' She stood up and pulled Charlie to his feet.

By the time evening came, Elsie was truly worried. Where was Ruby? Elsie hoped she'd find her house after she had gone to so much trouble with that frock. Something was troubling Elsie, but she couldn't put her finger on it. Was it something she'd heard? Please God, she prayed, don't let anything have happened to her. She's had more than enough to put up with in her young life.

Earlier Ernie had stood around waiting for Ruby to appear. He had a great deal to tell her. So much had happened since they last spoke. That morning he had looked again at the letter that had arrived last week. He still couldn't believe it: they never received letters. In one hand he had clutched the letter and, in the other, pound notes. He and his mother had discussed the contents of the letter all yesterday evening, and at breakfast he'd asked her once more: 'Are you sure this is what you want?'

She'd nodded. 'I always did like Richard. He was very kind.'

'So he couldn't get down to see us cos of the bad weather.

You sure that ain't just a excuse?'

'No, he's not like that.'

'How do you know?'

'From when I met him at the wedding. I loved your father very much, and he loved me enough to give up his family. But he always missed his young brother.'

'I still don't know why they didn't like you.'

'It's because I came from London and wasn't a Scottish lassie. The family had very strong loyalties over that.'

As a child Ernie had listened to the stories about the family in Scotland. There was a family home his father had lived in before he came – but not a grand castle or anything. His father had told him he'd always wanted to travel, to see the world, but then he'd met Jess and married her. His mother and father had been comfortable, as he always put it. Ernie didn't know at the time what comfortable meant, or why they never went to see his grandparents. 'So they cut him right off?'

'Yes. As the years went on, from time to time Richard kept in touch with your father, and he was very upset when he was killed.'

'Did they know about us?'

'Yes.'

'But they didn't think to help you after Dad got killed, did they?'

His mother bowed her head. 'No, they didn't, but Mr Wallis died soon after your father. Richard reckons it was from remorse.'

'So now my grandmother's dead this Richard wants us all to go up there to the family house?'

'Yes.'

'Will you marry him?'

'I shouldn't think so for one moment. I can't ever see any

other man filling your father's shoes.'

'But what if you don't like him?'

'I think I will. Your father was very fond of him.'

Ernie was at his wits' end. How could he explain to his mother how he felt?

'It will be a lovely home for you and the girls, but I'm not going.'

'What? Why?'

'Well, for a start, what job will there be for me?'

'I'm sure Richard will find something for you.'

'No thanks.'

'But why not? You will be away from all this poverty you're always going on about. There'll be no more taking people's washing to the laundry. And I won't have to skimp and scrape.' Tears began to roll down her cheeks. 'Please, Ernest,' she said, holding his hand. 'Please say you'll come. As you can see, Richard has even sent our fare.'

Ernie put the money on the table. 'I'm sorry, Mum, I can't.'

'Why not? What could keep you here?'

'I'll stay here and look after Daisy. She'll want somewhere to come home to on her day off.'

'She's coming with me and the girls. As far as I can see, it's only you that's the fly in the ointment. And I can't think of any reason why.'

He knew his mother was getting cross with him. 'You don't have to worry about me. I'll be able to make me own way down here. I don't want handouts from people I don't even know.' Ernie was also beginning to get angry. 'I reckon he only wants you up there to be a glorified cook and housekeeper.'

'Is that such a bad thing?'

Ernie couldn't actually argue with that. 'Look, I've got to go out.'

'Is it because you've found someone?'

He didn't answer.

'Ernest, you're young. A good-looking lad like you, you'll soon find someone.'

'I've got to go.'

'What if we don't go?'

Ernie felt the rug had been pulled from under him. 'So it's me that could be stopping you from this better life?'

His mother looked down.

'Please, don't let me stop you.'

'Where will you live?'

'I'll manage. Don't forget I'll be late tonight.'

'How will you pay the rent?'

'Something will turn up.'

'Think about this carefully, love. This could be a whole new start for you. Besides, me and the girls want you to come with us.'

He didn't know what else to say to convince her. Later he would talk to Ruby about it. He would tell her how he felt at last.

'Mum. Mum,' shouted Eve, the youngest sister. 'Me and Rosie are going to look at that funeral, you know, that girl what got murdered.'

'All right. But you be careful. They still ain't caught the bloke what did it.'

'You coming, Ernie?' asked Eve.

'No, I've got better things to do than standing gawping at a funeral.'

'They say it's gonner be ever so grand.'

But Ernie had to get ready to meet Ruby at the church. His mind churned over and over. He loved Ruby, but did she love him? Surely she wouldn't go with him to Scotland? She would never leave her father and brother. But could they have a better life up there together? No more living from hand to mouth?

He left the slum of a house he called home and as he walked along the road he stopped and took note of his surroundings. He began to whistle. Although they were both young, if he could persuade Ruby to come with him, soon it could be them who were walking down the aisle.

Chapter 30

As Ruby walked slowly behind Alfie she noted he was looking eagerly all about him.

'Ain't ever been in the back of a pub before,' he said.

Mr Thompson didn't make any comment.

In the back parlour, with one word, 'Sit,' Mr Thompson indicated with his finger to Alfie to sit down in the armchair, which he did very quickly.

Suddenly Ruby felt out of place and turned to leave.

'No, stay, Ruby, and take a seat.' Ruby also did as she was told.

'Do you know anything about this?' Mr Thompson asked her as he stood with his foot on the brass fender.

Ruby shook her head.

'But I know all about you, Ruby Jenkins,' said Alfie, grinning as he slumped back in the armchair.

'And I know you. I've seen you hanging about the buildings when I took washing back to one of me mum's customers.'

'I know, and me sister told me ter keep away from you and that brother of yours.'

Ruby looked shocked. 'I thought that was Mrs Bell's doing.'

'Na, it was me sister.'

'Just be quiet.' Mr Thompson took a cigarette from a

packet on the mantelpiece and then a wooden spill from a pot. Ruby watched him push it through the bars of the range and when it was well alight, he lit his cigarette with it. 'Now, Ruby, what do you really know about this?' he asked, puffing smoke into the air.

'I told you! I didn't know anything about Beth. She only told us her husband was in the Navy and was away.'

Alfie laughed out loud. 'That sounds like Lizzie. She certainly knew how to spin 'em.'

Ruby glared at him and, turning to Mr Thompson, said softly, 'After a while we guessed it might not be true as she never talked about him and she never had a letter from him, but it didn't matter,' she said hurriedly. 'We didn't care. We liked her.'

Alfie suddenly sat up. 'You know somefink?' he said slyly to Mr Thompson. 'That's why you ain't chucked me out.'

Mr Thompson drew heavily on his cigarette and, pulling a chair from under the table, sat down opposite Alfie and Ruby. 'When Beth first came to stay here she told me she was a widow, but I didn't think that was true. When your father got that job in the Green Man, Beth was very worried. She told me she came from round the buildings and wasn't married. That's all I knew about her, she never said any more, and I wasn't interested in her past. I thought that, once we were married, if she wanted to tell me more, that would be her business.' He threw the cigarette into the fire. 'Then this had to happen.'

For a few moments the only sound was the ticking of the clock.

'I couldn't find her birth certificate, so I put the name I knew her by on the death certificate. Danny's only got the small thrupenny one and the name on that is Norton. So, what is it you want?' he asked Alfie.

'Me mum wanted to know how it happened?'

'She was murdered.'

'So we heard. Who did it?'

'As far as we know, a certain Mr Cox.'

Ruby sat looking at Alfie. She could see now that there was an uncanny likeness between him and Danny. Like Beth, they both had fair hair and bright blue eyes, but more than that, they had exactly the same shaped noses and mouths. Surely Mr Thompson could see it as well?

'D'you know why?'

Mr Thompson looked at Ruby, then shook his head.

'Is he inside?'

'Not yet,' replied Mr Thompson.

'Me mum said she'd like to see the kid. That's why I'm here.'

'That could be arranged.'

'Me mum said, even though there's a few of us at home and me dad ain't at work, she'd be happy to look after the kid.'

'Thank your mother, but that won't be necessary.'

'You don't know who its father is, so who's gonner look after it now?'

Ruby stood up. 'I'll be looking after Danny.'

'How much is he paying yer?' He nodded towards Mr Thompson.

'I'm not doing it for money.'

'I bet. I know how hard up you Jenkinses is.'

'I shall be giving Ruby an allowance.'

'Me mum's better at looking after the kids than she is. 'Sides, we're family. Yer can't keep 'im.'

'And who says so?'

'It's the law.'

'You can't prove her name's Anderson,' said Mr Thompson.

Alfie looked agitated. 'She is, was, me sister. 'Sides, Ruby goes ter work.'

'How do you know?' she quickly asked.

Mr Thompson signalled for Ruby to sit down.

'I know a lot about yer. I used ter meet our Lizzie over the park sometimes.'

'Were you blackmailing her?'

'Come on now, Mr Thompson, that's a nasty word. She used ter give me a few bob now and again fer me mum. So you see we 'ave got some rights.'

'I don't think so, young man. If we don't know who Danny's father is, in the eyes of the law he is an orphan and I shall see about adopting him. He'll have a better upbringing with me.'

Ruby took in a quick breath.

'And we don't know if you're telling the truth about Beth.'

'She never said anything when you was bullying our Tom. Was she ashamed of you?' asked Ruby.

'I think we'd better leave it for now,' said Mr Thompson.

Ruby looked at Mr Thompson. As much as she loved Beth and Danny, she didn't want to spend the rest of her life looking after him. To her this was only a temporary measure.

Mr Thompson stood up. 'Now I think you'd better go. Tell your mother to come here tomorrow afternoon after closing time. I shall then take her up to the Jenkinses' house and she can see Danny. But don't have any ideas about trying to extract money from me.' He left the room.

'You think you're being very clever, don't you, Ruby Jenkins, but you wait. Us Andersons don't like being ridden rough shod over be anybody.' Alfie stood up and moved towards the door. 'And that goes for that wimp of a brother of yours as well. Tell him I know all what he gets up to with that Freddie Porter.'

Ruby watched him leave. Who was Freddie Porter? What did he know about Tom? It must be to do with the money. Ruby was angry. All this trouble was about money and the lack of it. Beth would still be alive if they had had money. 'I must get away from all this. I can't stand much more,' she whispered. But as she went out of the room she asked herself: Where can I go now I have Danny to look after?

As soon as she walked back into the bar Milly and Mrs Moss raced up to her.

'What happened?' asked Milly. 'Was she his sister?'

'Not sure. They want Danny.'

'What?' said Milly and Mrs Moss together.

'They can't do that, can they?' asked Mrs Moss.

'Mr Thompson reckons he's gonner adopt him.'

'Adopt? How can he?'

Ruby shrugged.

'What about his father?' asked Milly.

'Well, we can't find out who that was, can we?'

'But who'll look after him?' asked Mrs Moss.

'It looks like me for the moment.'

Mrs Moss pulled herself up to her full five feet. 'Well, I don't like to speak out of turn, but I think it's a lot to ask of you.'

'So do I,' said Milly.

'You're only a girl and you've got all your life in front of you. The last thing you want is a young child to bring up.'

Mrs Moss meant well. How could Ruby tell her she didn't have a lot of choice? That it was because of her brother that Beth was dead?

'Mrs Anderson's coming round tomorrow to see Danny.'

Milly could see that Ruby didn't want to discuss this so, looking across the room, she said, 'Mrs Moss, looks like they need those other sandwiches.'

'All right, love.'

As soon as they had walked away, Tom came up to her.

'What did that Alfie Anderson want?'

'Danny.'

'Why?'

'He said Beth was his sister.'

'She wasn't, was she?'

'Don't know.'

'He can't have him, can he?'

'I don't know.' Ruby felt drained. 'Who's Freddie Porter?'

Fear filled Tom's face. 'Who told you about him?'

'Alfie Anderson. So who is he?'

'Just a mate.'

'What's he like?'

'All right.'

'Is he the one who's been leading you astray?'

Danny began crying and Tom started to walk away.

'Just a minute,' called Ruby.

'I think this little 'en needs his bed,' said Mrs Moss, who had come back and picked Danny up out of his pram.

'Yes. I'll be off now.' Ruby looked round the bar; it was six o'clock. Mr Thompson had told his customers that he wasn't opening the pub tonight. Many of the people who had been to the funeral had begun to leave. 'You coming, Dad?'

'No. I'm staying to give Len here a hand.'

Milly gave Ruby a smile. 'I'll walk with you.'

'What about you, Tom?'

'I'll stay with Dad.'

'Milly,' said Ruby as she pushed the pram through the doors and out into the cold night air, 'd'you think it would be wrong? As it's not very late, d'you think Beth would mind if I went to the wedding?'

'I think she'd be tickled pink. You go and enjoy yourself. And wear that lovely frock. It'll be a nice change for you.'

'But what about Danny?'

'I'll take him over to our place.'

'Would your mum and dad mind?'

'No, course not. Besides, he's a dear little chap.'

'Thanks.' Although part of her was very sad, she was pleased she'd be seeing Ernie and Elsie. She had so much to tell them.

Outside it was very dark. The hissing from the street's gas lamps and foghorns from the river made the dank, damp night feel eerie.

'I only hope that fire's stayed in,' said Ruby as she pushed the large bassinet along the empty street. 'It can be freezing at home.'

When they turned into Hill Street Milly put out her hand to stop Ruby.

'Look. The lamp upstairs in Cox's place is alight.'

Ruby felt her stomach churn. She felt sick. 'He must be home,' she said softly.

'Shall I go back and get Mr Thompson?'

'No,' said Ruby forcefully. 'What if he tried to kill him or something?'

'Yes, you could be right, he's that angry. But what we gonner do?'

Ruby was pleased Milly had said 'we', she didn't want to confront him alone. 'I don't know.'

'We could go to the police station?'

'He might be gone be the time we got back.'

'That's true.'

They stood for a while looking up at the window.

'I'll go and get me dad.' Milly left Ruby standing.

It was only a short while before Milly's mum and dad came

out, but Ruby was freezing cold and had been banging her hands and feet to keep warm.

'Has he come out?' asked Milly's mum.

'No. I must go in.'

'D'you know you've got a dew drop hanging from the end of your nose,' said Milly light-heartedly.

'So would you if you'd been standing about here.'

'Now, girl, come on. We've got to think of something.' Milly's dad was a businessman and he was trying to be practical.

'What we gonner do?' asked Ruby.

'Let's get in first. He might come down when he hears us.'

'What will he say about his door?' Ruby manoeuvred the large pram up to the front door. She took the key from the shelf and opened the door.

They all stood in the passage looking up the stairs. Ruby could hear him moving about.

Milly's dad slammed the front door and they waited for a reaction.

'Who is it?' came a voice from upstairs.

Ruby looked at Milly's family. 'That ain't Mr Cox,' she whispered, then called out, 'It's me, Ruby.' Danny stirred and Ruby gently rocked the pram.

One of the policemen who had been before appeared at the top of the stairs. 'Sorry. I should have come down.'

'What are you doing here?' asked Ruby.

'Searching his place.'

'You ain't found him yet?' asked Milly's dad.

'No. But we think he might be in Southend.'

'Southend?' repeated Ruby.

'Yes. We found a bill from a guest house among his things – it appears he was there some time back.'

'He did go away once, but he didn't say where.'

'Does this mean you'll be arresting him shortly?' asked Milly's dad.

'We do want to question him.'

'How did you get in?' asked Ruby.

'We just felt around for the key. We knew you were at the funeral and we hoped we'd be gone before you got back, that way you'd be none the wiser. Everything's just as he left it, except the door of course.'

'What if he gets back before you get the chance to nab him?' asked Milly's dad.

'Don't worry, we'll catch him. He might not even know he's wanted for questioning about Mrs Norton's murder.'

'I bet he does. He reads the papers. Come on, missus. Let's get home.' Milly's dad looked in the pram. 'He's a bonny lad.'

'Don't you dare wake him,' said his wife. 'This poor girl needs all the rest she can get.'

The policeman and Milly's parents left. Ruby silently closed the door behind them.

'Come on, we'll see if this fire's still alight, then I'll make you a cuppa.'

'Thanks, Milly. I wonder how the wedding went, and if Ernie missed me?'

'You'll have a chance to find out soon.'

'I don't know if I should go.'

'Now come on. No second thoughts. You like Ernie, don't you?'

Ruby nodded. 'Yes I do.' But the thought that was going round her mind was: Would he want her now she had Danny to look after?

Milly must have read her thoughts as she said, 'Did Mr Thompson say what arrangements he was going to make for the boy's future?'

Ruby shook her head. 'Not really.'

'I suppose it's early days yet, but he can't expect you to look after him for ever, surely.'

'I don't know.'

'It's been a long day for you. You go and get ready.'

'Thanks. But I'm still not sure.'

'*Go!*' said Milly forcefully.

Milly gasped when Ruby walked back into the kitchen. 'You look really lovely. You certainly made a good job of that frock.'

Ruby smiled and twirled round. 'Now, you're sure it'll be all right? Dad and Tom shouldn't be that long.'

'Do I have to throw you out?'

'No. I'm going.' Ruby put on her coat and hat.

As they went along the passage Ruby looked in the pram. 'Good night, little 'en.' She kissed her fingers and placed them for a moment or two on Danny's forehead. Milly stood at the door and watched her hurrying along the road. She reflected on all that had happened to this young girl. She deserved much more than life had thrown at her. After Ruby left Milly quietly closed the front door behind her. She'd wait till Mr Jenkins and Tom returned. She wanted to be alone with her thoughts.

As Ernie made his way home he found that although he was worried, he was also angry. He went over the day. Earlier, before the ceremony, he had wandered around outside the church looking for Ruby. Slowly the congregation had begun to move inside, and he'd wondered if Ruby had gone inside already? Should he go in and look? He hadn't liked the idea of going in alone and she had said she would meet him outside. He hadn't been to church since going with his mother after his father had died. She'd said she felt she should pray even if she didn't have a body to bury. Ernie stamped his feet to bring life back into them. It was very cold. Had she gone in to escape the cold wind? He didn't know what to do. When Elsie and the bridesmaids arrived, Elsie had caught sight of him and had given him a little wave. Half an hour later everybody came out. There was much laughter and noise, but still no sign of Ruby. Ernie stood back as Elsie called for different members of the family and friends to join her and her new husband for the photographs. Gradually the crowd began to make their way to Elsie's house, and Ernie had followed at a safe distance. Inside the house was very crowded, but no Ruby. Had she changed her mind? After an hour or so, with his hands deep in his pockets to keep warm, he left the party. Why hadn't Ruby turned up? Something must have happened. Could it be her father? He was so unpredictable. She'd been so looking forward to this wedding it must have been something terrible to keep her away. It was then that he realised she might have had to go to work till four, but she would have made it to the house by now. If that was the case, should he go back? He would have a word with Mrs Watson about keeping his girlfriend working so hard. He smiled, he knew Mrs Watson was fond of him in a motherly way. She had told him how she wished she'd had a son. Should he have stayed at Elsie's house and waited for her there? But he didn't know Elsie that well and had felt like an intruder; besides, it wasn't the same without Ruby at his side.

As slowly he walked alone, he wondered about going to her house; he knew where she lived. But what if she didn't want to see him? Had she known she'd have to work today and this was a way of putting him off? His mind was in such turmoil. Should he hang about and see if she turned up? There was so much he had to tell her. He really did love her. He wanted to be with her. But could they have a future together?

Chapter 31

As Ruby hurried along the road to the church, part of her was sad, but she was determined she wasn't going to let it show, and she certainly wasn't going to tell Elsie where she had been today. She didn't want to spoil her friend's day. Ruby knew that this could be the most wonderful evening of her life. She felt grown up and although she was cold in the flimsy frock, she was burning with excitement. She was going to see Ernie and for the first time he would see her looking nice, except for her boots. She would have loved to have been able to buy a pair of fancy shoes, but it wasn't to be. Ruby remembered Elsie telling her that her house was near the church. She was pretty certain she'd be able to find it, and, sure enough, when she heard the sound of a piano and singing and lots of laughter, she knew she was at the right place.

The front door was on the latch and she pushed it open to make her way inside.

'Ruby!' screamed Elsie, throwing her arms round her friend. 'I was so worried you might not make it. Let me look at you.' Elsie took her coat and held her at arm's length. 'You look really lovely.'

Ruby blushed. 'Thank you. And what about you? That's a really wonderful frock. You look like a princess. Oh Elsie, I'm so happy for you.' She kissed her friend's cheek.

'I am pleased with it.'

'Turn round. It's gorgeous. I love the way the satin clings.' Ruby knew the frock must have cost at least a couple of pounds.

Elsie ran her hands over her slim hips. 'I feel ever so grand. Ain't had nothing like this before, that's why I don't wonner take it off. Come on,' she said. 'Come and meet my husband.' She giggled as she grabbed Ruby's hand and led her through the crowd. 'Charlie. Charlie,' she called, and a tall good-looking man turned and smiled. 'This is Ruby, my bestest mate, after you of course.'

'Hello, Ruby. I've heard a lot about you.' He kissed her cheek.

Ruby could see why Elsie had fallen for this man.

'I ain't seen Ernie since we got back,' said Elsie.

'Was he at the church?'

'Yes. He should be here somewhere, but you might have a job finding him in this crush. Try the kitchen, usually the blokes like to hang round the booze.'

After the introductions to her husband and her sisters, Elsie said she had to mingle.

Ruby had been scanning the rooms looking for Ernie, but she wasn't having any luck. After a while she sat on the stairs. She was enjoying watching people coming and going. The singing and the laughter got louder as the drink was being consumed and she smiled at the stolen kisses being enjoyed by many and wished she was sitting here with Ernie.

When Jenny, Elsie's sister, sat next to her, Ruby quickly hid her shabby boots under her frock.

'You've made a wonderful job of altering this.' Jenny picked up the hem.

'I hope you didn't mind.'

'No. As you can see I've got a bit large for it. If I ever get slim again and need any alterations, do you think you could do 'em for me?'

'I'd love to. I'll try to put this back as it was.'

'Na. Don't bother. You can keep it.'

'Are you sure?'

Jenny patted Ruby's knee and stood up. 'It looks far better on you than it ever did on me.'

The noise was ever increasing and Ruby began to feel hot and bothered. She wanted Ernie to be here. Why hadn't he stayed? Most people were in couples and she felt a bit out of place. When the bride and groom made their rowdy exit, Ruby too decided it was time to leave.

As it was Sunday Ruby didn't have to get up too early. Once she woke, she lay thinking about the previous day. How could so much happen in one day? She knew Danny and Tom were fast asleep, as in the dark she could hear their steady breathing. She would remember the wedding for ever. The laughter, the dancing. She had had a good time, but it would have been a hundred times better if Ernie had been there. Oh, *why* hadn't he stayed?

Danny let out a little sigh and her thoughts went to Beth. Beth's death was going to turn their lives upside down, but at the moment it was Tom that was causing Ruby the most worry. Yesterday every time she'd looked at him he'd been scared and busy biting his fingernails. She knew he blamed himself for this mess. So who was this Freddie Porter Alfie had spoken about? Tom didn't seem that eager to talk about him. Was he the one that had led Tom astray? She *must* concentrate more on his needs. Tom *must* go to school, whatever the cost. But she would wait till they were alone before she said anything.

Danny's cot was under the window. He still hadn't stirred. So much had happened in his short life. The house smelt of baby now. Beth had bought him lovely things, soap and creams she had never seen before. Mr Thompson said he would give her money to buy all the things Danny needed. Once again his large pram stood in the passage. Fear suddenly gripped her. Where would they live if Mr Cox went to prison? Her mind was flitting from one thing to another: next it went to Elsie. I hope everything goes well for you, she said silently. And what about Ernie? It would have been wonderful to have spent the evening with him. As she mused on all the day's joy, sadness, tears and laughter, Ruby buried her head in her pillow and cried softly to herself.

At four o'clock Ruby answered the door to Mr Thompson and Mrs Anderson. Ruby guessed she was wearing her best hat and had tried to look as smart as her circumstances allowed. Alfie was close behind.

'Come in.' Ruby stood to one side as they went down the passage.

'Hat,' Mrs Anderson barked at her son.

Alfie snatched the cloth cap off his head.

'Nice pram,' commented Mrs Anderson, running her fingers along the handle.

The kitchen door was open and they could see Danny sitting on Thomas Jenkins's lap.

'He looks a bonny lad,' said Mrs Anderson, going over to him. 'My Lizzie was bonny, and the spitting image of him.' She touched his head. 'I was very upset when I heard about what happened to my Lizzie. I hope they catch the bastard what done it – how could anybody do such a terrible thing? To murder a young girl.' She sniffed very loudly.

'Don't worry, Mum, he'll be taken care of.'

'It ain't my fault she wouldn't have anythink to do with us, it was her father, you see. He chucked her out when he found she was having a baby. She wouldn't tell us who his father was. Now he's sorry, but I told him, he's gotter live with that on his conscience.' She sniffed again and, taking a piece of rag from her tatty handbag, blew her nose hard.

'Don't upset yerself, Mum. I'm sure Ruby 'ere will let you come and see your grandson now you know where he is.'

She dabbed at her eyes. 'You do understand. I loved me daughter.'

Ruby quickly looked at Mr Thompson. She felt sorry for this woman who might have lost her daughter.

'I'm sure you did. Don't worry, we can make some arrangements,' he said kindly.

Mrs Anderson smiled. 'P'r'aps sometime I could take him fer a walk, or take him back home to see the other kids?'

'I don't know,' said Ruby. 'It ain't up to me.'

'Can I hold him?' She took Danny from Thomas and sat with him on her knee. 'He's a big boy.' She kissed his head. 'He'll be all right with us. The kids'll love him. And I could have him to sleep some nights if you wonner go out. It will be difficult for a young girl like you to have your own life and to look after a toddler. They get up to all sorts, you know.'

Again Ruby looked at Mr Thompson, searching silently for answers.

'What about your husband?' asked Ruby. She didn't want this woman to take Danny.

'I won't tell him it's Lizzie's. When he's tanked up he won't notice another kid in the place,' she laughed. 'He might think it's one he forgot about.'

Ruby was horrified.

'As I said,' said Mr Thompson quietly, 'it's early days yet.

It'll take us a little while to get things under control. I might get someone to help Ruby.'

'I could do that,' said Mrs Anderson quickly. 'I could come round and help her.'

'What about your family?' said Ruby, looking from one to the other.

Mrs Anderson then let everything slip. 'My lot are old and bloody ugly enough to look after themselves. They can't expect me to be pussyfooting round 'em all the bloody time.'

'Mum,' said Alfie. 'Watch it.'

'Oh yes. Sorry.'

'I have to go,' said Mr Thompson. 'And I think we should leave the little lad, he looks tired.'

'Yes. Well, all right then. Don't wonner outstay me welcome.' Mrs Anderson gave them all a big smile.

'I've got to be going as well so I'll see them out,' said Mr Thompson.

'You ain't letting her have him, are you?' asked Tom as soon as they were out of earshot. He was clearly agitated.

'I should say not.' Their father was on his feet. 'Don't worry, love. I won't let any of them get anywhere near him.'

Ruby picked Danny up and held him close. Whatever the outcome now, she knew that Danny would never go and live with the Andersons, even if they did keep saying Beth was one of them.

At six o'clock Thomas Jenkins put his coat on.

'Where're you going, Dad?' asked Ruby.

'To work.'

Ruby tried to keep her excitement under control. In the midst of all their troubles, she'd also been terribly concerned about her dad's job. 'But it's Sunday, you don't work on Sundays.'

'I know. I've got a lot of explaining to do. If George wants me to stop I may be late, so don't wait up for me.'

Ruby kissed his cheek. 'See you later.' Then she got Danny ready for bed. She put him in his cot, kissed her fingers and touched his forehead. 'Goodnight,' she whispered. As she closed the bedroom door there was a soft knock on the front door. She started. Every knock brought fear to the surface. But Mr Cox wouldn't knock; he knew where the key was. She opened the door.

'Ernie.' She wanted to throw her arms round his neck. She wanted to smother him with kisses. But all she could manage to say was, 'What are you doing here?'

'I wondered if everything was all right. When you didn't come to the wedding yesterday I thought something was wrong. Then I realised you might have had to work. Anyway, I was going to leave it till in the week and try and catch you at the laundry, but either I'm in a hurry to get some old dear's washing back to her, or I somehow seem to miss you on these dark nights, so here I am.'

Ruby's heart soared. He cared. He was worried about her. 'Come in. I didn't know you knew my address.'

'I remembered Tom telling us you had to move from up the road.' He lowered his head. 'I thought it served you right at the time. You know you was always stuck up.'

'Got nothing to be stuck up about now, have we?'

As he pushed past the pram he asked, 'This is nice, who does it belong to? It's too good to collect washing and wood in.'

'It's Danny's.'

'Who's Danny?'

'You don't know, do you?' she said softly as they moved into the kitchen.

'Know what?'

350

'You'd better sit down, I've got a lot to tell you.'

'I'm going to bed,' said Tom. He didn't want to listen to it all over again. It made him feel ill just thinking about it.

'I couldn't get to the church, but I went to Elsie's house in the evening, but you wasn't there.'

'Damn. If only I'd stayed a bit longer. But I didn't like hanging about, I didn't really know anybody and it looked as if I was just there for the free handouts.'

'Elsie wouldn't have thought that.'

'Maybe not, but that's how I felt.'

That was very sensitive of him: yet another reason, Ruby realised, why she loved him so much.

'You can sling your hook,' were the first words that greeted Thomas Jenkins when he walked into the Green Man.

Thomas stood at the door looking bewildered.

'You've got a bloody cheek walking your arse in here tonight after leaving me in the lurch all over Christmas and the New Year.' George was wiping down the bar.

'A lot's happened.'

'I bet it has. You been away with that old tom? She ain't shown her face in here either.'

'You mean Mrs Bell? Ain't she been in?'

'Thought you would have known that, so sling your hook. 'Sides, I don't ask you to work Sundays.'

'I know. But please, let me explain.'

'I was good to you, Thomas.' George pointed the dirty cloth at him. 'And you let me down. Now get out before me missus sees you. She had to work down here and she ain't that happy about it.'

'I ain't going till you hear what happened.' Thomas stood with his foot on the brass rail and felt very confident.

'Come on then, tell us what was so important.'

George stood open-mouthed as Thomas went into all the details.

'What can I say? I saw that in the papers. They said it was the girl from the pub, but I'd no idea your lad was involved. And you say your daughter – that the one what come here?'

Thomas nodded. 'I've only got the one.'

'She's looking after the girl's baby?'

'She has to go to work so me and me boy will have him all day.'

George poured out two generous whiskies and handed one to Thomas. 'Well, I'll be buggered. I reckon you've had more than enough on your plate. No wonder you didn't come in. Now, you sure you want to stay?'

'Yes, that's if you want me to.'

'Why not?'

'Evenings is all right, Ruby looks after the lad.'

'It must be bloody hard for you knowing you was living with a murderer. And you say you don't know why he did it?'

Thomas only shook his head.

'Ain't they caught the bastard yet then?'

'No. I'm worried that me lad might have to give evidence.'

'That could be upsetting for him.'

'Yes. So have I still got a job?'

George put his thick arm round Thomas's shoulder. 'I should say so.'

Ernie sat listening to Ruby in horror. He couldn't believe what he was hearing. He wanted to hold her, cover her sad face with kisses. Try to make everything better for her. He had wanted to take her away, but now she had this baby to look after any thoughts he might have had of taking up his uncle's offer had to be thrown away. Would his uncle want another mouth to feed? Would Ruby want to take the baby all that way? And would this Mr Thompson let her? There were so many things going round in his head, he couldn't think straight. 'My sisters went to see that funeral,' was all he managed to say.

'A lot of people did.'

'What's going to happen now?'

'I don't know.'

He ran his fingers through his dark hair. 'I guessed something must have stopped you yesterday. At first I thought it might have been your dad. Then I wondered if they'd made you work till four as usual on Sat'day.'

'I think they were going at lunchtime, but Mrs Watson let me have all the morning off as I had to help Mr Thompson.'

'I'd heard the girl from the pub had been murdered. Me sisters knew all about it but I didn't take a lot of notice, you know how they babble on. I had no idea it was anything to do with you.'

Ruby smiled at him. 'Well, you wouldn't. You didn't know Beth was Elizabeth Norton or that she'd lived here. There wasn't much about it in the papers. It's the Irish problem that's taking up most of the news, I'm glad to say. Don't want everybody coming round here having a nose.'

'It's going to be hard for you looking after a baby.'

'We'll manage. Elsie looked really nice, didn't she?'

'Yes, she did.' As he smiled, remembering the joy on the bride's face, his serious expression was dispelled. Ruby could feel the love she had for him brimming to the surface.

'Ruby, is there any chance of a cuppa?'

'Course.'

'Why did Cox hit Beth?'

'Don't know,' said Ruby as she took the kettle from the hob. 'How's your sister getting on in her new job?'

'She didn't start.'

'Why was that?'

'We had a surprise after Christmas.' He watched Ruby put the cups on the table. 'We had another letter from me uncle in Scotland. He wrote again instead of coming to visit.'

'That's pretty unusual.'

'I should say so.' Ernie played with the spoon in the sugar bowl. 'It seems me grandma's dead and he wants us all to go and live up there.'

Ruby dropped the tea strainer onto the cup with a clatter. In those few seconds she knew that any hope she had of them being together had just been crushed. 'Are you going?' she asked softly, dreading the answer.

'I told me mum I wasn't, but I don't know. Me mum said she'll worry about me being on me own. If we go it'll mean she won't have any more money worries and she'll have a nice house to live in. He's even sent us the fare.'

Ruby could feel her dreams slipping further and further away.

'Trouble is, if I don't go I won't have anywhere to live. I reckon our landlord would 'ave me out of those rooms as quick as blinking so's he can get more rent. Then there's a job. Things are as hard as ever for blokes at the moment.'

Ruby silently pushed his tea in front of him. 'Will there be work for you at your uncle's?'

'He seems to think so.'

'It's a long way away.'

'I know.'

'I bet Mrs Watson will be sorry to see you go.'

'Why? What makes you say that?'

'Well, if she wants an escort again, you won't be here.'

He laughed. 'There's a lot more than that I've got to think about.' He took a deep breath. He had to say it. 'Ruby, would you come with me?'

She closed her eyes. She wanted to pinch herself. Ernie Wallis was asking her to go away with him. 'But I can't,' was all she could say.

'I know it's a bit awkward at the moment. Just think about it.'

'I can't. I've got Danny now. And me dad and Tom.'

'I know I've sprung this on you, but *please* don't just say no. I want you to come with me. I want us to be together. I'm sure we could make a go of it. I ain't got nothing to offer you if I stay round here.'

Ruby felt her knees buckle under her. He must love her. He wanted to be with her. She sat down. Oh, this was so unfair. 'I'm sorry, Ernie. Besides, where would we get the fare from?'

'I'd ask me uncle.'

'Shouldn't think he'd fork out for my family to move in with him.'

There was a long silence. 'I suppose, thinking about it, it is a bit daft.' He finished his tea and stood up. 'I'd better be going.'

'When are you going to Scotland?'

'Not sure.' He picked his cap from off his chair. 'It'll be up to me mum, but I think it might be soon.' He opened the kitchen door. 'I don't want to go, but I ain't got a lot of choice. No work, no home, nothing.' His voice was bleak.

Ruby walked up the passage with him. She wanted to hold him back, tell him her feelings for him and how much she wanted to be with him, but it wouldn't be fair to land him with her family and Danny.

'You will let me know your plans, won't you?' She tried to sound calm.

'Course.'

At the door he held her in his arms. 'Perhaps something will work out.' He kissed her lips, then strode away.

Ruby wanted to cry, she was so happy and sad at the same time. She gently touched her lips, remembering the feel of his on hers. Scotland, a new life, no money worries: it sounded wonderful. But was it just another dream destined never to be fulfilled?

Chapter 32

When Thomas went to work that Sunday, most of the customers were hostile towards him at first, but when George told them what had happened they were like ghouls hanging on his every word, asking questions about Cox and telling him what they would do if they caught him.

Although it upset Thomas in some ways he was pleased at being the centre of the conversation.

During a busy evening the following Saturday, Thomas found a moment to roll himself a cigarette. As he wiped down the bar he glanced up at the clock. It was ten o'clock. The door opened and, with a lot of giggling, Mrs Bell walked in on the arm of a man Thomas knew wasn't a regular. She looked wonderful as she sauntered into the pub in a tight-fitting black coat with the large fur collar turned up framing her face. On her head she was wearing a silly little tight-fitting black hat. Thomas felt his heart take a little leap when she stopped and, parting her red-painted lips, smiled at him. He knew he shouldn't feel like this. But he also knew that deep down this was one of the reasons he had wanted to come back to work. Was it so wrong that he wanted to see this woman again?

'Thomas,' she beamed, coming up to the bar and blowing him a kiss. 'A little bird told me you've been a naughty boy and haven't been to work. I understand that George here was very upset about it, so where have you been hiding?'

Once again the story was repeated while drinks were being served and the conversation was interspersed with 'Oh my God', and 'How awful' from Mrs Bell.

There were lots of titters, bawdy remarks and laughing from the men as they watched Mrs Bell acting in such a theatrical way.

'It ain't funny,' she said, turning on them. Then, 'My poor darling,' she added, grinding her cigarette in the overflowing ashtray. 'You've had a terrible time. And where is the Christmas present I gave you?' she asked, looking at his cuffs.

Thomas was suddenly filled with remorse. He had pawned the cufflinks, but with everything that had happened over Christmas he had forgotten to give Ruby and Tom the presents he had bought them. 'I don't like wearing them at work, they look too expensive.'

She smiled and tapped the back of his hand. 'I can see you know the difference between the good and the rubbish.'

Thomas smiled back. He was very grateful to Mrs Bell for enabling him to buy nice presents for Tom and Ruby and couldn't wait now to give Tom the mouth organ and Ruby the locket. He knew it had been extravagant and the money should have been spent on other things, but those kids had gone without long enough. It was money he had never expected to get – and Mrs Bell must never know what he'd done.

Mrs Bell's companion had walked away when she sat at the bar, and throughout the next hour she sat talking to Thomas.

'You wonner watch yerself, Thomas. She'll make mince-meat of yer once she gets yer in her bed,' someone shouted out.

Thomas wanted to disappear.

'Shut it, you lot, you're only jealous,' she called out to the crowd behind her.

All too soon it was closing time and Mrs Bell collected the man she came in with and wished them all goodnight.

'You know you shouldn't have anything to do with her,' said George. 'You know what she does for a living. Well, if you can call it work. I reckon she must lay back and think of England.' He laughed; it was a loud deep guffaw. 'And she's got expensive tastes.'

Thomas polished the glass he was holding with fervour and laughed along with George. He wasn't going to let on he had been to her flat. 'I've got enough worries on me plate without adding to them.' His thoughts went to Mary. She had been a warm and loving wife. All the years he was ill she'd lain by his side and he had taken her whenever each other's need arose. She had been a passionate woman who had enjoyed him. Deep down he knew he could never love like that again, but he would like a woman to hold him once more. Mary. Her very name filled him with guilt that he was having intimate thoughts about another woman. He had been so content to sit back and let her work herself to death. If only she had got angry with him, made him see it was wrong for him to be how he was. But she wasn't like that. He mustn't make the same mistake with Tom and Ruby, he had to face down his fears and be a real father to them. He also knew he would never love another like he'd loved Mary . . . but a woman's touch would be so healing.

That evening Thomas hurried home as soon as he'd finished. Ruby, Tom and Danny were asleep. He took the presents from the cupboard in his bedroom and looked at them. For the first time in years he was giving them a surprise. It should have been something more practical, like a shirt for Tom and boots for Ruby, but he didn't care about being practical. He had some paper and wrapped the presents. He couldn't wait till morning.

Thomas was up well before Ruby and had the fire going and the kettle boiling when she walked into the kitchen with Danny on her hip. He looked at her; she'd had to grow up quickly. Suddenly she was a beautiful young lady. 'Good morning,' he said cheerfully. 'Tea's made.'

'Dad! I didn't hear you come in last night.'

'I'm not surprised. The hours you work, you must be exhausted be the time you get to bed. Sit down, I'll pour out your tea.'

She put Danny on the floor and sat at the table. 'What's this?' She picked up the small parcel and felt it.

'It's a late Christmas present.'

'A Christmas present?' She looked up at her father, her big brown eyes full of love.

'With all what happened it went right out of my head. That one's for Tom. Now don't you go telling me off for being silly and extravagant: I know I should have bought something more sensible.'

'Where did you get the money from?'

'I didn't pinch it. I had a bit of luck at work and I thought you both deserved some spoiling.'

'But . . .' Ruby suddenly put her hand to her mouth. 'I forgot as well.' She jumped up and rummaged in the dresser cupboard. 'Ugh,' she said as her fingers went through the silver paper and into the oranges that had gone mouldy. 'These were for you and Tom. And I've got a teddy bear for Danny.'

Her father laughed. 'He'll like that. Ain't you gonner open your present?'

'Can I wait till Tom gets up?'

'Of course. Come here,' said her father.

Ruby went to him and he held her tight. She felt happy and secure. It was years since her father had inspired such trust in her. 'I did get you a present as well,' she said. 'It ain't much. I'll go and get it.'

In the bedroom Tom watched Ruby manoeuvre herself round the room. 'What you doing?'

'I'm getting your Christmas present.'

He sat up. 'It ain't Christmas,' he said sulkily.

'I know, but with all what happened me and Dad forgot about presents. Come and see what Dad's got you.'

Tom jumped up and pulled on his trousers; he was already wearing his socks and shirt, it was too cold to take everything off at night.

Ruby burst into the kitchen with her precious parcels. 'Here y'are.' She thrust the cigarettes into her father's hand and the book into Tom's.

'Thanks, love.'

'I got you a present as well,' said Tom, standing with his hands behind his back. He brought out a small box. 'These are for you.' He handed his sister the chocolates.

Ruby took them and noted there were tears in Tom's eyes. Had he bought these for Beth?

'You ain't opened my present yet,' said their father.

Ruby couldn't believe her eyes when she saw the lovely silver heart-shaped locket, with a tiny ruby set in the middle, nestling in her hands.

'It's only small, and the ruby ain't real, but I thought it was, well . . . I just couldn't resist it. It was like it was made for you and I just had to get it.'

Ruby couldn't speak.

'Look, it opens. I thought perhaps you could put some-body's hair in it. I couldn't manage to get the chain as well, but one day I will.'

Tears spilt from her eyes. 'Dad, it's lovely.'

They were interrupted with Tom blowing on his mouth organ. He had a huge grin on his face. 'This is great. The best present I've ever had.'

'Make sure you play it outside,' Ruby said laughing as Danny clambered up on her lap trying to see what was going on. She lifted him high in the air and plonked a kiss on his cheek. He waved his teddy bear at her. 'That's all I can give you this year, but who knows what the next one will bring?'

'Ruby, you didn't mind me buying silly things, did you?'

She shook her head. 'I think we all deserve silly things at the moment. And I think we should all have a chocolate for breakfast.'

For the rest of the day everyone was happy. Ruby didn't ask where her father had got the money from for their presents. She knew it wasn't stolen so it didn't matter. And he would tell her one day.

After weeks of laborious sewing Tom was now in his father's room and Ruby had Danny's cot in with her. She was so grateful he was a good baby and didn't keep her awake half the night. She couldn't cope with sleepless nights and work all day.

In the middle of January snow came and tried to settle. It was Saturday and as Ruby left the laundry she put her head down and hurried out of the gate.

'You took your time. I've bin waiting ages for you.' Elsie was standing huddled under the arch outside the laundry.

Ruby ran up to her and hugged her. 'I'm so pleased to see you. How's married life?'

'Great.'

'Can we go to the market for a little while?'

'Don't you have to clean that old boy's place?'

'You don't know, do you?'

'Know what?'

'Let's get out of the cold. I've got a lot to tell you.'

'Sounds interesting. Anything to do with Ernie?'

'No.'

'Well, all right then, but I can't stay long. I have to get the shopping and do the tea for me mum-in-law and husband.'

They hurried to the market and made their way to the café.

Inside it was warm and the windows were steamy. As soon as they settled down with a cup of tea Ruby said, 'Did you read about Elizabeth Norton's murder?'

'Charlie said something about it. That the one that lived in the pub?'

Ruby nodded.

'My Charlie said he reckoned she was on the game and it was one of her punters.'

Ruby sat staring at Elsie. How awful. Did lots of people think that? 'She wasn't like that.'

'Did you know her?'

'Yes. She used to live with us.'

'Oh my God no! The one that had the baby and you thought she was . . . I didn't put two and two together, what with Christmas and the wedding. I didn't take much notice of what Charlie was saying. Was it one of her punters?'

'No! She didn't have punters. It was my landlord.'

Elsie's cup went down on the saucer with a clatter. 'Ruby! What can I say?'

Ruby shrugged. 'Don't know. He hit me brother as well.'

'*No*. Why did he do it?'

Ruby only shrugged again. She didn't want to say too much; she didn't want anyone to know it was through Tom.

'Was it awful?'

Ruby nodded and swallowed hard. It was still very painful to talk about. 'We spent a long while in the hospital and Beth's funeral was on New Year's Eve day. The same time as your wedding.'

Elsie quickly moved round the table and held Ruby close, knocking her hat skew-whiff. 'I'm so sorry. I had no idea. But you came in the evening. Ruby, that was so brave of you and you said nothing about it.'

'I couldn't spoil your day.'

Elsie held her ever closer. 'Thank you for being so thoughtful.'

'That's all right,' Ruby said, coming up for breath and straightening her hat.

Elsie sat down. 'So what's going to happen now?'

'I don't know. The police are still looking for Mr Cox.'

'Do they know where he might have gone?'

'Yes. Southend.'

'Southend?' repeated Elsie. 'What's he doing there?'

'I don't know. But that's enough of my problems.'

'I can't get over what a terrible thing.'

'I really enjoyed myself at your wedding. It was the most wonderful thing I've ever been to.'

'I'm glad. Have you managed to see anything of Ernie?'

Ruby nodded.

'Why didn't he stay?'

'He felt uncomfortable.'

'Daft 'aporth.' Elsie sat back.

'He came to tell me he might be going to Scotland.'

'*What?* Why?'

Ruby told Elsie the story.

'And you can't go?'

Ruby shook her head. 'Don't forget I've got Danny to look after now.'

'Surely that Mr Thompson can't expect you to look after the boy for ever?'

'I don't know. Who else is there? I can't let him go to the Andersons'; besides, Mr Thompson wouldn't let them have him.'

Ruby couldn't tell Elsie that she loved Danny and why she thought it was also her duty to look after him.

'Can he stop them?'

Ruby shrugged. 'I don't know. He's worried that Danny could finish up in an orphanage.'

'No. That would be awful.'

'Mr Thompson was talking about adopting Danny.'

'Can't you find out who the father is?'

Ruby shook her head. 'Mr Thompson has gone through everything, but our cheap birth certificates don't have the father's name on them.'

'That's true, but it's a lot for you to take on. Is he good?'

Ruby gave her a warm smile. 'He's lovely.'

'But not to be going to Scotland with Ernie. That would have been wonderful for you.'

'I know.'

'Poor you. But cheer up. You never know, it might happen – and I'd like to see Ernie in a kilt!'

Ruby laughed. 'I can't remember what his knees looked like.'

'Would you actually go with him if there was a chance?'

Ruby shook her head. 'I wouldn't leave Dad and Tom.'

'No, suppose not.'

They exchanged details about their new lives until Ruby said she had to get home.

As Elsie kissed her goodbye she said, 'Remember, there's always a silver lining somewhere.'

'I hope so,' Ruby said, but at the moment she couldn't see

where. She touched the locket her father had given her; it was on a piece of strong thread and she wore it under her vest. She didn't want anyone to know it was there. Ruby hoped it would be a sort of lucky charm.

At the end of the month Mr Thompson brought Beth's clothes down.

'I'm sure Beth would want you to have these,' he said, putting them on the kitchen table.

'It's very kind of you, but I can't take them.'

'Why not?'

'I don't know. It don't seem right somehow.'

'It's not that I'm getting rid of her. I have many keepsakes: she'll always be part of my life. But I know she would want you to have them.'

Ruby held up a coat, it looked lovely and warm.

'Everything should fit you, you were about the same size.'

'What can I say?'

'There's nothing to say. Ruby, about Danny . . .'

Ruby froze. Was he going to take him away?

'I know it's a lot of work for you and your family. If it gets too much, you will tell me, won't you?'

'Yes, but he's no trouble.'

'Not at the moment. At what age will he be able to start school?'

'He can go when he's four and a half.'

'You've got a couple of years yet then.' He picked up his trilby.

'You wouldn't let him go to Mrs Anderson, would you?'

He twirled his hat round in his hand. 'You can be very sure about that.'

As he left Ruby thought how lucky Beth had been. Len Thompson loved her and her son and was prepared to look after Danny, but for how long? What if another young lady ever came into Mr Thompson's life?

February was cold and wet. Although Ruby was warm in Beth's coat she was very depressed as she hadn't seen Ernie at all. Had he gone away without saying goodbye?

When Ruby got home one evening she found Tom upset. 'What's up with you?'

'Nothing.'

He was now at school and Ruby thought that was the reason he was so down in the mouth. 'I'll help you with any homework you've got. At least school keeps you busy and out of mischief. Where's Dad and Danny?' she asked, taking her hat and coat off. She ran her fingers through her hair.

'Dad's taken him up to see Mr Thompson. He's been there a long while.'

'Oh, right. Shall I make a cuppa?'

'Ruby, the police have been here. They've got Mr Cox.'

'*What?*'

'That's why Dad's up the pub. He's gone to ask what we've got to do. I've got to go as a witness. I don't want to go. I'm frightened.'

Ruby sat down. She had known that this would happen one day. 'I'm sure everything will be all right. Mr Thompson is very clever and he'll help you all he can.'

'But what about the money? Will I go to prison?'

'I can't answer that. I know it's wrong, but I don't think you should tell anyone about the money.'

'But Mr Cox will.'

'Let's wait till Dad gets back, he may have some ideas.' Ruby played with the spoon in the sugar bowl. Things had been getting a little easier for all of them. Although they should be saving the rent money, they had decided, after a lot of discussion, to spend it. Tom was at school; her father was at work and happy. Danny was a good boy and they enjoyed having him. Now this had to happen and all the worries had come flooding back.

Chapter 33

When Ruby heard the key in the lock she hurried to the front door.

'Well, what's going to happen?' she burst out, as soon as she saw her father.

Thomas manoeuvred the pram into the passage. Her father was one of the few men who didn't mind being seen pushing a pram; he happily took it up to the pub to see Len or across the road to Milly's. In fact he was rather proud of it as everybody knew the circumstances and would often stop and talk to him. 'I'll tell you in a mo. Let me get in first.'

Ruby took Danny out of the pram and followed her father into the kitchen.

'You're not to worry, son,' he said to Tom who was looking at him with large frightened eyes. 'Len is going to see about it. He'll try and find out if you can see the magistrate in private and not have to go into the court. I think Len's got a lot of friends in high places.'

'What did the policeman say when he came here?' asked Ruby.

'He just told us that Cox was at the police station and Tom here might be wanted as a witness.'

'Did he say when?'

'No. But they'll let us know.'

'I don't want to go. I don't want to see him, they'll find out it was all my fault.'

'All you've got to do is tell the truth, son.'

'But . . .' He looked at Ruby and his tears fell.

Ruby sat next to her brother and put her arm round his shoulders.

'Why did he hit Beth?' asked Thomas, settling in his armchair and unlacing his boots.

Tom looked at Ruby.

Ruby touched her locket. What could she say? 'Dad, I don't think you want to know.'

'Look, I'm better now, and as his father I should know what went on. What if I get called to the witness stand?'

'Why should you?'

'They might want to know what sort of bloke Cox was.'

Tom ran from the room.

Ruby stood up ready to follow him but her father told her to sit down.

'Len told me he thought Cox might have been . . .' He stopped and silently rolled a cigarette.

Ruby looked nervously at the kitchen door. 'I should go to Tom.'

'I know the old man was always looking at you.'

Ruby's head shot up. 'Who told you that?'

'Your mother. She was worried about it. I was going to have a word with him, but you know how scared she was of losing this place. Mind you, I don't know what's going to happen now Cox won't be around. He's got to have some relation ready to crawl out of the woodwork and lay claim to this property.'

'Mum told you?' said Ruby, ignoring the last part of her father's speech.

'Yes. We did have conversations about you both, you know. I know it seemed we couldn't talk, but we was very close. Ruby, tell me, did he touch Tom, you know, in an over-friendly way?'

'Let me get Tom.'

'All right.'

Ruby banged on the lav door. 'Tom. Tom. Come out. We've got to tell Dad the truth.'

Tom opened the door. 'I can't.'

'I think you'd better.'

In the kitchen Tom sat at the table opposite Ruby.

'Look, son. You don't have to be shy. Remember I was in the army and all sorts of funny things went on with some of the blokes. Some of 'em even committed suicide over it, but for you there's nothing to be ashamed of.'

Tom looked from Ruby to his father with wide staring eyes.

'Dad. You won't hit me, will you?'

'Why should I hit you?'

Ruby closed her eyes. How she wished he didn't need to know the truth.

'Well? I'm waiting.'

Tom stuttered, then looked at his sister despairingly.

'Ruby, you tell Dad.'

Ruby sighed. 'Dad. You know how you got upset with Tom over that coal business?'

'What coal – oh, that, what's that got to do with this? That was months ago.'

'Well, our Tom got in with the wrong lot.'

Thomas looked at his son. 'What have you been up to? Have you been stealing from Mr Cox? Is that it?'

'No. No,' yelled Tom. 'It was him what pinched my money and he said he was gonner tell the police and Beth said she'd see to it and that's when he hit her and . . .' He

371

put his head in his hands and wept.

Thomas sat looking at them both, bewildered. 'What money?'

Tom didn't look up. 'Money I pinched,' he mumbled.

'You've been pinching money?'

Tom nodded. 'I'm sorry. I'm sorry.'

'Who from?'

'Anybody who left it about.'

'How much was it?'

'Twenty-five shillings.'

Ruby gasped. She didn't know it was that much.

'That's a lot of money, son. So how did Mr Cox find out about it?'

'He found me hiding place in the lav.'

'You knew all about this?' her father said to Ruby.

She nodded. 'Not how much and not till Beth was in hospital.'

'But you didn't think you could tell your father?'

'We were worried what you might do to Tom.'

'Am I such a bad father? I know I've let you down, but this . . .'

'What could we do?'

'I was only doing it to help,' sobbed Tom. 'We didn't have any money and I wanted us to have a nice Christmas and Freddie Porter said it—'

His father took a quick intake of breath. 'Freddie Porter.' He stood up and Tom cringed.

'Don't hit me. Don't hit me,' he cried out.

'How could you get mixed up with scum like the Porters? Do you know who his father is?'

Tom shook his head. 'I only know he's in prison.'

'That's where you'll finish up, my boy, messing about with that lot.'

It was Ruby's turn to take a quick breath. 'Tom, how could you?'

Tom was shaking with fear when his father put his hand on his shoulder.

'Don't worry, son. I ain't gonner hit you. I think you've more than learnt your lesson. You'll have to live with Beth's death for the rest of your life and what for – a few shillings?'

'What you gonner tell the police?' asked Ruby.

'I'll tell them that Cox was going to interfere with my son and his friend stepped in to defend him.'

'But that's lies,' said Ruby, shocked.

'I know. But are lies worse than murder?'

'No. I suppose not. But ain't it against the law to lie under oath?'

'Yes. Yes, it is, but if it means it will save my son from being put away, then I think it'll be worth it. After all, it's only the three of us who know the truth – isn't it?'

Both Tom and Ruby nodded vigorously.

'Well, let's keep it that way.'

Ruby was seeing her father in a very different light. He had changed. He was being assertive. He was in charge now.

'When's Mr Thompson going to the police station?'

'Tomorrow. Now, I think it's well past this little lad's bedtime.'

Ruby looked at Danny who had been quietly sitting on the floor playing with his horse and cart.

'Has he had his tea?'

'Yes. I gave it to him before we went out.'

Ruby picked Danny up and kissed him. 'You're always wet or stinky. Come on, bed.'

'Ruby, kiss,' he said as he touched her face with a chubby hand. His grin was something that would melt any heart.

'Dad, should we take Danny to court?'

'Len thinks so. When the jury sees him and what Cox has robbed him of, he don't think Cox'll stand a chance of getting away with it.'

'Will he hang?' asked Tom.

'Looks like it.'

Tom shivered. 'That's two people that'll die cos of me.'

'Tom, you mustn't think like that,' said Ruby. 'He shouldn't have hit Beth.'

But Tom couldn't see it that way.

After Ruby had put Danny to bed she went over to the dairy. She had to talk to someone and as usual it was Milly who was prepared to listen.

'Poor Tom,' said Milly when Ruby told her the police had got Mr Cox. 'What's gonner happen to your place?'

'I don't know. Milly, I'm so worried, you see we've been spending the rent money. I know I should have kept it to one side, but it's so tempting to see it sitting there in the rent book, and once you start . . .'

'Well, don't worry about it, I'm sure something will turn up. After all, I can't see Mr Thompson letting you finish up on the street, not all the while you've got young Danny to look after.'

'I hope you're right. But I don't want him to think I'm only doing it so we'll always have a roof over our heads.'

'Course he won't.'

'I really love that little 'en. He makes us laugh. And he's been such a tonic for Dad. He's completely changed, you know.'

'I know, and I'm happy for you.'

'I'd better get back. Thought I'd just let you know how things were.'

'Thanks.'

As Ruby walked back across the road her thought went to Ernie. He must have gone to Scotland. Why hadn't he told her? Would she have found someone as friendly as Milly to talk to if she had gone with him? What were his mother and sisters like? Would they have liked her? All this was wishful dreaming. Ruby knew she had more pressing problems at the moment.

On Monday when Ruby walked into the factory Mrs Watson called her to one side.

'Ruby. You are going into the finishing room today.'

'Thank you. Will it be for long?'

'I think we could let you go in there permanently. For a young girl your work is very good. Would you like that?'

'Yes, please.' She liked the women in there; they were far nicer than Florrie and her friends. Lately, as she'd been wearing Beth's coat to work, they hadn't missed a day commenting on it, always wanting to know where she'd got it from.

As Ruby and Mrs Watson walked to the finishing room she turned to Ruby and said, 'I wonder if you know what has happened to Ernest? I know you two were friendly and he hasn't been here for weeks now. He did say something about his mother going to Scotland, but he said he wasn't going with her. I do hope he's all right.'

'I haven't seen him.'

'I pray he's looking after himself. I imagine with his mother away he doesn't have to worry about collecting washing now.'

'No, I don't suppose he does.'

'Does he have a job?'

'I don't think so, he would have told me. I think he must have gone to Scotland with his mum and sisters.'

'Yes, that could be it. If he should write to you, remember

me to him. He was a nice lad, always polite.'

'I will.' Ruby didn't think she would ever hear from Ernie again. If he was in Scotland he was going to lead a very different life to being here in Rotherhithe pushing a pram full of other people's dirty washing. She sighed. She had read about Scotland and it sounded wonderful, full of lakes and mountains. But it was and always would be just pictures in a book and a place on the map.

It was a Wednesday when the letter arrived to tell them the preliminary hearing for the case against Mr Cox was going to be on Monday 13 February. Ruby went to see Mrs Watson to ask for that day off.

'You'd better come into the office.'

Nervously Ruby followed Mrs Watson.

Ben Stone was sitting at a desk and looked up when they walked in. 'Hello there, it's Ruby Jenkins, is it not?'

She nodded.

The door opened and Frank Stone walked in. He nodded to Ben and Mrs Watson. 'What we got here, trouble?'

'No,' said Mrs Watson. 'Miss Jenkins wants next Monday off.'

'Does she now, and what for may I ask?' said Frank Stone, looking at the papers he was holding.

'I have to go to the preliminary hearing for the trial of Mr Cox. He was my landlord and he killed my best friend.'

Ben Stone sat up. 'That must have been a terrible experience for you.'

'It was worse for my young brother.'

'Mrs Watson has been keeping us informed. I hope everything goes well for you. If you have any worries we may be able to help. We do have professional people to look after our affairs, and if you find you need help, please call in.'

'Just a minute,' said Frank Stone. 'Are you a witness?'

'No, but my brother—'

'Sorry. We're running a business, not a welfare office. And with all these new orders coming in we can't let the staff off at the drop of a hat.'

Ruby stood with her mouth open as Frank Stone turned his attention back to his desk and began to rummage through some papers.

'Frank,' said Ben, but he was given a very black look.

Frank Stone simply said, 'Anything else, Mrs Watson?'

She shook her head and bustled Ruby out of the room.

Ruby was shaking with anger. 'He can't do that. He can't stop me.'

'He can and he will.'

'I was being honest. I could have just taken the day off, said I was ill or something.'

'I know.' Mrs Watson looked at the closed door. 'Come on.'

Slowly they walked back to the finishing room.

'What am I gonner do? I can't let Tom down.'

Mrs Watson put her arm round Ruby's shoulder. 'I'll have a quiet word with young Mr Stone. He's got a lot more compassion than his big brother.'

'Thank you.'

'Now come on, blow your nose and get back to work.'

Ruby stood at her ironing table with a heavy heart. She was grateful she was in this room, and didn't have to answer to Florrie any more, but how could she go home and tell Tom she wouldn't be there on Monday to support him?

In the end Ruby couldn't bring herself to do it. For the rest of the week she kept to herself the fact that she wouldn't be going with Tom.

On Saturday rain was falling and Ruby was full of despair

as she pulled her hat down and her coat collar up. She stood to one side as the new automobile van that Stone's were now using passed her. It had been the talk of the laundry when it first arrived and everybody had crowded round to admire it. Stone's were getting a very good reputation and everybody knew the laundry was expanding. They were being given work by some of the big hotels and their rich customers needed specialist washing done. Ruby was pleased when there was extra work.

Ben Stone jumped out and called her. 'Miss Jenkins! Just a minute.'

She stopped and looked around, but everyone else had gone.

'You always seem to be one of the last out. Why is that?'

'If Mrs Watson asks me to stay I always try to help out, which is more than I can say for Stone's.'

'Oh dear. We are angry.'

'Why shouldn't I be?'

'Yes, I admit I think my brother was wrong.'

'Excuse me, but I've got to get home. I have my murdered friend's baby to look after.'

He stood to one side. 'You're looking after her baby?'

'There ain't nobody else.' She wasn't going to tell him all of the family business. She went to move on but he put out his hand to stop her.

'Just a moment. I think we'd better have a talk.'

'I've nothing to say to you.'

'Please. Let me hear all of this story.'

'I can't stand around here, it's raining, in case you hadn't noticed.'

'Please, don't be angry with me. Let me take you for a cup of tea somewhere.'

'No, thank you.'

'I could give you a lift.'

'What, in that?' Ruby pointed to the laundry van.

'Only if you want to.'

Although it was against her better judgement she said, 'All right. But I mustn't be too long.'

He opened the door and with great difficulty she climbed in.

'This is very grand.'

'We're hoping to get another one day, but getting good drivers is a bit of a problem. You'd be surprised at some of the blokes I've taken out on test drives.' He laughed. 'Talk about taking your life in your hands. Most of them learned during the war and are only used to driving tanks and lorries through fields of mud. They chuck you about like peas in a pod.'

Ruby laughed. 'I don't believe that.'

'It's true. I couldn't even imagine what all that neatly ironed work would look like after they'd delivered it. No, we're certainly having trouble finding the right person, who's used to driving on roads.'

They only went a few streets when he stopped. 'There's a little café over there.'

Ruby jumped out and quickly made her way into the dry.

''Ello there, Ben. Everything all right then?'

'Yes thanks, Tosh. Two cups of tea please.'

They sat at a table and the tea was quickly put in front of them.

'Now, young lady, I want to hear all of this story. I've only read the bit they put in the paper, and that wasn't much.'

Ruby sipped her tea and went into most of the details.

After she'd finished Ben sat back with an air of decision. 'Don't worry about coming in on Monday.'

'But your brother said—'

'I'll see to him. And Ruby – can I call you Ruby?'

She nodded.

'Please come and tell me the outcome.'

'I will. Now I must get home.'

'I'll take you in the van, that'll save you from getting wet.'

'No, I can't.'

'Why not?'

'What will the neighbours say, seeing me come home in a van?'

He laughed. 'They'd say what a nice firm you work for, not letting their employees get wet.'

She really didn't want him to see where she lived. 'Please drop me off at the top of Hill Street. It's not far from there.'

'If you say so.'

Ruby smiled. Milly is going to have a field day over this, she thought.

On Monday, Tom was up and about long before Ruby.

Mr Thompson had been down the previous afternoon going over a few things with Tom and his father. Mr Thompson still didn't know the real reason Mr Cox had attacked Beth and everybody was determined to leave it that way.

Ruby dressed herself very carefully. She was wearing Beth's black costume and it fitted her like a glove. She felt very smart and grown up, and Beth's neat black felt hat just finished her outfit. She also dressed Danny very carefully. She wanted everybody to see him at his best. This man had to pay for what he had done to the little boy.

Milly came over and wished them luck. She had been more than a friend in all of this sorry business. 'Now, young Tom, just you look him straight in the eye and tell them everything. He's gotter swing for what he did.'

Ruby looked at Tom. Now Mr Thompson was giving them

more than enough money for Danny, and with no rent to pay, they'd been able to buy Tom a new shirt and trousers, which he wore to school, instead of his old cut-offs. He looked very smart; he'd even plastered his hair down with water. Ruby had checked his neck, just in case he'd forgotten to wash it.

Milly kissed the top of his head. 'You look very smart, young man, and don't worry.'

Ruby could see how nervous her brother was. 'I'll come and let you know what happens,' she said as Milly went to leave.

'You'd better. Good luck.'

Ruby closed the front door behind her. 'It's time we left,' she said, strapping Danny in his pram.

Chapter 34

Ernie looked all around him. Scotland must be a truly wonderful place when the sun shone, the snow cleared and the wind stopped blowing, but at the moment it seemed eternally cold and dark. He sat down and poured out a mug of tea from the flask his mother insisted he took with him while he cleaned out the barn. His mother and sisters were happy living in this big rambling house. In many ways they had really fallen on their feet. Richard was a decent man and had shown Ernie lots of the jobs that had to be done on a farm but farming wasn't for him. He wasn't happy. He wasn't cut out for the life – Ruby filled his thoughts day and night. He should never have left her. They could have worked something out if he'd been man enough to stay. But that was impossible now. He could never get back to London. The Thames, the docks, the fog were all a lifetime away. He would never be able to get the fare, and he couldn't ask Richard; although he was well off he had been more than generous already. No, Ernie knew he should never have left, but what choice had he had? His mother had refused to go without him. And without a job, or a place to live, he had nothing to offer Ruby.

The Jenkinses and Mr Thompson stood outside the magistrates' court and waited as a Black Maria turned down the side of the building. It stopped and they watched as two policemen got out. One turned and they could see he was handcuffed to another man. Ruby gasped as she realised the man was Mr Cox. She hardly recognised him. He hadn't had a shave for days; his eyes were staring and wild; he looked dirty and dishevelled. He caught sight of them, fear filled his eyes and he quickly bent his head. Ruby glanced at her brother. He had gone deathly white. She put her arm round him.

'It's all right. He can't hurt you now.'

'But what if he gets out?'

'Don't worry, son,' said Mr Thompson. 'Let's get inside.'

They made their way into the noisy building. Men were shouting and running about. Mr Thompson went up to the desk. 'Excuse me, but we're here to—'

'I'm sorry, sir, but we're too busy at the moment to see to anyone. Take a seat. Someone will be with you shortly.'

They sat on a hard wooden bench watching the police and other people rushing back and forth.

'What's going on?' asked Thomas.

'Search me,' said Len Thompson. 'They must have had a busy weekend and ain't got enough places for 'em all.'

A man carrying a black bag sped past them.

'Looks like somebody's got a beating, or had a heart attack. That was the doctor,' said Len.

'Do they hit people in prison?' asked Ruby.

'They do if they don't behave themselves.'

A while later the doctor came past again. This time he walked up to the desk, spoke to the man on duty and then disappeared into the sergeants' room behind the desk.

Tom was staring all about him. What if they found out about the money? He would go to prison. He didn't want to be beaten; he would confess. Should he tell the truth now? Could he lie? He felt sick.

Len Thompson looked at his watch. 'I hope they ain't gonner be much longer.'

'Should you be opening about now?' asked Thomas.

'Yes, but that don't matter. Monday morning ain't the busiest of times.' He looked about him and moved closer to Thomas. 'It's young Tom here I'm worried about, he's gone very pale.'

'Ruby, why don't you take Tom outside for a breath of fresh air? I'll come and get you when they call us,' said her father.

'That's a good idea. I'll take Danny as well, he's getting a bit fidgety – he wants to get out.' Ruby lifted Danny out of the pram and with Tom they slowly made their way through the crowds and outside.

'Ruby, why do we have to wait so long?'

'I don't know.'

'Do they always beat up the prisoners?'

'I don't know.'

'I'm very frightened.'

'I know you are.'

'Will they beat me and make me tell the truth?'

She smiled and went to ruffle his smoothed-down hair, but thought better of it. 'Course not.'

Ruby and Tom stood to one side as an ambulance drove up and two men got out.

'They must be ever so ill,' said Tom, his green eyes wide with fear and curiosity.

It was a while later when they finally brought somebody out. The person was covered all over with sheets and Tom suddenly burst into tears.

'Ruby. Ruby. Don't let them take me to prison. They've killed somebody. They're wicked.'

To the amusement of passers-by Tom was hanging on to his sister's arm and almost dragging her away.

'Tom, stop it,' said Ruby in a very cross voice. 'Everybody's looking at you. Come on, let's go inside. They might see us now this person has been taken away.'

Ruby could see Mr Thompson and her father in deep conversation with a man at the desk. Her father was solemnly shaking his head.

'Dad, what is it? What's wrong?'

'We've got to come back another day.'

'But I've taken today off. They won't let me have another day off.'

'There's been a bit of trouble. They've got a couple of violent blokes in there who've turned nasty,' said Mr Thompson.

As they made their way home, Ruby couldn't put that dreadful place out of her mind.

In some ways she was even feeling a bit sorry for Mr Cox. He could never have thought that that blow to Beth's head would land him in this mess.

On Friday afternoon Mr Thompson came again to see the Jenkinses. He was carrying a bottle of beer.

'This is a surprise, Len,' said Thomas.

'We've got a bit of celebrating to do.'

'Why? What's happened?'

'Get the glasses.' Ruby had been pleased when Len had given them some before Christmas. 'They always say you get your come-uppance in the end, well, it appears our Mr Cox has got his.' Len carefully poured out the beer.

'Why, what's happened?'

'Old Fred, he's one of the coppers at the nick, told me that Cox has had a heart attack.'

'*No.*' Thomas sat down hard at the table. 'Is he dead?'

'Yes.'

'Poor bloke. I'm sorry, but in some ways I can't help but feel pity for the wicked old sod.'

'I know how you feel. But at least it's let young Tom off the hook.'

'That's true.'

'Where is the lad?' asked Len.

'He's at school at the moment. He's doing very well,' said Thomas proudly. 'So what happens now?'

'Nothing.'

'What about this place.'

'Let's go up and look for the deeds, that's if he's got 'em. You do know his father won this in a gambling game, don't you?' said Mr Thompson over his shoulder as they made their way up the stairs.

'But can that be legal?'

'Gambling ain't, but if he's got the deeds, who's gonner contest it? 'Sides, the original owner can't still be alive. Not after all these years.'

'Suppose not. But what about the owner's family?'

'It wouldn't be something they'd be proud of, losing it gambling. They might not even know the old boy was the one who won it.'

'True.'

Tom was grinning from ear to ear when Ruby walked in. 'You look pleased with yourself,' she said, taking her hat and coat off. 'Got more good marks at school?'

Tom nodded. 'My teacher said I'm a bright boy.'

'Well, we all know that. What's this?' She picked up a bundle of yellow papers.

'Hello, love,' said her father, walking in from the scullery. 'Just been giving this little messy lad a wash.'

Danny ran up to Ruby holding out his arms. She picked

him up and cuddled him close.

'Sit down, love. Tea's ready.'

Ruby looked from one to the other. Her father and brother were grinning like a couple of Cheshire cats. 'What is it?'

'Mr Cox is dead.' Tom couldn't keep it bottled up any longer.

'*What?* How?'

'Seems he had a heart attack,' said her father as he poured out the tea.

Ruby gave a muffled cry and collapsed on the kitchen chair. 'No. When did this happen?'

'A couple of days ago.'

'Who told you?'

'Len. A bloke from the nick told him.'

'So what happens now?' asked Ruby.

'Nothing. It's all over.'

Ruby didn't know what to say.

'I still feel it was my fault.'

'Tom, I've already told you. He must've had a dicky heart. So you've got nothing to reproach yourself about. These are the deeds to the house,' said her father, picking up the papers.

'Who does it belong to?'

'Nobody.'

'It must belong to somebody.'

'It was won by Mr Cox's father in a gambling game. Look: it says here that "I, William Carlton, do hereby give these deeds to Thirteen Hill Street to Mr Harry Cox as payment for money owed." ' Thomas gave the papers to Ruby.

'Was his name Harry?'

'Dunno.'

'Len's gonner have a quiet word with a bloke what goes in the pub, he's supposed to be a bit of a legal bod.'

'Will we have to get out?'

'Len don't think so.'

'I must tell Milly.'

'Course, love. But don't forget I'm off soon.'

'I know. I'll just put Danny to bed.'

Ruby sat on the mattress looking at Danny as he snuggled down. 'What a lot I've got to tell you one day,' she said, turning the gas lamp down very low.

Milly called up to her mum and dad. 'You've got to come down here and listen to this.'

'What? What is it? You're making such a racket, Milly. Dad's trying to listen to the wireless.'

'Mr Cox is dead.'

As they exclaimed and chattered at the news, the atmosphere was almost jolly. Ruby couldn't help feeling sorry for this man. Although he had killed someone, she was beginning to see that Beth's death had been an accident. Mr Cox had no one to love or take care of him, and now he was dead, who would go to his funeral?

'Good riddance to bad rubbish, I say. What happens about the house now, Ruby?' asked Milly's mum.

'We don't know. Mr Thompson is going to try and find out.'

Everybody was seeing something good in Cox's death, and in a funny sort of way that upset Ruby.

The following morning Ruby arrived at work early and went straight up to the office. She hoped Mr Frank Stone wasn't inside as she knocked on the door.

'Come in.'

She almost gave a sigh of relief when she recognised Ben's voice.

'Ruby! How did things go?'

'You asked me to let you know how it went at the police station.'

'Yes. And?'

'We never got to court.' Ruby told him exactly what had happened and that Mr Cox had died from a heart attack.

'My dear girl. I can't believe that all this could happen to one so young.'

'I ain't that young. I shall be seventeen in September.'

He smiled. 'Yes, and you have lived a very full lifetime.'

'I'd better get to work.'

'Of course.'

'Your brother won't sack me, will he?'

'Course not.'

Ruby closed the door gently behind her. How old was he? She would try to find out from Mrs Watson, who was sure to know.

It was a week later when Ruby was called into the office. She knocked on the door full of apprehension. Was Frank Stone going to give her the sack for taking last Monday off?

'Come in,' called Ben Stone. 'Ruby, don't look so worried.'

'What have I done wrong?'

He smiled. It was the first time Ruby noticed his white teeth. He was a handsome man with straight slicked-back dark hair and dark eyes. She knew he was head and shoulders taller than she was. 'Nothing. I was just going to ask you if you would like to accompany me to the theatre. You see, I've been given two tickets and I don't know any other young lady I would like to take.'

Ruby could feel herself blush. 'That's very kind of you. I'd love to. Thank you very much.'

'I thought if we went straight from work we could go to a café for a bite to eat first.'

'Thank you. That would be very nice.'

'Right, that's settled. Come to work in your glad rags on Friday.'

'Friday? I can't come on a Friday; me dad works at the pub and there's no one to look after Danny.'

'Oh dear. That was a bit thoughtless of me. Can't a neighbour or someone see to the lad?'

'I can ask.'

'Please do.'

Although Ruby was thrilled at being asked out with Ben Stone she left the office with a heavy heart. Was this how her life was going to be? Would Milly look after Danny just for the evening?

That evening Ruby went into Milly's first before going home.

'Hello there, Ruby, everything all right?'

Ruby nodded. 'Milly, I've come to ask you a big favour.'

'If I can. What is it?'

Ruby suddenly felt embarrassed. 'Do you think you could come over on Friday night when Dad goes to work?'

'Why's that? You got some interesting scandal?'

'No. I've been asked out, but I can't go as I've got to look after Danny.'

'Who's asked you out? Here, Ernie ain't come back, has he?'

'No.' Ruby had told Milly that as far as she knew Ernie had gone to Scotland with his family.

'So who is it then?'

'Ben Stone.'

'What, the one what owns the laundry?'

'Well, his dad does.'

'Well I never. We are going up in the world. Where's he taking you?'

'To the theatre.'

'Lucky old you.'

'But I can only go if you look after Danny.'

'I think I could do that for you.'

Ruby wanted to hug her, but the counter was in the way.

'What's he like?'

'Very nice. Much better than his brother.'

'Is he good looking?'

Ruby blushed and nodded.

'You wonner play your cards right. After all, now Ernie's flown the coop this could be a good opportunity.'

'I don't think so. It's just that he was given tickets and he ain't got no one else to take.'

'That's what he tells you.'

As Ruby walked across the road her mind went over what Milly had said. Had he really had the tickets given to him? He must have, there was no way he was going to spend money on one of his workers. And what about Ernie? Why hadn't he written to her? If only it were he that was taking her to the theatre – but it wasn't and she should be grateful it was Ben Stone, since he was rather nice, not a bully like his brother. But she knew in her heart that it was Ernie she wanted to be with.

On Friday Ruby was happy when she walked into work. As she was wearing another of Beth's nice frocks, she was pleased she wasn't going to get comments from Florrie now she was working in the finishing room.

'You look very nice, Ruby,' said Mrs Watson.

'Thank you. I'm going out straight from work.'

'Anywhere nice?'

'I'm going to the theatre with Mr Ben.' Ruby didn't mind telling Mrs Watson; after all, he must have told her. Perhaps he'd even invited her before Ruby.

'Mr Ben Stone?' There was definitely surprise in her voice.

'Yes, somebody gave him tickets and he didn't have anyone to take, so he asked me . . .' Ruby's voice trailed off when she saw the look on Mrs Watson's face.

'I see. Well, don't let anyone else know. It's not good for the owners to go out with staff, we've had troubles before.'

Ruby watched her walk away. What did she mean about troubles before? She remembered that Elsie had been out with both of the sons and that Frank was married, but Ben wasn't. She wanted to say to Mrs Watson: What about when you took Ernie Wallis to the music hall, and gave him the money to get a suit out of the pawnshop? Ruby tossed her head back. What's good for the goose is good for the gander.

At the end of the day Ruby hung about till everyone else had left the building. The clattering of someone running down the concrete stairs told her that Ben was on his way.

'Sorry to keep you hanging about but I've just had a telling-off from Mrs Watson. She's been here so long she feels she's part of the family.'

'What did she tell you off about?'

'I didn't get a receipt for the petrol I bought for the van. But not to worry, I'm going to open an account there, so she won't have to nag me about that. All this extra paperwork is getting to her – I reckon we'll soon have to get someone in to help her. Mind you, she's not a bad old stick. Right. Let's be off.' He took hold of Ruby's arm and they made their way out of the laundry and up to the tram stop.

'This isn't a very posh place, but they do good food.'

To Ruby, after the café in the market, it looked very posh. At first she felt a bit like a fish out of water and imagined that everybody was staring at her; she was terrified of not doing the right thing. She carefully waited to see what Ben would do first, then followed suit. Fortunately she had read something about the way to behave, and, after all, everybody has to learn.

He looked at his watch. 'Now we'd better be off. Would you like to go to the ladies' room?'

It took a moment or two before Ruby realised what he was asking her. She blushed to the roots of her hair.

'It's through that door over there.'

When Ruby went into the ladies she couldn't believe her eyes. After the outside lav, everything was so lovely, from the deep red flock wallpaper to the shining silver taps in the washbasin. She pushed open the cubicle door; the lav had real toilet paper in a little box that had 'Jeyes' written on the outside. This was something she had seen in the shops but never been able to afford. It seemed such a waste of money to pay for paper just to wipe your bum on. She giggled to herself. This was wonderful.

Thomas smiled when Mrs Bell walked in. She was alone.

'Hello, Thomas,' she said, sitting on her favourite stool next to the bar.

Thomas could sense by the looks she was getting from the other customers that she was wearing one of these new shorter skirts and showing a bit of those lovely legs. He would go round and collect glasses shortly just so that he too could have a look.

'How's that family of yours?'

'Very well, thank you.'

A tall man came in and kissed the back of her neck.

'Darling. I didn't think you'd be able to make it. I was just about to ask Thomas here to take me home tonight.'

'Hard luck, mate. Better luck next time.' He took her arm and led her to a seat at the far end of the bar.

When she left with the punter Thomas felt very deflated. He'd been sure she was going to ask him to take her home.

Ruby was over the moon. All evening she had been sitting enthralled at everything she'd seen: dancers, singers, jugglers. It was truly wonderful. It must be lovely to have money to spend on such luxuries.

Ben was being a perfect gentleman and only took her arm to help her across the road or on to the tram.

'Did you enjoy yourself tonight?' he asked when they were seated on the tram.

'It was the best night of me life. Thank you so much.'

'The pleasure was all mine. You look very nice, is that a new frock?'

She nodded. She wasn't going to tell him whom it once belonged to. Deep down Ruby was wondering if some of Beth's luck was beginning to rub off on her. She would have loved to have her locket on show, but didn't think it looked right on the thread. Perhaps one day she could get a chain.

'We must do this again one evening. Do you think your friend will look after that little boy again?'

'I think so, but if it's in the week me dad will be there.'

'I'll have to see what I can arrange.'

'Did you really have those tickets given to you?'

Ben laughed and held his hands up. 'I must confess. I bought them. I wanted to make it up to you for all you've been through and for Frank being so nasty, but I didn't think you would come with me if you knew the truth.'

Ruby smiled. 'I was very flattered that you wanted to take me out when you have the whole of the laundry to choose from.'

'Some of them are too old for me and some, well, some are definitely not my type. This is our stop, I believe.'

When they got off the tram Ruby insisted on going home alone.

'Will you be safe?'

'When you've walked these streets pushing a pram full of washing, you feel more than safe. Just as long as I don't have to go near the docks or the buildings.'

'Thank you, Miss Jenkins, for your company tonight,' he said formally, but with a smile in his voice. 'I'll see you at work tomorrow. And, Ruby, I don't think it would be very wise to let any of the others know.'

'I won't do that. I only told Mrs Watson. Was that all right?'

'I know, she did tell me.'

Ruby stood waiting for him to kiss her, but it never happened. Was he being polite, or was it because he was her boss?

'Good night and thank you.'

He took hold of her hand and her heart gave a little flutter. Was he going to kiss her now?

Ben kissed her hand. 'Goodnight, Ruby Jenkins.'

Ruby stood and watched him walk away.

Did he like her? Really like her? He was nice, but it was still Ernie who filled her heart.

Chapter 35

It was April when Len Thompson came with wonderful news. He had been to see a friend of his about the house. The solicitor had put a notice in the paper saying that if anyone knew of a Mr William Carlton or a Mr Harry Cox, they had to contact him, but it appeared no one had come forward, so it was theirs. It had to go through some legal formalities, but Len was seeing to all that. No more rent. They could do as they liked.

When Len came with the good news he brought a bottle of beer with him. Ruby went over for Milly. She had to share their good fortune as she was always there for them. They danced round the kitchen unable to believe they would never be thrown out of the property again. Then Ruby sat and cried with happiness. She couldn't believe this was really happening to them.

Milly put her arm round Ruby. 'Come on, wipe those lovely big brown eyes. It's about time you had your share of good luck.'

'Yes, but it's only because of Beth dying that this has happened.'

'You mustn't think about that. Beth would be happy for you, and after all it's a home for Danny as well now.'

Ruby dried her eyes. She looked across at Tom. He had

been very quiet. It would take him a long time to come to terms with all this.

Life for Ruby was definitely better. She was now getting a little more money and her working conditions were much improved. Mrs Watson always had a smile for her and Ben Stone wasn't mentioned. Ruby was always willing to stay and finish any order that had to be out, so she regularly earned extra. But she was increasingly worried about Tom. He had become very withdrawn. He was always eager to go to school and appeared to be doing well. Night after night he would read his books and do his sums without any prompting. Was this his way of coping with all the tragedies that had befallen him in his young years?

Weeks had gone past before Ben asked Ruby out again. This time they went to the picture house. It was better than when she went with Elsie, as this time they sat in more expensive seats. She was thrilled at Rudolph Valentino in *The Sheikh*. His flowing Arab robes and dark smouldering eyes captured her heart. Ben thought he was daft and couldn't see what all the fuss was about. However, although Ruby liked Ben she knew she could never get fond of him, *really* fond of him, as they were worlds apart and he was her boss. Oh, where was Ernie? Why hadn't he got in touch? Was this his way of bowing out of her life? What would Frank say if he found out Ben had taken her out again? Ruby knew Ben hadn't told his brother: why was that? Was he worried about being seen with her?

Much to Ruby's surprise her father was continuing to work hard. He was now working for Len most mornings as well as every week night, but he still went to the Green Man on Fridays and Saturdays. On Sundays he spent the morning at the Royal Albert bottling up and behind the bar in the evenings. He told Ruby he enjoyed being with Len, and Len liked Danny running around, but he was getting to be a handful and into everything. Thomas never let on the real reason why he still preferred to go to the Green Man. It was because he was desperate to see Mrs Bell, despite what she did for a living. He wanted to get her alone to tell her he needed a woman but would she want him to pay? He didn't want to be a customer. He knew he was being silly, but he always felt hurt when she left with a punter.

It was the middle of April when Rita Bell, looking radiant, walked into the pub with a huge grin on her face and an old man on her arm. He was shorter than Rita, and fat. His long camel-hair overcoat almost reached the ground and a black trilby hat sat squarely on top of his head. Rita came up to the bar and, leaning over, said very softly, 'Thomas, I'll have my usual, and get my lover boy here a brandy and yourself and George a drink too.'

'Got something to celebrate then, Rita?' asked George.

'I should say so. I'm getting married.'

George almost choked on his drink. 'Blimey. What for? You up the duff?'

'No I ain't. Christ, that'd be a laugh and a bloody miracle at my age. It's young Charles here.' She smiled at her man friend and tenderly touched his flabby cheek. 'He's decided to make an honest woman of me. We're going to go to Holly-wood, that's in America. Charles is in the picture business. It's all very new and exciting.'

Thomas was standing with his mouth open. This news had quashed his ardour for ever.

'Ain't you gonner congratulate me, Thomas?'

'Yes. Yes of course.' He raised his glass. 'I wish you all the best. I hope it all works out well for you.'

'Thank you. I'm sure it will.'

Charles was looking round the bar grinning. 'I love the way you Limeys talk. I can see my lovely Rita in pictures yet. I have a lot of influence over there.'

'What d'you want our Rita for?' asked George.

'Now talking pictures are taking off, you Brits with your la-di-da accents are all the rage in the good old US of A.'

'La-di-da!' laughed George. 'Blimey, there ain't nothing la-di-da about our Rita.'

'Just you watch it, George. I ain't going all that way without a ring on me finger,' said Rita, grinning.

'Good for you, gel,' replied George with an equally broad smile.

Charles was loud and brash and all evening everybody was drinking Rita's good health and making crude comments.

It was almost closing time and Thomas was clearing the tables when Rita came up to speak to him.

'Why are you doing this?' he asked.

She stubbed her cigarette out in the ashtray. 'I'm sick to death of where I live and the life I've got, so when this golden opportunity came along I grabbed it with both hands.'

'But I like you, I was hoping . . .'

Rita Bell looked shocked. 'I'm sorry, Thomas. I didn't realise, and I seem to remember you spurned me once when I offered you comfort.'

Thomas quickly looked about him and continued wiping down the tables. 'Yes, that was a big mistake. I wasn't ready for the love of a woman then.'

'You're a nice-looking man. One of these days you'll find someone who will love you and take care of you.'

'I don't want another woman. I'm very fond of you. I could have taken you away from where you live. You could have lived with me.'

'What? I can just see your Ruby letting me move in with you.'

'She would have got used to the idea.'

She laughed. 'And what about me punters?'

'We could have managed.'

'I'm sorry, Thomas. I want more out of life than anything you could offer me.'

'Thomas, you'll be wearing that bloody table out before long,' shouted George. 'Hurry up and finish! I want me bed and Charles here wants to get his little Rita home.'

'When are you going to America?' asked Thomas as they both moved towards the bar.

'Next week. We're getting married on Monday and we sail on Tuesday,' said Charles. 'Can't wait.'

'That's a bit quick, ain't it?' asked George.

'Ain't no point in staying round here,' said Rita.

'No, s'pose not,' said George.

'What about your place and all your lovely things?'

George looked at Thomas. 'How d'you know what she's got? Here, you old dark horse, you been to her place?'

'Course he ain't,' said Rita quickly. 'I expect his daughter told him.'

'Yes. Yes she did,' said Thomas, speedily recovering.

'I don't own that much, and I'll be taking all I need. Charles has arranged a carrier to collect me stuff.'

'We're gonner miss you, gel, ain't we, Thomas?' said George.

Thomas nodded. 'Yes, we are.'

As Thomas Jenkins walked home that night he knew that he would be leaving the Green Man next week and working solely for Len. He knew Ruby would be pleased about that. He would never tell her the real reason he was leaving, but he knew George would guess.

★ ★ ★

The knock on the door sent Ruby scurrying along the passage. She was surprised to find a postman standing on her doorstep.

'Got a letter for you, girl. Couldn't slip it under the door, the mat's in the way. I reckon it won't be long before everybody will have to have these letter boxes fitted, the way everybody's sending letters and cards these days.'

Ruby took the letter. It was addressed to her but she didn't recognise the stamp: it was foreign. Carefully Ruby opened it. It was from Scotland.

> My dear Ruby,
> I feel I should write to you to tell you why I suddenly upped and come here with me mum and sisters. It was cos I didn't have anything to offer you. I've always liked you but it ain't fair if I ain't got a job and can't give you a home. I hope you will write and tell me how you're getting on. Did old man Cox get what he deserved? How's the boy? Remember me to your dad and brother. Hope we meet up again one of these days. It's ever so cold up here and there's a lot of snow so I can't help me uncle that much just yet. Mum and the girls like it.
> Take care,
> Your friend,
> Ernest Wallis

He had remembered her. But he wasn't coming back. She carefully folded the letter and put it in her pocket.

As April moved on so the weather became warm. Her father had left the Green Man and now worked at the Royal Albert.

Even when he wasn't working he spent a lot of time with Len, taking Danny with him.

One Sunday morning after her father had gone to work she asked Tom if he'd like to go to the park with her.

'I can't, I've got to finish this.'

'What is it?'

'Miss Tinsley asked me to write this story.'

'What's it about?' Ruby went to move closer but Tom quickly shut the book.

'Is it that much of a secret?'

'Not exactly.'

'Well, why can't I see it?'

'Cos I don't want you to.'

'I'm going to the cemetery first.' It was a year ago their mother had died and as soon as her father had felt fit enough he had made a small wooden cross to mark the place where she was buried. They had stood quietly together that day, all deep in thought. Beth was in the same cemetery, but she had a lovely headstone with the name everybody knew her by, Beth Norton, engraved on it.

'That what you got those flowers for yesterday?'

'Yes. I'll be going to the park after. Do you want to come?'

'No. I get upset to think Mum's under that pile of earth.'

'I know.'

'D'you think she'll mind?'

'Course not. I won't be that long.'

As she walked along she reflected on how their lives had changed this past year. No more pushing a pram with dirty washing. No more washing drying round the fire. No more cleaning Mr Cox's rooms. She had now moved upstairs into Mr Cox's room. She had been scared at first and had wanted Tom to go, but when he'd refused she'd taken her courage in her hands, and set about making it nicer. She washed the curtains and crocheted a doily to go on the bedside table. It was a bigger room so there was lots of room for Danny's cot. Tom had moved back into her old bedroom. Ruby couldn't believe they now had a bedroom each.

Today, in many ways Ruby felt content. She had one of the best jobs in the laundry and the sun was shining.

When they reached the park Ruby took Danny out of his pram and sat on the bench she used to sit on with Ernie. She enjoyed watching Danny trotting about, exploring everything that was new and exciting for him. Her thoughts always went to Ernie when she had time to muse: she still missed him so. Ruby felt in her coat pocket and her fingers curled round the letter that was always close to her. Although she had replied to his letter he hadn't sent any more. Had that been just a one-off? She knew every word that was written on the page but she just had to read it again.

She looked up when she heard someone talking to Danny and making him laugh.

'Alfie Anderson. What you doing here?'

'Just out for a walk. I see me nephew's getting on a treat.' He sat next to Ruby. 'Me mum's a bit upset you ain't brought him round to see her.'

'I work all week.'

'I know, but you're home Sundays.'

'I'm busy.'

'What, like you are now?'

'We're just going.'

'You know me mum's been round a couple of times but that old man of yours won't let her see him for more than a minute or two, or bring him home.'

Ruby knew Mrs Anderson had been to see Danny, but her father had always had an excuse ready, saying he had arranged to go up to Len Thompson, so she could never see him alone. 'I expect Dad's been too busy.'

'Well, I'm gonner take him to see her now and we might keep him.'

'You can't. You can't do that,' screamed Ruby, desperately looking round for someone to help her.

'Can't I? You just watch me.' He grabbed Danny and plonked him in his pram, not even stopping to put his safety straps on.

Ruby tried to grab the pram handles but Alfie was much too strong for her and he pushed her away.

Danny, whose laughter had turned to tears, looked bewildered.

'Bring him back,' yelled Ruby as she regained her balance and again wrestled with the pram handles.

Alfie grabbed her hand and bent her fingers back hard. He shoved her to the ground and her ankle was twisted under her. She screamed out in pain. As she held her ankle, she watched him disappear through the park gates.

She struggled to sit on the bench. What could she do? She couldn't catch him, and she also knew she was no match for the Andersons. She had to go to the pub. Her father and Mr Thompson would be very angry but what else could she do?

Slowly she limped her way to the pub. Tears ran down her face. What would they do to Danny? Would they hurt him? Ruby remembered the things she'd heard about Alfie Anderson. How he put his foot out to trip Tom up and laughed at him sprawled out on the ground. How he kicked people's gates in when he was angry. Was he hoping to take him home? Would he hurt Danny if he cried? Would he lock him away so she would never see him again?

'Hello, love, what brings you here this morning?' Her father was rolling a beer barrel across the yard. 'Where's the lad?'

At that Ruby burst into tears again.

'What is it? What's wrong? Is he ill?'

She shook her head. 'No. Alfie Anderson's taken him away.'

For a moment or two her father was silent as the horror of what she had said sunk in.

'He's taken him? Where?'

'To see his mum.'

'Don't worry. He'll bring him back.'

'I don't think so.'

'Why? What makes you say that?'

'I don't know, it's this feeling I've got.'

'I'm sure he'll be all right. Come on.' Thomas went into the pub with Ruby following on behind.

Len Thompson listened carefully to Ruby, then he casually said, 'Leave it to me. If he ain't brought him back be teatime, I'll arrange for someone to go round there.'

'Do you know where he lives?' asked Ruby.

He nodded. 'I made it me business right from when we first found out who they were, just in case something like this happened. Now go home and don't worry, he'll be all right. They won't hurt him.'

'How can you be sure?'

Len Thompson put his arm round Ruby's shoulders. 'Oh, I'm sure.'

Slowly Ruby made her way back home. She had suddenly realised just how much this little boy meant to her. These past months she had looked out for him and cared for him, but she hadn't realised she would come to love him as much as she did. That was it: she would write to Ernie and tell him that if his uncle could pay her fare she would bring Danny to Scotland. She had to get away from the Andersons even if it meant leaving her dad and Tom. Her dad could manage now.

Len Thompson would see that they were both well looked after. It was about time she thought about herself and Beth's child. She loved that little boy so much that the thought of anyone else looking after him – well, she just wouldn't let that happen.

Chapter 36

As Ruby approached her front door she looked across at the dairy. Should she knock and tell Milly what had happened? What good would that do? And hopefully Alfie would bring Danny back before long.

Tom looked up when she pushed open the kitchen door.

'Ruby. I'm sorry I didn't let you see me work, but . . .'

'That's all right.'

Tom put his pencil down. 'Where's Danny?' he asked, expecting the little lad to be trotting behind Ruby as usual.

Ruby looked away.

'What's wrong?'

'Nothing really. It's just that I'm a bit, I don't know, concerned, I suppose.'

'What about?'

'Alfie Anderson has taken Danny to see his mum.'

'And you didn't go with him?'

'No.'

'Will he be all right? Will he bring him back?'

'Course he will. Now I must get on with the dinner. Dad will be back after closing time.'

'Dad'll be ever so wild when he finds out what you've done.'

'He knows. I popped in the pub and told him and Mr Thompson.'

'What did they say?'

'Just that we mustn't worry. He'll probably bring him back be teatime. Now come on, let me lay the table.'

'Ruby, would you be upset if they kept him and didn't bring him back?'

'That's a daft thing to say. Course I'd be upset, silly.' She was trying very hard not to let Tom see how much this was worrying her.

The dinner was ready and Ruby opened the kitchen door quickly when she heard her father close the front door.

'Has he come back?' asked her father.

Ruby shook her head.

'What we gonner do if he don't?' asked Tom.

'Don't worry, he'll bring him back. Len will see to that. Look, if he turns up while I'm at work this evening, you'd better come and tell us.'

'Course I will,' said Ruby, but, without knowing why, she still had her doubts.

Dinner was a very quiet affair. They missed Danny shouting and making them laugh with his funny antics.

'I hope they've put him down for his afternoon nap,' said Ruby. 'And changed his bum. I don't want him getting nappy rash.'

'I expect they have,' said her father.

All afternoon they waited for the knock on the door, but it didn't come.

After her father had gone back to work Ruby sat and watched the clock. Would they change his nappy and cream his bottom? He had a very sensitive skin. Would they give him the right food and not fill him up with sweets and stuff? What if he got upset in strange surroundings, would they comfort him and make a fuss of him?

'Ruby,' said Tom, almost startling her, 'you know my writing?'

'Was it something I shouldn't see?'

'Well, yes. But it was something Miss Tinsley wanted me to do. She thinks I'll pass my exam and that I'm bright enough to go to the high school.'

Ruby sat up. 'That's wonderful. You must be very clever.'

'I am trying. Miss Tinsley was very surprised I knew so much. I told her it was you who taught me – she said *you* must be very clever.'

Ruby laughed. 'No, I'm not.'

'If I pass I'd like to go to high school but I don't think I'll be able to. She said it'll cost quite a bit of money.'

Ruby went over and hugged her brother. 'We'll all make sure that you do. I would have loved to have stayed at school, but it wasn't to be, but now Dad's working and I . . .' She stopped. 'We'll find the money somehow.'

After a while Tom said he was going to bed. He was pleased Ruby had gone upstairs, he didn't want to sleep in Mr Cox's bed. Ruby said she was going to buy him a proper bed soon. After Mr Cox died Ruby had gone through his things and given a lot of his stuff to the rag and bone man, but kept the sheets and blankets, which she had taken to work to be washed. It was nice for her not to worry any more. His thoughts went to Danny and he hoped he would be back soon. It was funny without him running about getting in to everything. Tom, as ever, was thinking of all that had happened since Beth died. He had never told Ruby about the nightmares he had because he remembered how upset she'd got over their dad's nightmares. Flashes of Mr Cox would have him waking up sweating. Then there was the one where Beth took his hand and told him not to worry. Just as she was about to kiss the top of his head he would wake up. Nor had he told Ruby he had seen Freddie Porter after Christmas and that Freddie had threatened him if he didn't stay in his gang. When Tom bravely told him he was involved with the police, Freddie quickly changed his mind and told him to keep away from them. It was when Ruby said he should go to school that he'd decided to work hard and show everybody he was clever. He was lucky his teacher Miss Tinsley liked him and helped him after school. She had said he should go far, and that's what he intended to do. He would get a certificate and then he'd be able to get a good job. He would show his dad and sister he wasn't really a thief; besides, he wanted to do it for Beth. The writing he had been hiding from Ruby was a book he was using to write down everything that had happened since Beth came to live with them. He had to do this; it was something he wanted to give Danny when he was older. He should know what a lovely person his mum had been. 'I hope they bring Danny back soon,' he mumbled as he fell into a deep sleep.

When Thomas returned home at eleven o'clock that night Mr Thompson was with him.

'He ain't turned up then?' asked Len Thompson.

'No. I'm so sorry. I'm ever so frightened. What if they've taken him away?'

'Don't worry, love, we're going round there now.' Her father put his arm round her shoulders.

'What, at this time of night?'

'Can't let it go on,' said Len.

'I'll come with you.' Ruby stood up and went to get her coat from the nail behind the kitchen door.

'No,' said Len. 'It's best you stay here, just in case he does bring him back a different way to the streets we take.'

'All right.' Deep down Ruby knew that Alfie wouldn't bring

410

him back tonight. He was going to make them suffer.

Ruby was dozing in the chair when the front door banged shut. She jumped up expecting to see the pram being pushed into the passage. But it was only her father and Len Thompson. They both looked full of rage.

'What's happened?' she asked.

'The old dear's only gone and taken him to her sister's.'

'What? Where does she live?'

'Down Brighton way.' Len Thompson was balling his fist and pacing the floor.

'She can't do that,' said Ruby.

'She can and she has,' said her father.

'Where's she got the money for the train fare? They're hard up. Will she bring him back?'

'The young kid said tomorrow. But if she don't I'll have the police round there so fast she'll wonder what's hit her.'

'This is all my fault,' said Ruby sadly.

'No, love. It was on the cards that it would happen one day.'

'I love him so much, I don't want anything to happen to him.'

'Don't worry, Ruby, nothing will happen to him. Your dad will be here. Now you go to work tomorrow as usual, the old dear should be back before I open up in the evening.'

'What if she's not?'

'Then, as I said, I'll have the police on to her for kidnapping.'

'Can you do that as she's his grandmother?'

'They've got to prove that.'

'Come on, love, you go to bed,' said her father.

'I don't feel like it.'

'I'll be going,' said Len. 'I'll see you tomorrow.'

'I'll see you out,' said Thomas.

Ruby sat waiting for her father to return. What could she do? She wanted to take Danny away. Should she write to Ernie again and ask him more about Scotland? Could she persuade her father to go with her? And could they find the fare? But what about Tom? His schooling had to be considered. She mustn't take this chance away from him: he deserved all the support they could give him.

The next day, after a restless night Ruby went to work with a heavy heart.

'Good morning, Ruby,' said Mrs Watson cheerfully. 'Anything the matter? You don't look very well.'

'I didn't get a lot of sleep last night.'

'Why was that?'

Since Beth's death Mrs Watson had been very kind, she had taken Ruby under her wing and Ruby felt she could tell her almost everything. Mrs Watson knew about the letter Ernie had written and at the time had been upset that she wouldn't be seeing him again.

Ruby told her most of what had happened.

'I'm sure you've nothing to worry about. His grandmother will bring him back, I'm sure.'

'I hope so.'

'Now come on, I've got some very expensive shirts for you to iron and they mean a little more money for you.'

Ruby smiled at her. 'Thank you.' So many things in her life had begun to go right, but also so many things could so easily go wrong.

That evening she hurried home hoping to see the pram in the passage, but it wasn't to be.

'He's not back then?' she asked Tom who was poring over some books.

412

'No. Dad and Mr Thompson have gone round there again.'

Ruby sat down. What could she do?

'Ruby, they will bring him back, won't they?'

'I hope so.'

'Dad said would you get something for our tea.'

'Yes. I'll go now.'

As Ruby crossed the road her thoughts were still on Danny. She stood to one side as Milly finished serving Mrs Mann. When Mrs Mann turned she gave Ruby a nod. 'Everything all right then, young lady?'

'Yes, thank you.'

'I saw your father pushing the boy the other day. I must say he's a credit to you. Always nicely turned out. I don't know how you do it. His mother would be very proud of him.'

'Thank you,' said Ruby.

'Must be off, can't stand about all day chatting. Bye for now.'

'Bye,' said Ruby and Milly together.

'So, young Ruby, what can I get you?' asked Milly.

'I don't know.'

'Are you all right?'

Ruby shook her head. 'Alfie Anderson's taken Danny.'

'*What?*' It was more of an explosion than a statement.

'I was in the park yesterday—'

'He took him *yesterday*?' interrupted Milly.

'Yes.'

'And he ain't brought him back?'

'No. His mum took him to Brighton.'

'Brighton? What's down there?'

'Her sister.'

'Bloody hell. How did she get all the way down there?'

Ruby shrugged.

'What's Mr Thompson doing about it?'

'He's gonner get the police on to her.'

'Can he do that?'

'He says they can't prove Beth was an Anderson.'

'I'll tell you what, you never have a dull moment in your house, do you?'

'No. And a lot we could do without. I need to get something for tea.'

'What d'you fancy?'

'Don't know. Don't really feel like eating.'

'Don't suppose you do. Don't worry, it'll be all right.'

'I hope so.'

'Now, what's for tea?'

'I'll have a bit of bacon, we can have that with an egg.'

Milly went to the bacon slicer and began turning the handle. 'You know what keeps going through me mind?'

'No.'

'What will you do if they put him in an orphanage?'

'Oh Milly. Don't say things like that.'

'Well, I suppose it could happen.'

'No. I wouldn't let it.'

'You love that little lad, don't you?'

'Yes I do. I can't think of life without him now.'

'Well, d'you know what I reckon? You ought to think about getting married and then he could be yours.'

Ruby gave a silly laugh. 'And who would have me?'

'What about the boss's son? He must be worth a bob or two. If you play your cards right I reckon you could have him down the aisle before he knew what hit him.'

'He's me boss. I don't think of him like that.'

'You told me you like him.'

Ruby had told Milly about the two times she had been out with Ben Stone. 'I know, that's cos he took me out, but not enough to marry him.'

'Well, I reckon it could work out just fine.' Milly slapped the bacon onto the greaseproof paper and put it on the scales. 'Tuppence, that all right?'

'Yes thanks.' Ruby picked up the bacon. 'I'll let you know what happens.'

'You'd better.'

As Ruby crossed the road, what Milly had said was going over and over in her mind. She gave a little smile and said to herself: I can just see brother Frank accepting me as part of the family. No, it was Ernie who held her heart strings, even if she could never have him.

Chapter 37

Ruby knew she wouldn't be able to eat anything till she knew Danny was safe. As soon as she'd given Tom his tea she hurried to the Royal Albert. She had to find out what was happening.

It was getting late and the pub was almost empty when she walked in. She could see her father busy wiping the shelves down behind the bar.

'Hello, Dad.'

'Hello, love.'

'Where's Mr Thompson?' she asked, looking round.

'He's gone to get the boy.'

'She's brought him back then?'

'We don't know. If she ain't he's going to get the police. Don't forget he knows a lot of the right people.'

Ruby was at a loss for words. 'I've given Tom his tea.'

'That's good.'

'Dad, I'm really worried. I hope they're looking after him.'

'I think he'll be all right. They know they'll have to face Len if not.'

Ruby knew this was a useless conversation, but she didn't want to leave till she was sure Danny was well. 'Can I do anything?'

'Nothing to do. Monday nights is always slow.'

'Has he been gone long?'

'He went at opening time.'

Ruby was filled with alarm. 'That was hours ago. You don't think anything's happened to him?'

Her father smiled. 'I think Len is big enough to look after himself, don't you?'

She nodded. 'I know, but there's a lot of them and I don't think they've much time for the law.'

'Don't worry, he'll be all right. He should be back soon.'

'He must have loved Beth a lot to worry about her son like this.'

'He did, and Danny is the son he's always wanted.'

She sat at the bar and watched her father. All of their lives had been turned upside down over these past three years. Who would have thought that her father would be working? And who would have thought he would be willing to look after someone else's son? And what about Mr Thompson? He was helping them too. Most men would have walked away from these problems, but he was different.

When the pub door opened and a pram was pushed in Ruby thought she would burst with happiness. 'Is he all right?' she asked, rushing over to them.

'He's fine. He's fast asleep.' Len Thompson looked lovingly in the pram. 'Ruby, I'm gonner let Mrs Anderson here . . .' He stood to one side and Mrs Anderson walked in.

'You can't let her have him,' she cried out, interrupting him. 'I won't let you. Where's he been?' Tears filled her eyes.

'No, listen. She's not going to take him away. She's coming here to help.'

'I don't want her to. I'm gonner look after him.'

'Don't worry, love, he'll be all right with me.'

'We've had a long talk. I've been to the house and seen the rest of the family and they love him.'

'So do I.'

'Ruby, I think you'd better go through to the back.' Her father's voice was strong and stern.

Reluctantly she pushed the pram behind the bar and, leaving it in the passage, went along to the parlour.

'Now sit down, both of you.'

Ruby and Mrs Anderson did as they were told.

'What I'm going to say affects us all.'

Mrs Anderson's worried eyes said it all as she looked from one to the other. She looked frightened and confused.

'Where's that bullying son of yours then? Why ain't he here throwing his weight about?' asked Ruby.

'Ruby, this attitude isn't gonner help,' said Mr Thompson.

'I don't care. I love Danny and I'm gonner get married and look after him.'

Both Mrs Anderson and Len Thompson looked at her with amazement.

'Does your father know you're getting married?'

Ruby shook her head.

'And may I ask who you're marrying?'

Again she shook her head.

'Ruby, I know you've been upset, but you mustn't be so childish,' said Len Thompson.

Ruby hung her head. She felt silly as well as angry.

'Ruby, I ain't gonner take him away from you. It's just that I think he should know who his grandmother is, and that he's got some sort of family. He ain't all alone.'

'He won't ever be alone.'

'Now, Ruby, listen to what I've got to say. I've had a long hard think about all this. I don't want to lose the boy, you know that, but we've got to start to be practical. As you know your dad brings him up here through the day when we bottle up and at lunchtime when the pub's open. I know Mrs Moss sometimes keeps an eye on him, but she can't be in two places at once, and I don't expect her to, she's here to clean my place and do me bit of washing. Now that Tom is at school it's getting harder for us to keep an eye on the lad. He wants to toddle about and I'm worried that he might get into some sort of trouble. There's a lot of things that are dangerous round here.'

'But she took him away without telling us. What if she takes him away again?'

'She won't. You have my word on that.'

Although Ruby could see there would be problems as he got older and into mischief she still wouldn't admit to it.

'I think you've done a lovely job looking after the boy. He's a lovely little lad and a credit to you. My sister loved him. She always liked Lizzie, she ain't ever had a lot of time for the others.'

'How could you afford to take him to Brighton?'

'Me sister's husband works for the railway and a long while ago she sent me a pass to go and see her. I never had cause to use it. Didn't want to go on me own and I wouldn't take any of my lot, so I thought this was a good time to use it. I'm sorry my Alfie never told you. He said he did. But then he can be a lying little bleeder.'

'See? That's why I don't want her to look after him. I don't want him learning to swear. We never swear in front of him. How could you let Beth down? She ran away from them, remember.'

'Now calm down, Ruby.'

Ruby could see the pain in his eyes and felt sorry for what she'd said.

'I'm not letting Beth down. I would never do anything to hurt her or Danny, you know that.'

'She did give me money sometimes, to help me out,' said Mrs Anderson.

'You mean your son used to waylay her and ask for money.'

'No. No. It wasn't like that. She didn't want to see her father.'

'And what if he harms Danny?'

'He won't. He's full of remorse over our Lizzie, and if that bloke hadn't dropped dead, then my old man was gonner see to him. So you've no worries there, ducks.'

'Ruby, Mrs Anderson is coming here to cook me and your father a bit of dinner and she can make enough so you don't have to worry about it when you get home from work, and she can look after Danny at the same time.'

Ruby sat and looked at them. Although she knew it made sense she didn't want to admit it and agree with the arrangements.

'I told you a while ago I was going to get help, and this is a good way for all of us. Mrs Anderson can work for me and you'll have Danny when you get home from work. I think it'll work out just fine.'

'I suppose so. But I didn't think you'd let her do it.'

'We had a long talk and it seems the right thing to do.'

'I'll look after him proper. I promise.'

'You'd better.' Ruby couldn't believe how nasty she was being to this woman. 'You won't let her take him out, will you?'

'You can trust me.'

'Ruby, you mustn't be so suspicious. You have to trust people sometimes. Now, while I go and tell your father what the arrangements are, perhaps you could make us all a nice cup of tea?'

Although Ruby wasn't happy, there wasn't a lot she could do about it. Why was Mr Thompson letting this woman into their lives? And what about Alfie? He wasn't nice and he might cause trouble.

'You'll have to show me where the things are and, Ruby, I promise no one will hurt that little lad,' she said, as if reading Ruby's thoughts.

'What about Alfie?'

'He won't get near him.'

If only Ernie were around. She could talk to him. With a heavy heart, Ruby filled the kettle.

As the weeks went on Ruby had to admit that the new arrangement was working. She would come home to a meal that Mrs Anderson had prepared warming in the oven, and with Len Thompson paying for the food, no rent to find and her father working, their lives were transformed.

Ruby had written to Ernie telling him all that had happened; she had also asked him what was Scotland like, and had he met a girl yet? But she hadn't had a reply. Was she wasting her time?

Tom had brought a letter home from his teacher saying how clever he was and his talent shouldn't be wasted. They sat and had a long talk about letting him go to high school if he passed the exam.

'I think we should try,' said her father. 'Your mum would be that proud of you, son.'

Ruby wished with all her heart that her mum were here. She touched the locket she always wore under her frock. She would have liked something of her mother to be near her: if only she had a photo, or a lock of her hair to put inside. But nothing like that existed.

Tom worked hard and every night he would pore over books Miss Tinsley gave him. On the day of the exam Ruby was more nervous than he was. All day at work she worried and wondered how he was getting on.

It was well into the summer when his results came through and the excitement when they discovered he had passed was shared by all. All that studying and worry was over. Milly had made a cake for him and Mr Thompson had given him five pounds. It was a fortune and Tom insisted they use some of it to help with his uniform.

It was with great pride that with their dad and Danny they went shopping for his uniform. It was a lot of money, but they were determined he would look the same as all the other boys. They had come a long way from when he wore his father's cut-downs. He looked so smart.

'Don't you dare get that in a mess,' said Ruby, trying to hide her true feelings.

Tom put his arms round his sister and held her tight. 'I promise I won't ever let you down again.'

A few days later Ben asked Ruby to go out with him again. Although she'd heard from her father that Mrs Anderson was making a good job of looking after Danny she still worried about it. She thought of what Milly had said about marriage. Ruby gave a little giggle. She saw very little of Elsie these days, she was so busy with her own life but Elsie would have told her how to use her womanly wiles to trap a man.

Ruby found herself laughing as she left the laundry with Ben. They were going to the picture house again. 'I wonder if we'll ever see Mrs Bell in a film?' Her father had told her about Mrs Bell going to America and hoping to be in pictures, and Ruby had passed it on to Ben.

'I don't reckon she'll be in films. I bet the old boy was just using it as an excuse to get her in bed.'

'He didn't need an excuse, just money.'

'Well, I expect she wanted to make sure she was married to

him before she took that big step. After all, America's a long way away.'

'Would you use an excuse to get married?' asked Ruby tentatively.

'No. I'd come right out with it. Mind you, I've got to find the right girl first.'

Ruby held her breath. 'So you've not got anyone in mind then?'

'No, and don't worry, as my friend and companion you'd be the first to know. Here's our tram, come on, hop on.'

Well, that made it clear he wasn't interested in her in a romantic way. Ruby was actually rather relieved.

The Sunday after she had been out with Ben she took Danny for a walk round the park in his pram. She sat on her usual seat deep in thought. When someone sat next to her she turned, intending to do no more than smile at this person who was dirty and looked like a bundle of old clothes. She did a quick double take. Was it Ernie? She held her breath and closed her eyes. Was it just her imagination? When she opened them he was still sitting next to her. He looked desperately scruffy and needed a shave.

'Hello, Ruby. You look very nice. You seem to have done all right for yourself.'

'*Ernie!* What you doing here?'

'Got fed up with Scotland. It's always cold and wet up there, or it is where me family is.'

'Where're you staying?'

'Here. This is me bed.'

'What? You're sleeping in the park?'

'Ain't got anywhere else, have I?'

'I don't know. How long you been here?'

'All week.'

'Why didn't you come to see me?'

'I did. I went to the laundry and I saw you getting on a tram with Ben Stone. You both looked very cosy, talking and laughing. I didn't want to interrupt.'

'I didn't see you.'

'No, I was hiding behind that new van they've got. Didn't know they was gonner get rid of the horses. They must be doing all right.'

'They managed to get work from a big West End hotel and the van's a lot quicker than the horse.'

'So, where was you off to?'

'We was going to the picture house.'

'You didn't say nothing about you and him in your letters.'

'There was nothing to say. Besides, you didn't answer them.'

'Didn't want to.'

'What's the matter with you? You used to be so full of bravado, now you sit there looking all filthy and acting like a spoilt kid.'

Ernie looked at her. Was this the little girl he'd left behind? Ruby was talking to him almost like his mother. 'You've changed.'

'I've had to. A lot's happened since you went away.'

'Yes, I guess it has. So are you and Ben going out together?'

'No. I told you, it's not like that.'

'So what is it like then?'

'We're just friends.'

He laughed. 'I've heard that one before.'

'Why should it bother you anyway?'

'Nothing. Is this that Beth's kid?'

'Yes. I think the world of him.' Ruby knew she shouldn't be saying this. What if Ernie had come back for her? He wouldn't want a young boy to be hanging onto her apron strings. 'Ernie, what have you come back for?'

He didn't answer her. Instead he took a tobacco tin from his pocket and set about rolling a cigarette.

'I asked you a question.'

'I heard.'

'Well?'

He lit the cigarette and blew the smoke high in the air. 'Me uncle's a nice enough bloke and now the girls have settled down Mum's happy about that. Daisy's got herself a good job in one of the big houses up there, so she's away all week. She's also seeing a boy from the village, so she won't be back. The other two are getting on well at school, and Mum – well, somehow she's just fitted in. But I was, well, homesick, I suppose.'

Ruby laughed. 'What kind of homes we got that you can't wait to get back to?'

'That's me. The fly in the ointment.'

'What are you gonner do down here?'

He shrugged. 'Don't know.'

'Look, come back home with me. You can have a wash and smarten yourself up.'

'What will your dad say?'

'We've had that many ups and downs that we can take most things in our stride now. Come on.' She stood up.

'Ruby, you've certainly changed.'

'I've had to grow up, fast.'

'And you've grown up into a lovely girl.'

Ruby stopped. Had he come down all this way just to see her? She wanted to hold him, make a fuss of him. Her heart went out to him; she knew she loved him and him alone, but what future did they have together?

As they wandered home Ruby told him all the news. She

pushed the pram into the passage and took Danny out. 'Go and see Tom.'

'Tom. Tom,' he yelled, rushing down the passage on his chubby legs.

'That's one of the words he can say clearly,' said Ruby, smiling.

Tom was standing in the kitchen. He looked up when he realised Ruby wasn't alone.

'What's he doing here? I thought he was in Scotland.'

'So did I. I found him on a park bench.'

'He looks ever so scruffy.'

'I've been living rough for a couple of weeks.'

'We can see that,' said Ruby. 'Here, take this kettle and go and have a wash and shave. Have you got a razor?'

'In me bag.'

'How did you get down here?' asked Tom.

'I was so keen to get back I used all sorts of ways, like jumping on trains after they started and jumping off before a ticket inspector came round.'

'Don't go telling him things like that. He's got enough imagination as it is.'

'I did find work in some of the fields, helping farmers and picking taters, that's hard work. But I'll tell you something: there's a lot of lovely things away from Rotherhithe. Green fields, tall buildings. A lot to see.'

'So why did you come back?'

He shrugged. 'Dunno, really.'

Ruby handed him the kettle.

Ernie smiled. 'I'd better go and do as I'm told.' He went into the washhouse and closed the door.

'Where's he gonner stay?' asked Tom.

'I don't know. He could stay here upstairs, I suppose.'

'What about a job?'

426

'I don't know, that's up to him.'

'Can't see him staying around here for long, not without a job.'

That thought had gone through Ruby's mind as well.

Chapter 38

The first thing Ruby did the following morning when she got to work was to tell Mrs Watson that Ernie was back.

'Where's he staying?' she asked.

'He's at our house for the time being.'

'What plans has he got?'

'He don't know. He'd been sleeping on a park bench.'

'No! The poor boy. Tell him to drop by one day. I would like to see him again.'

'I will do.' More evidence of the soft spot she'd always had for Ernie.

'Now back to work. And, Ruby, thanks for letting me know.'

'That's all right.' Ruby thought of the first time she'd come to the laundry and how she hadn't got a job because of him. How she had hated him for that. She shuddered when she remembered the horrible washroom and the wet feet and chilblains. She looked down at her boots. They didn't have flappy soles or let in water now. She was smiling to herself when she sat at her table.

'You look pleased with yourself, young Ruby,' said Mrs Turner.

'Yes, I am a bit.'

'How's that little lad?'

'He's fine.' Everybody in the room knew about Beth and Danny. They were a nice bunch of women who took great pride in their work, and they were always ready with any advice, from putting poultices on his chest when he caught cold, to making sure he had the right things to eat, and most of all, potty training. At the moment Ruby couldn't see that he would ever be clean, but Mrs Anderson had told her father she mustn't worry about it, she would try during the day.

In fact, to Ruby life at this moment was almost perfect. If only Ernie would stay . . .

She hurried home that night eager to see if Ernie was still around.

She pushed open the kitchen door and to her relief he was sitting laughing with her father.

Danny came running up to her calling out, 'Buby! Buby!' He couldn't say Ruby. He held out his hands for her to pick him up.

She took hold of him and swung him round. She was so happy at this domestic scene she thought she would burst.

'So what sort of day have you had?' she asked Ernie, putting Danny on the floor.

'Not too good. Been out looking for work, but ain't found much.'

Her heart skipped a beat. He's been looking for work, that must mean he's thinking of staying.

'I'll give it a few more days then if I don't have any luck I'll have to start thinking of moving on.'

She didn't want him to go. She wanted to hang on to him. She wanted to beg him not to leave, but knew she couldn't do that. 'Where will you go?' she asked.

'Dunno. Your dad here reckons there might be work round the docks, but I went there. I might try down the coast somewhere. I've even thought about joining the Navy.'

'Well, you can stay here till you find something, can't he, Dad?'

'That's what I told him.'

'I didn't know you owned the house now.'

Ruby smiled. 'We don't really own it, we can just live here.'

She didn't want Ernie to think she was better off than him. 'Now, what's for tea? By the way, Mrs Watson said she'd like to see you, so perhaps you could pop in some time?'

'Yer. I might do that. She wasn't a bad old stick. Here, do you remember when she took me out that time? I felt like a real toff, all dolled up and going to the music hall. If I play me cards right she might take me out again.'

'If you stay round here, you never know.'

The following morning Ruby said to Mrs Watson, 'Ernie Wallis said he might call to see you.'

She smiled. 'That would be very nice. Can he leave it till the end of the week? We are very busy at the moment.'

'Mrs Watson, could there be a job for him here?'

'I wouldn't think so. Stone's only employ women.'

'I see.'

'How's he settling down?'

'He's not. He's been out looking for work; he's talking of going to the coast to see if things are better there. He said he might even join the Navy.'

'That would be nice. He'll look very dashing in a uniform.'

That thought had gone through Ruby's mind. She wouldn't be able to hold him then. As the saying went: All the nice girls love a sailor.

A few nights later Ernie and Ruby were sitting in the kitchen alone. Tom had gone to bed and her father was working.

'Ruby, I'm thinking of moving on.'

'Why? What's wrong?'

'Nothing. It's been great here, your dad's made me very welcome, but I can't sponge on you. I can't find work and, well, that ain't my way.'

'I know.' Ruby was beginning to panic. 'Where will you go?'

'Don't know.'

She couldn't stop herself. 'Please, Ernie, don't go.'

He looked at her. 'You want me to stay?'

She nodded.

'I can't.'

'Why not?'

'It ain't right.'

'Ernie, do you like me?'

'You know I do. You was the reason I came back. I thought I could offer you some hope, but things have worked out fine for you.'

'I love you, Ernie.'

He looked at her.

'Marry me.'

'What?'

'Marry me, then you can live here. I know you'll get a job. We'll be happy, I know we will.'

Ernie stood up. He walked to the door.

Ruby ran to him and held on to his arm. 'I'm sorry.'

He gently took her arm away. 'No, Ruby. It's me who should be sorry. I shouldn't have come back to disrupt your life.'

'Don't you like me?'

'I do like you. I like you very much. But I've nothing to offer you.'

'I don't care.' Tears ran down her face.

He held her arms. 'I care. Be sensible. All your life you've struggled and been the backbone of this family. You are one in a million. I would even say you are a rare Ruby.'

She smiled through her tears. 'My mum used to say that.'

'I couldn't live off of you.'

'It don't matter.'

'It does to me. I'll be off in the morning.'

'Please, Ernie.'

He kissed her forehead and walked away.

Ruby sat in the chair and cried. She had lost the person she wanted to spend the rest of her life with. She loved him so much. Had she done the right thing? Had she lowered herself in his eyes? Women didn't ask men to marry them . . .

Ruby was up early the next morning, but to her dismay Ernie had already left. She did all the usual things she had to for Danny before she left for work.

'That lad went off early this morning,' said her father as he poured out the tea. 'Didn't even stop for a cuppa.'

'He told me last night he was leaving.'

'That's a pity. He's a nice lad and he's very fond of you.'

'I don't know about that.'

'Well, he told me it was you he came back for.'

Although Ruby felt elated she knew he'd gone out of her life. 'I can't mean that much to him, seeing as how he's gone.'

'Yes. A pity that.'

Ruby left the house and went to work with a heavy heart.

Mrs Watson came up to Ruby as soon as she walked in. 'Is Ernest still at your place?'

'No, he left early this morning.'

'That's a shame. I would have liked to see him again. Did he say where he was going?'

'No, he left before I was up.'

The rest of the day dragged for Ruby and she was pleased

to get home and even more so when it was time for bed, yet she had a restless night. Her thoughts were all of Ernie.

It was very early when Ernie left the Jenkinses' house, before Ruby was up. He couldn't stay. He didn't want to hurt her. He wandered round the streets, his mind in a turmoil. He desperately wanted to stay. When she'd asked him to marry her he'd wanted that so much it hurt. She loved him, but what could he offer her? She was a kind person, everybody loved her. He should never have come back. He had seen the way Ben Stone looked at her and he knew if he was out of the way one day he would see that she was the right girl for him. She deserved someone like him.

He went to the park and sat on their seat. He loved Ruby. He had loved her for years. He knew that was why he hadn't been able to settle in Scotland; he'd had to come back, he'd had to see her again, but now he was running away.

He leant back and closed his eyes. Where could he go? Life was so bloody hard.

A yapping dog running round the park brought him back to the present. He had to see Ruby just one more time before he left. He would go to the laundry; he wouldn't let her see him. He would stand in the shadows. He picked up his bag and moved on.

Outside the laundry Ernie looked up at the name over the brick arch. A van hooting made him jump.

When it stopped Ben Stone got out and walked up to him. 'Don't I know you?'

'Not really. I used to bring washing here.'

'So what are you doing now?'

'Nothing, well, I've just come down from Scotland—'

'You're Ernie. Ernie Wallis,' said Ben, interrupting him and shaking his hand. 'I know all about you. Or rather, Ruby

Jenkins has told me all about you.'

'She has?' Ernie was surprised Ruby would talk about him when she was out with Ben Stone.

'She spoke very highly of you.'

'She did?'

'Are you waiting for her to finish?'

'No. No. Not really.' This man had taken the wind out of Ernie's sails; he didn't know what to say. He couldn't walk away now.

'Look, why don't you come up to the office? I'm sure Mrs Watson would like to see you.' Ben took Ernie's arm and moved him on. 'I've got to hurry, another load to collect. We're so lucky to be busy at a time like this.'

'That van looks good.'

'We're very proud of it.' He pushed open the office door. 'Look who I found outside.'

'Ernest!' said Mrs Watson, jumping up. 'How lovely to see you. Ruby told me you were staying at her place. Have a seat. Are you waiting for Ruby?'

He was trapped. 'Yes.'

Mrs Watson brought him a cup of tea and they sat and chatted about Scotland.

When Ben left she said, 'That poor boy is going to work himself to death.'

'Where's his brother?'

'He's out drumming up work. I reckon we may have to move to bigger premises if this carries on.'

'With everybody out of work I would have thought it would be hard for you to get new orders.'

'No. Frank has managed to get in with some of the big hotels over the water and they're pleased with our services and prices. What about you? Ruby said you might be joining the Navy.'

'I was thinking about it. There ain't a lot of work round here.'

'You found work in Scotland then?'

'Only with me uncle.'

'What did you do?'

'Help around the place. I used to drive his car.'

'He had a car?'

'Yes. I enjoyed that.'

'So what made you leave then?'

Ernie looked in his empty cup. 'Ruby. I wanted to see Ruby. I knew she wouldn't come up to Scotland. She wouldn't leave her family, so I thought I'd come to her.'

'But she said you were moving on.'

'I've got nothing to offer her.' He stood up. 'I must go. I mustn't let her see I'm still around.'

'Just a moment. You said you could drive?'

'Yes. Why?'

'I know Ben is looking for a driver. He's only been able to find men who drove in the war and are used to driving lorries over muddy fields. But you've driven a car.'

Ernie sat down.

'Look, come back tomorrow. I'm sure we can help you, and you will be helping us.'

Ernie couldn't move. He sat and stared at Mrs Watson.

'Is anything wrong?'

'No. Do you really mean that? Does he really want a driver?'

'Yes.' She looked up at the clock. 'Ruby will be out shortly, why don't you wait outside for her?'

'Can I tell her?'

'I don't see why not.'

'What if Ben Stone says no?'

Mrs Watson smiled. 'He won't.'

'But what about his brother?'

'Be off with you, go and tell Ruby the good news.'

Ernie couldn't believe his luck. He stood watching the women go past.

'Why, if it ain't Ernie Wallis,' said Florrie, coming up to him. 'Waiting for our Ruby? She's really come up in the world. I think old Watson's got a soft spot for her. So you wonner watch it, she could put your nose out of joint.'

He laughed. 'Florrie, Mrs Watson knows pleasant people when she sees them.'

'Hark at him,' shouted Florrie. 'You saying I ain't pleasant to everybody? You wonner ask me boyfriends, they reckon I can be very pleasant, and I'm good at it. You wonner try me out sometime.' She came up close to him. 'I bet I could bring more than a smile to your face.'

'Save it for your friends. Hello, Ruby.'

Ruby had been standing back watching him talk to Florrie. 'What you doing here?'

He took her arm. 'I've got something to tell you.'

'But I thought—'

'Let's get away from this lot.'

Ruby was rushed along.

They were well away from the laundry when Ernie stopped and kissed her full on the mouth.

'What was that for?' she asked breathlessly.

'Ruby Jenkins, will you marry me?'

Ruby stood staring at him. 'But last night . . . What's happened to make you stay?'

'I didn't want to go, so I thought I'd sneak a last look at you. Ben Stone saw me and took me up to the office and Mrs Watson has offered me a job.'

'What?'

'I've got to come here tomorrow.'

436

'But they only take on women.'

'Not for my job,' he said proudly.

'Where will you be—?'

'I'm going to drive the van.'

'You can't drive.'

'Yes I can. I used to drive me uncle's car.'

'You didn't tell me.'

'Didn't see any reason to. So, Ruby Jenkins, will you change your name to Wallis?'

Ruby laughed through her tears. 'Yes, please.'

He wound his arms round her and kissed her again.

Suddenly, Ruby became practical. 'Danny. What about Danny?'

'I like him. I reckon we'll all be happy together, don't you?'

She nodded enthusiastically. 'We don't have to worry about where to live. We can be upstairs.' She clung to his arm. 'Come on, let's get home and tell everybody. I'm so happy.'

He stopped and stood in front of her. 'There is something I must say.'

'What is it?'

'That door upstairs will have to be repaired. There's a terrible draught through that hole.'

She laughed. 'I'll have a word with the person who did it.'

Everyone was overjoyed at their announcement. Milly was crying.

Tom held her close. 'I want you to be as happy as me,' he whispered.

'I will be.'

That evening they went with her father to the Royal Albert. Len Thompson was so pleased at the news. 'We must have the wedding reception here. It will be my gift to you.'

After they wandered back home, Tom went to bed and

Ruby busied herself putting Danny down.

Ernie held his hand. 'He is a lovely little feller.'

'You don't mind him being around?'

'Course not. With everybody helping, I reckon he's gonner end up having a great life.'

Ernie left Ruby to settle Danny. He was outside when Ruby came back down into the kitchen; she sat at the table quietly touching her locket. She couldn't believe all that had happened in just a few days.

Ernie came in and put his arm round her.

'Penny for them.'

'I was just thinking how everything has worked out for us.'

'We've had a lot of ups and downs to get here.'

'Ernie, Mrs Watson did mean it, didn't she?'

'Has she ever given you false hopes?'

'No.'

'She's not like that, and I think she has a lot more to do with that business than she lets on.'

'Could be.'

'Now, with my first week's wages I want to buy you something special. Can I buy you an engagement ring?'

'No, that's too expensive. We'll wait till you're settled in the job.'

'Please let me get you something. Is there anything you'd really like?'

'You mustn't go wasting your money on me.'

'Why not?'

'Don't know.'

'So what's it to be?'

Ruby dived a hand down the front of her dress. 'My dad bought this for me at Christmas but we've never been able to afford a chain. Could I please have a chain for it?'

Ernie held the locket in his hand. 'It's very pretty. But it don't look right on that thread. That's the first thing we'll go and buy.'

'Thank you. It opens.'

'Have you got a picture in it?'

'No. I would have liked one of me mum, but she never had her picture took.'

'You'll be able to put a picture of our wedding in there.'

'I really love you, Ernie Wallis.'

'And I love you. You are my rare Ruby. My jewel.'

He took her in his arms and kissed her.

Ruby could feel tears running down her cheeks again, but this time they were tears of happiness.

Sorrows and Smiles

Dee Williams

Pam King can't understand why her gran, Ivy, has forbidden her to see Robbie Bennetti. Robbie's a lovely lad, much less dangerous than Lu Cappa, who's always giving her the eye when he's out in his ice-cream van. Pam has to ask her best friend Jill to cover for her while she's out with Robbie.

When Ivy finds out Pam's been lying, she makes sure the relationship with Robbie is over for good. Then Jill falls in love, and it's loneliness that makes Pam accept a date with Lu Cappa. Before she knows it, they're married.

Even then, Pam knows Lu's still jealous of Robbie. And she can't help wondering what Lu's up to when he's out with his shifty brother. When Robbie comes back into their lives, it could be the last straw. One thing's for sure: until everyone starts to tell the truth, there will be as many sorrows as smiles in Pam's marriage . . .

Acclaim for Dee Williams:

'A brilliant story, full of surprises' *Woman's Realm*

'Flowers with the atmosphere of old Docklands London' *Manchester Evening News*

'A moving story full of intrigue and suspense, and peopled with a warm and appealing cast of characters . . . an excellent treat' *Bolton Evening News*

0 7472 6109 1

headline

Now you can buy any of these other bestselling books by **Dee Williams** from your bookshop or *direct from her publisher*.

FREE P&P AND UK DELIVERY
(Overseas and Ireland £3.50 per book)

Forgive and Forget	£5.99
Sorrows and Smiles	£5.99
Katie's Kitchen	£5.99
Maggie's Market	£5.99
Ellie of Elmleigh Square	£5.99
Sally of Sefton Grove	£5.99
Hannah of Hope Street	£5.99
Annie of Albert Mews	£6.99
Polly of Penns Place	£5.99
Carrie of Culver Road	£6.99

TO ORDER SIMPLY CALL THIS NUMBER

01235 400 414

or e-mail <u>orders@bookpoint.co.uk</u>

Prices and availability subject to change without notice.